ALSO BY DANIYAL MUEENUDDIN

In Other Rooms, Other Wonders

This Is Where the

Serpent Lives

✻

This Is Where the Serpent Lives

DANIYAL MUEENUDDIN

ALFRED A. KNOPF ✳ NEW YORK ✳ 2026

A BORZOI BOOK
FIRST HARDCOVER EDITION
PUBLISHED BY ALFRED A. KNOPF 2026

Published by Alfred A. Knopf, a division of Penguin Random House LLC,
1745 Broadway, New York, NY 10019.

Knopf, Borzoi Books, and the colophon are registered trademarks
of Penguin Random House LLC.

"Muscle" and "The Golden Child" were previously published in
The New Yorker.

LIBRARY OF CONGRESS CATALOGING-IN-PUBLICATION DATA
Names: Mueenuddin, Daniyal, author.
Title: This is where the serpent lives / Daniyal Mueenuddin.
Description: First hardcover edition. | New York : Alfred A. Knopf, 2026.
Identifiers: LCCN 2025009174 (print) | LCCN 2025009175 (ebook) |
ISBN 9780525655152 (hardcover) | ISBN 9780525655169 (ebook)
Subjects: LCSH: Social classes—Pakistan—Fiction. |
Pakistan—Fiction. | LCGFT: Novels.
Classification: LCC PR9540.9.M84 T48 2026 (print) |
LCC PR9540.9.M84 (ebook)
LC record available at https://lccn.loc.gov/2025009174
LC ebook record available at https://lccn.loc.gov/2025009175

penguinrandomhouse.com | aaknopf.com

Printed in the United States of America
1st Printing

The authorized representative in the EU for product safety and compliance
is Penguin Random House Ireland, Morrison Chambers, 32 Nassau Street,
Dublin D02 YH68, Ireland, https://eu-contact.penguin.ie.

For My Children

Eir, Neyàn

My two

I see through you,

You see me through

Contents

✳

Principal Characters

✻

BAYAZID (b. 1952?): Orphan found in Rawalpindi bazaar in 1955 and adopted by Karim Khan. Tea stall boy working for Karim Khan. Joined service as chauffeur to Colonel Khuda Baksh Atar in 1974 and subsequently chauffeur to his son Hisham Atar.

KARIM KHAN (b. 1920s?): Owner of a tea stall in Rawalpindi bazaar. A Pathan tribesman from Mardan.

KAMRAN KHOKHAR (b. 1951): Childhood friend and rival to Bayazid, son of a Rawalpindi ward boss. Later a boss of the Rawalpindi land mafia. Member of the Punjab Provincial Assembly.

MALIK KAMAL AWAN (b. 1930): Owner of the premium grocery in Rawalpindi stocking foreign delicacies and serving politicians, foreigners, and the diplomatic corps.

ZAIN AWAN (b. 1952): Son of Malik Awan, friend to Bayazid.

YASMIN AWAN (b. 1953): Daughter of Malik Awan.

MAI VIRO (b. 1910s?): Ageless crone working as a maid, cook, and cleaner to the Awan family, passionately devoted to them, and of a fearsome temperament.

COLONEL KHUDA BAKSH ATAR (b. 1922): Patriarch of the Atar family, landowner, industrialist, and politician. Father of Hisham and Nessim Atar. Dehradun, British Indian Army, 18th Cavalry. Member of the National Assembly, Federal Minister for Industries, 1981–83. Ambassador to the Kingdom of Spain, 1983–85. Retired in Lahore.

* * *

RUSTOM ABDALAH (b. 1966): Grandson of Mian Abdullah Abdalah, a great landowner of Punjab and son of "Tony" Abdalah, both deceased. Aitchison College, Columbia University. Second cousin to Hisham and Nessim Atar. Farming in South Punjab at Dunyapur.

CHAUDREY ZAWAR HUSSEIN (b. 1927): Manager at Dunyapur estate to Mian Abdullah Abdalah, to his son "Tony" Abdalah, and then to his grandson Rustom Abdalah.

MIR HASHIM HAYAT SANGHERA (b. 1952): Posted in 1988 as district superintendent of police (DSP) in Cawnapur, the large town nearest the Dunyapur estate of Rustom Abdalah.

SHEIKH SARKAR OF KHIRKA (b. 1920s): Patriarch of a gangster clan from Lahore, hereditary muscle to the Abdalah family.

SHEIKH SHARIF (b. 1961): Grandnephew of Sheikh Sarkar, later deputy mayor of Lahore.

* * *

HISHAM ATAR (b. 1954): Elder son of Colonel Atar. Educated at Aitchison College, Lahore, and Dartmouth College, U.S.A. Member of the National Assembly (1985–88). Landowner, industrialist.

NESSIM ATAR (b. 1955): Younger son of Colonel Atar. Aitchison College, Dartmouth College, Stanford Law School. Partner, Debevoise & Plimpton, New York City.

SHAHNAZ ATAR (b. 1957): Wycombe Abbey, Buckinghamshire, Dartmouth College, Hanover, N.H. Daughter of a career diplomat in the Foreign Service of Pakistan. Wife of Hisham Atar. Granddaughter of Begum Roshanah Imanullah, a grand old lady of Lahore.

* * *

CHAUDREY MOHAMMAD SAQIB (b. 1989): Son of a household gardener at the Atar family's agricultural estate at Ranmal Mohra. Subsequently, member of the Hisham Atar household staff in Lahore and then a farm manager at Ranmal Mohra estate.

SONYA AND SOHAIL HAROUNI (b. 1950s): Friends of Hisham and Shahnaz Atar. Industrialists. Owners of Samarra, a weekend house above Islamabad.

RANA ABDUL SATTAR (b. 1941): Manager of the Atar family estate at Ranmal Mohra, following the disgrace and removal of the previous manager, Sheikh Mohammad Abbas, in 1975.

CHAUDREY GUL NAWAZ WARRAICH (b. 1953): Progressive farmer from Faisalabad in Punjab province, promoted tunnel farming with imported materials and seeds in Pakistan in the 1990s. Businessman. Later, member of the National Assembly.

GAZALA ABBAS (b. 1989): Granddaughter of Sheikh Mohd. Abbas, the estate manager for Colonel Atar at Ranmal Mohra from 1939 to 1975. Married to Chaudrey Saqib.

INSPECTOR AFTAB SHAKIL JANJUA (b. 1973): Police "encounter specialist" on secondment in District Muzaffargarh, posted there to liquidate dacoit gangs operating in the riverine areas.

The Golden Boy

✳

RAWALPINDI, PAKISTAN

1955—1970—1979

*B*ayazid never knew how he came to be a little boy alone in the streets of Rawalpindi. He had a memory more of forces than of people, a crowd, a hand, a hand no more. Yet the bazaars in those early 1950s were not so crowded as that, and Rawalpindi a town small enough that a lost little boy should be found. That was a bitter day when he accepted years later that there might have been no hand, no desperate parent seeking him in the crowd. He might have been abandoned, not lost. Karim Khan, the owner of the tea and curry stall where his known history began, could tell him only that he had been sitting in front of the stall on a fine winter day, three or four years old, wearing just a shalvar kameez, barefoot and clean, holding a new pair of cheap plastic shoes tightly in his arms as if afraid they would be taken away, and scanning the crowds passing by. The shoes had caught Karim Khan's eye, not only because they were brand-new, but because the children of the streets, those sparrows, ran barefoot always. In those early years following the great Indian Partition, families drifted about, mothers dead, fathers dead, murdered for religion's sake, for politics, unwelcome children without parents thrown on some relative's mercy. Karim Khan thought this must be one of those stories, Hindus stuck on the wrong side of the border and on the run, an unwanted child—though that didn't explain the shoes.

Karim Khan kept an eye on the boy all through the afternoon and evening, serving customers by the light of a hissing pressure-gas lantern, dishing up dal or a meat curry that grew more delicious each year, for he never washed out the fire-blackened pots that sat over the coals, but replenished them with a double handful of lentils or meat, beef or mutton, whichever was cheaper, the mix of meat juices adding to its savor. The boy had a remarkable power of concentration, immobile all day and seeming quite unperturbed, but for the fierceness with which he held the shoes. He stood out even then as a person not to be treated lightly, as a being with resources of spirit if not of fortune. When Karim Khan finally approached him, the boy brushed him off, politely but firmly. He was waiting for his mother, who would soon be back, and must not move from this spot. Rebuffed, Karim Khan retreated back to his cook fire, the evening crowd getting a quick bite before taking a bus from the nearby station up to the mountains or out to the plains, for the shop served mostly travelers. Finally, when the crowds had died, when pye-dogs began sniffing around under the charpoys in front of the food stall for a last chicken bone or scrap of dry bread, when the lights in the shops along the road faltered out, and the cold came down from the Margalla Hills so that breath showed in a little cloud, Karim Khan went to the boy, and took his hand, and drew him away from the road and over by the fire.

"Come on, have a dish of my curry," he told the boy. "You're shivering, you'll get sick. Sit here and eat, you can still keep watch." The boy came along easily enough then, his will weakened by hunger, heavy-headed over food and then burrowing under a blanket that Karim Khan pulled over him, lying on a charpoy in the open-fronted veranda where the cook fire had just gone out, asleep so quick. At dawn he was back by the road, and for that whole day too he watched, not crying but just resolute, knowing that of course they would come back, his mother and father. Admiring the boy's remarkable tenacity, pitying him, Karim Khan fed him morning, midday, and evening with unsold chapattis and the leavings from customers' half-eaten plates—which otherwise would be poured back into the general pot. That evening Karim Khan said to him firmly, "Come on, little man. I'm not rich enough to feed you on charity. From now on you clean up and carry out the plates and then we'll see. Until your people come." Earlier he had been to the nearby police station but, as he expected, found the duty officer there quite uninterested in a street boy's troubles. In any case, the boy had struck his fancy, though no one would have accused that Mardani Pathan of being fanciful, with his wife back home awaiting money and three daughters there to feed, and this food stall his enterprise, and his pride too—he'd built it up from a little cart that he hawked around the train station.

Karim Khan, who was a good man, took the boy in and named him Bayazid, after a Sufi mystic who was known to him rather as a magician, *jhadoo ghar*—more fancy, indulging himself in poetry!—and treated him not like a son, perhaps, but like a cherished apprentice, miniature serving boy, dishwasher, runner, paid in food and treated unsentimentally but fairly, hardly any use at first, then gradually indispensable. Yazid grew up exceptionally large for a Pakistani, six feet tall by the time he first began shaving, and strong: big hands, big feet, a large head. He tended to be slovenly rather than unclean, ate enormously but without much discrimination, worked day and night slowly but implacably, and was a neighborhood pet as a little boy, and a person of accepted station by the time he was thirteen. He didn't banter or fling himself around, as teahouse boys often do—but had a humor that called forth smiles in return, and accepted all who accepted him, and damn the rest, and even them he forgave easily.

Most remarkably, Yazid had a long view of bettering himself, told to no one, an ambling bear moving to his own North. He taught himself to read, first learning the alphabet, buying government school grammars with his own money, encouraged and corrected by one of the regular customers, a schoolteacher who came in the afternoons for a cup of tea, and whom he treated with ceremony and respect that kept the tuition flowing. To the extent that Karim Khan thought of such things, he accepted this as one of the boy's caprices, a distraction in any station that he might achieve, but better than going to the cinema or flying kites. At ten Yazid would read aloud the Urdu newspaper to illiterate Karim Khan, a morning ritual after the shop was opened and before the customers came, choosing the stories that he knew his boss would like. At fourteen and fifteen he could be found whenever he wasn't working read-. ing gruesome stories of murder, or stories of thwarted love or lov-ers dying requited, bought secondhand from stalls and bound like magazines, with lurid pictures on the covers of fat-bummed girls and mustachioed men, lovers or enemies, kidnapped or eloping or on the lam, as only time and a hundred pages would tell. Yazid had charmed hands, became a master at making chapattis, hunkered cross-legged over the tandoor, slapping the flattened dough down into its orange glowing maw. He learned the technique of making nan, doing it so well that the shop became known for it, the local housewives bringing pots to fill with dal and curry, a treat for their poor homes in the nearby alleys, and a bundle of nan too, flecked with sesame seeds, oiled shiny, crisp and then soft inside, hot and wrapped in day-old newspapers. "Always your nose in a book," said the regulars, and were rather proud of him as he handed over the goods and picked up and resumed his reading, sitting under a lone bulb hanging from a wire.

*

The bazaar around the food shop had been established in British times, with some newer office buildings of two and even three sto-ries, a little park, and next to the park, the Sir Khawaja Nizamuddin Government High School, known simply as Nizamuddin College and acknowledged to be among the best in the city. The boys wore uniforms—blazer, straight-legged khaki pants, and pointed black shoes, even a blue-and-brown striped tie, which made them con-spicuous at a time when most Pakistanis wore shalvar kameez. They would come to Karim Khan's food shop in the morning for a rusk and tea, or in the afternoon after school for dal, standing around the lean-to and shoveling the food into their mouths, shouting and making a clatter, very conscious of their uniforms and their elite status. These were the sons of the wealthier houses nearby, of business owners, owners of the larger shops, local ward politicians, wholesalers, members of a rising middle class defined at the higher reaches by the ownership of a car, and at the bottom by the necessity of making hard sacrifices to buy their sons' uniforms and pay for extra tuition.

Sitting at the tandoor and pushing out piles of chapattis and nan, rising teenage Yazid had ample time to study these fortunate creatures. Gradually he began to bend his attitude and his appearance toward theirs, not quite affecting to wear pant-shirt, which would make him ridiculous in the eyes of Karim Khan and of customers, but cutting off his long hair, which had been modeled on gangsters in the movies, taming his rich sideburns, ditto adopted from the movies, and generally toning down his naturally exuberant style, though his loose walk and large appetite and size would always set him apart.

Rarely leaving the food stall, Yazid yet knew much about the world, for he was observant, and all sorts came through the bus station en route to their far destinations. Weary travelers dropped their bags and filled travel-starved bellies with savory curries and his hot-oiled nans and afterward unbuttoned themselves to the sympathetic serving boy, indiscreet because they would never see him again. Gradually, as he became familiar with the college boys, he understood that their views were rather narrower than his, and this gave him confidence. While they might have fine manners and live in proper houses, cosseted by their mothers and sisters, they were tame and didn't penetrate very far toward an understanding of the unforgiving streets and city. He formed friendships with the college boys, never presuming on his acquaintance, always ready to step back into character as the fellow behind the tandoor, sparing himself from any rebuff by this discretion. Yet he observed them closely and bided his time. He wanted to make friends among them rather than among the boys like him who worked the shops and sold cheap trinkets to travelers and ran the scams around the gullies, gutter princes, loud and quick to dodge a slap, smoking cigarettes, shouting after the begging girls who floated around the bus stop unchaperoned.

One spring when Yazid was seventeen or eighteen, the Nizamud-din College boys developed a passion for carrom board, poor man's billiards, played on a plywood square with the object of knocking round plastic pucks into corner pockets with a striker. Suddenly that year boys all over Pakistan were playing the game, in cities and towns, with federations and tournaments and newspaper coverage. Crowds of the college boys would gather around a charpoy set in front of the food stall, playing for cups of tea or plates of biscuits, standing in circles around the board with the seriousness of parliamentary debaters, discussing strategy, the real experts bringing their own favorite strikers. Yazid would serve out the snacks they ordered and stand watching, occasionally dropping in some humorous comment. Initially they had a miniature board, which they would carry to Karim Khan's stall, but when they banded together and bought a regulation-sized one, three feet to a side, Yazid offered to store it for them in the shop. He thus became the master of ceremonies, keeper of the board. He even found a rule book in one of the sec-ondhand bookstalls and studied it and so became the acknowledged umpire, his word on the finer points accepted as final. At night, alone, he would practice shots in his room, and so himself became an ace, rarely playing, because of his duties as a server, hard to get and therefore in demand, called when some outsider sat down and cleared the table of the locals. In the middle of a game, as he wiped out his opponent, putting away puck after puck with his striker, Yazid would say, chewing the tip of his mustache in the corner of his mouth, "I'm feasting on him, just feasting on him," and this became a catchall phrase for the college boys, used indiscriminately.

*

By the time summer came, when it was too hot to sit and play out in front of the food stall, a little core had formed around Yazid. Cen-ter of operations for the carrom players shifted to Yazid's shabby room attached to the food stall, formerly a storeroom, looking onto a gully on the side. For his first eight or nine years working for Karim Khan, Yazid slept rough on one of the charpoys lined up on a swept dirt apron in front of the stall, never even bothering to choose any one particular spot, but sleeping where he fell, cheerful under the stars, a fan to cool him in summer, and his clothes hung on nails in the filthy toilet that leaked sewage out into a little grassy plot at the back of the building, his comb on a shelf and then later a shaver and soap to make foam. He hadn't asked for the room. Karim Khan had told him one morning to empty the storeroom of the garbage lying there, empty Dalda ghee tins and piles of jute bags. Yazid had become too old, said Karim Khan, to be sprawled every morning in front of the stall, sleeping late as he often did and comfortably watching the street in front of him come to life as if in his own living room.

Now the room became a sort of clubhouse for the carrom players, so much so that several of the boys chipped in and had it white-washed inside by a withered opium smoker who made a living in the neighborhood as a handyman. There were two charpoys, with a table that held the board squeezed between them, teacups crowded to the side, players sitting cross-legged. The great luxury was a ceiling fan, given to Yazid secondhand by some buddy in the neighborhood, which made him the butt of his friends' jokes, who called it proof of his love of fine living. He also nailed pictures of actresses cut from the Sunday papers on the rough brick walls, although these soon were dust covered and flyblown and quite unregarded.

What the boys liked about this arrangement was that nothing was expected of them in that room. There were no rules, all came and went as they liked, they played carrom or they didn't, sometimes they played cards or just talked, sometimes one of them would be in a jam and would sleep there for a night or two. The college boys, who mostly came from respectable families, did not enjoy such freedom anywhere else. Yazid had the one indispensable quality for a man establishing a club: He was always at home, sitting in the veranda of the stall making nan and chapattis, or slumbering in his room if he had no guests, and even if he had gone off somewhere on an errand the room was never locked. Karim Khan had by now taken up another little boy off the streets, this one of known parentage but with parents who asked no questions and gave him up to this business as a riddance. Yazid thus assumed an emeritus position in the enterprise, though he still made the nan and still dealt with the cash when Karim Khan wasn't present. The old man—by then he would have been over seventy, wiry and likely to live forever—would go off to his home in Mardan for several weeks at a time, and when he returned Yazid would hand him every paisa that the shop earned, keeping a notebook with any subtractions carefully noted, cigarettes, a trip to the cinema, for he still took no salary, but asked for money when he needed it—never asking for much, a few times asking a lot, given over by Karim Khan without ever a question.

✳

One afternoon several of the boys had gone shares on a case of pilfered beer sold from the back gate of the Murree Brewery, a sideline for the brewery workers. Kamran Khokar, a senior boy whose father was a councilor in the Rawalpindi wards, knew one of the brewery managers, knew all sorts of tricks and could get his fellow students into scrapes and then out of them unscathed. A junior school student who served as Kamran's bullyboy and gofer brought the bottles in a gunny sack, the jute wet from being stashed in a nearby icehouse that belonged to yet another student's father.

"Is it cold?" asked Kamran, pulling one of the bottles out of the sack and putting it against his face. "Oh, it better be cold!" He pinched the boy's cheek and slapped him gently. "You're lucky, anyway," he said indulgently. "It is cold."

Yazid loomed over the carrom board planning a shot, his thick fingers dusted with the talcum powder they used to slick the surface. Without looking up he said indifferently, "Take some money, it's in that vest hanging up there."

"There you go again," said Kamran, sitting down and putting the sack under the charpoy, pulling out bottles and handing them around. There were three other people in the room, the boy who brought the beer and two others of the core gang. "You drink on the house, we all know you're broke."

"I am the house," said Yazid complacently. He took the beer and popped the top off with a quick smack on the wooden charpoy leg, catching it neatly in the air and shooting it into the corner—one of his tricks.

"You're not a house," retorted Kamran, "you're a barrel. It costs the rest of us a fortune keeping you full."

"I keep telling you not to bring all that garbage. You guys with your bags of samosas and God knows what. This is a tea stall, remember? I eat free."

The younger boys grinned at Yazid's insouciance with the big square-headed school bully. Kamran walked with a swagger and played the same role in the school that his father played in his ward of the city, keeping a hand in all the pies and pushing in wherever he could. He kept close to the powers above him, young Kamran trustee to the Nizamuddin College headmaster, unctuous when he needed to be, playing enforcer, too. They had nicknamed him Cuckoo, after the parasitic bird that drives its siblings from the nest, because sometimes for sport and to keep his hand in practice he would beat up his squeaky elder brother.

Soon a heavy fug of cigarette smoke hung over the players. They were betting for small stakes, Yazid winning, talking a bit of trash down to his opponents, studying the board the way chess players do, then cracking a shot, making cunning deflections and rebounds.

Another boy came in, Zain, whose grandfather and now father owned the old British grocery in Rawalpindi, selling fancy produce and select foods to the civil servants and officers and diplomats stationed there, the family distinguished by this commerce with foreigners and the wealthy, more worldly for it. He stood at the door, without entering, looked at Yazid and caught his eye, nodded.

"Hey mister, come in and slum around with us a bit," said Yazid affectionately, patting the charpoy beside himself.

"I'll come back later. I brought you something."

He stepped into the room and put a bag of apples on a charpoy, then continued standing by the door.

"From my father," he said. "We just got them in at the store."

"Look at him!" cooed Kamran. "He's so shy. It's adorable!"

Yazid and Zain had taken to spending time together, one of those odd couples, Yazid big and broad and hirsute, walking with his rolling gait, and Zain small and fine and finicky, with small hands, small feet, a long straight nose, and curly hair worn slightly long in the back as his single extravagance, even in this following the fashion rather than defining it. Zain brought Yazid serious books, not like the romances and adventure stories that formed his usual literary diet, histories and leftist political tracts, his father an old-school lefty from the days of the anti-British movement, despite or because of his regular interactions at the store with the blimps and pukka sahibs and their wives. Yazid jokingly called Zain the Professor and took pride in the connection.

"Tell your friend to sit down and join us," said Kamran. "Give him a beer, it'll do him good. Tell him not to be so ladylike."

"I can speak for myself," said Zain sharply.

Zain did in fact seem too prim for the situation. Slipping in, he perched at the edge of a charpoy near the door, legs crossed, then borrowed a penknife from Yazid and cut up apples and passed around slices fanned on the palm of his hand. The other boys all thought there must be something going on between him and Yazid, a common enough occurrence at an age and in circumstances where girls were quite unavailable and hormones in full raging flush, Pakistani boys and their boy crushes, and all forgotten when they married in a few years.

"Leave him alone," grunted Yazid. "Cut the bullshit and let's play."

"Playing with you is like shoveling money into a well," grumbled Kamran. "I'd rather bullshit."

"It's a paisa a point, man. Nothing for the rich politician's son! Anyway, it's good luck, tossing coins in a well."

"My coins and your luck, boy. I bring the booze, and then I pay for the privilege, too."

Boys came and went, Yazid playing or relinquishing the table if he lost, a freewheeling game. Only a few of the boys drank, the ones who knew they could slip past their parents at the end of the evening, Kamran and a couple of his close buddies. Yazid kept up too, chugging off bottles when challenged to by Kamran, the two of them rivals here as in other things, in carrom board, in cards, even in arm wrestling, the son of the ward boss ready to crack heads.

*

The quarrel began over nothing, as these things do. A couple of hours had passed, Yazid holding Zain back when he rose to leave. "Stick around, after a while we'll have food. I've got some of that marrow-bone nihari coming from Haji Noora's place." As he rarely troubled Karim Khan for money and so took hospitality from his college friends too often, whenever he had a windfall Yazid would spend the lot on a blowout for the crowd, clearing his debts all at once. That morning he had sold a big pile of the empty ghee tins that accumulated behind the tea stall, one of his perquisites.

Kamran continued to needle Zain, joking about the apples. Finally, he went too far.

"Tell your apple-cheek friend to cut up some more of that nice fruit. I wish he'd brought some peaches. He's a peach himself. He's like an egg, actually. Allah, I can imagine what that tastes like. We're all jealous, Yazid bhai. I suppose you tap that pretty often."

Whenever Yazid drank, his eyes, irritated from daily staring down into the tandoor's radiation, became extraordinarily red. He gave Kamran a heavy look. "Shut up, Kamran. You're drunk."

"You shut up, tandoori boy. I suppose when you're brought up in the street even a little priss like your Zain here seems a pretty classy fuck. Your mother must be proud."

Yazid usually moved so deliberately that they called him the Python. Now, as if released from a spring, Bayazid's enormous hand shot across the table and took Kamran by the throat and lifted him till he seemed to hover over the charpoy.

He was cool. "You should be careful what you say."

"Let me down, you fat bastard." Kamran could barely speak; he wheezed. Yazid plopped him down, then put his hands in his lap, awaiting events.

"Wait, I forgot!" said Kamran. He slapped himself on the forehead, miming. "You're actually a real bastard! Poor Yazid. We all know you popped out of one of those railway whores after your saintly Karim Khan snuck over to the wrong side of the tracks."

Still looking into Kamran's face, quite impassive, head tilted as if studying his expressions, Yazid reached calmly down with his right hand and took the penknife with which Zain had been peeling apples and took it between forefinger and thumb, put the blade close to Kamran's face.

"How about if I make you not so pretty?"

"You're fucking kidding me," gasped Kamran. The room had become very still.

Suddenly, as quickly as his hand had shot across the table, Yazid turned the knife down and stabbed himself in the leg, burying the blade in his thigh. Rising slightly, flipping the bloodied knife into the corner, he took Kamran again by the throat and lifted him bodily and threw him out the door with a single hand, not just pushing him but hard as if driving him into the ground, like a ball thrown to bounce.

The other boys in the room had stood up and now fled out the door. A surprisingly small red stain inkblotted Yazid's tan shalvar where the knife had gone in.

"Why don't you buzz off, Kamran," Yazid said evenly. "We'll talk tomorrow. Forget about it."

"You're finished," spat Kamran, rolling onto his knees and then quickly twisting up, athletic. "I'm going to fuck you up."

Yazid studied his bloody leg. "We'll see," he said mildly.

*

Only Zain remained behind. Yazid watched the other boys hurrying away, then turned to him and grinned.

"Ouch! That really hurts."

"Hurts!" said Zain. "You crazy person. You stabbed yourself."

"Better than stabbing him, I suppose."

"That's true. And now what?" He leaned down and peered at the bloody spot on Yazid's shalvar where the blade had entered, a look of distaste on his face.

"Don't worry, this is nothing. I've cut myself worse than this butchering chickens. That blade wasn't even two inches long."

Zain took a handkerchief from his pocket and tore it into strips.

"I'll have to take off my shalvar for this," joked Yazid. "Then you will be compromised." He was slightly hysterical, giggly at the sight of the now copious blood. Adrenaline. "You're the only guy I know who carries around a handkerchief."

The wound looked like a gill on a fish, a slim keyhole oozing bright capillary blood. Zain poured water over the wound till it ran more or less clear and then helped Yazid tighten the handkerchief strips around the massive leg.

"What are you laughing at?" asked Zain.

"Me sitting here with my shalvar off and your flowered handkerchief around my leg." Limping up, he took another shalvar from the tin trunk under the bed, where he kept all his clothes.

When he had dressed, he said, "Now what? Shall we keep playing?"

"You're still pretending, are you? I'll go get some spirit and a proper bandage."

"I'll come with you." Yazid didn't want to be alone after the beer and the excitement. The leg hurt.

"Absolutely not. Sit down, or, rather, lie down. You're an idiot. I'll be right back." Turning at the door, smiling at Yazid, he said, "Thanks, by the way. And the good thing is, we'll all remember this in thirty years. Now you're a legend."

After that, the two were best friends.

*

With the beer and the drunkenness and the verve Yazid had shown in stabbing himself, and not wanting to draw attention to the episode, Kamran didn't make a fuss. After a couple of weeks, he rejoined the carrom board mafia, and Yazid made no comment, treated him the same as he did all the others, all the others except Zain. If anything, Yazid and Kamran associated more closely after this, with the difference that Yazid treated the councilor's son with a slight familiarity. Zain stopped coming to the carrom board matches, but instead would slip over at the first school recess and have an early bite with Yazid, always accepting his hospitality of nan and dal and curry without demur, his good manners and perhaps a kind of admiration for Yazid shown by his willingness to be indebted so often, given food day after day. If he found Yazid snoozing he would lean over him and push on his shoulder, rolling him about, and Yazid would groan, "Oh, God, you're impossible. Lunchtime, is it? Where's that bloody boy with my food."

"You pasha! You used to be the serving boy here. What happened?"

These were happy days for Yazid. One of his bazaari friends, a taxi driver, had taught Yazid to drive, the friend generous to Yazid, as so many were, exactly because Yazid took as easily as he gave and had no expectations and was excellent company. Yazid now passed this skill on to Zain, borrowing the taxi and driving him out to the empty dirt tracks that spidered out into the scrubby plains around Rawalpindi. The boys made these excursions on the sly from Zain's protective if unconventional father, who had plans for his only son that extended to Government College in Lahore and a rich career—who knows?—in the civil service, or as a lawyer, a doctor, certainly something more than a grocer, however fancy the goods he sold to the increasing community of foreigners in Rawalpindi. His son fooling about with a taxi would not have amused Malik Kamal Sahib, who was a real Awan Malik, from Mianwali side, that martial land-owning race. He maintained a car himself, a temperamental but immaculately kept Morris Minor.

The first time Yazid went to Zain's house marked also the first time that he entered any respectable middle-class family's dwelling, if a higgledy house built up on four floors deserves that name, with a cracked wooden gate painted pistachio green leading into a courtyard too small for the car, which stood in the narrow gully outside. Zain had invited Yazid several times, but Yazid put him off, afraid that he wouldn't know how to behave, or that Malik Kamal might be offended to find his son entertaining a server from a tea shop. That afternoon, a Sunday, the boys had borrowed the taxi and Zain had driven on the blacktop road for the first time. They took the new avenue running along the outskirts of Islamabad and then drove up toward Murree on the winding, climbing road that followed the old Mughal horse and palanquin track up to Kashmir from the Punjab Plains.

In those days, just before the 1970 election, which brought Zulfikar Bhutto to power, Zain and even Yazid had grown intoxicated with Bhutto's socialist rhetoric, a promise that a new era of unimaginable possibilities would soon emerge before their eyes, that elite power in Pakistan would be toppled, the poor raised up, the system remade. Zain pulled over the car under a banyan tree beside the Murree road, and they ate samosas prepared by Zain's mother and drank tea from a thermos. Zain lay flat under the tree, with his head on a rolled-up coat, staring up through the branches and speaking of the future, of his plans. His father would support him next year at Government College in Lahore, if he were admitted.

Simultaneously shy and passionate, he spoke of his larger dreams, of making a significant life under this new dispensation, the reconfigured socialist system that Bhutto had announced, real justice for everyone, land reform, equality, power in the hands of the people, the freedom of the vote. Unfolding a newspaper clipping from his pocket, he read aloud a transcript of one of Bhutto's speeches, and Yazid was thrilled by the moment, by the dry rustling of the wind through the leaves and by Zain's handsome, earnest face in profile as he read.

"That's all very fine," said Yazid. "But I doubt it's for people like me. It's for you, your people, and that's good enough."

"No, it's exactly for people like you."

As they drove back into the city at dusk, Zain said, "I want to ask you a favor, Bayazid."

"Anything."

"I want you to have dinner tonight with me, in my house. I've asked my mother to cook something special."

"Another time. I need to dress properly and all that. Look at me, I've got samosa grease all over my shalvar leg."

"I insist. We'll stop and you can change at your room."

✳

In Zain's house, Yazid perched at the edge of his seat and stood up every time Zain's mother came into the room, bringing first pome-granate squash, then food, several dishes served on a low table set in front of the sofa, and even a dessert, carrot halva with clotted cream. The mother was small, with a very fair face, like a girl from the north, and a single dark mole above her lip, adoring toward Zain, and immediately familiar with Yazid, calling him "child," urging him to eat more, watching the boys after she brought each dish to see what they took, then retiring to the kitchen for refills. Yazid had not seen Zain like this before, both the pride he took in his mother's attentions, boyish that way, and also his brusqueness with her, slightly embarrassed, impatient, cool in response to her tenderness. Malik Kamal, the father, had recently bought an elaborate radio, square as a troll and as large, with a blond wooden case and speakers covered with tan cloth, a presence in the room. The boys listened to the news on Radio Pakistan and then to the BBC Urdu service, which was full of the upcoming 1970 election, and spoke also of tensions in East Pakistan, of strikes, political rallies, upheaval, war clouds, all the elements that thrill young men at eighteen and twenty. Malik Kamal came in when the BBC broadcast began and sat down, nodding to the mother, who brought food for him also.

"Take a seat, young man," he said to Yazid, and then, when Yazid still continued to stand, he winked at Zain. "Come on, tell this fellow it's okay."

"I cannot take a seat in front of you, Malik Sahib," said Yazid.

Malik Kamal looked at him shrewdly. "You're the one from Karim Khan's stall, aren't you? My son talks about you." He made an impatient gesture, flapping his hand downward. "Come on, don't annoy me. Sit down and eat."

They listened to the broadcast, and after it finished, Malik Sahib switched off the set and turned to Yazid. "So what do you make of all this?"

"What can I say, Malik Sahib. You know the saying, whoever holds the whip owns the buffalo. This is maybe just about some new people grabbing the whip from the old ones."

"And who's the buffalo, then?"

"People like me, I suppose. Karim Khan says I'm a buffalo, and I have to admit that even I can see a resemblance."

"And people like me?"

"No sir. You and yours are the new rising group, if you forgive my saying so."

Malik Kamal laughed. "You're a clever boy! I can see why my son speaks of you so often." He stood up. "Anyway, any friend of my Zain is always welcome here. Perhaps in Mr. Bhutto's new Pakistan you'll be the one holding the whip before long."

After that, Yazid regularly was asked to Zain's house, the radio broadcasts providing a pretext and an occasion. The mother took him in, pitying his orphan status and appreciating his straightforward manners, neither servile nor presumptuous, respectful and unembarrassed and warm. When Malik Kamal debated with Zain about the new socialist politics, he would call on Yazid to back him up, and after some time Yazid allowed his humorous side to emerge in front of Malik Sahib, and even his rough but serviceable philosophy. He could call forth delighted laughter from that quite jolly little man, a nice contrast between sparkling small Malik Kamal and large rocking Yazid. As Yazid discovered, Malik Kamal had developed liberal tastes while running his fancy-goods grocery shop and liked to play a bit of the radical, proud that he was educating his son for a great future, educating even his daughter, and willing to send her too for higher education.

✳

Gradually, Yazid began to understand the whole dynamic of the household, as if he had stepped into a wood and, in his wonder and appreciation, gradually perceived there a whole community of flowers and birds and shy woodland creatures. The mother's brother lived on charity in the house, smoking endless cigarettes up in his room and rarely emerging, coming down to listen to the cricket scores, wearing pajamas and a threadbare robe, thin as an end-stage tuberculosis patient, fingers yellow with nicotine, hacking cough, lighting a cigarette as soon as he sat down with trembling hands. The old humbug would remonstrate against the British, how they should never have given up India, and thought of Lord's Cricket Ground with the same reverence that Zain's mother offered to the Holy Places. Yazid's compendious memory included a remarkable store of cricket scores and batting averages and matches and catches and stumpings and right down into the weeds, balls faced, strike rates, all the minutiae that a quick-witted boy poring over the newspaper in a tea stall between customers might graze upon. It's a good thing to be in with the family dog—especially a snappish one—and soon Yazid and Uncle Rizwan formed a little exclusive cricket club.

They had only one inside servant, Mai Viro, an ancient crone with a bead of sweat perpetually on her upper lip, who washed and carried and ruled the household from the kitchen and might in her sleep have pedaled a generator to provide electricity, if that had been required. Ill-tempered, grumbling against Zain's mother, worshipping the father, she took a poisonous disliking to Yazid, be-damned that the family's status should be fouled by this jumped-up tea stall boy treated as an equal. She would come into the room, squatting along and flicking a filthy black rag reeking with disinfectant along the floor, and flick a couple of times at Yazid too for good measure, before retreating into the corner to hear the Urdu broadcast, mumbling irritably. Yazid tried everything, courtly language and shameless bribes of delicacies lifted from the tea stall and even once a little mirror with a beaded frame, but nothing would appease the old bat.

Finally, with a piercing note like a French horn rising up from the background of an orchestra, or like a deer that steps last of all and most shyly into a clearing, came Yasmin, Zain's younger sister, almost his twin. Yazid of course knew that his friend had a sister, and had seen her moving through the streets, his impression being mostly of a little froth of white, a white head covering, a girl so slight and floating that he had always assumed her to be much younger than Zain.

Because he had never had close contact with respectable girls or even with women, rarely spoken to any female other than brusque customers, women coming to take away food, he was aloof from them, lumped all women and girls together, creatures whose movements and concerns were unfathomably foreign. At fifteen he lost his virginity in a backstreet brothel to a woman twenty years his senior, to her greedy hands, her body in his imagination carrying the lion reek of all the men who had possessed her, went again like a man suffering blinding toothache, and fought against returning into the arms of those brutes, and failed. One day, after a particularly unsavory experience, involving an ancient greasy madam and an attempt at blackmail, he swore to go there never again, and kept his resolution in the face of all temptation and crude desire. Masturbation seemed to him like self-murder, wet dreams unavoidable. He tried to keep the blinders on and prayed, or would have, if he knew of any God that might relieve him of this rooted affliction.

Yazid would no more have associated Yasmin with this category of experience than he would compare shit on his shoe to a melody rising far away in the night, when he lay with his soul bared and receptive in his little room and dreaming. For many weeks, into the spring, into the summer, he was aware of her occasionally flitting past the open door at the corner of his vision, while he sat with Zain or Uncle Rizwan, hearing the news. Dimly he allowed that this other person also lived here, in his absence would own these rooms as much as any of the others. A young man would not ordinarily be invited into a house harboring a young girl. His status as an orphan, a tea boy, both made his presence possible and humiliated him, for his presence could not be misconstrued, must be exceptional. He could not compromise Yasmin. His rising awareness of her therefore seemed to him illicit, a betrayal, and he began to avoid the house, until Zain took offense and ordered him back.

"What's happened to your manners? My mother keeps asking if you're upset with us for some reason. Come with me right now, the cricket starts in twenty minutes. Uncle Rizwan sent me especially."

✳

One afternoon, Yazid and Zain had gone to hear the great Zulfikar Ali Bhutto give a speech at Liaqat Bagh, a park where political rallies were held. Bhutto cupped the crowd in his hands and shook them and filled them with his invective, until finally the young blades who had been bussed in from near and far lost all restraint and began throwing chairs and charging the police and were lathi-charged in return. The two boys happened to catch the attention of some zealous constable, and Zain received a cunning two-handed slicing blow from a cane whip, cutting the cloth on his back like a knife and leaving a stripe—the innocent always suffer in these circumstances, he and Yazid were in full retreat—a welt rising and blood weeping through, much more blood than might be expected. Zain added to his fine sensibilities a fainting aversion to pain and a spirit not equal to rough blows. He thought he'd been killed and had to be dragged by Yazid all through the bazaar and home, limping, sighing, Yazid tender and encouraging, both concerned and amused, glad of the opportunity to take his friend under his broad wing.

When they reached Zain's house, thankfully they found no one at home. Malik Sahib and his wife had gone off to see relatives, for once taking Uncle Rizwan with them. Even Mai Viro, who haunted the place like a resident ghost, had disapparated somewhere. The boys crashed inside, Zain throwing himself face down on a sofa still wearing his bloodied shirt, and Yazid nosing about looking for bandages and disinfectant.

"Cabinet next to the stairs," croaked Zain. "Third floor."

Yazid had never before penetrated into the sanctum beyond the living room. Tentatively he climbed the stairs, the house built around a shaft like an atrium, larger than he expected, dark and then open at the top, so that sparrows got in. On the second floor, passing a room, he saw Yasmin lying on a bed, curled, napping, back to him, feet bare and up on the bed, her little slippers tucked beneath. The bottoms of her feet glowed pale white. Yazid had never before seen her uncovered hair, which was long and black but had a reddish tinge. Later he would surmise that it was hennaed, to him a mysterious refinement. Silent, retreating, he went back to the stairway, down a few steps, and coughed, loud, a coughing fit. Nothing. Then he heard Yasmin call, "Who's that?"

"Excuse me, Bibi Jee. It's Bayazid."

He had frightened her. "Who? Yazid?"

"Nothing, Bibi. Just Zain has a little cut. I'll go back now. If you can bring some disinfectant."

She came out, putting on her dupatta, unperturbed now but brisk at this intrusion into the family quarters.

"Hello. How are you? Is everything okay?"

"It's fine. If you can come."

Yazid feared she would shriek or make a scene when she saw all the blood. Instead, she was perfectly composed, helped Zain to remove his shirt, told him to lie down again, studied the wound, and said dismissively, "You'll live, my dear."

Zain sat up. "You heartless thing. I'm in agony."

Yasmin laughed, the first time Yazid had heard this, for she had always been circumspect, self-effacing, slipping past and ghosting up the stairs if she found him sitting in the living room with the cricket fans. He expected her to be shy and tinkling, and instead her laugh was broad, a bit husky even.

"You're such a baby. Go on, lie down again. I'll be right back."

As he waited in the living room, smiling over Zain's recumbent form, Yazid's thoughts roamed. She had surprised him. Her reaction had been remarkably—how to put it?—normal. His only intimate experience of decent girls had been when Karim Khan invited him to each of his three daughters' weddings. Treated as family, he sat across from the girls singing around the bride and groom and smelled their musk and cheap desi scent, village girls dressed up in bright colors, and felt happily invisible to them, who could marry only within their families and knew him as the orphan boy from the tea stall, a favorite of their father. Yasmin was so much cooler, quicker, more assured. She was small, her face seeming to him very precisely cut, as if from some soft material, a silhouette. Near twin to Zain, his feminine face suited her better, though her notched chin expressed more strength and even stubbornness than the brother's sensitive mien. Yazid had never permitted himself to look directly at her before, nor to consider her personality, for any such thoughts would be a betrayal of his friendship with Zain.

She returned with a bowl filled with hot water and a cloth, crouched down beside her brother, and dabbed at the wound, an angry ridge weeping drops of blood that looked as if a razor blade had scored soft leather.

"Come on, can't you be gentler?" he hissed between clenched teeth as she applied the disinfectant. "I thought you plan to be a doctor!"

"I'm in a hurry. If your papa sees this your career as a political activist will end before it even began. It's an honorable wound, really. You've bled for your idol."

"Don't make fun of me."

"Notice how your friend here is too smart for whipping."

"That's what comes from being brought up on the streets," suggested Yazid. "I'm like one of those railway station dogs. You can't hit them with a stone if you try."

Yasmin cocked an eye at him. "You look pretty well fed for a railway station dog. I'd say you're more one of those fancy bulldogs that aficionados raise on butter and milk mixed with sugar."

"Not at all. Those are kept for fighting. Not for show. I'm not the fighting type."

Yasmin laughed, easily brought to it. "You're Karim Khan's great pet and luxury. I can see why he's never prospered much, keeping you in chicken curries."

"Stop it," Zain protested. "Poor fellow. He's a hero, and you're talking about chicken curries. He carried me out of there on his back, more or less. Another man wouldn't have stopped for the wounded."

"Tell me all about your rally," said Yasmin, who had finished wrapping a bandage all around Zain's chest and trunk, the wound stanched. Yazid held the knot with his blunt finger while she nimbly cinched it down. "I wish I could have been there."

Confidence in his storytelling powers overcame the reserve Yazid felt in front of this pretty girl. The college boys and others too grinned and pulled up to listen around the tandoor when Yazid began one of his meandering shaggy tales.

"I guess it began with those boys they bussed in from the university in Peshawar. They were all standing together, and they started making a fuss just out of sheer craziness. Bhutto Sahib kept pushing and pushing until finally they couldn't control themselves."

"You mean your Comrade Bhutto. And you should all be calling each other comrade too."

Yazid smiled, keeping company with his audience. "As you say. So, our Comrade Bhutto talked and he built it up and built it up for longer than you could imagine, soft and loud and taking it here and taking it there. It's like music, really, you should hear him do it in real life. And then finally he stops for a long time and looks all around and everyone is silent and waiting for him, holding our breath.

"Then out of nowhere he shouts, 'We'll smash it down, and we'll break it down, and we'll level it to the ground!' and he was standing alone on that big stage with one of those tall microphones on a metal pole, leaning over the head of the microphone to shout. He'd been sort of playing with it all along, a little metal head on a long shaft. He leans back and slaps the mike with his hand, and it teeters and wobbles over and almost falls flat and then it stands up again. He waits, and then when the microphone is standing up again he shouts, 'I swear to you. We'll smash it all to pieces and we'll make it new again!' Again, the microphone, a slap, and it teeters and almost falls over, and we're all watching that microphone, and we're all totally eyes on it, and there's perfect silence. Bhutto Sahib pauses again till the microphone rights itself and then suddenly, roaring—his voice had gotten hoarse, he could barely shout, but he did—'You'll own the world, we'll forge with fire a sword of steel from ice.' And he smashes the microphone and knocks it down slam flat on the ground and the crowd just went completely wild.

"That's when I started pulling your brother toward the gate. I knew what was coming. Those boys would have torn up anyone who got in their way then. Even I was about ready to start marching wherever that man told us to. I was ready to believe anything . . ."

Yasmin, watching Yazid's motions with amusement—he had acted out Bhutto slapping the microphone, once, twice, and then the third time hardest—interrupted him. "But tell me, bhai, what exactly is it that you believed in?"

"That we'd smash everything up and then we'd have it our way."

"And then the police step in and slice and dice my brother here. Wind you up and then beat you down."

Yazid relaxed, spread his big hands on his knees. "Anyway, my blood is already too cold for that. I was watching the exits the whole time."

"Thank God for good sense. And you, my beloved brother, should stay away from all this. You're not built for rioting in the streets."

"I should go," said Yazid. "Before Malik Sahib returns."

"Not at all," said Yasmin. "You're the hero. I was just joking about my father being angry. He'll be proud secretly that his son got a bit blooded. You should stay and bask in it. Now you really will have my mama eating out of your hands. And you know my father marched with our own Frontier Gandhi redshirts before he got sensible. He loves all this agitation, so long as they don't break shop windows."

Yazid felt confused, embarrassed. He couldn't bear to be so close to Yasmin anymore. "No, I must beg leave. I promised Karim Khan I wouldn't be late."

Without rising Zain waved his hand. "All right, then. Come see me in the morning. Yasmin can let you out."

Walking down the corridor, past the kitchen, which always smelled of spice and good food, Yazid thought of his ambling bulk and felt inadequate and experienced the loneliness that sometimes plagued him in the night. What right had he to be here?

At the door, he opened the catch and let himself out.

"Please, Bibi Jee, go in."

"It's nice," she said, coming partway out the door. "The air smells like rain."

"We can wish for rain," suggested Yazid, uttering the first words that came into his head.

"You're a good friend to my brother," said Yasmin quietly.

"Please." They both were embarrassed to be alone.

Yazid didn't know how to end it. "I'll go," he blurted out, and as he walked he thought he heard her trilling laugh behind him and hated himself and wanted to slam his head against a pole or bend a piece of steel or run into the countryside and not stop. "I'm such a fucking fool," he muttered to himself, hurrying through the dark streets to the familiar happy light of the tea stall.

✻

He had thought it must be late in the evening but found the evening rush at the stall in full swing.

"Come on, out of the way," he told the boy whom he had taught to make the chapattis and nan. "Let me show you how it's done!"

He set to work, and everything fell to hand and felt right, the balls of dough in his hands, the play of it, the liveliness of the dough as he worked it, and the satisfying whack as he slapped the wet cha-patti onto the orange glowing wall of the tandoor. Thousands of these tandoori rotis had passed through his hands, sometimes he thought that he'd fed half of Pakistan. That was his bounty, that was his gift. With his back to the wall, tandoor at his knees, sit-ting under the tin lean-to roof and surveying the charpoys arranged out front in the open all the way to the edge of the road, twelve by count, he felt himself sitting at the wheel of a bus, or even the cockpit of an airplane, seen in a movie. This was his domain. Thank God the customers rolled in, and each one got a signature piece hot from his hands, and no chapatti allowed to cool, but thrown to the scrap bin if not taken right away.

"Look at you up there," said Karim Khan, emerging from the inner room where he sat for hours doing absolutely nothing, perfectly content, shifting only to rise and say his prayers. "Make me one too, let's see if you've still got that magic touch."

"You're the one who should come up here, Khan Sahib. Let's try if you've got it still. A real journey into the past."

Yazid would tease him about his immobility, his hours that passed like a stream before him. "You Pathans have two modes," he would say. "Still as a stone, or shooting at your own cousins. But you, Uncle, never even wake yourself for the shooting part."

Karim Khan had just three teeth left in his mouth, the rest pink mottled gums, so that his spreading smile made him look like a little boy peeping out from a wizened wrinkled face. Nothing more beautiful than a happy face in an old man.

Now he stood for a moment with his hand on Yazid's shoulder, then went and got his hookah, pulled a charpoy closer to the tandoor, and began a desultory conversation, chewing the cud, wanting to bask in his apprentice's glow.

✻

Bayazid had never quite given up the fantasy he nurtured in boyhood, of discovering himself a child of some minister or prince. His romantic soul took refreshment from this impossibility, and his love for Yasmin could grow expansive and pure exactly because he looked at her from so very far away, and yet could imagine, dream, that he would rise to her station. She was immaculate, each little curve, her dimple when she smiled, her fine gestures, the way she moved her fingers idly in her lap when she spoke with animation. Once when a strand of hair fell into her face while her hands were busy, she blew it back with a little puff from the corner of her mouth, blowing it up only to have it drift down again in a falling grace across her forehead, and this seemed to him adorable. Yazid went to Zain's house only by invitation, and later, when he counted up the visits where Yasmin too had appeared and joined the conversation, there were not more than five or six of them, and it pained him that soon they all blurred together.

For many weeks he did not see her, keeping away as much as he could, called over by Zain, uncomfortable now while sitting talking of politics or of cricket with Uncle Rizwan. A couple of times he heard her passing through the house behind him, returning from school or from the market, and he prickled with anxiety and both wished and feared that she would come in. When next he saw her close up, she had just returned from the bazaar on a day so hot that drops of sweat dimpled her slender forearms as she raised her dupatta to cover her hair.

Now in front of Uncle Rizwan she was demure, quite different from her quick teasing on that evening after the rally.

"As salaam uleikum, Yazid Bhai. I hope you're talking cricket and not politics." Still, she had that impudent smile, amused by him.

Yazid had stood up when she came in and stood shifting from one foot to the other and looking unfocused at a spot in the air, not facing her.

"Look, they haven't even brought you water," she said, and went in the kitchen and made tea with her own hands. When she brought it, then he dared just for a moment to look in her face, as she handed him the cup. Nothing in his life had prepared him for her perfection.

He thought of her often, dreamed of her, the stories that he had read in those many romance novels now come to life, wishing that some mad chance should allow him to give his life for her or to worship her from a distance, but in sight of her. He was desperate and happy and shy, a tiny shivering piercing emotion inside him all the time. His throat ached when he thought of her, and at unexpected moments suddenly he would feel deep joy, gratitude. The world could not possibly be bigger than now.

✳

One Sunday morning Yazid came to pick up Zain for a trip to Rawal Dam on the other side of Islamabad, where there were rowboats for rent and a couple of stalls selling pakoras and samosas. Always before he had visited in the afternoon or evening. The house had a different morning feel, fresher, the single mulberry tree in the courtyard fruiting, so that Mai Viro stood washing away the fallen fruit catkins on the concrete slabs with a hose and a broom, her shalvar pants rolled up to her knees, hair uncovered.

"Hello, Auntie," said Yazid.

"Hello, young man. When did I have the honor of becoming related to you?"

"I'm afraid no one's related to me," replied Yazid, cheerily deflecting her temper.

That morning for the first time Yazid wore pants and a white shirt, as the college boys did, and black pointed shoes, pants, shirt, all new, the largest size in the little shop where the schoolboys bought their kit, the shoes cruelly laced.

"Those teddy-boy pants will split when you sit down in front of your tandoor," said Mai Viro, sweeping ferociously at the water bubbling from the hose.

"Let's hope not," said Yazid blithely. "Is Zain Sahib up?"

"This is an early rising house. The big Sahib's already gone to the store. Shouldn't you be at work too?"

"It's my day off."

"Well, then you're luckier than me," she said, and returned to sweeping.

*

Inside, the rooms were cool and a breeze seemed to blow through and into the atrium. He found Zain in the sitting room with the newspapers in front of him, still wearing a dhoti, and eating eggs with paratha.

"Come on," he said. "Tuck in. I'll go change. I'll tell Viro to make you something."

"For God's sake, don't! She'll add a dose of rat poison as flavoring."

"Yeah, we all worry about that, except the revered father. When they built that woman they injected her personality backward. The rest of us try to hide our bad temper, but she hides the good one."

Yazid sat down, throwing out his legs comfortably and slumping back, head tilted to watch his friend. "That's how you know she's loyal. She doesn't bother to try and win you over."

"That's a subtle thought. Anyway, I'll be right back. Give me twenty minutes. I'm sorry, I haven't shaved yet. I need to look smart with you all dressed like a bridegroom!" He joked, making his only reference to Yazid's attire, but it was a serious matter, the tea stall boy putting on schoolboy clothes.

Yazid sat listening to the sounds of the echoing house. Sparrows that had flown down into the roofless atrium chirped noisily. Zain's paratha, torn and dabbed with grease, looked delicious, and after satisfying himself that no one was around he got up and tore a piece off, sprinkled it with salt, and sat down, munching. He mustn't wipe his hands on his new pants.

A rustling behind him, and he knew immediately that it was Yasmin. He pretended he didn't know she was there, and she also stayed quiet for a long moment. Then she walked in and stood across from him, one hand touching the back of a sofa, the glass bangles on her wrist making a little chipping sound.

"Caught!" she said. "Go on, Yazid Bhai, chew and swallow. Don't pretend you don't have a mouthful of paratha."

He had stood up, heart fluttering. "Waste not want not."

"Will you have some tea?"

"Nothing, thank you."

"At least let me get you some water. To wash down all that paratha."

"It was just a scrap, not enough to need washing."

"But then you'd have to say that. You've probably had two or three of them. I notice the plate's empty."

"On my honor."

She went to the kitchen and returned with a tray and jug of water and two glasses, poured herself one, and offered him one also.

"There you go," she said. Again, they were embarrassed to be alone. Shy, after a moment she continued, "Have a good time at the lake." Still she didn't leave, but stood, her hand playing with a loose thread on the sofa. "Another time, I'd like to see it too." Her voice raised at the end, as if asking a question. Putting her empty glass on a table, she disappeared into the atrium. He heard her chappals on the steps going up, clattering, noisy where usually she drifted silently.

✳

Her glass glowed on the table after she left. The sparrows still were calling in the atrium, and still that delicious breeze, the one that blew through this house and funneled up the atrium, this house that included Uncle Rizwan and his cricket scores and Britisher humbug and the damp beautiful mother and the principled timid father and impossible brilliant difficult Zain and then Yasmin Yasmin Yasmin. And he couldn't help himself, though he knew he mustn't. He stood up—he had sat down again when Yasmin left the room, like a man shot, or whose legs go out from under him—and went over and took the glass that she had drunk from and put his lips exactly where hers had been.

And then he heard Mai Viro's voice.

"What's this! What's this!"

Yazid turned and faced her, the glass still clasped in his hand. She looked triumphant, impossibly old, her face settled down like a sack into her mouth, which turned stubbornly down at the corners.

"Nothing, Bibi. I was just putting the glass back."

"Don't lie," she seethed. "You're doing some magic with her glass, aren't you? Spit it out, what do you have in your mouth? You think I haven't been watching you? Just because Malik Sahib thinks there's no dirt in the gutter doesn't mean I do. I know about the gutter, it stinks and it sticks to your skin. Open your mouth and show me."

She thought he had some magic spell written on a paper in his mouth, to mix it with Yasmin's saliva. Hobbling over, she reached up with her bent crabbed hands and took him roughly by the face, barely able to reach high enough.

"Open it! Now! Or I'll scream."

He opened his mouth and she looked carefully, studied it. She wanted to put her fingers in there, and it seemed awful to think of her rooting around with those claws.

"You get in here, I'll have you in my kitchen. I want to deal with you right now."

He trailed her into the kitchen, then into the little room behind it where she took afternoon rest on a greasy mat lying on the floor, with rags for pillows.

When she turned, he put his hands together as if in prayer. It all would come tumbling down now, he couldn't bear it, for such an innocent trespass. Tears came to his eyes. "For God's sake, Bibi. What have I done?" He reached out to touch her knee in supplication.

"Keep your hands off me. I know what you are, and I know what you'll be. You should never have come into this house. Malik Sahib with his social this and social that, he's proof that too much education makes an idiot. I've been waiting for this. Don't tell me you weren't doing some magic on that little girl. See these hands?" She held her cupped hands in his face, slightly shaking, her anger. "See? These hands brought up that girl. I fed her, I cleaned her, I bathed her. No one else in this house has any sense. And I'll tell you another thing, I'd rather strangle her with these same hands than see a thing like you anywhere near her. I promise you, if ever you come again through those gates, I'll say such things about you that you'll not make that mistake a second time, and I'll tar you and shame you forever. I'm an old woman, and I've served them all my life. They'll believe me over you, no matter how much you've tricked them with your tongue and your made-up manners. Look at you, coming here with those pointed shoes and those pants like a college boy. You'll never be that. Go away." And she spat on the floor, and then even slapped him on his head, which he had bowed before her.

"Out!" She picked up a broom lying there and poked it at him, driving him. "Out!" And she poked and pushed him out the door and to the gate and stood there watching him, eyes blazing with righteousness and triumph.

When he stopped at the gate and turned, huge bulk of him, she looked him in the eyes and began screaming, "Thieves, robbers, I've been killed," shrieking it now so loud that people would come running soon.

Unmanned, he turned and scooted away.

Where could he go? He walked through the streets, still hurrying, turning left and right without thinking, moving away from the center. It seemed to him that he might be pursued. He had forced his feet into the new shoes, which pinched at the front, and now they hurt terribly. Finally, he could walk no farther. Sitting down on a boulder, he removed the shoes, then also his new checkered socks. His big feet popped out, seeming to inflate as they pulled loose, twice the size that would again fit those pointed shapes. Even in his sorrow, he thought, *They'll never make me wear that shit again.*

He remembered then the shoes he had held in his hands the day that Karim Khan found him, new shoes in a little boy's arms, as much as he knew of his arrival on earth. They threw those away before I ever saw them, he mourned. He had never wept for that boy as he did now, for his new shoes, people hurrying past, this big man wearing pants too tight and barefoot, holding a pair of shoes clasped against his chest, back shaking, how sad he felt for himself, whatever name he once had—he must have had a name. Yazid. Bayazid. His pain ran its course and subsided, it was over. He stood up, began walking, barefoot. People looked sideways at him hobbling along. Finally, he threw the shoes that he'd bought with such a buoyant heart into an empty lot.

*

Yazid left a few days later, with Karim Khan's blessings, blessings given against his will, for he had begged Yazid to stay, to take over the stall. He would retire and give Yazid the whole thing, just ask for a monthly payment. But Yazid said no, his resolution stood firm. He told his friends, including Zain, that he'd been called away, and answered no questions. Zain looked sharp, might have guessed the cause of this wild retreat, began to speak and then stopped himself.

"Well, go then," said Karim Khan, coming into Yazid's little room, as he rarely did. "Here's money. I owe you much more, for all the years."

He tried to give a very large sum, but Yazid would take only bus fare and a bit extra.

"I'll be back, Uncle." It would have meant everything if he could say the word "Father."

Yazid took the bus to Murree, then farther up to Azad Kashmir. A couple of years ago he had made friends with a Kashmiri who was involved with smuggling along the permeable border into Indian Kashmir. This man had said, "Yazid, the way you look and as big as you are, and with your cool temper also, you're exactly what I need. I'll pay you well, there's a fortune to be made shifting in gold from India."

Now Yazid resolved to try his hand at becoming rich.

*

Time passed, Yazid made some money and lost it and blew about the country, landed up in Lahore. He had not been to 'Pindi for coming on ten years except passing through. This was 1979, the year General Zia hanged Bhutto, and all the scent had gone off the flowers the boys wove in their hair when they danced that politician's tune. Since '74 Yazid had been chauffeuring Colonel Khuda Baksh Atar, landowner, industrialist, till recently one of Bhutto's backers, and who had now switched alliances to the new man. Yazid had driven him up to Islamabad from his house in Lahore that morning for an informal assembly of power brokers called by the dictator.

Allowed the night off, Yazid resolved upon a little sentimental turn, to revisit after all the intervening years his old haunts in nearby Rawalpindi. It was a cool spring evening, and he covered himself with a shawl and a cloth on his head against recognition, for he still wasn't ready to meet old friends and acquaintances. Karim Khan had died—Yazid went for the funeral up in Mardan—but there were others he wished to avoid in his childhood town, not yet ready to make a prodigal's return. Most of all, of course, he thought of Zain and Yasmin, the image of that girl flickering in his mind for all these years. He had entirely forsaken the connection, occasionally met someone in Lahore who would have known them, but avoided all inquiry, a rankling wound in the memory of that first decent house where for a few months they allowed him in. Just for a moment then the rising up that Bhutto Sahib promised had seemed possible. That too had been like love and failed like love.

There had been no other woman, not in Kashmir, not in Lahore, and just briefly one of the servant girls in Colonel Atar's house, who looked at him with longing eyes, and whose advances Yazid pushed aside after a first incomplete encounter, finding her ignorance and village manners distasteful when measured against his ideal. Just approaching thirty, Yazid affected to be beyond the age of romance, and even believed it himself.

The tea stall had been torn down and a block of buildings had come up there. He walked along, breasting the crowd. In these years, at the height of his young strength, Yazid had become massive, huge chested and bellied out and powerful, quick despite his bulk, moving easily, a noticeable figure. Lights in the stalls along the Mall Road came on, selling oranges and kinoos, the old British buildings closing up for the night, new stores here and there. The massive trees along the Mall had been cut down, the mood of the city had changed. Yes, he was growing older.

Walking ahead of him he saw a figure instantly familiar, the back of the head, the motions of the walk, and knew it was Zain, older too and yet the same. Drawn to the flame, Yazid's movements had circled toward the house that figured so brightly in his memories. He followed behind, keeping enough distance to avoid being recognized. Zain looked somehow shabby, and this is what decided Yazid to reach forward and touch his shoulder. It should not have been that way. Zain should have come into a position of importance, doctor or lawyer, civil servant. Why should he be trudging along the old Mall Road in the waning light, seeming without purpose?

The instant Yazid touched him, Zain sprang forward, turned, and pulled a revolver from his pocket, raising it up, but awkwardly. Up in Kashmir Yazid had many times handled weapons, brandished them, though he'd never fired one in anger. He reached and took Zain by the wrist, pointed the gun up.

"What the devil are you doing, old friend?" he whispered. "It's me, Bayazid! It hasn't been as many years as that."

Zain struggled for a moment, but Yazid easily twisted the revolver away from him, like plucking an apple from a tree, took it, and shoved it into the pocket of his shalvar.

"For God's sake, people will see you. Stop it."

Zain declined to recognize him, and then he did, visibly scared and distressed, eyes wild.

"Are you okay?" asked Yazid.

"What are you doing here? Give me back my gun."

"I would rather ask you, Malik Sahib, what are you doing with that piece. Aren't you going to greet me?" Yazid was angry with him, an anger that had gnawed him all these years. Whatever else Zain might have become, Yazid could see this boy was no gangster.

The two looked at each other, conflict between them, and then Zain did embrace him, coldly at first, and then as warmly as Yazid could have wished.

"Come on," said Yazid, overcome. No embrace had felt like that in many years, not since he said goodbye to Karim Khan. "Let's go have a cup of tea. I don't like this business with pretending to carry around a gun."

They walked without talking, Yazid leading his friend by the elbow. He wanted so very much to know what brought his friend to this current dilapidation, and yet understood that Zain must be given time, knew delicacy well, an orphan boy whose own happiness always had that original crack in it. When they were seated on a charpoy outside a tea stall, finally Zain spoke.

"I'm not the man you knew. It's all different now."

"And yet you look the same." But the brightness that Yazid once loved had gone off him.

Zain said no more, sat as stubborn as Yazid knew he could be. Filling the silence, Yazid told his own story, unhurried, expansive, continuing to elaborate as he observed Zain calming down. He had moved gold and even wheat up in Kashmir, different prices on the other side of the border, cooperating with the border force on both sides and with police connections all the way down to Rawalpindi. Then, when it became too big, the racket fell apart. An army general commanding there stomped in and took over the business. Yazid went to Lahore, driving a HiAce van he bought with his smuggler's share on a main-line Lahore city route. A chance encounter led to proud Yazid going into private service because he found the terms respectable, a temporary and then permanent job chauffeuring the great Colonel Khuda Baksh Atar, whose name appeared in the papers.

Finally, when Zain seemed almost to be dozing, as if exhausted, Yazid wrapped up his tale.

"That's it," he said quietly. "I told you everything. Now you tell me. I see you're in trouble. Let's hear it and see what we can do."

"It's not that kind of thing. It's over for me. When you hear my story, you'll give me back my revolver."

"Perhaps. Let's hear it."

Zain was shivering. Yazid took off his shawl and put it around the boy's shoulders, standing over him, then sitting and putting his legs up on the charpoy, becoming smaller that way—a trick he learned doing business up in Kashmir, if he sought not to intimidate.

A man brought tea and Zain said, face wan, "That used to be you."

"Once a tea boy always a tea boy."

What could have been a joke made them both sad.

"Now you say you drive a Mercedes limousine. I might as well say it. It's about Yasmin."

Yazid's heart quailed at this mention of the name that concerned him most of all.

"You remember Kamran? That boy where you stabbed yourself in the leg?"

"Of course I remember him. The Cuckoo. I hear he's in the Provincial Assembly. He did well."

"He's the biggest motherfucker in 'Pindi. They're doing all that land grabbing where the maps are for the new Islamabad. They force the owners to sell it and then the government acquires it from them. Speaking of Mercedes, he drives one now."

He stopped.

"Please, Zain. If it's Yasmin, you know that I'm a brother to you, though we've been apart. You have to tell me."

Zain sat with his head in his hands, elbows on his knees. His voice broke.

"I don't know if it was my fault. She wanted to study. Wouldn't marry. And for a while I became one of the people hanging around him, I don't know how or why. That motherfucker, he would see her because of me. Just at the end, quite a while after you left. Then for a long time he was gone doing his politics. Recently again he started bothering us, and he even would send people to the house with presents and things. And I'll tell you the truth. I think Yasmin also had some part in it. Though I won't believe it ever. Three days ago, some of his men came and they took her. Right from in front of our gate. They took her away and Kamran took her up to Murree. And then yesterday they let her go in front of our gate again. Last night she tried to cut her wrists, but she couldn't."

Yazid's body had become tense and huge and he stared down at his bare feet crossed on the charpoy.

"Fuck. That dirty fucking piece of shit."

Zain was blubbering. "What's the point? What's the piece of shit? I'm the piece of shit. Give me that gun. I'm no use. I'm going." He tried to stand up, and Yazid held him down. "Wait." He found his shoes with a wandering foot under the charpoy, looking Zain in the face, then stood and threw money on the table.

"Let's go, you're coming with me. You can't be trusted."

He took Zain to a cheap travelers' hotel he knew and said he wanted a room, and in that room he made Zain lie down.

"You're going to stay here for a few hours."

"I've got to go home. They're all there alone."

"Not till we've sorted this out. You're a mess. Come on, give me your shirt, give me your shoes. I can't have you leaving." Forcibly he took off Zain's shirt, and Zain was hysterical, but Yazid had a grim look on his face. "No, I won't let you. You'll do something stupid. I'm going to talk with someone."

Finally Zain sat down bare chested and shoeless and began murmuring over and over, "Allah, Allah, Allah."

Yazid left without looking back and locked the door from the outside.

"Stay there," he ordered through the door.

Back from his days running gold up in Kashmir he knew a

policeman, had done good business with him, and now he went to the Central Police Station and found the man.

They chitted and chatted and drank tea and Yazid took his time, putting his feet up on the desk, as if he owned the place.

"So, there's a guy who's pissed me off, Inspector Sahib. It's an old issue, but I want to deal with it now. I need a favor. Pick him up, put him in the chiller room. Don't hurt him, just keep him for a couple of days. Don't say anything about me, he'll figure it out. I want him to think of me on his own."

All teeth and smiles, the inspector said, "Bayazid, that's between you and me and a done deal." Then, cunningly, "He's not any big fish, is he?"

"He's a nobody. This is personal, don't worry. He can't hurt you. He's in a ten-rupee hotel nearby."

"A ten-rupee hotel. And you say you're working with Colonel Atar Sahib now."

"I'm his driver."

"Drivers have the master's ear. You're a smart guy. Well then, I remember you now, and someday you'll remember me."

Yazid stood up. "How could I forget? We're agreed. Thank you."

"No thanks needed. It's our daily bread."

Yazid gave him the name of the hotel where he'd confined Zain, and the room number.

*

That night and even years later in recollection, Yazid didn't know quite what he thought in all those brazen hours, what gave him that mounting power arising up through his legs, into his stomach, diffusing through his arms and hands, as if he had drunk some violent potion. Of course he knew where Kamran had his dera, that family's headquarters. There was a guard, just one, but he didn't move from the charpoy where he sat smoking a hookah and then sleeping, and he didn't notice the man sitting quietly half a block away, who arrived before dawn and sat on a curb smoking cigarettes.

At nine the guard emerged from his little booth and went to

open the gate, and Yazid rose and went over, standing there like someone with a petition. Men like Kamran often had business with strangers; no one took any notice of some wretch who needed a favor, blood or money.

The car nosed out, and Yazid made a motion with one finger, asking for a moment of time. Annoyed, the driver stopped, Kamran lowered the window. He wore glasses and looked like a respectable businessman, had that polish.

"Don't I know you?"

There was recognition in his eyes, uncertainty. Yazid liked to think forevermore that also there was an instant enormous knowledge of what was to happen very quickly then.

He raised the revolver, fired once. The bullet struck low, through Kamran's jaw, making a mess, bone and blood, like a bloodied thigh of a chicken under a cleaver. It shocked Kamran, and then he really did recognize Yazid. His eyes haunted Yazid later, but in a way that felt like victory, a blaze in them that wetted out so fast. Correcting, Yazid fired again, and this time plugged right into the forehead dimple. A little hole appeared as if dotted with a black marker, powder burn, then blood piping out to shocking red.

Everything that Yazid had ever felt of anger went into that second shot, the insult of his childhood, his thwarted impossible love. He would never have to do this again, nor could he, the power to do this act flowed out through his arm and left him. Never blood again.

Arms loose by his sides, still holding the gun, not looking at this work of his hands anymore—the bloody man askew—Yazid looked around and even up at the sky, as if a bolt might come down upon him. He thought with pain bordering distaste of Yasmin, utterly confounded that she came to this pass. Why had she not married? What had filled her days and months and the years since Yazid last saw her? And what of her now?

Aware again of the street and the shock of this violence, coming at the end of a night where his mind circled one thought, of placing those two little coned bullets in that one square head, and now hearing the screaming, the guard shouting, the driver shouting, Yazid walked away ten paces, turned and pointed the gun, and said, "Your turn next, my darlings."

He said it very calmly, and maybe that's why they ran so fast back into the house.

Hurrying around a corner, around another, he walked half a mile, took a bus to Islamabad, to the grand mansion where Colonel Atar spent the night with friends.

Yazid read about it in the papers, but the story died in a day. These gangsters played this game, and no one really minded, one down and another one rises up. If it occurred to Kamran's family that Zain had a grievance, an inquiry would have found that he'd been in jail. Business didn't stop, the funeral was well attended, even a minister came, a federal minister.

Muscle

✻

DUNYAPUR—LAHORE

1988

*B*ack in the 1950s, when old Mian Abdullah Abdalah rose to serve as Pakistan's Federal Secretary Establishment, a knee-bending district administration metaled the road leading from the Cawnapur railway station to his Dunyapur estate. They also pushed out a telephone line to his farmhouse, the first phone on any farm in the district. Even now, thirty years later, there was no other line nearby. A single wire ran many forlorn miles from Cawnapur city through the flat tan landscape of South Punjab, there on the edge of the Great Indian Desert, then alongside the packed-dirt farm tracks laid out in geometric lines, and finally entered the grounds of a small, handsome residence built in the style of a British colonial dak bungalow.

Now, for the second time in a month, the Chandios had stolen a section of the telephone wire, which served for all the area as a symbol of the Dunyapur estate's preeminence. The Chandio village sat far from the road at the back end of the estate, buried in an expanse of reeds and derelict land, dunes that had never been cleared. Testing Mian Abdalah's grandson, Rustom, who had returned from college in America six months earlier and moved onto the estate, they had been amusing themselves and bearding him by cutting out lengths of the wire that passed near their village and selling them for copper somewhere across the Indus.

Rustom drove in to Cawnapur with the farm manager, Chaudrey Zawar Hussein, to see the superintendent of police about the matter. Despite the alarming state of the farm's finances—brought home to him over many afternoons spent sweating through deviously knotted accounts, woven by Munshi Zawar Hussein as a screen to hide his thefts—Rustom had bought himself a used jeep, not a sleek vehicle that would impress the locals, but a boy's toy, a jacked-up four-by-four with a ragtop. Chaudrey Zawar Hussein always seemed comically unsuited to the vehicle, a tall man with steel-gray hair, never smiling. His heavy demeanor and black-framed square glasses made him look for all the world like a mid-century European intellectual, with that gravitas and that ponderous air of having threaded a way through complex revolutions. Rustom took a grim satisfaction in watching the manager clamber up onto the front bench seat, his dignity ruffled. As they drove out, he would say, "But, Mian Sahib, why not take my car? You'll be more comfortable, and it looks better. After all, what's mine is yours."

Rustom left unsaid the corollary, What's yours is mine. So much that belonged to the Abdalahs had through the years been tickled over with a catfishing guile to the munshi's portion.

*

The deputy superintendent of police, the senior-most policeman in Cawnapur, had offices in a crumbling whitewashed-brick building near the old city, with deep verandas and archways. Various additions made the place gaudier and more in keeping with a policeman's appreciation of his own dignity, including a tin-roofed portico painted with glossy red-and-blue stripes, like a wedding marquee, sheltering the DSP's official jeep. Gilded with insignia and sirens and lights, the vehicle defied the general dilapidation. A peon wearing a dirty white uniform resembling a sailor suit, with brass buttons, guarded the door.

Rustom had never been to this office. "Mian Rustom Abdalah," he said to the peon, putting on an air of importance. "Please tell the DSP Sahib."

Chaudrey Zawar Hussein leaned forward and whispered in his ear, "You can just go on in."

In the room, five or six men were sitting in chairs arrayed in a line in front of an enormous desk decorated with a pair of crossed miniature flags of the Punjab police, blue and red. Behind the desk sat the DSP, a short, plump Punjabi with very thick black hair parted at the side, wearing elaborate golden-framed glasses, with the interlocking Chanel monogram on each side. His uniform had been starched to the stiffness of sheet metal, and his numerous badges were matched for brilliance only by his gold pen, which lay on his desk in front of him, pinning down some papers. By contrast, the guest chairs were rickety, the floors bare concrete and slippery with dust. A strong smell of urine escaped from a little toilet that had been built by walling off a corner of the room, the DSP presumably being unwilling to enter the even fouler common latrines.

The DSP looked up owlishly, regarded Rustom, and continued speaking to one of the men arrayed in front of him.

"So, he told the son of a bitch that, judge or no judge, they were confiscating those filthy videotapes . . ."

Rustom took one of the seats pushed against the wall, uncomfortably aware that the other visitors were of a crude social class, hangers-on to government officials, penny lawyers, and various kinds of fixers.

With a sugared smile on his face, Chaudrey Zawar Hussein stepped forward to the desk.

The DSP jumped up and, not content with shaking his hand, walked around to the side of his desk and embraced him.

"As salaam uleikum, Chaudrey Sahib. What a pleasant surprise, what an honor!" Still looking into the manager's face, he reached blindly around on the desk with his other hand, found the telephone, lifted the receiver, and muttered to the steno to send tea. Chaudrey Sahib beamed at the DSP; the DSP rebeamed at Chaudrey Sahib.

"Please, please." The DSP flicked a hand at the men sitting in front of the desk, who instantly vacated their chairs. Rustom awkwardly rose from the seat he had occupied on the periphery and moved to one of the places of honor, facing the officer.

The officer for the first time looked with interest at Rustom.

"You must, in fact, be the young master of Dunyapur, Mian Rustom Abdalah."

With half a dozen pairs of amused eyes upon him, Rustom launched a long-winded description of his recent movements. "Yes, I've come to take control of the farm. I've only been here a few months. And I'm afraid it's all new to me, I've been out of the country, in college and then before that in high school abroad also." He spoke through a fixed smile, intimidated by the setting, the officer and his uniform, the spectators leaning forward in their seats, as if expecting something tremendous, not wishing to miss a word. "Abroad. In America, I mean. My parents sent me, you know."

"So sorry, so sorry." The DSP cut him off. "I see, very sorry. And you are most welcome, I see. So, Chaudrey Sahib, how are your crops? All is well?"

"With your blessings," the manager replied, lowering his eyes piously, as if right there receiving the blessings of the DSP.

The peon brought mixed tea in small, crudely made cups, with a rose design, and also a little plate of biscuits. He served Rustom first, and when Rustom proffered the biscuits to the DSP he demurred, in English, "Please, you take some, I take after you." He even put another biscuit onto Rustom's plate. "Have more," he said, again in English.

One of the men sitting on the chairs backed against the wall asked, "Are you then the grandson of Mian Abdullah Abdalah?"

The DSP gestured. "This is Mr. Aftab, whose father-in-law is both a leading advocate of Cawnapur and our vice-chairman district council."

Aftab leaned forward and shook Rustom's hand.

The DSP removed an imported cigarette from a box lying on the table and snapped open a trick lighter shaped like a tiny pistol. "Do you smoke?" Rustom declined. Fixing his eyes on Rustom, the DSP gulped the smoke greedily, held it, allowed trickles to escape his mouth, and inhaled it again up into his nose, a cycle. His eyes blazed with interest.

As if he had come to some decision, he stubbed the full cigarette in the ashtray, excused himself, and went into the improvised toilet at the end of the room. Because the walls didn't reach to the ceiling, the bystanders could hear him moving about, then silence, and more silence.

"Should I come give you a hand? Just a little tug? I'd love to do that for you," called Aftab.

"If they're really coming over, they don't stop to ask," the DSP riposted over the wall.

They heard him pissing, and then the DSP resumed his desk, buttoning his fly as he walked across the room. Rustom was unsure how to respond to this strange insult. Awkwardly speaking up, he said, "I'm sorry to bother you, but I've come because of an issue I have. The Chandios, you know them, next to my farm."

The policeman laughed merrily. "Oh dear. I should have introduced you properly. This is Mr. Aftab Chandio, in fact. His uncle is the senior member of the Chandio clan. He was just speaking to me of this whole matter. Don't worry. We'll have it all sorted out. It seems someone else has been troubling you and been blaming the Chandios. They respect you, sir. They respect your grandfather's name. You rest assured. And I'm here for you, too. We're all here."

He turned now to Aftab Chandio and began discussing something about a new watercourse, very clearly having finished with Rustom, who finally stood up and said he must go.

"How dare he treat me like that?" Rustom said to Chaudrey Zawar Hussein as they drove through the bazaar. "And what's that with the Chandio happening to be there? Did you tell them we were coming?"

"Oh, Mian Sahib, not this again," the manager lamented. "Of course I didn't. What would be in it for me? You know how it is. These people are all politicians. There are two or three hundred houses in the Chandio village, and every old lady and every baby and even the fresh graves in the cemetery can be counted on for a name and an ID card when it comes time for us all to fill out ballots at election time."

*

Back at the farm, at dusk, Rustom sat in the living room before a rosewood fire, typing away at a letter to Klara, his first love, the American girl he'd dated his last two years at college. He wrote too often, too many pages, while she increasingly sent little more than a note, written in haste, late for class, going out with friends, and the poverty of his own nights seemed so much greater for it. In the fall she had begun a master's at Columbia, and already he glimpsed through the scrim of her letters that her concerns were drifting away from him, as she settled in the city and found her way. He knew that he thought of her much more often than she thought of him, and that made him angry at the farm, made his troubles here more galling.

From Cawnapur it took hours of dialing and negotiating with the operators to call Lahore, much less abroad. Even from Lahore, international calls had to be booked through an operator, and were limited to ten minutes, Rustom booking another as soon as the operator cut off the first, Klara sitting in her New York apartment waiting for the phone to ring, becoming frustrated, and always the line would get cut just when they reached some crux, or some resolution, as if the operators took a gremlin pleasure in impeding this love. They spoke of her coming to Pakistan next summer, but Rustom knew what the villagers would think of his bringing a single woman here, what the servants would think, and Zawar Hussein. On the phone during his last visit to Lahore, when he described his projects at Dunyapur, hinting at a political role, she had laughed and said something about his being a big frog in a small pond, silencing him. He couldn't write to her of his visit to the DSP's office, of all the men sharking around him. He wanted to make the place seem attractive, romantic, and his own role benevolent. She glowed there across continents and oceans, competitive among prickly hyperpolitical graduate students, discussing Lacan, eating vegan, and proud to be broke. Seen from New York City, his feudal preoccupations must appear so crude, and he imagined her pitiless and dared not speak of his vulnerability.

Looking up, he startled at the face of the old majordomo, Fezoo, framed in the windowpane of the door.

"For God's sake, Fezoo," he shouted. "I've told you, knock."

"Yourself, sir, you told me," Fezoo mumbled, aggrieved. "Just this morning. No knocking."

"I told you not to hammer as if you were trying to rip the door from its frame."

Fezoo's square head, with a single wart above his left eye, his odd gold-colored skin, and his green eyes, like an Uzbek spy, had made him since Rustom's childhood an unsettling figure, sidling about the house, sullen and always seeming weighted down by unspoken reproaches.

"Anyway, I'm sorry. What do you want?"

"Chaudrey Zawar Hussein Sahib begs a moment of your time."

Few things spoiled Rustom's evenings as completely as these managerial visits, which always signaled some unpleasantness— overturned tractors, oxen thefts. With each passing day, emergencies on the farm seethed up with greater regularity, a gathering storm that had not yet reached its fury.

"Why in God's name doesn't the Munshi Sahib come tomorrow, during the day?" Rustom moaned. It irked him that the manager came and went pursuing his own agenda, with some irrefutable excuse always ready if Rustom questioned where he had been.

Fezoo looked at Rustom with a dull expression. "Allah knows best, sir. Perhaps his personal business in the city keeps him busy?"

"Are you trying to be humorous, Fezoo?"

"Sir?"

"Forget it. Seat Chaudrey Sahib in the living room. I'll be there in a minute."

*

Zawar Hussein sat in front of the fire that had been lit in the long, high-ceilinged room, in anticipation of Rustom's dining there. He sat with one leg extended and his gaze fixed in the flames, as if considering weighty matters, in repose wearing a much shrewder expression than the one he invariably presented to the young master of these lands and villages.

"Hello, Munshi Sahib," Rustom said, declining to use the Chaudrey honorific. "What can I do for you?"

The manager hesitated a beat before rising to meet Rustom, expressing something between reluctance and tired bones.

"Mian Sahib."

"Please sit down."

They both faced the fire in carved wooden wing chairs, flickering light on their faces.

"So what is it this time?"

"The Chandios, sir. That young one who's been throwing his weight around, one of Ghuman's sons. Sadique."

"Not again! Now they're doing it every other day."

"No, much worse than just stealing wire. Sadique Chandio found Bahadur Khan drinking tea by the bridge this afternoon and beat him up. Then his brother came and started brandishing a pistol around. Firing shots in the air."

To his shame, when he recalled it later, Rustom felt panic, an impulse to flee. He thought of New York and America, those havens. This was the dreaded violence that wriggled about his mind at night and kept him from sleeping.

"Shots! My God! And why would anyone hurt Bahadra?"

Bahadur Khan had been Rustom's childhood servant, the man in Dunyapur most identified with him. They had secrets together, which the little boy knew not to tell. The old man would spirit Rustom away on his shoulders into the village, a row of mud-walled compounds where the field-workers lived, to see the hutch of rabbits, the newborn goats, Rustom finding intimacy there, playing in the dust with Bahadur Khan's ragged children. Before Rustom's father entirely abandoned himself to hard daily drinking, the family would come from Lahore to Dunyapur every winter for a week or so—Rustom, his parents, and a couple of their drinking buddies. His father's father, Mian Abdalah, never joined them but came separately on formal tours of inspection. The drinks cart would come out at noon, and the adults would be tight as lords by evening, shooting off guns and having huge fires made in the garden, once ordering tractors to be brought after dark and hilariously racing them on the cricket pitch, smashing one into a tree. During all those years, when otherwise Rustom might have been quite untended, Bahadur Khan had been his keeper, his protector and playfellow, with his long white beard even then and rheumy eyes, a simple man, willing to sit for hours and sail leaves down the watercourses with a little boy, conjuring up countries and great storms. Thinking of all this, his man, the lap where he rested, the arms that held him, Rustom choked with anger. He walked away to hide the tears that had started into his eyes, going to a side table and pouring himself a glass of water.

"Those fucking bastards."

Zawar Hussein made a clucking dismissive sound. "Mian Sahib, what good is swearing now? It's less than a year since we said your grandfather's funeral prayer, and already this is how they're toying with us. I've been saying for months that we need to have them pulled into the station and then run the rod over them a few times. They're begging for it."

✻

This had been a refrain for the past six months, that he needed to take a firmer hand. Chaudrey Sahib put very little credence in Rustom's ambition to manage the farm according to new humane principles. He would say, "All that works fine in your America. Here they only understand one thing."

"And I keep telling you, I came here to make things better. Otherwise what's the use of all my education?"

Rustom circled around the humiliating fact that, this morning, when they called on the DSP, he had barely been offered a cup of tea.

Since he moved here, it had been getting worse. The Chandios cut down and carted away overnight a massive rosewood tree planted on the boundary of Rustom's land, with the claim that the bulk of the roots grew on the Chandio side. A motorcycle disappeared from the dera, the administrative center of the farm, and everyone said they'd taken it—a couple of their boys ran a business in lifting motorcycles. Then the phone wire. The first time, with the rosewood, when Rustom summoned the Chandio elders they came and touched his knees and pulled at their beards, saying that it was beneath him to notice such a minor issue. They trooped with him to the site and showed him the particulars, convinced him, belittled Zawar Hussein. He saw their point of view and accepted it. The tree wasn't worth more than two or three thousand rupees. When he summoned the Chandio elders about the motorcycle, they sent just a couple of men to declare that they had nothing to do with it, even becoming testy at being accused. Lying awake at night, Rustom had been fearing this—an affront that couldn't be borne. He wanted to help these people, to show them a better way, and he would wonder, as he sat alone at dusk after coming back from the lands, why must they be this way? Why this press and urge to test him and expose him?

"Let this pass," Zawar Hussein said, "and we won't be able to leave the farm after the sun goes down. All those guys are armed. And the police are right with them." The Chandios moved all the heroin and hash in the area, and made drums of booze from industrial spirits, selling little plastic shooters of it—three of those and you were ready to kick cobras and uproot trees, and fuck the laws against alcohol. The police wouldn't act against them unless forced to. At best a pickup with a few constables would roll up for a pro forma raid, giving plenty of advance notice, and that would be the end of it.

Worst of all, Rustom had to go out to the servants' sitting area and see the old man, ashamed to be so powerless that people beat his own Bahadur Khan. He lay groaning on a charpoy outside, next to the garages, and would not be stopped from painfully rolling off the bed and falling at Rustom's feet, his arm in a crude sling.

"Mian Sahib, there's only you below and God above—" He broke into racking blubbering sobs, sorrow rather than pain. They had told him Rustom would come; he had awaited this moment to let himself go. "I beg you. I carried you on my shoulders. All the ministers and presidents know you. The Chandios will eat me up—that was just the first bite." His sobbing fell into a rhythm, turning inward.

Tenderly, Rustom lifted him back onto the bed, inhaling his heavy sweet smell, so well remembered. Pity and sadness pricked Rustom's anger.

How thin the old man had become, light, as if hollow boned. Rustom himself needed comforting. In this very spot, on this same oversized charpoy built from Dunyapur wood, Rustom had sat on Bahadur Khan's lap and been allowed to sip tea clotted with milk from the old man's share. They hid this tea-drinking from his mother, another of the festivals in their private world, their play.

In the light of a bare bulb hanging from a tree branch, several people stood watching this scene between Rustom and Bahadur Khan—the old man's useless son who drank and kept getting fired from the estate, a sweeper, one of the gardeners. Rustom should be enraged, resolute, dramatic, and instead he listened with one ear to the breeze in the leaves overhead and felt strained and fearful and dissociated, as if this violence could be wished away.

He patted Bahadur Khan's cheek, couldn't imagine what to say.

"Now those guys will hear from us," he said finally through gritted teeth. "Don't worry. We'll fuck them up. They'll beg your forgiveness."

Just a flash of incredulity passed through the injured man's eyes, humoring Rustom, as when he was a boy and railed against his nap-time. None of the people watching this scene knew what to believe.

✳

Zawar Hussein had not followed when Rustom went out to see his old keeper. Now he sat in front of the fire in the shadowed living room, leaning forward and warming his hands as if at a campfire.

Rustom threw himself into a chair, shook his head. "These people are animals, Chaudrey Sahib. There's not a single fucking person I can rely on. No one!" In his frustration, he encompassed the manager in this lament.

"Mian Sahib, why do you think I'm here?" Zawar Hussein asked theatrically. "If you don't trust us, who can you trust? Here you don't need to be afraid of anyone."

"I'm not afraid. I'm frustrated. I came here to help, and all you people do is push at me and pull at me. Look at that old man, lying there. His only fault is that he took care of me as a little boy. It's disgusting."

"Anyway, it's not so bad as that. These villagers are like cats. You can smash their heads in and they crawl into some hole and live for days."

Smashing cats' heads! thought Rustom. What a fucking shithole.

He said nothing, the moment heavy between them. Zawar Hussein's jaw had tightened, defying Rustom's general condemnation. Rustom recalled that this, too, was a man who would personally beat peasants caught stealing.

✳

"Go on, you should rest now," the manager said. "I'll put guards outside. Tomorrow we'll figure out something."

Rustom rose and went to the fire, savagely kicking at a log, which threw out a shower of sparks.

"No. I'm not going to take this. We'll do it the old way now. I'm sending you tomorrow to Khirka. I'm bringing in Sheikh Sarkar. I don't like to, but that's what these Chandios want."

"Sheikh Sarkar Sahib! That's a name to frighten children with. But your grandfather never brought any of that lot here. And then, will he come? He must be eighty now."

"My grandfather went himself to see the governor about a pardon when they were going to hang Sheikh Sahib's nephew for a murder. These goondas remember such things. They'll make this right."

"You know better than we do, sir."

"Oh, for God's sake, Chaudrey Sahib. Don't pretend. I've told you a hundred times what I want. You people won't follow me."

"Well, it's the police or do something ourselves."

"All right then, I've decided. Call Sheikh Sahib."

The munshi stood up to leave. "It's as you wish, sir. Show your hand once and be done with it forever."

With Munshi Zawar Hussein off in Lahore to deliver the summons, Rustom did nothing all day. Outside the walls roamed the Chandios. He wasn't afraid, he assured himself, but he mustn't allow them to insult him unprotected. In truth, he found it not frightening but somehow embarrassing to face the villagers without the manager present. He felt fraudulent, the villagers touching his knee and making the correct obeisance, but with a sullen look on their faces, as if they didn't quite know who he was. He had once caught Zawar Hussein motioning behind his back to a group of the villagers to come and make their salaam.

Throughout Rustom's childhood the garden had not been walled. When Mian Abdullah Abdalah, rising up through the ranks of the civil service, came to the farm, the entire district administration waited upon him, and villagers came from miles around and sat in the garden as if in a public space and watched the proceedings, Mian Abdalah holding court. Then Rustom's father, Tony Abdalah, had thrown a wall around three acres of orchard, not wanting the villagers to see his buddies and their wives drinking and lounging, the women in sundresses with arms and legs bare. Those party weeks still imbued this property with a melancholy glamour in Rustom's mind, his father and mother members of the fast set in the Lahore of the 1960s and '70s, boozing, sleeping around, flying to London to gamble, importing fabulous cars. They had recently died in one of those cars, too, in Rustom's first year at college— moving between parties on New Year's Eve, rammed into a truck full of steel rebar on Lahore's Main Boulevard.

His mother had wanted him schooled in America, the farthest place she could imagine from the parties and all the excesses of her life with Tony, the little boy seeing them drunk and disorderly once too often. Her great stroke, very much against her father-in-law's inclination, had been sending Rustom to a boarding school outside

Boston, which she knew would lead inevitably to an American college. She went alone to see the old man when he refused money for the fees, and said, "They'll make him clean and hardworking and then he'll come back and do what you wish. It costs me a lot to say this. I don't want him spending his life like his father." Mian Abdalah nodded sourly and said nothing, but the next day sent a check to her private account. Five years playing lacrosse and wearing a jacket and tie to chapel with Boston Brahmins and the older New York money had made Rustom nostalgic and romantic about Pakistan and the farm, so that returning for holidays seemed an adventure and a release from schoolboy insecurities, traveling alone on the flight through Europe, landing in the comforts and privileges of Lahore and Dunyapur. Now his encounters in Dunyapur were quickly teaching him new manners and sensitivities, for he saw aroused in the beady eyes of the DSP and all the Zawar Husseins of the district a hunger to pluck and swallow this little foreign pullet.

His parents' violent deaths, followed by his grandfather's passing just three years later, made Rustom master of these lands at twenty-two, the only son of the only son. His father would have kept selling land if he had lived, till it all flowed away, after him nothing. Throughout Rustom's childhood, as they were selling, there were huge fights between his parents and his grandfather, who could not finally resist them—his mother and father forming a team against the declining old man. When Mian Abdalah refused to sign some deed or document, his parents would seethe and say they would rather live as free paupers than under the thumb of despotism. Blowing up, they would withdraw to London, first class, staying in good hotels, and then later in a flat that they bought—fruits of selling land here at Dunyapur, the London flat itself sold at the end. Mian Abdalah always gave in, wanting them back in Lahore with him, living in the big house, settled in their separate wing, having dinners together, warming his old age.

Rustom walked around the garden, thinking of his parents, gone these past five years. A November wind, fresh and almost chilly, blew through the hundred-year-old rosewood trees that stood at one end of the garden, home to a vast swarm of crows, which came from miles around at evening and settled in noisily. Yes, this was home to him too, as much as Lahore was home. He'd been based here at Dunyapur since June, and now it was November. Every three weeks he drove down to Lahore in the ragtop Land Cruiser, which had no air-conditioning and was incredibly hot in summer, but rather pleasant now in the cool fall days, smoking cigarettes, sharing cigarettes with Mustafa, his driver—or, rather, Munshi Zawar Hussein's driver, who came to Rustom on secondment. In Lahore, however, the large, fusty house made him sad. The old bearer brought in the cocktail trolley that all through his childhood had signaled the commencement of his father's daily drinking session, tinkling into his parents' sitting room. He had no close friends, only a cousin who would invite him over for a drink, a few others, five or six whiskeys, rolling up joints of black-tar hash. Sent abroad at thirteen, he had lost touch with the boys his age who had gone through grade school with him.

✳

The following afternoon, Rustom sat in the garden, wisps of trailing cloud screening the pale blue sky very high up, the sun just too warm for a sweater. He heard the slamming of car doors. Munshi Zawar Hussein must be back. Two cars stood in the circular drive, not intruding into the curving portico. Walking down the steps into the sunlight, Rustom went to embrace Sheikh Sarkar, a tall, very straight-backed man with one of those lined faces that are old yet seem boyish, a boy grown old, wearing an immaculate white dhoti wound around his waist, a costume that very few still wore, a man of the fading generation. He held Rustom with one hand on each shoulder and looked into his face, studying him, then broke into a smile.

"Mian Sahib, you look exactly like your grandfather now that you're almost grown."

"The way he looked at my age, I suppose, which you would know better than anyone."

"I served him then, I serve you now."

The Sheikhs from Khirka had been Rustom's family muscle for

a claimed six generations, called out when some land mafia threatened a property—force used against crude force. Their dera lay outside Lahore, but within striking distance, Gujranwala toughs going back to Sikh times, and for generations they had preyed upon the weak and the foolish around those districts, like wolves circling a herd of bison and pruning out the stragglers, serving themselves and also serving Rustom's ancestors, symbiotic. For Rustom's family, certain challenges could be met no other way, with holdings so large, shops and tenements in Lahore, or strips of city land liable to adverse possession. His grandfather had treated Sheikh Sarkar with a ceremony just a degree less formal than he reserved for the heads of great families, the Boranis and the Watwans and the Jhaggas and the rest, the Mians of Bhagbanpura. Rustom had once asked his grandfather about such distinction bestowed on a killer, and was told sharply, "These are hard men who served us in hard times. They've done what we couldn't do. They live on their pride, remember that, young man. I've never once failed to ask Sheikh Sahib to be seated when he visits me, and he's never once accepted. Or only once, when they hanged that poor boy."

Three men emerged from the second car, a beat-up old Toyota Corolla. They stood stretching, spitting, adjusting their balls, retying their turbans, looking around at the house with its rounded portico and columned veranda, the massive old rosewood trees filled with a chorus of bulbuls and crows, parakeets that fed on the guavas, sparrows hopping around in the dusty curving driveway, enjoying dust baths in the warm sun reflected off the whitewashed building.

A fifth man stood behind Sheikh Sarkar. He alone was dressed in city clothes, a starched white shalvar kameez, paired with a blue blazer, like a senior district official or a sharp businessman of the rising class.

"My nephew," Sheikh Sarkar said offhandedly, gesturing at him. "Take a look—even the Sheikhs of Khirka have become gentlemen in this generation. Rather, my grandnephew. Sheikh Sharif."

The man, six or seven years older than Rustom, stepped forward and made a formal obeisance with the old feudal gesture, bending his knee slightly as he took Rustom's hand in both of his own. His slender figure and the quickness of his movement lent him grace, and he finished it with a disarmingly sweet smile showing his small, very white teeth.

Rustom had debated with himself the delicate question of whether Sheikh Sarkar should be lodged in the guesthouse—which ordinarily would not be offered to a person of his class—or in the dera, the complex of buildings and stores in the village itself where lower-status guests would be entertained by the munshis and brought to meet his grandfather as required. Under the circumstances better to bow too low, he had concluded, than not low enough, easing his sense of propriety with the thought that Sheikh Sarkar had been of his grandfather's generation.

"I'll say my prayers now and rest, thank you," Sheikh Sarkar said, "but I'll go back to Lahore this evening. Old men don't like to spend the night away from home. If I am to die tonight, I wish to be in Khirka."

At tea, Rustom contrasted the old man's dignified bearing with his rough manners, pouring tea into the saucer and slurping it up. When Rustom insisted that he at least stay for dinner, Sheikh Sarkar couldn't manage a fork and knife, but called for chapattis and ate with his hands.

"This is no time to be on the KLP road," Rustom said, when Sheikh Sahib took his leave. "You won't be home before dawn."

Sheikh Sarkar made his only reference to his calling. "Don't worry, Mian Sahib. Men like us are accustomed to traveling in the night." When Rustom had broached the Chandio issue, Sheikh Sarkar said, "Tell this all to my grandnephew. Now these boys handle everything. I've only made this journey to pay Mian Abdullah Abdalah's grandson my respects. You summoned me and I came."

Young Sheikh Sharif did not eat dinner with them, and he kept back in the shadows when Rustom saw off the old Sheikh. Rustom remembered so many other nighttime departures from this veranda, returning to Lahore after a week's sojourn with his father and mother, last drinks and running late, a line of jeeps sputtering and spicing the air with their exhaust, managers waiting to say their salaams, off to catch the up-country train from the old colonial railway station at Cawnapur—the Khyber Mail, Tezgam Express.

Turning just as he stepped into the car, Sheikh Sarkar took Rustom's face in both his hands, almost tenderly, and said, "This is my first visit to your family's Dunyapur. This land is your gold mine. Thank you for showing it to us. And don't worry, we'll settle everything now." The look that passed across Sheikh Sarkar's face reminded Rustom that he had certainly killed men in his long career. His flamboyant mustache extended from tight lips, a thin mouth. "Now you will be the one we call Mian Abdalah, since your father and grandfather have left us." Then he kissed Rustom on the forehead, and touched his head, a gesture of blessing more commonly extended to a daughter or a niece or a young child.

*

When Rustom asked at breakfast if Sheikh Sharif had eaten, Fezoo replied, "What can I say, Mian Sahib? They asked for food at two in the morning, and they called me twice more to make tea. They kept saying, 'What's this watered-out railway-station tea?' Everything's a joke to them."

After breakfast Rustom walked with Zawar Hussein on one of the distant farms, where they would not run into the Chandio brothers. At lunchtime, Sheikh Sharif still had not emerged, though he and his men had called for food, so again Rustom went out, now rather annoyed. He carried a revolver, his grandfather's Webley from his service days, as he walked among fields of mature sugarcane standing more than head high. The land, so flat, so dusty, had a mood that he loved at evening, when the light settled down upon it, and he thought of the horizon, of the desert just to the east, open there all the way to India, to Jaisalmer, Bikaner. He felt his family's uncertain place here as a longing. The people still called them Punjabis, implying that they were carpetbaggers from the north—the villagers all long settled here, most of them Riyastis, lieges to the Bahawalpur nawabs whose reign had passed just a few decades ago.

Driving into the dera, he saw Sheikh Sharif sprawled on a chair

in the sun, reading an Urdu newspaper, and his three men on a
charpoy. The young man's shalvar gleamed white, his shoes polished
as if dipped in some bright black substance, hair smoothed back
and rather long, foppish. He had no more the deferential air that
he assumed in front of his grand-uncle, but strolled up to Rustom
wide-armed, an easy, open approach.

"Mian Sahib, oh Mian Sahib. You farm like an Englishman! Our
people never bother going out to their lands." He gestured around
at the dera. "Why not do your business here? There should be guys
tied upside down in the trees and a line of their families come to
beg their release."

His men continued to lounge on the charpoy, one of them smoking a hookah. "Get up, you donkeys! Are you blind, or didn't you
see Mian Sahib come in?"

They grunted themselves up, grinning broadly. One of them carried a stubby little Kalashnikov, cradling it under his arm, barely
showing.

"Glad to see your men came prepared."

"What can I do? I have so many enmities."

"I hope I don't add another one to your list."

"Don't worry, your Chandios are just a snack for my boys."

"Come to the house and have tea. Let's talk it over."

"I didn't know the lands around here were so rich," Sheikh Sharif
said. They were sitting in the middle of the garden that fronted
the house, looking onto the cricket pitch laid out by Rustom's
father. "This garden itself would be a good-sized field, if you put
in sugarcane."

"That's a fine idea, Sheikh Sahib. I'll plow up the flowers and put
in something better paying."

Sheikh Sharif looked at him sharply. "Do you really think so,
Mian Sahib?"

"I was planning on getting some horses, actually. I could graze
them here."

"That's better. It's a good safe place for riding if things get ugly.
You wouldn't want to do that out on your farm with the Chandios

and the Kandios and the Bandios and God knows what else. Thank God for your nice high wall. But you need more guards. You don't have any fighting men at all."

"But I have you!"

"Yes, you do. And lucky I'm here. We need to show these Chandios exactly who's boss on this farm. Then you'll be free to ride wherever you want. After my fellows are done, these bastards will salute you by shitting their pants when you pass by."

Rustom winced at the phrase, yet he felt almost for the first time since he came to the farm that with these goondas he outgunned the many desperate men plaguing the district. Going out on the farm that morning had been an act of bravura. Walking through alleys of sugarcane, he had been thinking that surely the Chandios must have a plan of escalation, if they had gone to such extremes as to beat up his childhood caretaker.

"In a minute I'll call in Munshi Zawar Hussein," Rustom offered. "The Chandios have a pretty good connection with the DSP in Cawnapur. As you know, under their uniforms the police are cousins to the thieves. That's why I didn't bother calling them before I sent to Sheikh Sarkar Sahib."

Sheikh Sharif looked at Rustom appraisingly.

"You didn't call them, eh? Better not to unless you know they'll come. And another thing. Your Zawar Hussein is too clever by half. He's been here for quite a while, I gather. We have a saying, new cars and old munshis beggar the rich man's son. You should change your manager every two years. But let's not worry about him; we'll sort him out later."

This tickled Rustom's sense of loyalty to the manager, almost family over the years.

"My grandfather used to say that there's as much beneath the ground where Munshi Sahib stands as above."

"What's buried under there, Mian Sahib? All the money he's stolen?"

"My grandfather meant that he's solid, he's planted," Rustom said, bristling.

"Of course," Sheikh Sharif said soothingly. "But we'll be careful with him. Your grandfather's generation were very trusting, and they could afford to be."

*

Rustom felt obliged to invite Sheikh Sharif for dinner. He tried not to drink at the farm, for he knew all the stories, going back to British times, of the dangers of drinking alone out in the field, one drink at night leading ultimately to whiskey for breakfast. That evening, however, he made an exception and sneaked in a couple of stiff ones before calling in the gangster.

"Come in, come in," Rustom said, having put away his glass when Fezoo announced his guest.

"You have a fire," Sheikh Sharif said. "Your own wood, so you can afford as many fires as you like. And yet my men are swimming during the day. That's your desert weather." Munshi Zawar Hussein had brought this up earlier with Rustom, that the three goondas had been sporting at the old swimming pool, built near the village in the 1960s, not just swimming but lathering up and then lying around in the sun with cloths around their loins. In Rustom's childhood, the whole family would swim there in the afternoon, unmindful of the villagers, who must have thought it strange that his mother would bathe quite naked, as they considered it, for all to see. Rustom's father, an aristo to his fingertips, would have been amused to think of a Dunyapur peasant having an opinion on the matter at all, and might have called him over to enjoy his discomfiture in the presence of the Begum Sahiba's bikini.

"I actually wanted to mention that," Rustom said. "The village women walk past there all the time. Only the little boys swim there."

"Say no more, say no more. I'll keep them cooped up in their room during the day."

"But that's not what I meant. It's just that the women have to pass nearby."

"Did someone complain?"

"Nothing like that. Maybe you could suggest to your men that they bathe at the canal. Or there's the shower right where their rooms are."

"They're city boys at heart. They think the canal is dirty. Nobody more fastidious than these bloods. Anyway, I'll keep them on a tighter leash, Mian Sahib. I'll cut them down an inch or two. I went off into town to see the DSP Sahib, and they started playing around in my absence."

Rustom thought back to his own experience with the policeman, taking a loud piss and bantering with the Chandio about it.

"So you know the DSP?" asked Rustom.

"Of course. I know the police all over Punjab. Sanghera Sahib's last posting was in Kasur, just next to us, and we used to see him all the time. He's a good guy."

Fezoo brought in glasses of lemon sherbet, but Sheikh Sharif declined to take one. When the servant left the room, he said, "Mian Sahib, I don't suppose you have something a bit stronger in the house. In the evening I like to have a little glass, if you wouldn't mind sharing one with me."

"Not at all. I should have asked."

"And you were just having one?"

Rustom laughed. "You're right, I was."

Though Rustom didn't like to advertise that he was drinking with the goonda, he was obliged to ring for Fezoo, ask him to bring the drinks.

"How will you have it?" Rustom asked.

"However you take it. Give me the same as yourself."

"Cheers," Sheikh Sharif said, lifting his glass and making a little moue—the first time Rustom had heard him speak English. He drained half the glass at a go, with the same abstracted expression that Chaudrey Zawar Hussein wore when downing a glass of water after a meal, as if taking medicine. It seemed to do Sheikh Sahib a world of good, for he immediately relaxed, sat back in his chair, and smiled, showing his small, even teeth. The living room in which they sat was packed full of heavy, carved-teak furniture that had been banished from the Lahore house by Rustom's mother. Three poorly painted family portraits hanging above the fireplace showed large plush men of the late 1800s, muttonchops and mustaches all around, one of them holding a sword, one with a double-breasted jacket that might have suited a captain on the P&O Lines, with epaulettes and big buttons.

"These must be your elders?"

"The one on the left is my great-great-granduncle, who bought this land."

"There it is. They were buying land, and now you're selling it."

"I'm not selling. That was my father."

"God bless him."

They were silent for a moment.

"Do you know, they're watching over you," Sheikh Sharif said gravely. "You must believe that. Yet why would you bother with this farming and dealing with Chandios and danger and inconvenience? You've been in America. You can never be settled here. You weren't brought up for this. Bad things happen—you could lose everything."

"Well, we've been farming in my family for six or seven generations."

"Your grandfather wasn't farming. Your family have been in government. Do you know, I met your grandfather only once. Sheikh Sarkar Sahib always went to see Mian Abdalah Sahib alone. None of the rest of them would have known how to behave. But, when my cousin was going to receive the Black Warrant, then we all went, every single member of my family. Our village was empty. Your grandfather himself went to the governor, not once but twice."

"You all camped in the garden," Rustom said. He remembered his grandfather, long retired, with no power left, connections lost, going off and coming back, the men from Khirka camped out on the driveway of the big Lahore house for days, the coming and going. "I remember my grandfather visiting Governor's House. He tried very hard."

"He tried. Ten years earlier the governor would have listened. Or if your father had followed your grandfather into service. But Tony Mian was a prince." He laughed. "I remember Tony Mian's car, from that time. We boys were naughty, at night we snuck into the garages and sat in it. It had a machine in it to make tea and a spotlight that you could move from inside. I even remember you. One day you kept riding a bicycle around that big circular drive in front of the house, and every time you passed we all stood up. Your grandfather wondered why all of us were jumping up and down, and then he saw you and took your bike away."

"That's so funny!" Rustom said.

"Later we used to tell that story, us young ones. The older ones could never joke about those times. After they carried out my cousin's sentence no one in my village laughed for a year, at least not in front of my grandfather." He leaned over and touched his glass to Rustom's. "Cheers," he said again in English. "Mian Sahib, we used to talk about you. When Tony Mian and your mother passed away, God receive them in heaven, Sheikh Sarkar Sahib said that now no one would protect our clan, that we'd lost the cover that had shaded us for six generations."

"I would like to protect you," Rustom said, on the verge of tears at the memory of his parents, just four years buried side by side in the old family graveyard in Lahore. "I will protect you, if I can."

"Of course you will," Sheikh Sharif said.

"You must come and see me whenever you like in Lahore. Times are changed. You should meet some of my friends."

"Yes," Sheikh Sharif said. "Do you know, we Sheikhs have perhaps as much land as what's left here in Dunyapur. It's not good land, not like this. But now the property dealers all want to buy it from us. Lahore is growing in our direction. It might be worth even more than your Dunyapur. So I'm a landlord, too, in a way," he said, proud of it.

"Why not?" Rustom answered, nodding in agreement, though he could see no equivalence. "Who cares about landlords anymore?"

· · ·

When Fezoo came in to ask about dinner, Sheikh Sharif said to him, before Rustom could answer, "Not yet, boy. Mian Sahib will call you."

Though Sheikh Sharif had been rattling the ice cubes in his empty glass, Rustom did not offer him another drink, minding this presumption with the servant. Still rattling the glass, Sheikh Sharif stood and went to the sideboard, poured in three fingers of neat whiskey.

"This is how we drink. Straight. But we don't usually have this nice liquor. We take what we can get. If my father knew, I'd be beaten. Still, even at my age."

Rustom had drunk two whiskeys before Sheikh Sharif came, and another one now. He had warmed to the young man, wanted to understand him, to make common cause with him even. The Sheikhs of Khirka had been loyal for generations, and it seemed right that, now, in these modern times, there should be less formality, more acknowledgment of that bond.

"Really, did your father beat you?"

"Mian Sahib, you don't know how we're brought up. We're brought up with slaps and blows. There are more things happening all around than you can dream of, Mian Sahib. These Chandios of yours are nothing."

He shook his head, as if embarrassed by the disclosure, and Rustom noticed for the first time that he had a dimple, like a little cut framing his lip on one side.

"That's how we were brought up, Mian Sahib. That's our school in America."

Rustom flipped another chunk of wood into the fire, then stood for a moment with his back to Sheikh Sharif. When he turned, he saw Sheikh Sharif's eyes intent upon him.

"If the wood falls out, you'll burn your valuable carpet," Sheikh Sharif said.

"Well, anyway, the house is made of brick. It won't burn."

"Let's hope not."

In a single gulp Sheikh Sharif finished the glass of whiskey. He stood up, unsteady for a moment. "Now that's enough, Mian

Sahib. You've unbended yourself too much for me. Thank you for this liquor. It's not my place to eat dinner with you. Your Munshi Zawar Hussein wouldn't like it."

"Please don't—have dinner with me." Rustom did not want to end it this way.

"Thank you. We eat differently, my guys and me. We use our hands. I'll eat with them." Then, looking at Rustom's concerned expression, he laughed. "Mian Sahib, don't get all serious. We go back a long way, and a few drinks can't come between us."

Leaving, he shook hands making the same deferential gesture as on the first day, holding Rustom's hand with both of his own.

✳

The next morning, when Rustom went out after breakfast, he was surprised to find Sheikh Sharif awake and standing by the jeep in the portico, smoking a cigarette. The previous evening, smoking cigarette after cigarette as he did when drinking, it had not occurred to Rustom to offer one to Sheikh Sharif.

"Do you smoke, Sheikh Sahib?"

"Forgive me for smoking in front of you, Mian Sahib. But now the ice is broken between us."

"Of course it is. I should have offered you one last night."

"Well, perhaps it's better you didn't. Your servants might think I was taking liberties."

"Would you like to come out on the farm with me? See the crops?"

"I think not. Keep business and pleasure separate. But I'll send a guy with you."

"Do I need it?"

"No. It would be just for show. While I'm here these Chandios won't make a peep. Last night the DSP Sahib's men made a raid on them. They're all scattered across the river now, hiding in mud up to their necks. For good measure DSP Sahib hauled in some of their women to the station last night."

"Why take the women?" Rustom said. "My grandfather wouldn't

like it. We never did any of that. We never bring the women into it, not in this village."

"Is that right?" Sheikh Sharif said, grinning. "Don't worry, these ladies are like sisters to the sepoys. Not sisters. Like distant cousins. It wouldn't be the first time they were invited to a dance party at the station."

*

When Rustom drove in to the dera in the afternoon for his daily session with the accountant, he found that Sheikh Sharif had ordered that one of the farm tractors should be hitched with a plow and made ready.

"Mian Sahib, it's time to turn up the heat a little bit more. My boys are getting bored, and that's not good for their appetite or their temper. I'm told your Sadique Chandio owns an acre of fodder on the other side of your orchard. Let's go over there and plow it under, and if the boy shows up then we'll have a chat with him. I sent him a message to come see me here in your dera, and the motherfucker hasn't shown up. Didn't even send a reply. Makes my throat dry just thinking of it."

"I thought all those guys had gone into hiding. Maybe he didn't get the message. Why don't we give him a bit of time?"

"He got the message. Anyway, what's the harm? We'll beat the bushes and see what pops out."

"Let's go have a cup of tea, anyway, and make a plan. We can talk it over with Zawar Hussein."

Sheikh Sharif let out a big false laugh, like a gangster in the Bollywood movies. "Again with Zawar Hussein! We should hitch him to the plow and make him pull it. It would be good for him to oil the earth with his sweat. He's fat but he's strong, eating all the nice biryani around here. Forget it, Mian Sahib. It's time. It's too late now. I've been insulted.

"And look at you. They beat your personal servant days ago and haven't heard a word about it. I insist that your Sadique Chandio comes and touches the old man's feet and begs his pardon.

Otherwise, people will say that the grandson of Mian Abdullah Abdalah summoned the Sheikhs from Khirka but they came and did nothing."

They were standing under a tree, at a slight distance from the drivers and from some villagers who had gathered in the dera to gawk at the armed outsiders. The goonda put his hand on Rustom's arm and squeezed the muscle, then led him to the jeep, still holding his arm.

"Let's not waste time, Mian Sahib. I'll ride with you."

*

They drove to the Chandio field in procession, Sheikh Sharif and Rustom in one jeep, Zawar Hussein and the goondas crammed in another, and the tractor behind, going through the little Dunyapur bazaar with mute-faced villagers watching. Everyone knew of the ongoing confrontation, and Rustom felt their hostility as a tightness in his throat, the people unfriendly, not greeting him.

"All the people in the bazaar should salaam when you pass," Sheikh Sharif said laconically as they pulled up to the field. "It's respect."

The tractor driver balked at plowing into the fodder. "I've got little children, for God's sake. Don't get me involved, I beg you."

"Look at this guy!" Sheikh Sharif said. He went and whispered in the driver's ear, then called over one of his men. "Are you more afraid of the Chandios or this gorilla?"

The goonda pointed at the tractor with the barrel of his Kalashnikov. "Come on, sweetheart. Saddle up. Do it."

Sheikh Sharif turned to Rustom. "And you, Mian Sahib. Go home and relax, have a cup of tea. There's no need for you to be here anymore. Everyone will know you came and showed us the spot. Now it's time for my guys to do their thing. Tell your cook to make some samosas for them. They'll be hungry. I'll be with you as soon as I sort this out."

Relieved, abashed, Rustom got back in the jeep and let the driver take him back to the house. The people in the bazaar knew something was about to happen.

*

A little running track ran along the perimeter of the garden, another of his father's follies, since no member of the family had ever jogged. Rustom strolled the circuit, birds in the trees clamoring, while he thought of the tractor plowing up the Chandios' fodder. He shouldn't have let that happen. What happened to college days and marching for justice in South Africa and in solidarity with ship workers in Poland? Worst of all, he was afraid, relieved not to be standing there while they ruined the field of ripe fodder. It was out of his hands.

He had just completed a fourth round of the track when he heard voices. Emerging through the trees, he saw Sheikh Sharif sitting at the tea table on the lawn and Chaudrey Zawar Hussein standing behind him.

"Come, Mian Sahib," Sheikh Sharif shouted, without rising. "Have a seat."

The goonda looked different, enlarged, and in a buoyant temper.

"What happened, Zawar Hussein?" Rustom asked. His hands trembled as he lit a cigarette, for he had been expecting that there would be unpleasantness, and that he would have to get involved— that the Chandios would have driven Sheikh Sharif away.

"Ask Sheikh Sahib," the manager said.

"These things happen," the young gangster said offhandedly. "Don't worry, we'll sort it out. I'd say you go to Lahore in the morning. You'll need to talk to someone."

"But what happened?"

"My man, you know, the one with the Kalash. He's got a terrible temper. It's really too much of a good thing."

"Mian Rustom Sahib," Zawar Hussein whined. "Mian Sahib . . ."

Sheikh Sharif looked meaningfully at the munshi. "Don't you get in the middle of this, Munshi Sahib. Don't exaggerate."

The munshi shook his head from side to side, as if shaking off water.

"So what exactly happened?" Rustom asked, again.

"Nothing, really. The boy came, and he started insulting my

men. And my guys just don't know how to put up with that sort of nonsense. So that big one, you know the one? The one with the AK? He, I don't know. Let's say that he hit the man."

"It seemed pretty bad," Zawar Hussein muttered. "I didn't watch. I left."

Now Sheikh Sharif turned and stood halfway up. "Are you trying to piss me off, Munshi Sahib? Are you trying to make me angry?"

The munshi had put up his hands, as if fending off a blow.

"Anything more, Munshi Sahib?" Sheikh Sharif asked. He lowered himself comfortably, crossed his legs, lit a cigarette, and smiled at Rustom.

"Go on, Zawar Hussein, check on the samosas for my guys. Try to calm down. Mian Sahib will handle this."

They drank tea, Rustom alarmed and fearful and yet not wanting to know the details.

"Tell me about America," the goonda said. "I'll go there someday. You can get me a visa."

Rustom told him of the orderly people there and the discipline, too voluble, running away from the awful subject at hand. In his telling all the American policemen were honest and all the politicians virtuous. If anyone dropped a gum wrapper in the street, he would be stopped; it had happened to Rustom himself. He exaggerated and then saw that Sheikh Sharif didn't quite believe him, had lost interest, kept saying, "Well, well, well" and "Oh, my."

As they parted, Sheikh Sharif said, "Good, now you've told me everything about America. And you ask no questions, that's also good. But, Mian Sahib, now you have to do a little bit of work. Please go to Lahore tomorrow first thing and talk with one of your relatives. Just have them phone to the DIG Police in Multan. He's the real boss in this division. Just so it doesn't get blown out of shape. There's some Chandio on the other side of Multan who's in the provincial assembly. We better keep him out of it. I'm sure these guys will go to him."

*

Rustom left at dawn, eager to be in Lahore and to read a foreign newspaper, to have a phone line to America, to call Klara, after six weeks without hearing her voice. He borrowed Chaudrey Zawar Hussein's car because it was faster and more comfortable than his own jeep. Rustom wryly remembered his father joking with his own father about the manager having a nicer car than the master.

"Really, Daddy," Tony would say. "If you're not careful he'll steal your false teef, and then we'll be feeding you on bananas and porridge." The lisped "teef" was always good for a laugh.

Smoking cigarette upon cigarette, lighting one each time for the driver, Rustom felt his anxieties fade as he left the farm behind. It would have been unthinkable for a driver to smoke in front of his grandfather, or even his father. The only child of an only child, sure to inherit the property, Rustom should never have been sent abroad, certainly not for boarding school as well as college. Even as a teenager he had been aware of the vultures circling around—the boy too soft, too mannered, too Westernized. His grandfather, anyway, had always taken the position *après moi, le déluge*, a principle that Tony Abdalah had embraced in every sinew of his soul, if his soul were judged by his behavior. Bold bold Tony sold, those sorts of nonsense word games rang in the air, as Tony and his racy group of lightfoot lads gambled and drank, Rustom's mother retiring early, her little pills washed down with a last drink to make her sleep. Sitting alone at Dunyapur these past months, the scorpions nibbling at his heels, Rustom had sometimes reflected bitterly, *I wish I'd been the one burning away the money all night.* Dunyapur when Rustom arrived was really just the rump of the estate, so much had been sold over the years.

These were the thoughts passing through his mind as the dawn light scraped his eyeballs, the sun orange in the Punjabi haze of a late fall morning, driving the rutted KLP road, the old British road from Karachi to Lahore, the life of the country awakening into the fields. They drove through little ugly towns made of concrete, steel-gated shops clanking open, men sitting on their haunches pissing into little clumps of greenery, crowding around tea stalls.

When asked by Rustom at dinner about the incident with the goondas, Fezoo claimed not to know anything.

"Come on, Fezoo. A mouse doesn't fart around here without everyone talking about it."

But Fezoo wouldn't speak.

*

Now, as they drove along, the usually loquacious driver kept his silence, until finally Rustom asked him, "Really, Mustafa. You have to tell me. What happened yesterday?"

"Nothing happened."

"Oh, come on, you're one of the few guys who talk to me straight. I need to know."

"What do you think happened, sir? They grabbed the boy and laid him out and thrashed him till he cried like a dog."

"I guess that's what he did to Bahadur Khan."

"Maybe. I hear they broke Sadique's leg. Or legs. There's all kinds of stories going around. No one who was there would talk."

"That's unusual."

"This was unusual. Someone said they drove the tractor over the boy's knees."

"Don't be ridiculous. That's not possible."

"Everything is possible."

They drove on. After a few miles, the driver broke his silence. "Mian Sahib, please take things into your own hands. Take control. I've eaten Chaudrey Zawar Hussein's salt, but I say this to you. We all beg you. In the village. Then you'll have the police to do these jobs. They know how much to do and how much not to. These Sheikhs don't know where to stop."

*

Entering Lahore in the late afternoon, they drove along the canal that bisected the city, then into the shaded neighborhood where a few big houses stood next to old British government bungalows. The same bent chowkidar from Rustom's childhood saluted them through the gates of al-Abdalah, a large pinkish pile built in the 1930s in the Art Deco style that prettily touched down for a moment in this corner of the Empire. The house wearied him, the committee that would trickle out to greet him, his grandfather's old phlegmatic secretary, who lived on in a suite of rooms capping an administrative building near the stables, all the old servants, and the sense of failure that hung over the house, of lives passed by and glories not to come again.

Dismissing everyone, he slipped up to the room he had occupied since his parents died, his mother's retreat—she had called it her *pinjra*, her cage—up a flight of stairs and onto the roof. A wide balcony overlooked a side garden, now unkempt as it had been since her death, her roses blown and leggy, the seasonal flower beds empty. Afzal, his grandfather's old majordomo, followed behind on the stairs, mumbling through his ill-fitting false teeth. He grumbled that he had been informed only at midday of Rustom's arrival, so that the cook hadn't gone to the market, only dal and chapattis to eat, the house still shuttered.

"Come on, old man. You're losing it, I swear. Don't worry about it. Bring me a whiskey, or, better, bring the bottle and ice and water."

The room had still the scent he remembered from childhood—to him the sweetest scent—of the woven reed floor mats that his mother ordered specially made in Rawalpindi. He remembered her at the desk, typing, writing her novel, which had never seen the light of day, cigarettes overflowing the ashtray, her long hands, long face, sadness. When the servant came back he said, "Afzal, go on, twist one up."

"One?"

"Make it two."

Old Afzal, himself a late-night toker, looked up at Rustom affectionately. "As you wish. I'll do it here, so that no one smells when I heat it."

"Oh, come on, as if they didn't know. Anyway, sit down. I need company."

The servant sat down on the floor, emptied cigarettes, heated the hash, refilled the tubes, while Rustom sipped whiskey and read the *International Herald Tribune*, which he had picked up at the Intercontinental Hotel on the way into town, the first news he'd seen in six weeks. A review of a Bonnard retrospective at the Musée d'Orsay in Paris—Bonnard, his mother's favorite. She had that, those choice tastes, had taught him that—perhaps too well, he had reflected in the past months as he waded into the combats around Dunyapur. In the back of his mind loomed the horror of the Chandio confrontation, which seemed now very far away, all those miles driven across the plains of the Punjab, all those towns, villages, crops, orchards behind him, between him and the rude fact of Sadique Chandio lying on a charpoy with mangled legs, his clan around him, and Sheikh Sharif and his men prowling the old house that Rustom's great-grandfather had built. It horrified him that he'd done this, allowed a man to be beaten, becoming just like the other landlords. When Afzal learned of it, as he certainly would, he would approve of the beating administered, a line drawn. Six months taking care of business in Pakistan, and already Rustom was coming to accept these violations.

And what of Klara? He thought of her living, breathing, at that exact moment on the other side of the globe, and it gave perspective to his troubles. In New York it would be morning. How bad could the Chandio incident be, if she was still there? He could board a flight and be with her in a day, and perhaps make a life in America with her—or at least it soothed him to think so. He wished for nothing more than for her to come here and live with him, give him strength—for what? The strength to do the right thing. Soon, before he smoked the first joint, he would book a call to her in New York.

One of his mother's oldest friends, a courtesy aunt, had once invited them to tea at her Upper East Side apartment. Under this scrutiny, Klara had been mannered, slightly false, and expansive about her ambitions: to publish, to teach, making no reference to Pakistan. Watching the two women fencing, Rustom had felt excluded, felt that the two were fighting over him without any consideration of his presence, as if he were a child. Afterward, when Rustom asked his aunt what she thought, the old lady cagily suggested that Klara was perhaps a personality too strong for him.

The booze helped, one drink and then another. Later still, he would call Hisham, his older second cousin. He did not like going hat in hand, though his parents and Hisham's had broken bread on many nights in many dining rooms. He had nowhere else to turn. Hisham's senior branch of the family held the original ancestral lands nearer Lahore, the family jagirs from before the British annexation of the Punjab. Both Hisham and his father, the legendary Colonel Khuda Baksh Atar, had been in the National Assembly. If only he would, Hisham could help clear up this case, could settle it as such things had always been settled by Rustom's grandfather, a phone call to someone at the top, and an order sent down like a thunderbolt.

Rustom lay back on the bed, working through the newspaper, which brought to mind again all that lay a twenty-hour flight distant—an afternoon taxi in from JFK to Klara's studio somewhere on the Upper West Side, described to him in letters but never yet seen. He imagined them making love under an open window with drapes blowing, for in his fantasy it was always summer when he returned to her. After lovemaking, dinner, a slow descent down Broadway to one of those restaurants where they serve decent Italian food, good enough to make Dunyapur seem an illusion, though he would have been away from Pakistan for less than a day. He remembered what his aunt had said, in final dismissal. "She wouldn't make a go of it back in the home country, my dear. She couldn't or wouldn't be bent to our weird shapes."

✶

"This is the thing, my boy," Rustom's cousin Hisham said as they sipped their drinks the next evening. "This is the thing you must understand. In Pakistan, every problem is a lock, and to that lock there is a single key. Your job is to find that key—that's what farming is all about. Or business, whatever you like. Politics." He shook his cigar more or less in Rustom's face. "That, Rustom, is your job."

Hisham's abstract response to Rustom's plea for help made him feel again his own helplessness. He had been counting on Hisham as a one-stop solution to what was, after all, a rather minor issue, a man thrashed who had first unprovokedly beaten Rustom's personal servant. It made him squirm, ashamed to approach his cousin as a supplicant, ashamed of his role in Sadique Chandio's beating. He must characterize the issue as serious enough to merit Hisham's full exertion, while trying not to show himself as an old-school landlord—dentists and surgeons, as they called them, rearranging teeth and dismounting knees and elbows. Hisham would laugh it off, even approve, and that seemed worst of all.

"Good boy," Hisham said. "You'll get the hang of it in no time. Maybe we should put you up in the next election. It's pricey, but it pays in the end. With your education we'll get you a ministry after a few years. Most of our respected members sound like one of those Hollywood desi bad guys when they start letting off speeches in English. You can be one of the gentlemen we set up facing the Americans. You can't go wrong fiddling for them."

They were sitting in Hisham's drawing room, arranged with white-upholstered sofas, glass-topped tables, a bar at one end of the room, many mirrors, spectacular modern Pakistani art mixed with old miniatures and old objects, and an entire elephant's tusk as an accent piece on the fireplace mantel, a finial of beaten silver cupped around the massive base end. A dozen or so years older than Rustom, Hisham always glittered and made the right moves— a measured harvest of wild oats as a teenager from an old Lahore family, no more than a bit of trouble in the vicinity of the Punjab Club and the polo ground. After that, a degree in America, something vague at a good university. Back in Lahore, he took to farming with that initial modernizing enthusiasm so common to these returnees, ditto his attention to the family spinning business, and then within a few years he won his father's seat in parliament. His father had been in the army, retired as a colonel soon after Partition, his retirement something in the way of a protest against that rash withdrawal of British discipline. In the course of his political career, gadfly or insider, sometimes holding a ministry and sometimes courting jail, Colonel Sahib had set up the spinning business that made his branch of the family richer than many other farmers. There had been nothing illegal in this engrossment, nothing that could be termed corruption, rather a matter of opportunities offered to the minister, and opportunities taken. There were also stories current in the family about Hisham playing hardball with his younger brother's property, shoving him off to America, and that, too, added to his gloss, made him appear a man willing to do whatever it took, princely in that way.

Getting up to refill his glass, Hisham rang a bell.

A young man entered. He knew Rustom, greeted him as a family member, touching a hand to his forehead, sly and informed as the servants of powerful men are.

Throwing a fistful of peanuts into his mouth, Hisham said, "All right, Hassan, tell them to put me through to Mian Salah. He's in Multan, not the Karachi number."

After a few minutes, the phone on the table next to Hisham softly buzzed. He settled back with an alert, amused look on his face, as if about to tell a joke, a hand toying with his cigar, tapping it in the ashtray. Very quickly, leaving out all the details that Rustom had so painstakingly explained, and mixing up the facts, Hisham described the problem at Dunyapur. The voice at the other end spoke at length, almost audible to Rustom, while Hisham nodded, took a puff of his cigar, said, "Yes, yes, yes," and then, "All right, excellent, I'll tell him." He spoke a mixture of English and rich Punjabi, some words not comprehensible to Rustom, who had been brought up on servants' Urdu.

About to hang up, settling into the choreography of goodbye, body relaxing, suddenly he leaned forward and put down his cigar.

"Oh, by the way, sorry. What happened with that Nazim Shah thing? Have you spoken to the DC?"

Again, like a fire almost extinguished and then blazing up, the conversation became animated, complex, something to do with a shipment of machinery held up in Karachi port. Rustom watched with admiration as his cousin worked through his own business, joking about the other man's lack of initiative and pressing him, listening and then remonstrating, "But, Mian Sahib, these are your men. Who but you?" He laughed. "Who but you, my dear?" and then, with no more ceremony, hung up.

Turning back to Rustom, he said, clucking his tongue, "There, that should help. He's a good man. God willing, he'll sort this out for you. But he says the best thing may be for you to go through the courts."

✻

Just then, Hisham's wife came in, a suave woman in evening clothes, appearing intimidatingly grown-up to Rustom, glittering as his own mother had.

"Hello, Rustom," she said, coming up and kissing him lightly. "I didn't know you were here." Her enigmatic tinkling laugh always seemed to Rustom both a flirtation and a judgment.

Rustom had stood up when she came in.

"Look at you being so formal. Next you'll be calling me Auntie Shahnaz."

Turning to her husband, she said, "We're going to be late, you know. I can't understand what takes you so long in that dressing room of yours."

"Come on now. When have you ever been on time for anything, my darling?"

"When am I ever anything but on time?"

"True. Your understanding of time is finer than the rest of us. Peasants like us can't make these nice distinctions."

"Poor you."

"Quick drink?" Hisham asked.

"And make one for Nisa, too. She's just coming."

✻

She sat down and began asking Rustom seemingly rote questions about his health and his state of mind, yet teasing out little intimacies along the way. After a few minutes, the door opened and a younger woman came in, also dressed to go out.

"Come sit. Rustom, Nisa is the younger sister of my oldest, closest friend. And Rustom is Hisham's cousin. He's back from America and running his farm."

"Amazing," Nisa said.

"Nisa and you must be the same age, but I suppose you went off to school too soon to know each other."

"Actually, I know you, Rustom. You're exactly a year older. I came to your birthday once when we were in primary school. And when I was little my parents would bring me to al-Abdalah at Eid, and your grandmother would always give me a hundred-rupee note, which was more than anyone else did. I always loved that house, I suppose because I associated it with the hundred-rupee eidee."

She cut into a wheel of brie that the servant boy had brought, smeared a dab onto a cracker, and offered it to Rustom. "Here you go."

As she passed it to him, he became uncomfortably aware of her proximity, of her rounded biscuit-colored bare arm and the red-polished fingernails on the hand holding the cracker.

"I'll be right back," Shahnaz said. "I have to see to something."

Hisham sat back in his seat, heavyset but sleek, smoking his cigar reflectively and watching the two young people.

"I say," he observed. "You two are about the same age. Maybe Shahnaz should get you two hitched up."

Nisa made a clicking sound. "Great idea, Hisham. And you're so subtle, too."

"What's subtlety got to do with it? He's got land and a nice house in Lahore, your families have known each other for generations, and you're the prettiest girl of your batch."

Rustom found himself blushing, much to his discomfiture.

"Look at that," Nisa said. "How sweet!"

Just then, Shahnaz swept back in.

"All set," she said. "Rustom, I'm throwing you out. My husband has to get ready. Why don't you come for dinner tomorrow?"

"I'm afraid I have to get back to Dunyapur in the morning."

"What a bore. Oh, well, we'll see you next time, then."

"I'll walk you out," Hisham said.

As they left the room, Nisa called behind him, "Bye, Rustom!"

✻

Driving home, Rustom's relief at having unbuttoned himself to his cousin warred with his sense of having been hurried away, treated with less ceremony than he had hoped. Go through the courts! Nobody ever went through the courts unless they had no power. If he would only do it, Hisham could solve this thing in a minute.

People said that Shahnaz, the wife, was the real brains of that operation. That's what Rustom should do, of course, marry one of the girls whom he'd seen around the polo ground since childhood, the girls of his class, someone like Nisa. Choose one with connections, not like his father's legacy friends, his drinking buddies, all the gilded youth of that Lahori generation, who spent their lives pawning off the gilding. He needed someone like Shahnaz, someone to pull the wires behind the scenes. It would be no hardship to see that dimple and that smile over breakfast every morning, however double-edged the mind behind it. Perhaps Nisa's presence had not been accidental, he reflected. As Hisham had observed, it would be just like Shahnaz to set him up, take the credit for a useful marriage.

✻

The long driveway to the Dunyapur house ran near the old swimming pool. Through the trees Rustom saw Sheikh Sharif's men bathing, one of them bare-chested in the water, another sitting and combing his long hair in the afternoon sun. They had piled their Kalashnikovs on a charpoy beside them, and, when they saw Rustom they watched him pass with blank faces.

"Look at that," Mustafa, the driver, said. "The village women go past to get water, and these guys are sitting half-naked."

Back at the house, Rustom called in Chaudrey Zawar Hussein.

"What's the story with Sheikh Sharif's men bathing in the old swimming pool? I specifically asked them not to."

"What can I tell you? All they do is order beef pilau and chicken pilau and sit around smoking hashish."

"They're smoking hash?"

"Openly. And walking around with their guns."

"What about Sheikh Sharif? Where is he?"

"He went into Cawnapur this afternoon."

"Did he take the jeep?"

"No, he's got a car now. Some more of his guys drove in last night. That makes five of them total plus Sheikh Sharif."

"Tell Fezoo to give me dinner right away. And, when Sheikh Sahib returns, tell him I've retired for the night."

*

That evening Rustom received a phone call, with much crackling on the line, which once again had been patched up.

"Hello, Mr. Robinson Crusoe. It's Shahnaz."

It surprised him that she should be calling, rather than Hisham.

"Is everything okay?"

"Of course it is. Listen, Hisham has some business in Bahawalpur, of all places, and so we're all going to see old Begum Latifa. For some reason she insists on living there. And we thought we'd first come and spend a couple of nights with you. If you're not too busy. I was going to mention it the other night, and then I forgot."

"Busy doesn't happen in Dunyapur. Please come and never ever leave."

"It's just us, and then Nisa, my friend from the other night. And her father, old Uncle Tiffy."

"So that's who Nisa is! You should have said Uncle Tiffy's daughter. He was part of my dad's whole group."

"Group indeed. Look, this connection is terrible. We'll be there tomorrow afternoon. Thank you a million. I've heard so much about Dunyapur, and now I can see it. Big kiss." And she hung up.

*

They arrived in a convoy, Hisham's black Mercedes with MNA plates—Member, National Assembly—and then two other vehicles, Nisa and her father in a little sports car, and a big jeep with

Hisham's people, a bodyguard and his valet and a couple of managers from his factory. Hisham had brought his friend Shehryar Salauddin, known as Bumpy, a slim, groomed business type from Karachi in a blue pin-striped shirt and cream slacks, milk from the top of the bottle. Flicking open a gold lighter and inhaling a deep drag from a cigarette, he looked placidly about, as if waiting for the show to start.

The group stood in the portico, stretching, gazing about as people do when arriving at a place that they have heard spoken of.

"Nice wheels," Rustom said to Nisa.

"Not bad, right? I drove all the way myself."

"That's a major effort. I was wondering how you could fit a driver in that thing. The back seat there would be like eight hours in a dog carrier."

Shahnaz drifted over. "What are you two laughing about?"

"Nisa driving from Lahore by herself."

"I know. Isn't she a nut? We couldn't keep up with her."

Showing them around the house and then the garden, Rustom saw through their eyes the hundred-year-old banyan tree around a pavilion at the far end of the garden, its aerial roots dropping from branches all around the bole, so that the single tree formed a mysterious grove. It gave him weight, that this belonged to him—the ancient trees, the mellow brick of the walls. The guesthouse at the far end of the lawn had been yet another of his father's follies—an architect manqué, people said, flattery to cover his idleness—with three domed rooms and a round, sunken bathtub that was more like a swimming pool.

"This is so much nicer than your Ranmal Mohra place," Nisa said to Hisham. "Your farm looks like some industrialist plonked up a brand-new, mega-sized Lahore house with a helicopter and dropped it in the village."

"Come on, that's so unfair! At worst it's Indian colonial with an update, and actually it's better than that. Anyway, I have to overawe the locals. Rustom here is a prince like his father, he can live any way he likes. I doubt he knows the name of any revenue official in the district."

Rustom laughed. "Not yet! I've still got that fussy American stomach. I get queasy."

They went and sat in the middle of the central garden, where Uncle Tiffy had been waiting for them, with the sun just going down.

"Well, young man," he said. "You think that you're the master here, but in fact I got here long before you. I came with your father and mother the first time in 1971, during the war. Everyone thought the Indians would be in Lahore in a few days, eating lunch at our tables and using us for footstools. A whole caravan of us came up here, showing our bravery by showing our backs." He greeted his own story with a huge laugh, his face marmalade golden and shining, satyric, and curling lovelocks around his ears, hair just slightly too long. "I hope you don't mind," he continued, stretching his legs forward and looking up at the sky and into the branches of the old pipal tree. "I've asked Fezoo to bring the drinks cart and something to eat. Excuse my taking the liberty, but I feel I'm at home here."

Rustom did mind but brushed it aside. This Uncle Tiffy had been close to his father, and that counted for a lot. Still, he remembered something that his grandfather had said, when Tiffy showed up once too often exactly when the drinks were laid at al-Abdalah. Tiffy had gone to the toilet, and his grandfather made one of his very rare jokes, and even rarer criticisms.

"Do you know what Tiffy brings to a potluck dinner?" he asked. "A spoon."

✳

The servants lit a bonfire in the garden, and later served an immense meal that Chaudrey Zawar Hussein had conjured up from the city, chicken tikkas and beef tikkas, a pilau, chicken karahi, all the food that a group of boozers would need to keep themselves from going bottoms up, as Uncle Tiffy remarked happily. He called in Zawar Hussein and became familiar with him, saying, "You rogue, you used to spoil us with these dinners back in Tony Mian's day, didn't you! You villain!"

"Thank you, sir," Zawar Hussein said, his expression less benevolent than his words.

In English Tiffy said to the group, "The old dog's probably lap-ping it up himself out back there in the servants' area. A bottle disappears and nobody knows the difference!"

Bumpy, the friend from Karachi, laughed. "Brilliant, Uncle Tiffy. That should be on your coat of arms: A bottle disappears but nobody knows!"

After dinner the women were cold, and so they all went into the living room, had the fire lit. The conversation turned to the problem on the farm with the Chandios, and Rustom described what had happened, making his own role seem more judicious and strategic than vindictive, and diminishing the Chandio beating to a couple of well-deserved slaps.

"Quite right, to bring in these goondas," Tiffy said. His accent grew more and more British as the evening progressed. "That's all these people around here understand. The stick. The carrot and the stick. You have to show them who's in charge." He poked a finger toward Rustom. "Young man, remember, you're the grandson of Mian Abdullah Abdalah, and these people should be grateful to you and your family for all you've done in this area. You're like a father to them."

Nisa sat next to Rustom, making a little corner with him, watch-ful, amused rather than amusing. Shahnaz slowed down, but Nisa drank one for one with the men, chain-smoking cigarettes. Slur-ring and confidential, Tiffy launched inconsequentially into a story about one of the village women back in the old days, calling her the Pride of the Punjab.

"Whoops, mixed company, mixed company!" he wheezed.

"Come on, Abu," Nisa said, standing up. "Time to go to sleep."

"But why!" He clenched his teeth and made a stand, but she managed to lead him out.

"It's all right, Uncle Tiffy," Hisham said. "I'm going, too. I've got to make some calls."

"To your bookie?" Tiffy warbled. "Put down a thousand for me."

Nisa managed to lead him out, helped by Hisham, who winked and whispered to the room, "I'll be back."

Returning after a few minutes, Nisa said, "All right, bring it out. Who's got the dope?"

"Why not?" Bumpy said. He had been egging on Uncle Tiffy as he became more and more sodden, refilling his drinks. "Come on, Rustom Mian, if you don't have any dope, then amuse us somehow. Show us your weapons or whatever it is you get up to here. What about this Punjab Pride? Or her daughter. Or granddaughter."

"Are you serious!" Nisa said. "That's offensive."

Shahnaz clapped her hands and began to stand up. "All right, gentlemen, I'm off, then. I know where this goes. It's straight downhill from here."

"Calm down, Shahnaz," Bumpy said. "If you go, we'll all go. What about this goonda, then? Bring him out, offer him a drink." When telling them about his evening of drinking with Sheikh Sharif, Rustom had made a joke of it, exaggerating his own coolness and Sheikh Sharif's deference. "He's a bit of a tough guy," Rustom had told them. "He has to be. But you'd hardly know it—he can fit in. He's actually not bad company."

Nisa had been looking at the books on the shelves, a lot of mysteries and P. G. Wodehouse and old books that might have been found in a gymkhana club library back in British times, but also the books of Rustom's mother, her poetry and novels. "What a nice collection," Nisa said to Rustom, calling him over. "It's a time capsule, isn't it? It's beautiful. The books of that moment in the sixties and seventies. I wonder if your mother wasn't lonely here, with my dad and your dad and all that. It's a place to make a home, you know, if it weren't for all the nonsense."

She had picked Mary McCarthy's *Birds of America* from the shelf. "I love this."

"Truthfully, I'm surprised you've even heard of it," Rustom said. "I always wanted to read it, because of the title, but I never got around to it. For the longest time I thought it was one of those field guides."

She laughed and put her hand lightly on his arm. "I'm not as dim as they make me out to be, you know."

. . .

Rustom took Nisa to his study, to show her his mother's collection of poetry first editions, and when they returned to the living room Bumpy had taken it upon himself to ring the bell, sending Fezoo to ask Sheikh Sharif in for a moment.

"For the record, I warned him against this," Shahnaz scolded. "My husband won't approve when he gets back from wherever he's disappeared to."

Rustom didn't want to ruin the fun. "Maybe the women should at least put away their drinks."

"Oh, come on," Bumpy said. "Don't be a bad sport. It's not as if this chap doesn't know that Lahori women drink. In Karachi these gangsters give the best parties."

"We're not in Karachi," Rustom said. "But it's fine—you're the guest."

The men made a great show of politeness to Sheikh Sharif, rising when he came in, offering him the best chair.

"Please, I'm comfortable here," he said, slipping toward a sofa placed against the wall.

But they wouldn't allow it and insisted he sit in front of the fire. Without asking, Bumpy poured a drink and brought it to him.

"Sheikh Sahib, will you do us the honor of joining us?"

He sat too far back in the low, deep seat, then struggled forward and set himself upright, his feet together on the floor. "As you wish, sir."

They spoke of generalities, Sheikh Sharif clearing his throat with low humming noises between sips of his drink, Bumpy with an amused expression on his face.

"Isn't this exciting!" Nisa, who sat curled with her feet under her, whispered. She put her feet on the ground, found her shoes, stood, and went over to the bookshelf again.

Sheikh Sharif watched her walk across the room, then turned to Bumpy. "May I ask where you come from?"

"We drove from Lahore. But I'm based in Karachi."

"Are you doing business there?" He spoke in Urdu but said the word "business" in English—"bijness."

"Yes, bijness."

"And do you know Hajji Jajji Baba Soreja?"

Bumpy laughed. "The One-Eyed Hajji!"

"Yes. Hajji Sahib is a friend of ours."

"You have powerful friends! Come on, drink up, and we'll have another."

After taking Sheikh Sharif's glass and returning with the refill, Bumpy stood by the fire, examining Rustom's family portraits.

"So, tell me, Sheikh Sahib, what is your business?"

No one moved. Sheikh Sharif looked around the room, over at Nisa, who was standing by the bookshelf, watching the men ranged by the fire, a little smile on her lips, very delicate, very pretty, waiting to hear what the gangster would say.

"Does your friend speak our tongue?" he asked Rustom in Punjabi, indicating Nisa.

Directing Sheikh Sharif's attention away from Nisa, Rustom pretended to think that the question referred to Bumpy. "Bumpy Sahib here is a businessman, so he knows all the languages."

"But he's not a Punjabi," Sheikh Sharif said. "I'll speak in Urdu. I'll explain it this way. Our business is your business. Wherever you have business we have it too. Let me give you an example. Mian Rustom asked me up here to settle a little dispute with one of his neighbors. Now, it happens that the DSP in Cawnapur is obliged to my grandfather for something that happened in Lahore a few years ago. The DSP is Mir Hashim Hayat Sanghera; he used to be in Kasur, outside Lahore. You may have heard of him. Rustom Sahib knows him. These policemen are also businessmen, like all of us."

Sheikh Sharif commanded the city people's attention, none of them moving, all eyes fixed upon him, the room still but for the wavering fire.

"So I drove to Cawnapur and went to see this friend of ours, this Sanghera Sahib. We had tea, we spoke of mutual acquaintances. Then he said to me, 'You've come, and I need you to do something for me. We're going to pick up this badmash who's been causing trouble in the area.' It was nothing to do with Rustom Mian's Chandio guys, someone else. We get in his private jeep, three or four police wagons with us, we drive to some village, and when we get there Mir Sanghera says, 'Please, do this. For you it's all in a day's work. Or maybe you've never done one before.'"

Shahnaz, who had been sitting back in shadow, stirred up. "What in the world are you all talking about?"

Though she spoke in English, Sheikh Sharif understood her. "Encounter, Bibi Jee. This is the way they settle this business. The police wish someone else to do the job. That way they put the blame a little bit away from themselves, for the enmity, you know. This man in that village had fifty-six cases against him, and not one could be settled, because the judges are afraid or they're bought, and he keeps getting bail. So they pulled him out, threw him in the back of a pickup, we drove out to the desert to a quiet spot, and then we finished the job."

"And did you? Do it, I mean?" Bumpy asked, offhand, still looking up at the family portraits on the wall.

"Someone had to do it, anyway. Who knows? When you eat a chicken someone has to cut the neck first. He got in the way of business, and that's how we dealt with it. An inch of lead, nice and hot. They couldn't pry him out of the back of the pickup. We just did it in there, finally."

Nisa called over, "Seriously, Bumpy. You can tell this one in Karachi. About dining with panthers."

A look of revulsion on her face, Shahnaz stood up. "That's so awful," she said, also in English. "It's disgusting. All you men are disgusting. It's horrible."

Wrapping her shawl around her shoulders, not looking at Sheikh Sharif, she whisked up and out. From outside the door she called back, "You're an idiot, Rustom."

"But why blame poor Rustom?" Bumpy murmured.

Sheikh Sharif sat unmoving, a muscle twitching in his jaw, looking fixedly at the corner of the room in front of him.

"I'm sorry, Sheikh Sahib," Rustom said, after a moment, going over and taking the gangster's glass. "My cousin's wife isn't feeling well. You know how women are. Let me get you another drink."

"I think not, thank you. I'll beg my leave, so you can see to her. Your women seem to require more attention than ours do."

"At least have some dinner, Sheikh Sahib. Join us. Let me tell them to put it on."

"Thank you, Mian Sahib. Thank you, no." He went and shook Bumpy's hand with an excess of politeness that bordered on insolence, standing in front of him, bowing his head for a long moment. Coming to Rustom, he closed his eyes as if in prayer. "I was just remembering your grandfather and Sheikh Sarkar Sahib," he said, in Punjabi, and then backed out the door, giving it a last loud jerk as he pulled it shut behind him.

✸

"Not cool, Bumpy," Rustom said, when he was sure that Sheikh Sharif had left.

"He's right," Nisa said. "Now I'm a bit nervous. Call Hisham, please."

Returning from making phone calls, Hisham listened to the story with a grave expression.

"How well do you know this guy, Rustom? Is he going to keep boozing it up out there? This was not a good idea."

"I agree. I was in the other room when they called him. Bumpy here thought it would be entertaining." Rustom tried to make light of it. "Anyway, Sharif is old school, or at least his people are all old school. They still have that respect. He's Sheikh Sarkar's grand-nephew, as I said. You know all about it. From that old connection."

"You told us you'd been sitting with him the other night, and that seemed fine," Hisham said. "I wish I'd been here, but then it wouldn't have happened. Let's hope he's more evolved than the run of them. And let's get to bed, tuck in tight, and everything will be better in the light of day. I'll meet him tomorrow, just to settle him down."

Bumpy evidently felt himself unfairly blamed. "I'm sure he didn't understand what Shahnaz said. His English isn't good enough."

"Dream on," Hisham replied. "He knew exactly what she thought of him. From what you told me, my wife didn't mince her words. That fellow could take 'You men are disgusting' pretty far in the wrong way, bad English or good."

"I hope Rustom won't need goondas to relieve him of his goondas!" Bumpy tittered.

As she left, Nisa squeezed Rustom's hand. "Thanks for the excitement."

Waking early, looking up at the high ceiling in the chilly, still room, overcome by a feeling of dread, Rustom considered that last night Sheikh Sharif had been insulted in his living room.

He rang the bell, and when Fezoo came he said, "Is Sheikh Sahib awake?"

"Sheikh Sahib left early this morning for Lahore. He got called away."

"And his men?"

"He left them all behind. They're shouting for breakfast."

✳

Hisham and the little party stayed another day. After a boozy lunch in the garden, with champagne that Bumpy had brought as a host present, Hisham asked Rustom to call in Zawar Hussein and then interrogated him about Sheikh Sharif.

"You better get to Lahore and call this man and put him in his place," Hisham warned, after dismissing the munshi. "There you'll be in a fourteen-kanal house right in the middle of GOR, with the commissioner's residence a few houses down, and all your staff around you, and he'll be intimidated. Don't let him be familiar. And then you better get his men off your farm pronto."

They went to sleep early, the party too long by one day, the conversation stale, everything already said. Rustom's room seemed particularly bleak that evening. Life alone here could dry up so easily; his plastic slippers fussily lined up by the bedside told him that, the bare bulb and his face in the mirror in the stark bathroom as he brushed his teeth. Fezoo had not lit the fire, as he usually would, and Rustom knew that if he brought this up in the morning the

servant would put on a pained expression and refer to the burden of
the guests. He reflected that Fezoo had no real attachment to him,
despite having worked in this house all his life, seeing the family
come and go, never here for long.

They had all agreed to sleep late, and, though Rustom sat in bed
reading for almost an hour after he woke, he heard nothing. After
dressing, he went to the kitchen and called from outside. He tried
never to go in, for the place was filthy, village style, and he couldn't
bear in these early days back at the farm to tackle these matters of
housekeeping.

It surprised him then to hear Nisa's bright voice responding.
"Hey, you, you're up! Come and check it out."

Rustom went in. "Good lord! Look at you in this grubby corner
of my little kingdom."

She was standing in front of the stove, the cook beside her flus-
tered. "It's fine. In Lahore now all the houses have two kitchens—
one for the begum sahiba, to play around at making her little
desserts or whatever, and the other one that they call the dirty
kitchen for the servants to do the real cooking. They actually call
it that. I'm teaching your guy how to make pancakes. I thought I'd
work on your breakfast menu."

"I guess it's true—breakfast isn't our strong point. They hardly
eat it themselves. The only thing this guy knows is greasy omelets
with that awful bread."

"Bunny's Bread. The worst brand in the world. It sounds like fun
till you taste it. You should eat parathas and honey for breakfast,
you know. Your cook could manage that. Anyway, the dinners have
been excellent."

"I'm not sure. Bumpy picked out one of the bones from the
curry last night and wondered if it came from a brontosaurus."

"He's a jerk, isn't he, just between us. He'll dine off that goonda
story for weeks when he's safely back in Karachi, telling them all
about how he was roughing it in South Punjab."

"And look at you, sleeves rolled up in my unwashed kitchen and
cooking over coals. A real pioneer."

She made a little curtsy, bobbing her head. "Thank you, thank you. Give me a few weeks and I'll turn your cook into a cordon bleu."

"And then you can teach him the tango. Better yet, you could polish up Zawar Hussein, and then get to work on the rest of my munshis too."

✵

In a corner of the garden, Rustom's mother had made a breakfast nook, sheltered and with the sun coming off a whitewashed wall, so that it warmed quickly. Rustom took Nisa there after she had turned the pancakes over to the cook. Walking behind her on a little bridge over a watercourse, Rustom had been free to look at her neck, her shoulders, and the blue ribbon in her black hair. Now he said to her, "You know, the last woman I remember sitting here is my mother. You look a bit like her. Or you act like her. Like a foreigner almost."

In the morning sun, Nisa glowed sleek, and her presence made him feel happier than he had in weeks. He tried not to look at her and felt a delicious embarrassment at being alone with her, his face stiff as if involuntarily smiling. They might have kissed in the night after drinks, she might have slipped into his room so easily, he might have touched that body, though he wouldn't do it, wouldn't be unfaithful to Klara. His body ached, not just with desire but with the desire for connection, for the comfort of touch.

"I remember your mother. You're right, there was something foreign about her. She was a little bit apart; she didn't quite join in. Mostly I remember your father. One time I woke up in the morning and went into the living room at our place, and he was sitting there with my dad and the rest of the gang. The room was all smoky, with drinks lying all around, and they were playing Monopoly for real money. They'd been at it all night. You've probably seen that."

"Seen rooms like that a hundred times. I don't remember the Monopoly."

He was sitting back, looking up at the morning sky. As always in South Punjab, it would be fine weather, the sky turning from blue to a mare's tail of milky white when the light turned flat at noon, and then in the evening to orange. A chill in the morning breeze reminded him that it would soon be real winter, too cold at night to sit out, and the breeze in the rosewood trees spaced around the large garden poured down and cooled and emptied the space. Fezoo came with tea, put it on the table, and stood with his hands folded.

"That's fine, Fezoo. Put on the breakfast in half an hour in the dining room. And light the fire."

When he'd gone, Nisa said, "You've got quite a collection of old-time servants around here. Your parents' old people. Or probably your grandfather's. You're lucky, even if they're inefficient or corrupt or whatever. It's continuity."

She made him tea, and her gestures reminded him again of his mother. Handing him the cup, catching him in the act of watching her, Nisa looked him in the eyes. "You're lonely here, aren't you? Poor Rustom, and you're all alone. I can imagine."

Taking the cup, looking away, Rustom felt exposed, as if he would confess and break down. He wanted to say something light, but his emotion prevented it, not just his loneliness but his fear, and the knowledge that after lunch Nisa would go, along with the rest of them. He would be alone, with Sheikh Sharif's men prowling outside, and all the concentric rings around him, all the people looking in toward him, the villagers, the Chandios, and the rest.

"Look at you," she murmured. "I'm sorry."

"It's fine. I was just thinking of my mother."

"Of course you were. Let's talk about something else. Tell me about Klara. I'm so curious. She sounds like such an intellectual."

Rustom had dropped the name several times, expressing the hope that Klara would soon visit Pakistan.

"If she comes, we'll take her in hand," Nisa continued. "We'll doll her up for you and take her around."

Rustom made a joke of it. "That doesn't sound good. But let's talk about something else. Tell me some Lahore gossip. I don't know anybody or anything. You can tell me all the worst stuff and I won't know who you're talking about."

Just then they saw Bumpy at the far end of the lawn, looking about, seeing them, waving and striding toward them.

"Oh, great, here comes Mr. Plastic. I should have told you some of the gossip about him," Nisa said. "I hear his dad's got some dealings in Karachi port that would make your goonda's eyes water."

They all spoke for a few moments, and then Rustom went to see about getting the breakfast, Nisa reminding him to order honey for her pancakes. Wanting a moment alone, troubled still by the emotion that Nisa had awoken in him, he returned to his room and took off his shoes, slipped under the covers. He thought of Klara, of having her there with him. That evening he would write a letter to her, telling of this visit and hinting about being set up with Nisa. Having kindled Klara's jealousy, he would put it to rest. Watching Nisa when she was unaware, he had traced her figure with his eyes, and noticed how well she was put together, all the way down to her feet. But her feet were long, shaped clumsily, and she had thick ankles. He would say that, the ankles. Lying in bed with Klara he would sometimes encircle her ankle with his finger and thumb and say how delicately she was built. "You're such a racist," Klara had exclaimed, reassured, when he said before leaving her in America that he could never marry a Pakistani.

Yet in the past couple of days Shahnaz had been laying out Nisa's merits and demerits, subtly but with purpose, and very much in the context of the predicament in which Rustom found himself, with the goondas and the issues with his neighbors.

"No doubt," Shahnaz said, "her papa's a tiny bit dotty. He props up the bar at the Punjab Club, and that's about all he's useful for. But Nisa's a tough girl, and she's a very good sport, and, if she has a bit of a past, well, that's what happens when you send a girl abroad for schooling. She's got ten first cousins, half of them in the army, and all of them know how to skin a cat ten ways."

"I like the way you put things," Rustom said. "Is that even a phrase?"

Then Shahnaz laughed her little tinkling laugh, her face lit and yet cold. "I think you understand my meaning. A girl like Nisa comes complete with an army, literally. She's spent a lot of time abroad, not as much as you, but then you need some local masala in your mixture. I'll be straight with you. You've been away since you were what, thirteen? If you're going to put down stakes here, that's a decision, too, just like going away."

"I didn't make that decision. My mother did."

"I'm just being straight. I'm speaking as your cousin's wife. And then I've known Nisa since she was a little girl."

Yet seeing her father pouring himself drinks and making himself at home, and seeing Nisa's little flirtations, done so well, Rustom couldn't escape the feeling that he was being haltered and led. He was damaged goods—parents dead, schooled abroad too long, cut off from the oxygen of living in this place. Propertied as he was, he must prove himself, one way or another. Lying in bed the previous night, he had thought of Nisa's body, her tight bodice, small breasts, how that might open to him, and, as he closed his eyes, imagined a tiny scarlet forked tongue darting out of her mouth.

After he had seen off his guests, the garden and the house seemed barren. He read all afternoon, didn't go on the farm, ate his solitary dinner. Falling asleep, he remembered his loneliness, the insuperable difficulty—it terrified him to admit this—of bringing Klara here. And even if she came she would never stay, with her feminist principles and her thesis on Christine de Pizan. It had been so hard, especially at first, living alone in these rooms, where in all the years before he came here and set up camp no guest or even any member of the family had ever stayed more than a week.

The days streamed by him, like a flowing liquid, and he put off going to Lahore from one day to the next. One night he called Fezoo and told him to bring some bananas. That had become his ritual—dinner, green tea, and then just before sleep a banana, eaten slowly, voluptuously, while reading in bed. And, when Fezoo told him there were no bananas, none in the bazaar, he sent the servant away, turned out the lights, and began weeping, the quiet tears one sheds when perfectly alone.

✳

Rustom had been back in Lahore for a week. He had brought Chaudrey Zawar Hussein with him, and twice sent him to invite Sheikh Sharif into the city from Khirka.

"Mian Sahib, this thing could become serious," Zawar Hussein said, returning after the second fruitless mission. "I'm not sure what happened between you and Sheikh Sahib, but you should go yourself to his dera."

"Did my grandfather ever go to Sheikh Sarkar's dera?"

The munshi made a dismissive gesture, holding up both hands and shaking his head. "Mian Sahib, forget about what used to be. These days, the District Commissioner Lahore goes to call on the Sheikhs of Khirka. They summon the superintendent of police and make him wait half the morning."

Then, one evening, late, Afzal came up to Rustom's room, after he had already gone to bed.

"Sheikh Sharif has come, Mian Sahib."

"What does he want at this hour?"

"He's brought someone with him, a policeman I think, and they came in a police jeep."

"Put them in the drawing room."

To Rustom's great surprise, the DSP from Cawnapur was with Sheikh Sharif, both of them in civvies, white shalvar and waistcoats, so that at first Rustom didn't recognize the policeman.

"I'm afraid we've disturbed you," Sheikh Sharif said, rising, saying the word "disturb" in English but mispronouncing it "dish-turb." "It seems that you go to sleep very early, even in Lahore." They had seated themselves on a sofa next to each other, got up to shake Rustom's hand, and then dropped back down, Sheikh Sharif sprawling, the policeman upright and alert.

"Mian Sahib is careful with his health," the policeman said.

"Please," Sheikh Sharif said, "surely you remember my good friend, Mir Hashim Hayat Sanghera, who is also DSP Cawnapur."

"I've been meaning to come pay my respects to you in Dunya-pur," the expressionless policeman said. "When you were so kind to visit me first."

"Mian Sahib is a very keen farmer," Sheikh Sharif said. "He gives a lot of time to his lands."

"It's very difficult," the policeman said. "These boys come back from abroad, and it's so hard out in the sticks. You and I, Sheikh Sahib, we were born out there, it doesn't bother us. That dust! And the heat!"

Despite their bravado, the two men seemed to Rustom diminished in this drawing room that had witnessed the great life of this city, ministers and generals coming in and out, sitting irritably playing bridge all through Rustom's childhood.

"What can I offer you? Tea?"

Sheikh Sharif put his hand on the policeman's arm and squeezed it, as if giving a signal. "DSP Sahib only drinks tea at night when he's working."

The policeman nodded gravely. "It helps keep me awake."

Fortunately, at that moment Afzal brought in three glasses of sherbet on a tray.

"Nothing," Sheikh Sharif said. "We can't stay. We just came to say our salaam to Mian Sahib. Now we'll let him go back to sleep. Sanghera Sahib wanted to see Mian Sahib in his Lahore house. I had been telling him of it."

Although he hadn't wanted to, Rustom said, "Would you like a drink, perhaps?"

Sheikh Sharif, standing up, said with satisfaction, "Now Mian Sahib is offering us a drink."

The policeman also had stood up and looked around and up at the twelve-foot ceiling.

"Big rooms! How much land is with this house?"

"Fourteen kanals," Sheikh Sharif said. "It's massive."

"And whose name is it registered in?" the policeman asked Rustom.

Sheikh Sharif let out a big, thigh-slapping laugh. "Why, San-ghera Sahib, are you a buyer?"

"Only if Mian Sahib is a seller."

✲

Out on the circular drive, Rustom watched the departing taillights of the police jeep, followed by a second car that had four men in it, also in plain clothes. As they were leaving, the DSP had said gravely, "Thank you, Mian Sahib, for allowing us to see your golden palace," and then Sheikh Sharif, getting into the jeep on the other side, had said in vulgar Punjabi, "Oy, you, hop in, buddy. Leave him alone."

They drove very fast down the long drive, so that the old watch-man leapt to open the gate in time.

As Rustom turned back into the house, a siren began to wail, then drew away and gradually diminished, gone in the direction of the river and the Old City. This too was intimidation, the two men hooting away. The sound blended into the background hum of Lahore at night in winter.

Rustom dismissed Afzal, walked through the many rooms lead-ing up to the roof, and stood on an open terrace at the very top, taking a moment beneath the stars, gathering his thoughts. There, far away, were the lights of the Intercontinental Hotel. He could map the quadrants of the city, the Governor's House in its fifty-acre grounds, where he swam as a boy when his grandfather's closest friend became governor. Lawrence Gardens, then the zoo, with its lions calling all night. Caped around al-Abdalah, like a village at the foot of a fort's battlements, stood the commissioner's house, the district commissioner's house, all the officers' residences since British times. He remembered the governor visiting his grandfather, other grandees calling, easy with one another, running the coun-try by right. The goonda and his pet policeman would be going perhaps to the dancing girls in the Old City, or on some violent errand, pulling a trigger, breaking an arm. Prisoners in chains. All this was surely a lesson for him. Finally, if he would pay the price, all the power was his—or would be, could be.

The Clean Release

✿

LAHORE—HANOVER, NEW HAMPSHIRE—
KAGHAN VALLEY, NORTHWEST FRONTIER PROVINCE

2005–1972–1976–2005

You're a glutton for company!" said Shahnaz brightly to her husband, Hisham, kicking off her heels and curling up on a sofa with her feet tucked under. "Aren't you on the zombie flight to Karachi?"

Now late January, it was the wedding season in Lahore, and they had just returned from yet another *valima* dinner.

"Relax, my love. That's exactly why I invited old Rustom to drop in. You go to sleep. The flight's not till four a.m. I'll chat with him a bit and then I'll go to the airport."

"You mean booze and puff on cigars and keep our long-suffering servants awake all night."

"I tell Rustom stories. He loves to hear the family gossip, it makes him feel more plugged in."

A servant boy came in with ice and soda on a tray, opened a cabinet gleaming with bottles, and laid out the drinks.

"Chelo, Saqib," said Hisham. "Make two whiskey sodas and a glass of white wine for Begum Sahiba. And bring my other shoes, and then sort out my Karachi bag. I'm on the dawn flight. And tell Bayazid that I'll need some cash and to call and check the flight's on time."

Shahnaz wagged her finger at the servant. "Only the sahibs' whiskey, Saqib. I'm off to sleep."

Just then, their guest, Hisham's second cousin Rustom, returned from the toilet. The two men, both wearing suits, had removed their ties and hung them around their necks. White upholstered sofas and chairs formed several enclaves in the room, the space designed for parties, striking contemporary art on the walls, arrangements of miniatures, family portraits in silver frames on tables, clever ashtrays fashioned from antique brass stirrups or heavy silver tribal bangles scattered to be near at hand.

Removing her sapphire earrings with a neat quick motion then cupping them in her hands, Shahnaz looked appraisingly at their guest, who was uncertainly watching her.

"My apologies, Shahnaz," offered Rustom. "I'm keeping you people awake. Hisham asked me but I should have waited for an invite from you. I was just passing on the way home."

"Come, Rustom," she said amicably, having rearranged and softened her expression. "I'm off to sleep. You guys keep it up as long as you like. If Hisham is still woozy in the morning he won't be bothering me. I just hope it's some mullah in the seat next to him breathing the fumes."

Hisham had been standing pensively at the French doors leading into a garden, neither in nor out, smoking. Now he flicked away his half-smoked cigarette onto the grass and briskly turned. Sitting down on one of the white sofas, he straightened out his legs so that the servant kneeling in front of him could take off his dress shoes and put on his loafers. With his hands locked behind his head, he indulgently studied his wife, a handsome woman coming up on fifty.

"My darling, how do you stay so pretty?"

Uncoiling herself from the sofa, she stood and went over to a vase of long-stemmed roses on the sideboard and rearranged them idly. "Don't, Hisham." Her voice had an edge. "You're feeling sentimental, you've been in a mood all day. It doesn't become you. And then, you make me sound like one of your antique cars. There you are at these little functions, swilling in some hidden barroom, and the ladies are parked under the hothouse flowers comparing handbags. It's very trying."

"You're so right," said Hisham, fanning himself with his hand. "The hell with weddings! Let's skip the whole rest of the season."

"Fine with me. You're the one who has to go around and fly the flag. I do my side of the business more privately."

Turning again to face the two men, she went over to Rustom and brushed her cheek lightly against his. "Come, sit down, Rustom. Don't be all formal. Stay as long as you like. Really."

Almost of a younger generation, Rustom made a deferential gesture, tilting his head down. "Thank you."

Going out, Shahnaz called over her shoulder to Hisham, "Say hello to everyone. Say hi to Karina!"

Behind her back, Hisham made a cat face at Rustom. Everyone in Lahore knew about these things, his special friends.

Rustom followed her with his eyes as she exited, his little smile lingering as she disappeared.

Taking a cigar from a humidor lying on the table, Hisham snipped it with deliberation and lit it and then looked up at his friend with an amused expression.

"When the hell are you going to get married, Rustom? All the matrons of Lahore think of you like a dog without a license. You're a danger to the establishment."

"Fortunately, I'm sitting with one of the pillars of the establishment. You can vouch for me."

*

An hour had passed, the two men capping each other's anecdotes, Hisham's broad laugh a ready chorus, for he had the largest and most encouraging laugh in all Lahore—a talent that won him friends wherever he went.

"Come on, I want to show you something," Hisham said.

"I suppose Shahnaz has made another of her great discoveries."

"Nothing like that. A new toy. Come on."

The fruits of Shahnaz's quick eye and open purse hung on the walls here and there throughout this sprawling old house, modern paintings from the emerging Pakistani artists of the last fifty years, her first acquisitions from the '70s, when she was just married and barely out of college, keen-eyed young. Above the mantel in the dining room hung an enormous flame-red satyr by Sadequain that had been her tenth wedding anniversary present to herself, presiding over her collection. A crop of small, brilliant paintings and drawings tucked here and there among the old family miniatures provided a lively and sophisticated counterpoint to the ivory-handled swords and rhinoceros-hide shields from Ranjit Singh's time, all the baggage of a family emplaced in Lahore for several hundred years and farming out in the districts on a large scale. Now, in these first years of the twenty-first century, she was spoken of as a collector, and several of her pieces had recently traveled to New York for a group exhibition at the Whitney that included a young Pakistani artist just making a splash in the larger world.

Puffing on cigars like locomotives, they went through the house to Hisham's study, a cluttered room with a bookshelf of outdated economics textbooks from his time studying abroad mixed up with books on farming and paperback novels and leather-bound classics, a deep and shabby chesterfield sofa in red leather, green-shaded lamps, tottering piles of official papers, and a cabinet of shotguns and rifles with glass doors to show them off. Opening a drawer in the gun cabinet, Hisham took out a case and put it onto the desk. Clicking the latches, opening the case with a flourish, he lifted out a tiny black submachine gun. Cycling the bolt once to prove it wasn't loaded, he handed it to Rustom.

"What do you think?"

Rustom took the gun and aimed at the corner of the room, one eye closed. "Brilliant! Where does a man pick up a thing like this?"

"General Jehanzeb got it for me, actually. Heckler & Koch, but imported, not that license-built crap the army makes in Taxila. You probably heard about our little issue at the farm."

"I did. That sounded exciting."

"Very. When they say *cousinage-dangereux-voisinage*, I think they had my cousin Ali in mind. That boy's a menace."

"Did you get that sorted out?"

"Judge for yourself. My well-wishers are sourcing weapons for me, so it's not completely settled."

Rustom handed the gun back to Hisham. "What a dandy you are, Mian Sahib. This isn't a gun, it's men's jewelry."

Leaning over the desk, Rustom studied a lithograph that had been spread out, weighted down with several of the knickknacks that were lying about.

"And what about this?" he asked. The lithograph depicted a withered old man in bed, sitting up and touching the forearm of a kneeling boy.

"Guess."

Rustom looked carefully.

"I get it! Look at the sheepskin or whatever it is wrapped around the boy's arm. It's that mess of pottage story, isn't it? From the Bible. The father giving his blessing to the wrong son, the younger one. Stealing the birthright."

"I'm impressed!" said Hisham. "Exactly. Jacob stealing the elder brother Esau's birthright. I bet the bishop of Lahore and you are the only people in this godforsaken town who would figure that out. You spend too much time at that farm of yours, young man. And we all assume you're playing doctor doctor with those pretty little girls who pick your cotton, not studying the Old Testament."

Pleased at his little feat of memory, Rustom settled himself down on the sofa and took a sip of whiskey.

"I remember from college. A course on the Bible as literature. That story was my final paper, the birthright and all that. It's the classic Pakistani story, actually. I don't know a single family in Lahore that hasn't been completely screwed by fighting about property."

"At least the ones that have property to fight over! That's exactly the point. Guess who gave this to me."

"It doesn't look like something Shahnaz would buy. It's too antique, for one."

"And not enough drama. Or the wrong kind of drama. No, it's from my brother, Nessim."

"I didn't know you two have the sort of relationship where you exchange presents."

"We don't, or we didn't. Since his visit last winter, it's been better. I call him every few weeks, and sometimes he even calls me. He plans to come again next year."

"That's nice. I loved the way all of Lahore got booted and suited and showed up for that dinner you gave."

"That's just boredom and curiosity. Anyway, he sent the picture with Auntie Azra a couple of days ago, with a little note. She was staying with him in New York. A peace offering, I suppose, with a barb. It's quite valuable, it's old. The note was meant to be funny. You know how people do that, making a joke of the truth. He said something about how I may have gotten the birthright free and clear, but he got New York City."

Rustom said nothing, for the estrangement between Hisham and his brother was not openly discussed in the family, certainly not with Hisham. There had been a break some thirty years ago, in the '70s. Soon after the two brothers finished up at college in the States, the younger one, Nessim, had abandoned country and family and gone to live in America. Stories abounded, that he was gay, that he was schizophrenic, that he was on drugs. All Lahore had turned up to peer at him when he made a ceremonial return the previous year and been disappointed to find an affable and dryly humorous man with no obvious eccentricities other than his disinclination to live in Pakistan and enjoy his considerable property.

Hisham rang the bell beside the door, and when the young servant appeared, almost comically fast, he said, "Oh well, Saqib, blame Rustom Sahib for keeping you awake. Bring the drinks tray here, will you? And tell them to get the car ready in an hour."

"Yes, sir," said the boy, a tuft of his hair standing up on one side, suggesting that he had leapt from sleeping in some nook, waiting for the sahibs to call it a night. "Bayazid Sahib asked me to inform you that the flight is delayed."

"Surprise surprise. Anyway, bring the drinks."

When the boy left, Hisham turned to Rustom. "Dear dirty Pakistan International Airlines, there's a metaphor for the Pakistani soul. Won't fly, don't fly. I swear it would be easier to drive, even all the way to Karachi. I could bunk with you overnight at your Cawnapur farm on the way."

"I wish you would. I'm stuck there alone in Paradise, as you know. And then you remember those gangsters I got tangled up with who kept overstaying their welcome. It's good for me when you guys show up and demonstrate what big guns I have on my side."

"Well, anyway, tonight it's in for a penny in for a pound. I'm not keeping you up, am I? Are you captivated or just captive?"

Rustom laughed. "Always captivated."

"All right then, I'll have Saqib light this fire, and you can keep me company."

*

The servant boy came in with an armful of wood, dropped it with a crash into the fireplace, poured kerosene and then threw a match, the fire exploding, the dry wood burning instantly. For a minute he sat on his haunches before the fire, grave before this immemorial mystery, then broke the spell, rose, and left the room. The two men, sitting facing the fire, were quiet till the boy had closed the door. Finally, Hisham spoke.

"Good old Nessim. I wish you'd seen us together when we were little. I'm not sure where it began between us," continued Hisham. "With Nessim, I mean. I was the elder, and you know how that is in a family like ours—you're lucky not to have siblings—the sibs, as they call them. Two little princelings, and he was the understudy."

"And look at you now," exclaimed Rustom. "The prince has become the Awami Party kingmaker!"

"Come on, Rustom, don't rub in salt! It's more like, always the bridesmaid never the bride. But that's another story. No, I think with Nessim it began with our parents. Too bad you didn't know my mother."

"One has heard so much about her." Rustom shook his head with a pious expression, trying to look sympathetic and vague.

Hisham's mother had been killed in a hunting accident near their family farm, just before Rustom was born, another of those stories that inspired much gossip in Lahore. The father remarried too soon—the funeral baked meats served cold for the wedding supper, as some waspish and literate old lady put it, encapsulating the general view of the thing. Not knowing what more to say, Rustom leaned forward and patted Hisham awkwardly on the knee.

"I was just nine," continued Hisham. "And of course it's difficult even to think of her. In a way, Nessim was her favorite. I was the first one, but he was the baby. That's just the way it was." Pausing, he sighed heavily, yawned, and silently mouthed the word "Allah," a moment of involuntary candor.

"I think she felt she needed to protect him," he continued. "I was ten pounds at birth, and my mother nearly died having me. Nessim was tiny. There's a story, one of those family lore things. My mother was sitting reading, and Nessim was playing on the floor. I was probably three, so he was two. Still in diapers, just playing quietly on the carpet. And I came in, with a toy train on a rope, pulling it behind me, a wooden train. I came up to him, and walked around him in a circle, once, twice, and my mother is watching. And then *bam*, before she could jump up, I took the train and swung it and hit him over the head. My first attempted murder, so to speak!"

Leaning forward, Rustom tapped his friend on the knee. "But not your last, Masha'Allah."

"Well, let's hope it was, anyway. He had a scar on his forehead for years." Hisham launched his big laugh. "I was always more like my father. You know how he is."

Rustom grinned and stroked his chin. "Colonel Sahib is a legend, sir. More than willing to break a few eggs to make an omelet."

"Legend or not, he treated Nessim and me like a couple of his ponies, ran us against each other and let the best one win. When I pushed my brother around, my father refused to take sides. He would tell poor Nessim, 'Well, fight back and make it hurt enough and he'll stop.'"

"And did he?" asked Rustom.

"He wasn't built like that. It made me angry. He wouldn't get his hands dirty. I used to call him the Blade, the way he could cut into me. You've probably noticed that my father's sense of humor is so dry that it only blossoms once a decade, like those desert flowers. But my mother, Nessim could make her laugh, even though we were just little boys. And then she died. I was nine, so he would have been eight. And poor Nessim, it was the sound of one hand clapping, after that. He became very silent for a long time. For a year he barely spoke. That's when we became really close."

"Whenever I pass through New York, he's kind enough to invite me for a meal. He's a thorough gentleman, but you know that. Though there's not a lot of Punjabi in him."

"Not anymore," said Hisham. "Maybe after my mother's death that all got squeezed out. After she died we learned to divide the world, and pretty evenly too. It was like generosity between us."

Rustom gestured around the room, at the carpets and guns. "I suppose the division fell along the temporal and spiritual lines. You got the books, and he got the ideas."

"Hardly!" Hisham also took in the room, with a pleased expression on his face. "Maybe. It's true, I like nice things. I collect."

"The way you collected me."

"Well, you're my cousin. I already had an ownership stake."

"Second cousin."

"Own up, buddy. We even sound the same, the way we talk. The only real difference is you guys drank the Kool-Aid when you followed us to school in the old U.S. of A. Your generation bought in. I wonder if it ruined you for Pakistan." Hisham reached over and patted Rustom's shoulder. "Anyway, cousin or not, you're the best friend I have, Rustom."

Rustom had it on his lips to joke and say, *Then God help you*—but imagined the expression on Hisham's face, the look of sincerity and hurt, the welling up. He kept it to himself. And then, they were in fact true friends, so much as Hisham allowed such intimacies.

Instead Rustom said, "You're feeling sentimental tonight."

"I am," answered Hisham. "It's Nessim, you know. That lithograph from him has got me thinking. I wonder where to hang it, or if I'll ever hang it at all. I haven't shown it to Shahnaz."

*

The fire had taken and was burning nicely, and the two men became comfortably untethered from each other in the warm room, Hisham speaking as if to himself. Going into an anteroom, where he had a camp bed, Hisham brought a pillow, allowing Rustom to stretch out and get comfortable. Then, relighting his cigar with much flaring of matches and clouds of smoke, Hisham focused cross-eyed on the tip.

"You won't believe this, but as a boy I was mad about polo. And now I haven't ridden in years. I was big for my age, right from the time I could first get up on a pony, and that was part of it. I got into the rhythm of it before Nessim could, and at the polo I had my dad's attention, and half of the rest of Lahore. And then Nessim started playing too, just hitting the ball around, and the old man would go and watch him and shout at him to do this and do that. You know how my father is, but it was attention. So I would insist on riding Nessim's pony and then saw at the reins to make it vicious or hit it on the legs to make it shy from the ball. One afternoon, with my dad watching, I managed to drill Nessim twice in the back with the ball and knock him out of the saddle both times. And then he refused to ride anymore, and my dad let it go. My mother wasn't there, and my dad didn't have time to follow up on us—and I was the eldest, so no harm done. Instead Nessim played tennis, every day for hours, summer or winter. Even on holidays the marker would come from the gymkhana and play on the courts here at the house. He ended up captaining the school team. And strangely enough that's how we ended up in America."

Mian Sitaruddin, the boys' grandfather, was an old-school civil servant from the British days. He had a friend, an opulent Virginian, acquired while he was posted in Washington for a couple of years negotiating a treaty. Passing through Lahore on a Subcontinental grand tour, this gentleman benefited from the large hospitality that is easy in Lahore for such families, where dinners for twenty are arranged with a word to the cook. In the afternoons, the American worked off his supper playing tennis with Nessim, who showed his good manners and his good form by stretching out the game with long volleys, keeping the old man in the game but never quite letting him win. Sipping a beer one afternoon after a hard-fought match, the Virginian squire gestured at Nessim and promised—and insisted—that he would arrange admission for the boy to a university in America. He was on the board of trustees of Dartmouth College, his alma mater, and that's where Nessim must go, he said, exactly the best place to be dipped and dyed in the American virtues.

But Mian Sitaruddin made a provision. He wanted both his grandchildren to go, not to break up the pair. And so the bargain was made, Hisham riding to America on his younger brother's coat-tails, despite his indifferent grades.

*

Hisham went first, shoveling off from Aitchison, the old British Chief's College stretching along the Mall Road next to the Punjab Governor's House. The American friend had proved as good as his word. His secretary mailed Hisham a packet festooned with bright stamps, enclosing the college application and with a cover letter emphasizing that the response should be sent through her. This at least felt comfortably Pakistani, working through channels to ensure a happy outcome.

Hisham's grades at Aitchison left much to be desired, though he and his buddies more or less ran the place, on the strength of their backgrounds and late-teen swagger. He played the title role in *Julius Caesar*, and made the part his own if not Shakespeare's, his delivery clapped and bravoed with a relish due more to his popularity among the junior boys than his acting skills. After a few homesick days on the Hanover plain and lonely meals in the dining hall, Hisham found that his devilish streak, grown florid while pranking around Lahore late at night with his schoolmates, played equally well in America, and that the confidence formed while meeting the high and mighty at his grandfather's dinners and at tea in the Lahore polo lounge covered up the gaps in his knowledge of American form. He had the benefit of a generous allowance—for old Mian

Sitaruddin, who was footing the bill, felt that this thing shouldn't be done by halves, and in any case had little understanding of what constituted an appropriate state for a freshman showing up on the Hanover Green.

By the time Nessim matriculated the next fall, Hisham had already made a success of the project. He drove a white convertible— bought secondhand but still a beauty—and had pledged Alpha Delta, which a few years later would serve as the model for a movie about wild times on campus. He had even managed to form a sentimental friendship, teasingly platonic for the moment, with one of the female undergrads from the first batch ever admitted to the college.

Nessim took a different path. He befriended a couple of Indian boys—unlike Hisham, who avoided Subcontinentals on principle— and played on the tennis team and worked hard. Hisham had gone native, grew a beard and took 'shrooms a couple of times while pledging his frat and wore bell-bottoms, for '60s fashions had finally crept north up to New Hampshire; but Nessim kept himself pitched at a slight angle from his classmates, more fastidious than alienated, occasionally sharp-tongued, speaking up in classes more in a semester than Hisham did in his entire career. Nessim came and went in Hisham's busy life, going often to parties at the frat and almost a mascot there, the sober one. Three years passed, each of the brothers slightly condescending to the other, Hisham indulgent toward his bookish younger brother, Nessim raising a supercilious brow toward the elder's beer bongs and gentleman's C average. They went home each Christmas and summer, and then were inseparable, camping way up into the Himalayas on fishing trips, swanning about Lahore. They were bound by their feudal background, which no one at Dartmouth could understand, but their charged childhood closeness repelled more than it attracted; they defined themselves against each other.

✷

One morning, in the fall of his senior year, Hisham strolled down Wheelock Street under elms just turning red and yellow, down to

Nessim's apartment near the river, in a pillared building occupied mostly by grad students.

"There he is!" he said to Nessim at the door. "And I haven't seen my studious brother for donkey's ages."

"It's cruel how you neglect me."

The immaculate apartment had three rooms, dark reddish pine floors, a rickety stove, and a wheezing Frigidaire that came on like a power plant being kicked into operation. Nessim had painted the bentwood cane furniture white, and on a table put a collection of photographs in silver frames, several of their mother as a girl and as a woman, one of her with a shotgun standing over an array of antelope and sand grouse and bustard shot in the desert, and then old ones with groups of men standing and seated by rank at weddings, their grandfather as a boy cross-legged at the feet of the English district commissioner, another of their now ancient grandmother in her twenties, looking unimaginably vampy and glamorous.

Stamping his feet on the mat and scraping the edge of his boot, Hisham countered, "Or you've been neglecting me! Anyway, I've come to do my puja at your little ancestral shrine. We can light a candle together."

He stood in the vestibule pulling off his army surplus trench coat, threw it on the floor, and saw—sitting at the desk with a pile of books in front of her—a South Asian girl, her long black hair swept up and held back by a white headband. He had the impression that she was unusually tall, although she wasn't, a fact only gradually borne in on him during the following weeks, as she came into focus in his mind. She had kicked off her shoes under the desk, wore stockings and a skirt and a black turtleneck sweater, and had a long straight nose and one of those long Callas faces that grow upon you, first too singular, too emphatic, and then gradually suffused with her particular beauty. It struck Hisham that she seemed remarkably at home and a bit put out by his loud entrance. She carefully marked the page in her book with a notecard, then swiveled around to face him.

"So you must be the famous elder brother," she brightly said.

Hisham stood holding the two ends of his scarf hanging around his neck, sawing them back and forth.

"I hadn't seen it that way, but you're right."

Nessim watched this scene unfold, enjoying his brother's surprise. "Anyway, yes, this is my brother. And this is Shahnaz."

To cover his discomposure Hisham threw himself on the sofa and stretched out his legs, sprawling. One hand toyed with a pencil lying on a table beside him.

"Usually I find old Nessim here reading Aristotle or astrology or otherwise studious. You see me reeling with amazement."

"Not astrology, anyway," murmured Nessim.

"Well, reading whatever it is that makes you want to keep at it for another three years."

"In the leafy groves of academia," said Nessim, nodding. He was planning for law school, subtly encouraged by Hisham, who found it pleasant to imagine his brother happily distant from Pakistan for another few years, uncoupled from politics at their farm, known as Ranmal Mohra, and all the property that came with it, orchards and a spinning business.

Hisham continued with Shahnaz. "Are you from India, then?"

"Lahore, actually, to start with. Then all over."

Hisham raised his brow in surprise. "Lahore? Really?"

"I guess so."

"You guess? And yet I haven't met you. I thought Nessim and I and some Karachi guy that no one but my brother has ever physically seen are the only Pakistanis between here and Boston. We're easy to recognize because we're the ones shivering under two sweaters and an overcoat as soon as the first snow falls."

"You weren't looking hard enough. I'm a sophomore, so you should have caught up to me by now."

"You're right. I need to comb through again. I trusted myself to have dug out all the Lahoris, at least, and know their parents and grandparents too."

"Well in that sense then you probably know me. I'm Begum Imanullah's granddaughter. I've only lived in Pakistan when I was little, at my nani's house and then in Rawalpindi, before they built

Islamabad. My father's in the foreign service. We've been posted all over, Belgium and then Czechoslovakia. And then for the last three years I was at school in Buckinghamshire."

At the mention of Begum Imanullah, Hisham's manner changed. He sat up a bit and put his hands on his lap and looked at Shahnaz with a different kind of interest, correcting his posture toward her.

"Finishing school in Buckinghamshire, was it?"

"Bars on the windows and our little faces peeping out."

"Lucky for the groundskeepers peeping in," said Hisham. Decisively snapping down the pencil that he had been twisting about in his fingers, he leaned forward and laughed his generous laugh. "Wonderful!" he exclaimed. He turned to Nessim. "You devil! Come on, make us some tea."

Nessim seemed disinclined to draw out this encounter. "No milk. Why don't we meet later for lunch?"

"I'll have it without. I don't mind."

"But you always have milk."

"I'm a man of surprises, my dear," he said in Urdu. "And you are too, it seems."

"You know, of course, that I speak the lingo," offered Shahnaz, lighting a cigarette and studying Hisham through half-closed eyes.

*

"That was the fine springtime morning of Nessim's life, I suppose," Hisham said to Rustom those many years later in his Lahore study. "They were awfully attractive. She was surviving on dining hall food, and their first date he took her to dinner at the Hanover Inn. They were dressed up and shy and everything. She was on a partial scholarship. Her parents more or less lived on that pittance of a Pakistan Foreign Service salary—with occasional dollops squeezed out of her tight-fisted moneybags granny." That night in Lahore, recounting this story to Rustom, Hisham said quietly, "For years Shahnaz wouldn't tell me about all this, and then she did. She made me terribly jealous."

Shahnaz had made a joke, not even meaning to be cruel. Her love for Hisham had become like a public building, she said, compared to the unvisited ruin of her season's love for Nessim, that first love, abandoned and picturesque. The first snowfall of that winter in New Hampshire threw a light cape of snow on the shoulders of Shahnaz's long green coat when she came to his room, and the snow like toecaps on her little red boots, feet frozen. That afternoon they made love, each for the first time. She stood at the door of his room all serious and almost severe, just for love. When she threw off her coat a cold fragrant air from out of doors escaped the crevices and folds. It had been that kind of wooing, gravity and quiet emotion and solicitude, certainly on Nessim's part. This was 1976, the American Bicentennial, and that year's Winter Carnival ice sculpture of the Statue of Liberty spread benedictions over the Green long after the snow all around melted, an early spring, unseasonably warm throughout till Commencement Day. Their plain supper afterward, that was the detail she told Hisham, the one he could not forget. "And we were very wonderful," that's what she had said.

That spring Hisham found himself often seeking out Nessim and Shahnaz, though he was absorbed in his last year, in squeezing out every bit of pleasure—a party king with a Poseidon beard, vice president of his frat, with all his expectations back home to buoy him. He took his Georgia girl to formal dances, made slightly mournful by the fact of their coming separation, the relationship weakened by their understanding about that final parting. They shed tears and she gave herself to him, once, twice, again, but they would wake one morning soon and it would be over. He and his friends beat the drum more loudly because they all had plans, were marching out from this place, growing up, getting away, grad school, jobs at their fathers' businesses. Hisham would move back to Pakistan, maybe take the civil service exam, certainly move into the business.

Nessim and Shahnaz studied together in the eighth-floor stacks of Baker Library, sitting next to windows looking north high over the campus. Hisham found them there the first time almost by accident, meeting his brother at the card catalogs in the main hall and coming up to the stacks for a coffee. They kept a plug-in water boiler hidden behind books, with instant coffee and sugar packets and little plastic creamer containers, a whole kit.

"I bet you never had this," said Shahnaz, beating together coffee crystals and sugar and a bit of cream in a mug, a full minute's work with a spoon, the mug held between her legs. "It's Indian cappuccino, my mother called it." She gradually poured in the hot water at the end, stirring, and with a flourish handed it to Hisham, watched him take the first sip.

It really was good too, Hisham remembered, incredibly good, sweet and foamy, a little bit of crunch from the crystals. "You two have quite the domestic situation here," he observed.

A fleck of foam splashed on Shahnaz's white stocking when she beat the coffee between her legs, drawing Hisham's eyes to her. That was when he truly became aware of her as a woman, and then it wouldn't leave him. She looked up at him, and he saw amusement in her eyes and a sly recognition, as if saying, "So you just noticed . . ."

✳

There were three months left till graduation. Maddeningly, Nessim and Shahnaz behaved toward Hisham with vague indifferent generosity, including him in their excursions, inviting him around, as if he had no other place to go. "I remember," Hisham said, with wonder in his voice all those years later, "exactly how she looked then, every detail. If I knew how, I would paint her. She's always beautiful, but then she was nineteen. I remember a pair of bright orange corduroy jeans, bell-bottoms, and her long black hair cut in bangs, falling loose on one side and on the other tucked behind one ear. One day the three of us had finished lunch in the dining hall and then she went off somewhere, running late as always. Watching him watching her move through the room, I told Nessim that he looked saturnine, and with his eyes still on her he corrected me, said that saturnine means gloomy. I had meant to say sardonic, and even that was wrong. I felt foolish. As you see, he was the one with the vocabulary. I meant that he looked too proud for my taste.

Triumphant. And truly he was so proud of her, very formal, open-ing doors and all that, and quiet, letting her shine. And behind her directness and her manners she was an imp."

✿

One day, sharing a coffee in the dining hall, Hisham asked Nessim, "Why the devil would you choose a Pakistani girl for your first plunge? You guys seem to be moving pretty quickly. Remember, she's one of us. You break it you bought it, that's the rule back home."

"It's not about choice. Don't talk about it. Don't say anything."

"Why not? You guys are great. You're starting to look like each other. That usually takes at least two years."

"Her loss!"

"Or your gain."

"I've promised myself to take it day by day. That's my new philosophy."

"You're a lucky man. But philosophy won't go very far when her granny puts the screws on you. And you're going off to grad school, you might be halfway across the country. Then what about her? What's her plan?"

"She wants to move back to Pakistan. She's coming this summer, I've been meaning to tell you. She'll be staying with Begum Imanul-lah. I want to show her around. We can get together a group and go to the farm. I want her to see Ranmal Mohra."

"You can't take a girl there just like that. What will Daddy-o say?"

"No one will know, if there's a group of us. He won't pay any attention. And Begum Imanullah's eighty years old. I doubt she'll be keeping a very sharp eye."

"Are you kidding? It's the old ladies who police the whole thing and haul you up in front of their marriage council. That girl would be followed by bloodhounds wherever she went."

"I don't think so. They don't have any property to speak of, for one thing, so she's hardly a catch. The grandmother's stuff will end up with Shahnaz's uncle, he's got it tied down. All their lands were in Jalandhar, across the border, and they lost it all at Partition. If only the Brits had drawn the border fifty miles to the east—her grandfather died with those words on his lips, and even Shahnaz says it."

"More reason to watch out. You're the catch. To restore the family fortunes." This all seemed dangerously impertinent to Hisham, now when his own plans were just forming, Nessim turning his attentions back home to the property, with a clever woman to stiffen his spine.

"Anyway, you can't take her to the farm. The whole district would be buzzing about it. I've got a position to keep up there, you know. It's easy for you."

"Why easy for me? I've got as much interest there as you do."

Hisham stood up. "Really? Your interest?" He paused for a moment. "That girl's leading you a dance, isn't she. Watch out!"

Nessim had a smile on his lips. "You're jealous."

✻

One day, just at dusk, the electricity suddenly failed in the library. Students caught in the deeper recesses of the stacks, away from the windows, screamed and pretended to be scared. Hisham, who was studying on the floor below Nessim and Shahnaz's carrels, groped his way to the eighth floor, running his hand along the bookshelves.

Shahnaz was alone there, standing at the window looking out, turning in the gloom when he came up.

"Hello," she said.

"Lights out and you're alone. Nessim must be just finishing up at his nationalism seminar."

"You've memorized his schedule, have you?"

"I like our private coffee breaks."

"I've noticed. Very brotherly of you."

"Why not? Maybe you mean brother-in-law."

"You never talk like this when he's around!"

They stood, shoulder to shoulder. The last of the light hesitated over buildings and trees.

Their arms touched, and Shahnaz laughed.

"You're bigger than Nessim. It's like him, but a half size up."

They said nothing, for a long moment. Usually they bantered with each other, Hisham could make her laugh. In the dark Hisham could just perceive her outline.

She broke the silence. "In a few weeks, it's over, isn't it? Your party."

"For what I plan back home I got what I needed. A degree and enough economics so I can talk the talk. Like your finishing school. And then, I had a blast."

"That's the point, is it?"

"I always have fun. Otherwise, what's the point?"

"Of parties?"

"Of everything."

"Well, duty, I suppose. Doing the correct thing."

"I'll leave that to Nessim."

"Doesn't sound like it. You're the one who's going back home to run some factory."

"You're right, that is my duty. Elder brother. I'll do the business, and he'll go off to grad school. And someday a minister's flag on my car. At least that's what my father wants."

Shahnaz paused for a moment, thinking. "You two brothers. It's pretty desperate between you two, isn't it?"

"I don't think so. We don't interfere with each other too much. And then, I'm the elder."

"So you keep saying."

"Me and my brother against the world. It's a Pakistani thing."

"Duty. That's quite nice," she said, "if it's true. So you'll take care of him?"

"Does he need it?"

"I may not have lived in Pakistan much, but I've heard all about it. The elder brother plays judge, jury, and executioner too. Taking care of business."

"You're a funny girl!" exclaimed Hisham.

Unexpectedly, she took his hand, looking into his eyes, their eyes now accustomed to the gloom. He returned the look, and she slowly raised his hand to her mouth and bit the ball of the thumb, just a touch of her teeth and then harder and then—when he didn't react—suddenly biting down hard.

"Fuck!" He jerked his hand back and cradled it, anger flashing in unfiltered. "You little . . ." He stopped himself.

She put her palm on his shoulder. "You little what? You thought I'd kiss you, didn't you?"

Just then, Nessim came up behind them, they heard his footsteps—he must have been already in the stairwell when the lights went off, taking the stairs up eight flights, as he often did. He called in the dark. Hand squeezing Hisham's shoulder, she drew him a little toward herself, then pushed him gently away.

*

Flying into Karachi on the PIA jumbo jet, Hisham and Nessim folded back into the privilege of their childhood, ushered through the VIP lounge at the airport, then a night at a cousin's house in Clifton with a congratulatory party laid on, barely catching their flight next morning to Lahore. All the aunties of Lahore were gearing up to find Hisham a suitable girl, and sooner or later his father would call him in for a conversation about business, the farm, the spinning mill, and politics at Ranmal Mohra. All this seemed to him interesting, possible, inevitable—but not yet.

The brothers moved together through the city, to the polo, swimming at the Punjab Club, flogging their grandfather's venerable Mercedes—a cruelty, the old girl like a spinster aunt, never been to the races till they beat her up near one hundred miles an hour going past the Governor's House on the Mall one night. In the rush of being back, and with the common experience of America between them, their old roles dissolved for a moment, Hisham more solicitous, Nessim demonstrative.

Nessim spoke of Shahnaz only a few times, wishing desperately that he could phone her. In those days in the 1970s people called overseas from Lahore only to announce births and deaths, booking the call and then sitting for hours, sometimes days, awaiting a ring back from the operator. Letters too were difficult, sent to her parents' house in Vienna, where her father was posted, subjecting Shahnaz to questioning from her mother.

✻

But even in Lahore after Shahnaz finally arrived it wasn't easy for the couple to meet. Nessim of course couldn't be at the airport, where the old granny herself showed up, as she would not have for another much grander visitor, and so he sat by the phone all morning till finally Shahnaz called. Then all day, the next day too, her grandmother kept her close by, while Nessim moped at home, bones aching for his lover's embrace. Though Begum Imanullah had herself fifty years back scandalized Lahore, wearing a tennis skirt halfway showing her calf on the gymkhana courts, she was not a woman to be trifled with. Fussy and yet imperious, she had outlived her old-guard cronies, kept a good cook, and watched her pennies. She lived in one of those lugubrious houses where half the rooms are shuttered like knights' tombs, dark with old wooden furniture, with no air-conditioning except in the best guest bedroom, in a part of town no longer fashionable. There were half a dozen gossipy old servants who couldn't be let go but who were more fed than paid, parked in nooks and crannies of the house and certain to sniff out any secret trysting around the premises.

The front gates of Hisham and Nessim's house, Al-Unmool, opened onto a lawn as public as a government compound, visitors high and low passing through all day, watched over by a spoon-chested Pathan with paintbrush whiskers and an Old Testament beard. A smaller gate fed by a little lane at the back of the compound was, however, left open and unmonitored, the servants' quarters back there a separate little village, with its own bustling traffic. During their school days the boys used that channel to sneak in their friends late at night, though in any case their father took little more notice of the boys' private lives than he did of the servants'. On Shahnaz's third night in town the boys gave a small party, inviting a couple of girls they knew from school days, who themselves had to be sneaked in, and then a couple of boys, Hisham's old posse. Shahnaz was spirited from her grandmother's house by a girl who pretended to know her from abroad. At around eleven, one of the girls looked at her watch and shrieked, "Oh my God, now I've done it," and rushed out, Shahnaz then taken home as part of the general dispersal. Even so, her grandmother asked pointed questions about who exactly she was seeing so late at night, and why wouldn't she take the driver?

Finally, ten days into Shahnaz's visit, the lovers could take it no more.

"What do you think about Faletti's?" Nessim asked Hisham one morning over breakfast.

"What about it? I suppose it's turning into the No-Tell Motel for the woolier Punjab parliamentarians, since it's right behind the Assembly. Our senior legislators of course prefer to fornicate at the Intercon."

Faletti's had been the best hotel in Lahore for a hundred years, tall-ceilinged rooms scattered about a large garden, till the Intercontinental Hotel on the Mall Road was built in the '60s.

"Well, then it's perfect. We won't meet anyone we know."

"Who's we?" asked Hisham. "I assume you mean Begum Imanullah's granddaughter."

"It's true, I'm getting pretty desperate. All I want is a whole afternoon with her. I swear, this isn't working out. Yesterday we finally managed to sneak into my room and were just getting comfortable and then that cat Ghulam Rasool knocked and asked if I needed anything. He knew I wasn't alone. She got embarrassed and said it ruined the mood and asked me to take her home."

"Ouch. I'll go myself and reserve you guys a room. I'll tell them I've got guests coming from America, if they ask. Pretend you're flying in. That way they won't ask any questions."

*

Toward evening Hisham was in the boys' upstairs living room, sorting through fishing tackle and camping gear, getting organized for a trip to the mountains after Shahnaz left, when he heard rapid footsteps on the stairs. After their mother died the boys had gradually moved their operations upstairs, away from the ground floor, where their father lived and entertained, these upper precincts of the house unvisited by him for years at a time.

"Hello, Mian Sahib, how's that boom-boom business?" he called over his shoulder, fitting together two sections of a fishing rod.

Nessim burst into the room, and then Shahnaz slipped in behind him, sitting down on the edge of a sofa, holding her arms tightly around her body, knees together.

"Pardon me, Shahnaz," said Hisham. "I assumed Nessim had already dropped you home." The lovers were on slightly easier terms now with the grandmother, who had sniffed out Nessim's presence around Shahnaz and tentatively approved the connection to the Atar family.

She said nothing, but looked around the room, as if checking that no one else was present. Putting her elbows on her knees and fingers together, she touched them to her lips, an attitude of concentration.

Nessim stood with his arms clasped behind his head, leaning back. "Big problem. Big big problem."

Hisham had gone in the morning to Faletti's, registered Nessim and Shahnaz under an assumed name, gotten the key, so that they could go straight to the room without seeing any of the staff.

"What happened?"

"We're fucked, that's what happened."

"Calm down. Let's hear it first."

"I'll tell you what happened," said Shahnaz. "We went to the room and your brother opened a bottle of wine and brought out glasses and we sat down and then suddenly there was a pounding on the door. Two goons pushed in and started shouting adultery this and adultery that. They wanted Nessim to show them a marriage certificate. They kept saying it's not that kind of hotel. I was sitting down on the bed, while they talked about me as if I wasn't there."

Nessim walked over to her and stood behind her, leaned over the sofa and put his hands on her shoulders, kissed the top of her head. "I'm so sorry, Shahnaz, really. That was so ugly."

Shahnaz had taken out a cigarette and now sat tapping the filter against her thumb, sitting forward, elbows on her knees.

"It's fine, it's fine. Just fix it." She kept tapping the cigarette. "This isn't how I imagined it. I feel gross."

"Back up," said Hisham. "Tell me the whole thing."

"They took me outside," said Nessim. "They pointed to a policeman sitting in an unmarked car. Then they asked how much money I had. Only dollars, no rupees. I had like a hundred rupees on me. I didn't even have ID. And they wouldn't believe me."

"So how'd you settle it?"

"They said I should go and get money from wherever I like. But they wouldn't let Shahnaz go."

"He was trembling," said Shahnaz. "When he came back in. And then they took my passport. Luckily I still had it in my handbag. They wouldn't let us go otherwise."

"I told them I'd bring over five hundred dollars by tomorrow. In the parking lot at noon. Otherwise they were taking us to the station, right then. They even tried to push me into the car. Obviously I didn't want to tell them who I was. I pretended we were from America visiting relatives. They didn't believe it. We need to talk to somebody right away, like tonight. Maybe one of your buddies. We can't get any of Dad's people involved."

"It was disgusting," said Shahnaz quietly. "The way they looked at me when we were leaving. And then, just when we were getting in the car, the guy got all fatherly and said, 'Don't do this, you look like a girl from a decent family.' Like the good policeman in those Hindi movies. One of them had a camera, and he took a picture of me."

They were all silent for a moment. Hisham said, "I am going to personally see that these guys are sitting on a block of ice with chili peppers shoved up them before sunrise tomorrow."

Then, to Shahnaz, "I'm really sorry. This shouldn't have happened to you on our watch. Those guys just didn't know who they'd messed with. They thought it was some little shop owner's son or something. It was a mistake."

"It is what it is," said Shahnaz. "Like I said, please just fix it."

"I will," said Hisham. "You'll have your passport back by morning, and those guys will be wishing they'd chosen a different line of business."

"So what's the plan?" asked Nessim. "I was thinking I should talk to Tariq. He was my doubles partner in the tennis, we're pretty tight. He's got those police connections, his uncle was IG Police. But he's the sort of guy who makes big promises but doesn't do much."

"No, he won't be able to sort it out. I'll talk to Zaqi. He's a good guy, he'll see it the right way and keep his mouth shut. Remember when he had that thing with that girl from Kinnaird? He owes me. He's already starting to take over his dad's racket in the Old City. Their guys don't worry about breaking kneecaps."

"Wasn't she some doctor's daughter?"

"It wasn't a doctor, it was a fucking member of the Provincial Assembly, one constituency over from Ranmal Mohra, and the details weren't pretty. I saved his ass."

"There's a reason I never liked that guy."

"Well, now you've got a good reason to like him a lot. Or you will have."

Hisham went over to Shahnaz, kneeled, and locked eyes with her. "Look at me. Please. Don't worry about this anymore. It's settled. Nessim can take you home now. I'm really really sorry."

She returned his look, defiant. Dropping her gaze after a moment, looking into space, her posture softened, and her voice. "All right. Thank you."

*

Returning home late, Hisham went into Nessim's room and found him lying on his bed, listening to music.

"Cheer up, man," said Hisham brightly. "The cavalry showed up." He sat down and began massaging Nessim's legs, squeezing tighter and tighter, then slapping his thighs.

"Remember when Ditta used to do this to wake us up for school?" asked Hisham.

"Stop it. I'm in a shitty mood."

"Well, you had a shitty day."

"What happened with Zaqi?"

"He said he'd have the guys brought to his compound and do it there and be there himself while they did it. As he said, the Faletti's manager has to know all about it. It won't be hard to trace those goons who came to the room. Zaqi's got this guy who's like his main muscle, and he sent him to the hotel. A big motherfucker with a scar across his face like the movies. We'll have the passport by morning. They were planning to pick up the hotel manager from his house if they needed to."

Nessim touched Hisham's hand. "Okay, I'm impressed. I'm glad you hung out with the wrong crowd at Aitchison."

"One of us had to. Anyway, let's hope old Zaqi does the right thing thoroughly—meaning the wrong thing. But he will. Poor Shahnaz."

"She was already getting sick of the situation, trying to keep it cool with her grandmother and all that. It's just not the same here after Dartmouth. She says she wants to go to Islamabad for a few days and think it over and spend some time with her Aunt Tasha. Not her real aunt, her guardian from school in England. Shahnaz used to stay with her in London on school holidays, when the aunt lived there."

Hisham gave Nessim a final slap on his leg, gently now, then stood up and went to a little fridge, took out two beers, gave one to Nessim, and began pacing across the room.

"What about you two?" he asked.

"She said maybe we should cool it for a bit, till we get back to Dartmouth. She's sort of disappointed. It's worse than if she were angry. She'd get over that, she's got a temper, as you may have noticed. She had these romantic ideas about us running around Lahore and me showing her the place. Remember, she hasn't lived in Pakistan since she was a kid, just coming for vacations. And of course she blames me for this thing at Faletti's." He shook his head. "You should have seen it, those two fucking guys crowding in the door and then they pushed in and she's sitting on the bed and the wine and whole scene. It was scary and awful and just disgusting. Thank God we weren't in bed."

"You did put her in a pretty bad situation. Imagine if Begum Imanullah heard about it."

Nessim's voice rose. "I put her in it? You mean you did. I asked you if Faletti's would be okay."

"Come on, you're a Lahori too. This isn't on me."

Sitting up on the bed, Nessim crossed his legs and sat staring at his feet. "I think she might break up with me."

"Oh, come on, man. Be tough, take charge. Why don't you go down to Islamabad too?"

"And do what?"

"I don't know. What's this aunt like? She can't be as much of a bloodhound as old Begum Imanullah."

"That's the one good thing. She's not. The aunt used to cover up for Shahnaz when she got in trouble at school, and she'd take her out in London and all that. Aunt Tasha, that's her name. She's the cool aunt, she got Shahnaz drunk the first time. For a while she was dating some drummer in a band, a guy twenty years younger than her."

Hisham nodded appreciatively. "That is a pretty hip aunt. I'm surprised old Begum Imanullah would pick her as a chaperone."

Nessim's mood brightened. "Begum Imanullah has no clue what happens in London. Shahnaz said this Auntie Tasha would go out wearing leather pants and a bright red fake-fur jacket and not come back till morning."

"Whoa! Your troubles are over, my friend. That's not a chaperone, that's an enabler. What about taking Shahnaz up to Murree or Nathiagali or something?"

"And stay in a hotel? Isn't that what people do with hookers? Go up to those hotels and do it like rabbits all day and all night. We've already tried that. Shahnaz might not go for it a second time."

"That doesn't sound too bad. But all right. Be creative. Take her up to Kaghan. Go camping, stay at the Armoured Corps hut. General Habib keeps telling us we can use it."

"Just the two of us would look very weird. And suppose something happened, car breaks down or whatever."

"Well, obviously you'd take Yazid." Bayazid, their father's chauffeur, always went on mountain trips with them, halfway between a servant and a friend, companion to their escapades, who had covered up several car crashes and seen them through their teenage wilding.

"You could come with us, I suppose," said Nessim, mulling it over.

Hisham had not dared to propose this. Quite the opposite, he knew that he should refuse. "I'd just be the fifth wheel in that adventure."

"If it's all of us I think Shahnaz might agree. If she can swing it with her aunt. Shahnaz was saying how comfortable she feels when you're with us. Two guys and a girl doesn't look like a romantic situation."

"We can pretend we're going up to stay with a friend in Nathiagali. I'll tell Yazid to call the farm in the morning and have them send the jeep. You talk to Shahnaz. I'm sure you can convince her, tell her about the mountain air and all that. We'll fish and cook over coals and live off the fat of the land. We'll look at the moon in the clear night sky. We'll sit by the fire and tell stories. You know, get into it, sell it."

"Maybe I should send you over."

"Unfortunately, this part you'll have to do on your own."

*

When they picked up Shahnaz in Islamabad, the aunt insisted they come in for a cup of tea, this courtesy aunt, an old friend of her mother's.

"So which one of you is Nessim?" she asked, looking him over, then told a story about their grandfather from when she was a little girl. She treated it as quite natural that they should be taking Shahnaz up with them for a few days in the mountains, asked vaguely about the girl with whom they were staying. When they were getting in the car, she looked at Hisham and said, "You're in charge here. Bring her back in one piece."

"That's ambiguous," commented Hisham, as they were driving away.

Shahnaz turned—she was sitting in front, Nessim driving. "I told her the truth, that's the only way I could get her on board. She's a romantic, she liked helping out the young lovers. Auntie Tasha is pretty crazy. I told her we were going up to Kaghan and staying at a government rest house. I suppose it doesn't hurt that you guys are who you are."

Once they got up in the hills, Hisham drove all day, with Shahnaz sitting in front beside him, because she couldn't sit in back next to Bayazid. Nessim didn't like to drive in the mountains. Every time Hisham shifted the gear, he was aware of her knee near his hand. She fed him slices of oranges that she peeled, sips of water from a bottle, opening the cap first.

In the afternoon, Nessim and then Bayazid both fell asleep, each leaning sideways against the window. Hisham said to Shahnaz, "Hey, tell me stories, I'm getting sleepy too."

"What should I tell you about?"

"How about telling me about where you lived as a girl? You must have stories about being an embassy brat and all that."

So she told him about the Prague Spring, the commotion in the streets and the embassy closed up, the markets closed, and their Pakistani cook bringing a Czech friend into his quarters to avoid a curfew. The intimacy of the jeep brought them close, the road steep and wooded on the sides. Once for emphasis she put her hand on his, as he rested it on the gear, and he looked at her and raised his eyebrow. Glancing back at Nessim and Bayazid, she whispered, "All sound asleep."

In those days the pavement ended in Mansehra, and the last seventy miles up into the Kaghan Valley passed along a crumbling single track. They crept up against a wet ferny bank while a column of British-era four-wheel-drive logging trucks growled past smuggling Himalayan cedar out of the valley, the logs fifteen feet around, scenting the air with pine pitch. Great herds of goats and sheep blocked the road every few miles, the khana badosh nomads taking their animals up into the mountains to graze them, their lean, enormous dogs following, hanging their heads, and the sheep crowding.

Coming into Naran just at dusk was like riding into a frontier town, a few straggling huts and then flickering kerosene lamps hanging in the mud-built shops, the light fallen behind the mountains, this Karakoram building up to the Pamir Knot, where five of the world's great mountain ranges meet. The jeep splashed through sheets of glacier meltwater fingering down from the slopes. Yazid was driving now, because he could do it so much faster than the boys could, working his way through ditches and streams and around rocks with a beautiful rhythm, his big square hands draped over the steering wheel. Nessim and Shahnaz in the back played music on a little cassette deck, Reshma again and again, the village girl from Rajasthan. As soon as the shadows fell it became very cold. When they opened the windows to throw out cigarette butts the chill mountain air poured into the jeep. Tired at dusk, they drove in silence but for the music, Yazid intent on the road in front, his large face, long hair, drooping mustache, and sideburns like a villain in a Punjabi film. This was his bread and butter, driving well, driving fast.

*

They slept the night in a little two-room army rest house next to the Kunar River, then after breakfast went fishing, Shahnaz sitting beside the river with a book unopened, first expectant, then bored. They caught nothing, and in the afternoon under drizzling rain Nessim and Shahnaz trudged back to camp. Hisham continued fishing with Sufi, a teenaged boy from a village up on the slopes who had attached himself to them, showing up in camp at dawn and hanging about at the edges, being helpful. Yazid took him in— he had a genius for this—sent the boy for eggs, a rare commodity up here at eight thousand feet, and paid him well for them, then set him to chopping onions. Sufi had gone to his village and returned with a dozen eggs in a dirty cloth, unwrapping them tenderly, shy to offer so much, as if they were wild eggs found in a hidden nest.

At nightfall, Hisham finally returned, empty-handed. The rain had stopped, Nessim and Shahnaz were sitting in front of a camp-fire lit beside the hut, a mile or so past the last shops in Naran bazaar.

"Now what?" asked Hisham. "The river's tapped out. The locals net the whole fucking thing in the winter. That boy Sufi was telling me that it's easy when the water's low. He wanted to go home and get a net and show me how to do it."

Hisham had been thinking of Shahnaz all afternoon while he fished. "We should probably head back down," he said. "We can go back to Islamabad."

Shahnaz stood up, animated, picked up a chunk of wood, and threw it on the fire. "Come on, guys. Don't be such wimps. I thought you were such mountain men and all that. There's got to be someplace where it's better. Ask that Sufi guy."

"There is one place," offered Hisham. "Yazid was talking to one of the jeep drivers when he went into town. There's a valley where the shepherds go sometimes. It's far up, a full day's walk. None of your ordinary desis will sweat that hard, they all fish from the side of the road."

"Are you kidding?" said Nessim. "We'd be sleeping in tents. Shahnaz would hate it."

"Don't talk as if I'm not here," she said. "Anyway, I'll love it. I want to go."

"Fine with me." Hisham grinned. "Let's go where the fish are. Yazid can go back into town and get a tarp for Sufi and him to sleep under. We've got two tents, and we've got all the other stuff. You guys can finally have a space to yourself."

*

The torrent fell almost vertically, water frothing over rocks. They climbed switchbacks up and up, long curving capes of scree, trig-gered to slide in a sheet down to the water, a fall in that ice-green turbulence likely to be fatal. In the afternoon they came over a crest, Hisham and Nessim under packs, Shahnaz strolling in front, and found a valley opening before them, green with summer grass after the stony cliffs of the narrow approach. Yazid and the boy Sufi, driving a laden pony, had lingered far behind. The river glittered here and there across a plain under the sun, wind off the water lending a fresh scent to the air. Burrows of golden marmots were scattered all across the valley floor and partway up the mountainsides, the marmots whistling warnings as the brothers made their way past.

They found a likely place for camp and stood the two packs high up on a boulder so Yazid would see them and then put together their rods and picked their way down to the river. On his third cast with a spinner, Hisham caught an eighteen-inch brown trout. Trembling and afraid it would thrash off the hook and be lost, he threw it up on the bank. He killed the trout with a blow to the spine, then put it in his creel with wet grass to keep it cool. Shahnaz sat cross-legged and looked at the fish. "Look, it's changing colors," she said. "Now it's just gray." They were all alone there in that immense theater, standing beside a fisherman's ideal of a stream, too wide and deep to wade across, and sandbars, deep holes at the bends, big boulders with water rushing on either side, then the meandering progress that promises fish. Hisham lost touch with Nessim and Shahnaz, fishing one deep curving stretch and catching three more browns in the next hour, one more than twenty inches, speckled and glassy iridescent, swimming there in that high place and living out their lives.

✥

Meeting, putting up their rods, they picked their way along the valley flank and found the camp from the smoke rising straight above it in the still nightfall. Walking along with Nessim, seeing Hisham in the falling light, Shahnaz had been girlishly excited and skipped forward, holding up a stringer heavy with four large trout. "Look what we got!" she called singsong across the dusky water meadow. Yazid offered them little plastic cups of hot sweet tea as soon as they came in. They each had a sleeping bag, and Yazid had bought two cotton-filled quilts in Naran bazaar. He and Sufi would sleep together under a tarp rigged between two boulders far around a little ridge, to give the sahibs privacy. Hisham lay down in his dark tent, exhausted, while Yazid cooked dinner, an old hand frying the fish in ghee as he had done for them on other mountain trips. Nessim and Shahnaz had gone down to the river. Nessim might freeze, but he'd wash before going to bed. Finally, Yazid stuck his head into the tent. Hisham had fallen asleep.

"Mian Sahib," he whispered. "Come. Eat."

Nessim sat in front of the fire with a mug of whiskey in his hand.

"Where's Shahnaz?" asked Hisham.

"She wanted to be alone a bit beside the river. She's in a strange mood. Come on, I'm having a drink."

The brothers were silent in the heat of the fire, waiting for Shahnaz to return before they ordered the dinner.

"So what do you think?" asked Nessim.

"Fishing's good," answered Hisham carefully. "You seem tense. Are you okay?"

"You keep asking that. Why wouldn't I be?"

"Forget it. Let's have another drink."

All day Nessim had been complaining of feeling unwell, been uncommunicative. On the trail he had fallen behind throughout the morning, catching up with Hisham and Shahnaz when they laid out a picnic lunch in the shade of a rock, walking up on them and throwing down his pack without speaking.

*

After a few minutes they saw Shahnaz's light, wobbling up from the river, and Nessim went down to guide her. When Shahnaz sat down, Nessim put a shawl around her shoulders, squatting behind her to tuck it in, and rested his arms on her for a moment, leaning his body against her back.

"Stop it, your guys will see," she whispered.

He pulled back and stood up. "Sorry."

"I'm sorry," she said. "Just. Please don't. I feel all yucky without a shower after the walk up here."

"I'm impressed, actually," said Hisham. "I can't believe you've been wearing those pants all day, and they're still white. The dirt won't stick to you."

Shahnaz had not brought the right clothes, wore a pair of white canvas sneakers and white bell-bottomed pants. As Hisham had said, she looked immaculate, as if she were going yachting.

"Let's hope not," said Shahnaz. "Metaphorically. If they find out in Lahore that I went up to the mountains with you two, the aunties will definitely assume the worst."

"Are you worried about that?" asked Nessim. He had sat down at a distance from her, so that the three of them were looking at each other across the fire.

"I don't know," said Shahnaz. "Are you?"

"Well, at least you've got the elder brother as a chaperone," joked Hisham. "Come on, drink up. Look at where we are. Listen to the river."

They were silent, and in the background the river made a grinding dragging sound, the sound of the water drawing away and down the valley and down the gorge. The stars above were brilliant and unblinking in the cold clean air.

Nessim didn't drink very often, but that evening he kept pushing the bottle around, good whiskey that the boys had abstracted from their father's extensive liquor hoard. Crunchy from the hot pan, cooked in ghee, the fish juices sopped deliciously into the rice. There was plenty for all, Yazid standing there at the end with yet another plate of fish, saying that he and Sufi too had eaten more than they could hold.

"Go to sleep," said Hisham affectionately to Yazid. "You've earned it."

Yazid made an obeisance to them each. "Salaam, Bibi," he said to Shahnaz.

When he was gone, Hisham said, "You know, Shahnaz, he doesn't know what to make of you. He can't imagine a girl walking up here voluntarily, definitely not the chicks that he's seen Nessim and me hanging out with."

"Your Lahori princesses! He probably thinks that I'm a loose woman."

Hisham waved a finger. "Don't worry, he wouldn't presume to have opinions about you or any of this, really."

Nessim had become heavy with the alcohol. Now he spoke with a thick voice. "Don't be an asshole, Hisham. He's a friend."

"He's on salary, man. He's only a friend when we're on camping trips."

"Well, he's my friend, anyway."

"That's true. You're the democrat, aren't you."

"Fuck you."

Shahnaz sat up and put her hand on Nessim's arm. "Come on, guys, stop it."

"I'm tired," said Nessim, shrugging off her hand. He stood, unsteady for a moment. "I'm going to bed."

"Take some water," said Hisham, also standing.

"Do you want me to come?" asked Shahnaz.

"Whatever you want."

"I'll just sit for a moment, sweetheart. I'll be there soon."

They heard Nessim scrabbling around in the tent, then coming out again, his light going a little distance away, the sound of him brushing his teeth by lamplight over a little rivulet that came down from the slope above, where they had been taking water for the camp. Crawling back into the tent, he called hoarsely, "Don't stay up too late."

For a long time, surprisingly long, neither Hisham nor Shahnaz spoke, and neither looked at the other.

Finally, Hisham whispered, "You should go."

"Why?"

"I don't know. He seemed upset all day, he's not right. Something's going on."

Whispering. "You mean with him and me?"

"I don't know. Yeah."

"It's fine. It's just . . ." She stopped herself. "I'll go see if he's okay."

Returning, she sat down again cross-legged, her knee touching Hisham's.

"He's snoring. I think he was exhausted."

"Aren't you?"

"No, I'm completely not exhausted. I could stay up all night."

"All right, then, let's have another drink."

As if by agreement, neither she nor Hisham had drunk very much. Nessim had complained to Hisham, "What's wrong with you? Finally I want to drink, and you don't."

Hisham and Shahnaz pulled their heavy rough shawls around them, shawls that Yazid had bought in Naran bazaar when they decided to come up to this valley, the same ones that the locals wear when traveling in the wild, tent, blanket, and rain gear all in one.

Shahnaz shivered with pleasure. "These things are so warm."

They were still whispering.

"Should I put on more wood?" asked Hisham.

"Yes, do."

She stared into the fire while he carefully put two more logs onto the coals. They had carried up wood on the pony, and Sufi had gone down again and brought thick knotted brush from lower in the valley, which burned hot and fast.

Now they spoke, but too inconsequentially, more emotion between them than their words expressed. And yet the conversation felt to them vital and significant. After a second drink, Shahnaz began shivering.

"Oh, you're cold," said Hisham, as if worried.

"I'm fine. Give me some of your shawl."

She moved closer to him, and after a moment, they both turned and smiled at each other, their faces chilled and awkward, expressions not matching emotions. "This is so bad," whispered Hisham. Her small body fit next to him.

"Why?" asked Shahnaz, but she couldn't help grinning again, though she tried to stop it.

"Well, bad is as bad does, I suppose."

She rubbed her shoulder against his. "It's just that it's cold."

"So what do you think about all this?" asked Hisham. He felt sober, deliciously so, as if the mountain air swept all the liquor from his brain.

"I think you know what I think. I'm really fond of your brother. He's a really good person."

"Fond? He's in love with you, you know. That's no secret."

"Coming here means a lot to me," she replied. "Not just up here in Kaghan. Coming to Pakistan. My parents and everyone assume that I want to live abroad. But I think I want to live here. This feels like home, it always has. Even though I haven't spent that much time here since I grew up."

"Your Urdu's perfect. It's amazing."

"Just amazing!" She laughed. "You can thank my dad for that. He always insisted. He spoke Urdu with me, even though it drove me crazy. I used to be embarrassed when he spoke Urdu to me in front of my friends. I would answer him in English."

"So he must have thought you would come back."

"I don't know. He's wounded by the place. He hates it and loves it. And then, he hates that we lost our property and all that."

"Well, your grandmother still has some."

"Give me a cigarette," said Shahnaz. "Let's not talk about property, for God's sake. Let's talk about something else. Let's talk about love."

"We were talking about that, and that's how we started talking about property."

Shahnaz laughed, a happy drunken laugh.

"That's true. So I really am Pakistani blood just like your Lahori girls."

"Hardly!"

And just as he was saying this, she leaned over and kissed him on the mouth, sat up on her knees to do it, threw the cigarette that Hisham had lit for her into the fire. He looked into her eyes, and saw them widen, and then closed his own eyes and tasted her mouth, sweet with whiskey. They had been wanting this for a very long time, and now the distance between them crashed away, and she moved close to him, sat on his lap facing him, and whispered to him, "Mr. Hisham Atar."

"I am."

"I know."

A flutter of movement in the dark, and they both looked over and saw Nessim in front of the tent where he had been sleeping, his face in the open flap orange and yellow from the firelight. He looked for a moment, hard-faced, and then pulled himself back into the tent, withdrawing silently, and they heard him moving and then silence.

"Oh, fuck," whispered Shahnaz. She was still sitting in his lap.

"That's bad," said Hisham.

She kissed him once again, hard, mashing her lips against his, and then stood up.

"Now what?" He too was whispering.

"I don't know. I'm going. I'll just go in as if nothing happened. He was drunk, maybe he didn't see."

"No, he saw."

Still they were tender to each other. "Good night," he said.

She held his hand, slowly pulling it away. "Good night." Walking off, she returned and said into his ear, very softly, "It's okay. I'm glad. It'll be fine. Good night."

*

Hisham threw on more wood, once, twice, then sat cold by the fire till it quite went out, even till the white silhouette of dawn finger-nailed the dark peaks to the east, feeling rather than thinking. He imagined Shahnaz's body warm as she slept so close by, immaculate, and dreaded the morning when he must confront his brother. There would never be another night like that for him, so full of hope. Under the dawn star finally he crept into his tent and fell into a heavy slumber, waking only when the sun beat yellow through the nylon of the tent and heated it beyond comfort. He had emptied his water bottle before going to sleep, and the cigarettes lit one from another beside the fire were scratchy in his throat, his thirst raging. It must be faced. Crawling out into the day, blinking against the bright sun, he saw Yazid sitting next to the fire with a kettle of tea on the embers.

"Good morning, boss," said Yazid in English.

"Oh God, Yazid, please, no humor. And give me some water." He felt ashamed, as if Yazid might know what had happened.

"I was about to wake you, sir."

"You would have gotten a shoe around your ears for it."

"Poor man's earrings, sir. We're used to it."

Drinking long gulps from a bottle of icy spring water, shading his eyes, Hisham looked toward the river, just turning golden below them as the sun glanced across it.

"Where's Nessim Sahib?"

"He left even before I was awake. He didn't have tea or anything. The boy saw him."

"Well, if it wasn't till you were awake then he can't be far away."

Yazid looked at Hisham complacently. "What a place for sleeping, Mian Sahib. Look at where you've dragged me!" He threw both huge arms open and offered up the landscape, the purple tinge of the high-mountain sky that morning, and the summer grasses of these rarely visited pastures, the encompassing gesture belying his words.

"Is Bibi with him?"

He blinked and returned to the conversation. "No, sir. She had breakfast and then went back into her tent."

Yazid knew there had been a crash—his humor served as an interrogation around this. He understood their moods so well and how to manage them.

"All right, I'll take a tea thermos and a paratha for Nessim Sahib then."

*

Hisham could see no one, not down to where the river fell into the gorge, nor upstream to where it curled around a rise. Nessim would have gone upstream. The distance up deceived Hisham in this clear air. Climbing for almost an hour, coming around a bend, he saw above him a glacier that extended laterally a thousand meters across the valley and then all the way across the river, the river tunneling through it underneath. Nessim sat on the arch far out across the ice, dark against the white, the immense snow-crowned headwall at the end of the valley looming over the scene. He was staring down at the water as it emerged below him, the ice turquoise green at river level, the surface of the glacier dirty with rubble, scalloped by the wind. The thought flashed in Hisham's mind that he seemed poised to jump, or that he resembled some ancient figure put to die on an ice floe. In childhood they spent long summer days in the swimming pool at the Ranmal Mohra farm. Nessim would shimmy up on the roof of the changing pavilion and take a running leap over the broad concrete apron, landing feetfirst in the water, nearly clipping the edge. He had this solitary courage, jumping between buildings at the Lahore house, a violence in him that seemed desperate and inward, taking risks for himself, rarely following when Hisham and his friends made dares.

Keeping his eyes fixed on Nessim, as if to pin him there, Hisham trotted up, and when he got close Nessim motioned him over, Hisham reluctant. The glacier, rounded on top, steepened on the flanks to vertical. Sliding one foot in front of the other, Hisham made his way along the crown.

Standing just two arm's lengths above, he called. "How the hell did you get down there?"

The water poured through, a great volume of it.

"Come down here." Fury in the tone.

It didn't feel right. Hisham wanted to shout that he was sorry, but it seemed ridiculous to apologize hovering above the roaring of the water running through the glacier. It would not be possible thus to speak the phrases he had planned. Yet he must do it, as Nessim waited, looking him in the face, motioning with his head. Hisham sat on the ice and inched down. Nessim sat at the point where the ice got too steep, no grip, and a fall in that rushing ice-chilled water meant death.

"Just unfocus your eyes," shouted Nessim. "Look at the flow."

"Are you crazy?"

"Stare at the water. It's like time passing."

They sat together for a long minute, and then Nessim carefully stood. He touched Hisham's shoulder, caressed it, leaned down and kissed him on top of the head, somehow keeping his balance on the slick ice. This was madness, the least pressure and both would be gone.

Afraid to move and afraid not to, Hisham listened to Nessim climbing up behind him.

"Come on, then," called Nessim. "It won't get any easier."

Fighting panic, Hisham scrabbled himself backward up to the crown crab-fashion on his seat, seat of his pants wet, hands like claws.

Nessim kicked a rock, which tumbled past into the seething water. It was over. Hisham's skin prickled with cold and tension. The glacier lay barely in shadow still, the sun rising behind the headwall, the wind and the light working off each other.

They came off the glacier and emerged into sunlight, Nessim hurrying in front.

"I brought tea and parathas," called Hisham, wanting to move slowly, to gather himself. "Slow down."

Nessim jogged down the path as if running away. Stopping in a wind-sheltered hollow, he turned and looked around, up at the headwall, down to the gorge, then sat back against a rock. "Okay. Let's have it, then."

Hisham opened the thermos and poured tea, steaming and milky and sweet, took the parathas wrapped in greasy newspaper from the cargo pocket of his fishing vest.

Both were silent while they laid out the food, the silence heavy, the break imminent.

"I understand," said Hisham finally. "Let's talk. You tell me and I'll tell you. But that's the stupidest thing I've ever seen you do."

"What are you talking about? Don't talk to me about stupid things," said Nessim. "Do you know what I was thinking when you came up on the glacier?"

"I suppose you're about to tell me. I'm sorry, you know. I'm really sorry, but it's not what you think it is."

"Just listen. Remember the story of Napoleon and the barber?"

"Napoleon?"

"Napoleon the Emperor. The barber was shaving the emperor with a straight razor. He's just getting those difficult hairs around the throat and he whispers, 'Do you know, Your Majesty, right now I'm the most powerful man in France. You hold the Empire in your hands, and I hold you in mine.' And the Emperor says nothing and lets the man finish and as soon as he steps away calls the orderly and tells him to arrest the man. No one is allowed to think such things about him."

"I don't get it."

"When you slid down beside me, I thought, just a little push and off you go, away and down the gorge and out to the Kunar River."

"I said I'm sorry. Please, let me explain."

"Well, it was just a thought. Just a little push. But I'm just saying that. What I was doing, I was watching the river flowing out, and I was saying goodbye. I was thinking that this same water, in a few weeks, when it joins the Indus, it runs right past Ranmal Mohra. That exact same water under my feet might flow into our canal and into the orchard. The gardeners might be watering the lawns with it. That's what I was thinking. And that this is the last time I'll ever come up here. Last time ever."

"Come on now. We were drunk, if that's any excuse. It wasn't even a kiss. And this is our new secret spot. We'll come up here every summer. We'll bring our wives. We'll bring our kids."

"Don't talk about wives. Forget it. This feels like the end of the line. You and I, all our lives, you've been pushing me out. Don't interrupt me. You know you have. And you're the natural, aren't you? You're the golden boy. I don't like standing in the shadows fingering my dagger. I don't want to feel resentment anymore."

Nessim paused for a moment, playing with grass between his knees.

"I wish you'd just get angry," said Hisham.

"What's the point? It wasn't just last night. I was waiting for it. I even thought about it before we all came up here. You two are alike. You're no good."

Hisham for years regretted what came next. Of course she had been playing with him, with them both, that was the funny part. Yet when he should have been serious, an idiotic smile that he couldn't control spread across his face, a grin.

Nessim had kept tearing up bits of grass between his legs, and then he glanced over and saw. "Fuck you," he said, quietly. "Fuck you. I'm not doing this anymore. I want my own life."

"Don't be so melodramatic. It's just a girl."

"That's fine. Take her. You can have it all, and choke on it too. Though you won't choke, you'll just get fatter and fatter sitting on it like a poison toad."

Hisham put his hand on Nessim's knee. "Come on now, steady. It's you. You never wanted any kind of real response from that girl. That scared you. You were afraid to own her. You're desperate, and no girl likes a desperate man. Anyway, you're not good at possessions. You're right, that's more my thing." He knew he wasn't making sense, but better to attack than to defend.

Nessim stood up and stood over him.

"Whatever," he seethed, whispering. "Your loyalty should have been to me." He stopped for a moment, thinking. "You know what I think? I think I came very close to pushing you in the river and watching you float away."

With a shake of his head, blowing out as if blowing away this thought, he turned and walked back up toward the camp.

Ten minutes, twenty minutes, Hisham sat looking at the river, eating paratha and sipping tea. No point going back until Nessim cooled a bit. Hisham knew all about how to handle his little brother. He lay back. Nessim had always been the forgiving one in this relationship. *And needed to be*, thought Hisham with grim satisfaction. He looked around, appreciating the valley, the water, the sun, the river brimming with fish. It would be very awkward, but Shahnaz would win him over, by afternoon those two would be sitting somewhere out by the river talking and making it up. Hisham would keep out of the way, fish alone, come back to camp late. They would catch more fish than they wanted later today, they would be filing the barbs from their hooks and releasing their catch before evening. That's how they would get over it, with the fishing. Thank God for sport. And he thought of Shahnaz. Nessim had a point. He lost his virginity to that girl, after all. He hadn't said so, but Hisham knew it.

✳

Sitting in Lahore with Rustom, Hisham fell silent. After a moment, he said wonderingly, "And there it is. Coming on thirty years ago!"

Reaching over, he gave Rustom a little punch on the arm, breaking the spell.

"Hey, are you sleeping?"

"Are you kidding?"

"I think you fell asleep."

"Just a bit."

"So what did you hear?"

"Two brothers and a girl and a bottle of whiskey."

Hisham stood up, went over and studied the lithograph that lay on the desk.

"Brothers and birthright, I guess. That's what it's all about."

Rustom yawned. "I've said it before. I'm glad I'm an only child."

"I don't know. Over the years it's been lonely."

"My sympathies to you, poor sir," he said, softening the words by patting his host on the knee.

"Don't be sarcastic, it's not attractive. And anyway, between us brothers it was all quite civilized. We went back to Lahore, and you can imagine the fuss when he told the old man his plan. It came out slowly. He didn't say forever, but he said that he would go to law school and then look for a job over there. He did it that way too. He was always one for making a plan and then following it. My dad finally got over it. Now he goes and stays with him for a month each summer."

"Do you guys meet at all over there?"

"Of course. He was all right about it. I went once and stayed with him, right at the beginning, the very next spring, in that same little apartment down near the river at Dartmouth. Where I met Shahnaz the first time. I slept on the floor, and we ate pizza and drank beer, and then we were all fine. He'd completely broken with Shahnaz. I saw her a couple of times, but secretly. Maybe that was bad of me. He went off to law school over at Stanford, and then he began working in one of those white shoe law firms. You've seen him in New York. Old Nessim has the whole setup, a pretty American wife and the brownstone on the Upper East Side and the whole thing. He puts companies together and takes them apart and never soils his hands while he does it. He looks like he's made of silver, and so does his wife. You must have met her. She terrifies me, she makes me feel seedy and provincial. I get all the details through the desi grapevine. I was busy too, you know, the business and then soon the politics. When I go abroad it's always London. Like all good Pakistanis."

Rustom laughed. "And what about the woman in the case?"

Hisham had been pacing in front of the fire. Now he stopped and raised an admonishing finger. "Careful what you say about my wife. Don't annoy me. The only reason I've told you all this is because I know how you are. You've got the discretion of a barnacle."

Rustom winced. "A barnacle!"

Just then, the servant boy came in. "Mian Sahib, it's time. Bayazid Sahib rang the airport, and the duty officer said you should come."

Rustom stood up. "I'll beg my leave then. I wouldn't want them holding the plane for you. I've heard stories about that. Rina was saying that she was flying from Multan to Lahore, and they held the plane for you half the afternoon, while the rest of them sat baking on the runway."

Hisham snorted in deprecation. "It wasn't even ten minutes. That woman is always making things up. Come on, I'll see you out."

Out in the portico they stood for a moment, Rustom's driver holding open the door of his car.

"What a beautiful garden you have," said Rustom. It was that moment right after dawn, the light pale and hung up in the trees, a wet thick winter fog descending.

Hisham put his arm around Rustom's shoulder, walked him forward a few steps.

"It's true. I love this garden. Shahnaz really loves it. She brings plants from all over the world. Last year she got the embassy in Canberra to ship her over some sort of rare Australian trees, and not little ones either. And look at that big banyan there in the corner. Nessim and I had a fort there when we were kids. A magic fort. But don't get me started again. As you said, I'm feeling sentimental. Then they will have to hold the plane."

Putting his arms up and stretching, Rustom pulled away. "There's that word again," he exclaimed. "'Sentimental'!"

*

Piercing the greasy winter fog that blanketed the city, the plane rose into sunlight. There were just three other passengers in business class, all strangers. Twenty years ago, Hisham would probably have known each of them, at least well enough to greet. Lahore was changing that fast, and businessmen who recently would have thought it a great thing to take an overnight sleeper compartment on the Khyber Mail to Karachi now buzzed around upcountry and down on these flights.

The freshness that came of showering and shaving had faded, of dashing his neck with lemony cologne, slipping on shoes polished to brilliance, of sitting back in fragrant leather as the car became warm on the cruise to the airport through empty streets. He felt stale, raw from the night's intimacies. In Karachi he would as always lodge with a boozy extravagant friend who kept open house in a dilapidated mansion and whose servants rolled in the drinks cart exactly at noon. The party would carry on, Hisham slipping away for his meetings, welcomed back by a chattering crowd. He had his girl in Karachi, someone known to them all, and she too would be there later, everyone getting tight around sunset. That had come too soon after his marriage to Shahnaz, his little first forays into infidelity, and then her more suave love affairs, carried on with mannered discretion and no drama and thus even more painful to him, more final.

The stewardess coming around offered him tea or coffee, addressed him by name—had looked him up on the manifest, or knew him from the newspapers. Pretty little thing, daughter of some middle-class family, and a party girl from the look of it, here in business class among the politicians and moneymen, flirting, and probably available, and that too wearied him. Imagine the trouble of it, the withering small talk. The sun poured through the plexiglass window of the airplane too bright, and he lowered the shade halfway, thinking of his long evening. He should have known better than to share his troubles with someone like Rustom, who had drawn all the wrong conclusions.

Last night it had all come back to him vivid and sadder than he expected. Thirty years had passed since that Hanover winter and spring, thirty summers gone. Remember Shahnaz that first morning as he found her sitting at the desk in Nessim's apartment down by the river? And was that such a final blow received from her in that room, or was he just remembering it that way? She had a slight British accent, and she leveled her eyes, looking him in the face, her challenge and her particular strange beauty, and that at least felt like destiny still. He'd always believed that the glory ran with the land, with Ranmal Mohra, and she'd helped him to it. Yes, he had it all, land, business, politics. It meant so much to have power. And yet here he was on the dawn PIA flight, dropping into the smoking hulk of Karachi, and Nessim flourished untouched in a faraway city that by contrast seemed to float clean above the clouds.

This Is Where the Serpent Lives

✡

LAHORE—SAMARRA—RANMAL MOHRA—KÈRALA

2003–2005–2010–2013

*S*aqib was born at Ranmal Mohra, the estate in central Punjab where Hisham Atar's family had grounded their fortune several generations back. Only son of the head gardener at the centuries-old village house, he had reason to come and go in the servants' area there because of his father's job, and one fortunate day he passed under the gaze of Shahnaz, the wife of Hisham, during one of the family's winter descents on the farm. Like most Lahori women of her class, Shahnaz battled constantly to find and train and keep household servants. They began so well, and then stole or knocked up some neighbor's ayah or collapsed into a well of apathy—Oh, the disappointments of these begums!—and so she kept an eye out for likely recruits to the household when visiting the farm, for almost all of their servants came from Ranmal Mohra. Summoning him into the presence, Shahnaz asked little Saqib a few questions, then ordered him given a more or less unpaid job washing dishes in the farmhouse kitchen, a dark busy place furred with the smoke of coal fires. Like barnacles catching on rocks, these little boys of fortune are swept away by waves or stuck in one place forever. Some few have a better chance, which in Saqib's case meant that he crept by inches closer into the light of Shahnaz's regard, became something of a pet among staff and masters, useful around the place because of his mousy insignificance, until one fine day, when he was a mouse-mustached fourteen, he was summoned on approval to the family's Lahore mansion.

There he is, Saqib still almost a boy, standing out by the garages at the back of the compound. His shalvar pants are rolled up and feet bare, as he soaps and buffs one of Hisham's fabulous glittering cars of a chill spring morning, ankle deep in the foaming water and hopping around like a crane. Like most servant boys, his ambition at that age was to be a chauffeur, and by God he must earn it, doing slavish duty as apprentice—*shagirdh*—to the great Bayazid, the head chauffeur, whose seniority, vying with his immense inertia, prevented his trifling in that detail work.

Early on Yazid taught Saqib to drive, though usually *shagirdhs* can pass years doing the most menial duties before they are allowed so much as to slide behind the steering wheel and make vrooming engine noises—and early on Yazid described Saqib to Hisham as his quickest pupil of all, which was saying a great deal, for Yazid had legions of disciples in the art salted all over Lahore among Hisham and Shahnaz's friends. Saqib had been at the elementary school in Ranmal Mohra set up by Colonel Atar, but after he came to Lahore Yazid took pains to school him further. The two would sit together nights in Yazid's quarters over schoolbooks, the boy attentive and quick to please, Yazid's hungry soul encompassing the boy.

Slight and tall and eager, soft and intelligent, sensitive, quietly humorous, Saqib had charm, a quality not often found in boys of his class. Charm ripens in the sun of youth, lineaments and color— but for those millions of poor boys all over the country, brought up in the arms of no matter how loving a mother, in villages, in tenements, in slums, it is a quality that withers. It is taken as proof of loving glittering things too much, of a corruptible mind; and so the quick ones, the ones who will get ahead, conceal themselves behind an air of servility or bumptiousness or at least a featureless impassivity.

And yet Saqib did have charm, at ten and fifteen and twenty, though increasingly it was masked by his efficiency, the quickness and seriousness with which he bent himself to whatever task he was given. He got away with his graces and appeal partly I think because of his peculiar appearance. As thin as he was, he seemed very tall, and half of it seemed to be neck, studded in the middle with an enormous Adam's apple. You would think it would pulse like a metronome whenever he gulped—yet by some lucky chance his was entirely fixed, a rabbit-bump in a serpent's length. It would have been comic if, every time he was caught at a fault, it slid up and down and gave away his emotions. But Saqib gave nothing away, not if he didn't intend to.

On top of that neck, imagine a head of blue-black hair, boyishly coiffed with a clean part at the side and always in place but for a single punkish unruly lick at the front, this bird-tuft of disorder a reflection perhaps of a duality within. Finish it off with high Asiatic cheekbones, a little scrub of a mustache that never did grow much further, fine-grained skin, no hair anywhere else on his body but on top and presumably at the middle, and a nose that jutted out toward extravagance—and command. Indulgently pleased with this protégé, Hisham joked with his friends that at seventy Saqib would look like a particularly ascetic Roman emperor. Saqib was more than happy, he was joyful those first years, at sixteen and seventeen and eighteen, then nineteen and twenty, almost a man, learning each new trick of service, earning trust, sensitive each minute so as not to err. Hisham and Shahnaz would sometimes hear him singing to himself very quietly while dusting or doing some other repetitive work.

Although she didn't like doing it, even Shahnaz found herself succumbing to the frictionless ease that Saqib provided. He studied her moods, coming to understand that she preferred the muted to the bright, valued silence, insisted on the best or nothing, and wanted no fuss made at all. She would send him on personal errands, say to the Khussa Mahal, a shop in Liberty Market where they made the sandals she preferred, and he would return with samples of the designs most likely to suit her taste, from which she could pick a few and send the rest back. Though he might have presented them to her with a flourish, he instead simply left the package on her desk, to be found by her later, her heart leaping at this pile of goodies. Trying them on in front of the mirror—nine or ten pairs of pretty sandals, all different, brightly colored—she appreciated Saqib's gesture of leaving the sandals there unremarked, allowing her the pleasure of the surprise, drawing no attention to himself.

It went on, and Shahnaz would half complain to Hisham that the boy was ruining their initiative. One afternoon the two of them were drinking a cup of tea in the garden and had just been exposed to one of Saqib's little courtesies—he'd been to the jewelers and brought back a necklace that Shahnaz had sent for restringing, sitting by while the jeweler did the work so that he wouldn't be tempted to substitute cultured for her natural pearls. "Look at him floating along," she groaned, tucking the string into her handbag and watching him recede across the lawn. "He's becoming smug. You're ruining him, my love."

"Ah, but you're the one who sends him around Lahore with your ornaments!"

*S*aqib's evolutions as a boy in the Atar house had many points of inflection, but one experience in the early years bore more weight than others, as first impressions do.

Hisham and Shahnaz usually took no one but Yazid when they drove out from Lahore on long excursions, to their farm down south at Ranmal Mohra, or to Islamabad for a wedding or a party or to say their condolences over the relics of some old family friend. On this occasion, however—they were making the six-hour haul up to Islamabad for a party—Saqib had been taken along for the first time, just a couple of years into his service at fifteen and already a favored pet, his presence so weightless that Shahnaz herself had proposed he should be brought, to learn his manners and duties from Yazid.

They pushed six hours up through the Punjab toward the mountains, speeding along on the new Korean-built motorway, stopping just once, for fuel. Hisham sat in back looking out the window, playing with his cell phone, which then in the early 2000s had just become ubiquitous in Pakistan. An early adopter, he was one of those gadgety wealthy men in Pakistan, having a phone installed in his car way back when no one else did, and recently taking delivery of this superb jeep, ordered in London with all the trimmings, cooler-box and dual AC and locking diffs and all that. Sitting beside him, Shahnaz read all the way across the June plains, then napped, then read again. The AC blew ruffling cold air, but the windows were hot to the touch, for outside the landscape lay hammered breathless and flat by the Punjabi sun. Bayazid flashed along trimmed for speed, relaxed, a pro at this, the long haul.

✳

They were driving up to a party at a summer house belonging to a foreign woman and her industrialist husband, a blowout. There would be music and girls and God knows what. People would swim after dark, fireworks, that kind of thing. Some of them would spend the night, just a little crowd, the real intimates. Yet the mood in the car was tentative, for Hisham and Shahnaz had drawn apart in the matter of parties as in other things, husband still unreformed in his appetite for the charging night, and Shahnaz increasingly finding these excesses not so much unseemly as uninteresting.

Climbing up into the hills from Islamabad, the road becomes narrow and winding after the motorway's surge north across the Punjab, the route following the old British alignment up to Kashmir, curves and switchbacks originally contoured for cavalry and carts. Partway up the mountain, they were caught for turn after turn behind a Bedford truck rolling black smoke out its side-facing exhaust, laboring up at a walking pace under a load of cement. Tired after the long drive, Yazid glimpsed an opening and punched forward hard. Just as the jeep came abreast, with a huge drop-off next to it, a truck shot down from above and blared its airhorn and jammed its brakes, wheels-locked slide, tall as a house above them, road too tight, and Yazid just managed to slip back and safe, the truck shooting past with inches to spare, so big a thing to move so fast.

Hisham and Shahnaz, half dozing in the back, startled as the two vehicles almost smashed, the truck flashing past close enough to touch.

"You'll kill us all like that, Yazid," commented Shahnaz dryly.

She was the sharp one, the one who caught things, the one the servants knew to mind.

Hisham, equable in his present mood, said mildly, "Well, that could have gone wrong."

"Yes sir," said Yazid, unperturbed, piloting the jeep around the truck at a better spot, smooth. He wore his mustache long and low, a bit Fu Manchu, and had laughing eyes, one of the few servants who spoke to Hisham in Punjabi rather than Urdu, informal in that as in other things, most trusted man.

"I startled you, Bibi," he said, not changing his accustomed pace. He was addressing the boss, meaning Shahnaz. "Forgive me. I lost my patience."

They were silent, her Bach partitas playing on the elaborate stereo that Hisham had specified in England.

Finally, Shahnaz relented and broke the tension. "And then you never make mistakes, Yazid," she remarked offhandedly.

Yazid had forgiven himself, anyway. He knew it was true, he rarely did make mistakes, in driving or in any of the many ways he handled his masters' business.

Hisham laughed. "Look at the boy! Mr. Saqib here didn't turn a hair. Too cool for school."

Riding shotgun, so thin that he barely filled a third of the seat, in sharp contrast with Yazid overfilling his side of the vehicle, Saqib stared straight ahead and gave no indication that they were speaking of him.

Yazid looked over at Saqib cheerfully. "He's just a boy, sir. It's all new to him. He thinks whatever happens is right. He wouldn't know to be afraid."

Feeling buoyant after a nap on the motorway and looking toward his first vodka tonic in half an hour, Hisham became chatty.

"What about you, Bayazid. Why don't you have children? A long-established man like you should be thinking about a young wife."

Yazid caught his master's eye in the rearview mirror, just for a moment, and then focused again on the road. If Shahnaz weren't present, he might have offered a joke, just for companionship's sake.

Two years older than Hisham, Yazid had already been in service with Hisham's family for thirty years, joining as the chauffeur of the father, old Colonel Atar, in 1974. He wore that date proudly like a badge, for in Colonel Atar's household servants of twenty years were still newbies, and the ancient valet, Subhanullah Khan, so venerable that he never did any work at all except to dress Colonel Sahib, could boast sixty years in attendance. Now, in their silver-sabled fifties, Hisham and Yazid had been through many revolutions together, hunting and mountain trips and business done well and badly, and even Shahnaz trusted him completely, though she thought him indulged and sometimes joked with Hisham that they should call each other sweetie and admit they were a couple. "If he weren't so high on his dignity," she said, "he would squabble with you like a village wife."

"Nope. He's not the squabbling type," Hisham demurred.

✳

The question of having children was a delicate one in this group, for Hisham and Shahnaz too had none, a fault in her fertility. In a family such as Hisham's, to be without heir risked grave consequences for so many people. No children meant no clear succession, and Shahnaz, coming up on fifty now, would have no issue. Other masters might destroy the estate, squander it, or fall into violence. Many minds and many hearts were troubled by this problem, the tenants at their Ranmal Mohra estate, and even more intimately, the servants peopling—infesting, said Shahnaz—the Lahore house.

It said much about their relationship with Yazid, that Hisham should jokingly broach this subject with him in front of Shahnaz, for over the years they had rarely discussed it even between themselves, each unable quite to take comfort from the other in this sorrow—this bitter "might have been."

"What can I say?" answered Bayazid carefully. "I never had the chance. You know my story, sir. I'm an orphan, I was brought up in the streets. I've always had luck, I've always found good men and women too who valued me more than I deserve. But who would find a wife for me, with no sisters and no mother and no cousins? You know how our people are. Our manners are all backward."

Hisham continued his interrogation. "Come on, Yazid. I'll find you a nice little Punjabi girl at Ranmal Mohra. It's not too late. My great-grandfather had his last child in his seventies. And think of the size of the ones you'd father!" Yazid was something near being a giant, and in medieval times might have been the warrior called out when someone was needed for single combat.

Even Shahnaz couldn't resist joining in. "What about the little sweepress? That itty-bitty Christian. What's her name?" she teased. "They tell me she's always hanging around that clubhouse you drivers have set up in our garages."

Yazid was relaxed now and driving as fast as he ever did, slicing up the hill but without any impression of speed, hands loose on the steering and in perfect control.

"Well, Bibi Jee, the boys like the carrom board, it's a disease with them. They play it all night, and for some reason they like to do it in my room."

"Oh, come on, Yazid," laughed Hisham. "Everyone knows you're the master."

"That was a long time ago, sir. Now I'm just a spectator. And I don't have time, I can't put in the hours." His eyes in the rearview mirror merry, Yazid's fingers played on the steering wheel, a ring with an enormous orange agate in a crude silver setting on his pinky, the sort of thing usually worn by Sufi holy men trolling the country with begging bowls.

✳

They would be spending the night at a house perched on the mountain slope overlooking Islamabad, a mysterious tarmac driveway squirreling off the busy road and upward into a vast garden, where several jeeps and cars stood parked on a lawn. The gatekeeper knew them and saluted as Yazid gunned up to the landing, bringing the jeep to the base of a staircase leading upward through a series of terraces. He unpacked himself from behind the wheel and maneuvered out, went around and opened the door for Shahnaz, who was pulling together her things in her neat manner, sunglasses, book, hand cream. Saqib in a single motion unclipped his seat belt and flowed out of the car, around, and quickly opened Hisham's door.

"Thanks, boy," said Hisham, touching him with two fingers on the shoulder. Saqib bowed his head, an attitude respectful but not servile, a fine nuance. Hisham had been increasingly pleased with this new recruit's manners, and it added to his satisfaction at their arrival on this scene of merriment. Though he considered himself free from old-fashioned views of the relation between master and servant, like other rich Pakistanis he took the position that he anyway deserved to be well attended, paid well and expected good service. He would indulgently tell his friends what rascals his people were, the subtext being that in fact they were all a big happy family—which in his case they more or less were. Boyish, blurred by travel, Hisham looked up the hill toward the immense stone-built house. A woman's voice called down in English, "Who's that, then. Is that you, Shahnaz? Hey!" She had a soft, friendly voice, easy with them.

The woman, a foreigner, came down carefully in the fading light, her high heels unsteady on the flagstones. She was taller than most Pakistani women, energetic and pretty, kissing Shahnaz once on each cheek. Hisham came around and stood smiling at her till she turned and kissed him also, then took Shahnaz's hand and led her upward. Saqib had seen her before, in Lahore, when she and her husband stayed with the Atars, in a room that even was called by their name, Harouni Sahib's room—each of the guest rooms at Al-Unmool was named after a regular visitor, for many of the Atars' friends from Karachi and Islamabad invariably quartered with them in Lahore.

Climbing partway up toward the house, Hisham turned and looked down, the view all the way down to Islamabad and Rawalpindi, which could vaguely be seen smudged at the foot of the Margalla Hills. In an hour, when it grew dark, the two cities would be bright and twinkling thirty kilometers and many million cubic feet of air below them.

✳

Down by the cars, Yazid shook hands with the watchman, who had followed them up the driveway. When Hisham and Shahnaz could no longer be seen, he called to Saqib.

"Come on, boy, jump to it. They'll want the bags right away. Grab a couple and I'll take you and introduce you to this crew."

Two rough men had already descended to the car and were stand-ing ready to carry, Paharis not Punjabis, mountain people, as Saqib could tell by their accents. Seasoned now by running around the household at the farm in Ranmal Mohra and then in Lahore for a couple of years, Saqib knew these men as outside workers, gardeners and such, not the more consequential cadre of inside servants who would be running this complex establishment. They shook his hand deferentially, their fingers hard and ridged like horn from working with shovel and spade—after all, he was riding in the sahib's car, he must be of some importance. Saqib inclined his head, saying "Hello, Uncle" to each of them, then standing up very straight. The two Paharis even in summer wore rough-spun woolen vests infused with woodsmoke, rather pleasant and familiar, the way Saqib's own mother back at Ranmal Mohra might smell on a winter evening, of cook fire smoke and a tang of cow manure. Yazid watched this all shrewdly, for he was keeping an eye on the boy. He'd been at other parties here at Samarra, as the house was known, and knew the antics of the place, disgraceful scenes among the sahibs and the servants nipping about like pye-dogs at a banquet. Their host was an industrialist's son, Islamabad people with different manners than those of Hisham and the Lahori feudals, the tone more citified and smoother, the servants not drawn from a single village as Hisham's people were but sharked up from all over Pakistan.

Hisham followed Sonya, their hostess, and Shahnaz up to the main level of the house, which was built in the style of Frank Lloyd Wright, fifteen-foot ceilings, a large living room fronting onto a veranda, with glass doors that were thrown wide open that evening.

Their host, Sohail Harouni, was standing on the veranda with several others when Hisham and Shahnaz came up. He turned and put down his tumbler on the parapet, stepped forward with arms wide, and gave Hisham a big embrace, his face shining, a prosperous-looking man dressed in summery white.

"Aha, aha, my dear!" He turned and kissed Shahnaz. "And even the boss has come!" He touched his cheek to hers. "Bibi Jee."

Hisham looked over at a servant standing impassively to one side, a commanding figure wearing a full black achkan and white shalvar and a starched white turban with the *turrah* standing a good two feet above his large square head, like a swan's wing.

"As salaam uleikum, Ghulam Rasool Sahib. How are you holding up? You look like the old Nawab of Kalabagh in your togs."

"Mian Sahib," answered the majordomo, keeping it simple.

✻

When the drinks came, Sonya and Shahnaz drifted into the living room, which was separated from the terrace by sliding doors that extended across the room and made outside and inside one. Hisham remained outside chatting with Sohail and another guest, a foreign woman, perhaps coming up on forty, wearing a flowing plunge jumpsuit of silk with flared legs, her magnificent back nude almost to the bum, an elegant look but one that a Pakistani woman wouldn't venture upon.

Hisham offered the woman a cigarette and then lit it for her. "So what brings you to Pakistan?" he asked. "Business or pleasure?"

"Well, both and neither," laughed the woman, her French accent especially piquant in Pakistan, where such things were prized, redolent of life abroad.

When the Frenchwoman drifted away briefly, looking for her bag, Hisham said to Sohail agreeably, "Nice one, Mian Sahib. She's easy on the eye."

"She's a friend of your buddy Bilquis Sheikh."

"Lucky man!"

"Friends in need are friends indeed, I suppose." The comment didn't make much sense, but Sohail covered that with his generous laugh, which found a ready echo in Hisham's own merriment.

"So what's the plan?" asked Hisham.

"Just a few of us. Rahila and Shafqat should be here in a while. He had to pop in at some drinks party in Islamabad."

"Double dipping, is he?"

"Exactly what I said. Anyway, he's bringing the supplies."

"Oh no!"

In the past few years, cocaine had become the drug of choice among a certain segment of the fast set in Karachi and Islamabad, slightly less of it in Lahore, even among these old hippies who had been using drugs since their college days in America. Hisham was a latecomer onto that scene but took to it like a baby to barley sugar. He had known, as they drove up, that it was likely some selected group would pass around lines late in the evening.

"What about Shahnaz?" asked Sohail. "I don't want to cause any tension." He jokingly pronounced it "tan-shun," the way villagers used that word, which had become a part of Urdu vernacular.

"No, she's fine. I hinted at it, and she said she was peeling off early. You know how it is, she always scoots when the shooting starts."

Sohail laughed. "Nice that she lets you off the leash! That's why Sonya put you chaps off in her new wing. It's like another village over there, out of sight and out of mind."

"Sonya's a sensible girl," purred Hisham. He raised a finger for another drink to Ghulam Rasool, who stood in the shadows, barely present.

*

With the sahibs gone up into the house to their recreations, the servants relaxed, chatting, the night soft and humid. The Paharis had insisted on carrying all the luggage, taking it from Saqib's hands, as if a fine city fellow like him should not be dragging heavy cases around. He stayed back a little, savoring the moment, shivering though it wasn't cold, walking the dark path toward the servants' area, the house above lit. He had never been in the mountains before—not even into these foothills of the Himalayas, up in these pine forests, which gave an unfamiliar scent. It seemed to him a luxury beyond price, to be in summer away from the heat just like that by driving up and away, the culmination of that race through miles of burning heat in Hisham Sahib's extravagant Land Cruiser. In Ranmal Mohra, where he had been planted all his childhood until being plucked away to Lahore, there was no escaping the flesh-blistering heat from May till September. Often for weeks at a time in the summer there were not even fans running in the little village, the electricity cut off by load shedding.

Built under the great house, like pilgrim cells in a monastery, a row of servants' rooms stood with doors open to allow in the night air, each with a single lightbulb hanging from a wire. At the end of the row a door led into a much larger common room where the gardeners and other lower-status servants bunked on charpoys laid out in a grid, enough for visiting servants too. The door was so low that Yazid stooped to duck into the room, found it empty, and went out again. The gardeners and some other drivers were squatting out on a flat rooftop, circled around a card game under a bare bulb attached to the wall.

"Hello, sir!" said one of them. He rose and embraced Yazid, and several others called to Yazid and stood, familiar from parties over the years. "Come on, we're setting up a little barbershop here. Help me give these kids a close shave next to the skin." No one paid attention to Saqib, who perched on a charpoy out of the way. Earlier Yazid had told him, when word came down that the boy would be joining for the trip up to the mountains, "You've seen them in Lahore. They're good people. The wife is a foreigner, and that means the servants all live easy. It's good grub and soft bedding."

Yazid stood over the card players, studying the game. After a minute he said, "I like what I see. But first things first. Could one of you boys put a charpoy for me off to the side? Somewhere quiet, this is sleeping weather." He looked at Saqib, forgotten there. "Put the kid next to me."

One of the gardeners, about the same age as Saqib, had attached himself to Yazid as soon as they arrived, knowing him from an earlier visit. He leapt up and said to Saqib, "Give me a hand, I know your guru sahib's habits from when they came last summer."

They each balanced a charpoy on their heads and maneuvered down the path to a little secluded terrace. A buffalo and her calf chained to one side under a lean-to stirred and snorted but didn't get to their feet.

"So they're training you for a driver, are they?" asked the boy, impressed.

Saqib looked full in the boy's face, saw there a reflection of the raw bumpkin that he used to be back in Ranmal Mohra. "Something like that."

The boy left Saqib there and then returned with two pillows, greasy with hair oil, and a couple of heavy shaggy blankets.

"You'll need these, you'll be surprised at the chill around dawn."

Yazid had told Saqib earlier, "As I said, it's a good house, you shouldn't worry. But still. Different sahibs make different manners, and there's all kinds about. And don't talk about home things. There's one hard rule, never say anything about Mian Sahib, and even more, not a word about Bibi, what they do or where they do it or why they do it. Nothing. If ever Begum Sahiba finds out you've been running your mouth, you'll be back in Ranmal Mohra with a shovel in your hand."

Saqib didn't need to be told twice. He had seen that Yazid's low-key manner overlay a great force, and that when it came to loyalties the big man was inflexible. Anyway, discretion came easily to Saqib, for he was essentially a loner.

*

Inclined to make conversation, the boy offered to bring tea, but Saqib refused. "I'll be up there in a moment."

"There's a full-on banquet tonight, and for us too," the boy said. "Once the sahibs finish eating the Begum Sahiba allows us to have the rest. There's no leftovers in this joint, you'll see. They've got a guy up specially from 'Pindi to make that Baloch sajji. He brought three lambs and butchered them right here and everything, a real pro. And another guy for the nan. Tonight we'll live it up."

Saqib allowed himself a bit of humor. "Well, if we're waiting for the sahibs to eat then it's going to be more like breakfast."

"I know what you mean. They'll keep it up for sure. Party all night. They won't eat till they're staggering."

This seemed to Saqib too familiar. "That's none of our business, anyway. As long as the sahibs are happy."

The boy grinned. "You're right," he said, "I get it." He went away, disappointed that Saqib wouldn't join him for a bit of gossip.

· · ·

The stars shone bright in the mountain air, through the branches of the pine trees, a soughing wind flowing through. Saqib felt shiveringly alive. He must savor this; he lay down in the dark, hearing occasional bursts of laughter above where the others were playing cards. *I'm lying at night in the mountains!* he thought, feeling the loom of the heights around him, boy of the plains. There were many stars above, and among them one for him alone, his particular star, as his mother had told him often, that wise village woman.

He stayed there a long time, half an hour, his thoughts wandering. One of his qualities always had been to spend time thinking, planning, even when he was quite little. This shrewd mother, who sent him to learn his prayers and to learn to read too, taught by the village maulvi, always kept a special hand on him, her little warrior. He thought about his behavior in the car, about the many hours, listening to the desultory conversation between Hisham and Shahnaz, carried out in English, incomprehensible. Bayazid and he of course had not said a single word as they drove up to the mountains. And yet funny how they could be so familiar with Yazid— Yazid, who knew all the secret workings of the Atar business, so they said. That was a power worth having!

✻

As the night wore on there was much ringing of the servants' bell, men running up into the house, calls for ice, for cigarettes. The Baloch men sitting by their coals waiting for the sajji to be ordered pulled out a few skewers for the servants.

"Come on, you good people might as well eat these, they're getting cold. It's not the same reheated. There's plenty for the sahibs later." They kept in good with the servants, for they knew that the sahibs' whims were unpredictable—or, rather, predictable only to the ones who watched them closely. With a word at the right moment in the master's ear a servant could ensure a summons to another of these dinners, and that meant a clear ten thousand rupees, twenty, even more if the sahib came out in the night flushed and threw around largesse.

When they finally called for the food, one of the servants brought out a brimming glass of whiskey and gave it to the Baloch who was doing the grilling. "The big sahib sent this for Karamat Khan. They're loving your tikkas. Go on, take it, the sahib says that it's fuel for your cooking, he remembers from that time at Khanpur Dam." The Baloch didn't say anything but put the glass next to his foot and took surreptitious sips as he squatted in front of his coals, putting skewers in the flame and then sending all kinds of kebabs and tikkas steaming up into the house. Saqib had insinuated himself off to one side, cross-legged on a charpoy, and watched the proceedings, too excited to sleep.

✶

The Baloch had shut down their operation and gone off to bed with the rest of the staff, the fire burned low, and Saqib alone lay near it dozing, eyes shut but not asleep. The boy who earlier had offered him tea had lingered last. Then, finding Saqib incommunicative, he too went into the big smoky common room to his charpoy. Like a roving hound that waits till all around are sleeping, Saqib's eye opened. He had the capacity to be instantly awake, and he loved the night. Back in Ranmal Mohra, in the years before he was summoned to Lahore, Saqib had developed a dangerous habit. He would slip late on moonless nights from the little mud room where his parents and sisters and he slept and steal into the orchard that caped the village, after even the watchmen had abandoned their rounds, slipping into places not permitted to the villagers.

In later years, as he drew closer to Shahnaz's world, waiting through each season for the Atars' arrivals at the farm, he found a secret ingress to the garden at Shahnaz and Hisham's house in the fields beyond the Ranmal Mohra village, the house known as Kèrala. He would slip in at night, gardener's son and thus familiar with the layout, sitting at the edges of the great lawn there and watching the play of shadows on the grass expanse, or dabbling his legs in the swimming pool. This trespass pleased his sense of being special to the Atars, and as he prowled near the rooms where Shahnaz spent her nights, rooms familiar to him because increasingly he was given the freedom of the house when they came, he felt intimate with her and them, as if he watched not just the garden and glimmering white house but watched her sleeping place unaware, the master sleeping beside her. Stealing this contact gave him secret power, as theft does, the overwatcher's power.

On this night up at the mountain retreat of the foreign woman, Saqib felt the same thrill that he experienced penetrating the master's house at Ranmal Mohra. The pleasure lay in the violation, entering their world and enjoying it by this secret design, his subterfuge, his cunning. Now, as he raised his head, he heard far away up toward the house a strange wailing sound, at first thinking it some mountain animal calling, not familiar to him, but then identified in the sound the beat of a drum. Yes, he would go, he trusted himself to move silently. His senses keen, thrilled, this was a drama that he liked, the night offering itself.

Very carefully, he went into the servants' common room and surveyed the bodies lying on the charpoys. All were sound asleep there, the two Pahari gardeners, drivers belonging to guests. Along the row of servants' quarters, the doors were open to the night air, and in each he saw through the gloom a head in a bed. Yazid below would be sleeping oblivious. Saqib knew how deeply he went into the mountain of his body, and how difficult it was to rouse him from that journey into his capacious dream world.

Slowly, very slowly, he crept around to the front of the house, where he knew he must not go. That was a woman's voice playing on a stereo, now he could hear it, a bewitchment in this clear mountain air, the voice projected out. On one of a series of terraces cascading down the mountain, fire in a huge metal pan had burned down, and next to it two chairs stood empty, a bottle in the grass half full, and two glasses, and on a table a speaker playing the strange music. He should not proceed, but his demon led him forward. For minutes at a time, he watched from hidden places, then moved quietly into the open, up one set of stairs, then another. No, they were all asleep. For a moment, this place could be his, where during the daylight he would never intrude except to bring some item, a lighter or a bottle of water or a phone. From the terrace he could see forever, it seemed, down to the west, to the twin cities, Islamabad and 'Pindi. Lately his horizons were growing wider in many ways, just a couple of years removed from Ranmal Mohra to the house in Lahore. This Islamabad capital figured more numinous still, a place of power, parliamentarians in their assembly on television, army parades with jets, men speaking into bunches of microphones like steel bouquets. There must be some undefined wickedness too in the same measure, he was coming to grasp that, the powerful serving themselves, quarters of pleasure to serve them. Saqib's lively imagination was drawn to stories of that place, where it seemed great destinies met their beginnings, his mind older than his age. Going back down to where the fire guttered in the metal brazier six feet across, he crouched and looked into the flame. The music above him continued strange, unlike any sounds he had heard before.

Then, far below, he heard another sound, only when the wind blew uphill, not like voices, but rhythmic. Instantly he slipped back from the fire, into a shaded place near the wall, perfectly motionless. Knowing then that a man might pass two paces from him and not see him, he sat for two and then three minutes, and the sound continued and resolved in his mind. It was a woman. Back in Ranmal Mohra he had once spied upon one of his neighbors going out into the sugarcane fields on an assignation with a young married woman. He followed them at a distance, saw them going into the field where the cane grew more than head high, sat listening to them, and in the daytime went into the field and found where it had been cut to make a little safehold. Now, this night, he knew this sound must be a woman like that.

Making a long detour, he moved down the hill, approached the sound. It was a woman's voice, saying not words but little cries. There was a tank of water, like the swimming pool in the lawn of the big house at Ranmal Mohra, and next to it also like the pool at Ranmal Mohra a daybed with an upright back. It was distant through the trees at first, but he approached still along a swept path of stone, shaded by a row of bamboo alongside.

A woman lay on her back on the bed, naked from below the waist. There was a shaded sconce on a pole that cast an indistinct light. Kneeling on the ground in front of her, with his face buried between her legs, a man's head, the man fully dressed. Saqib had never thought that a man might do this to a woman in real life, not people known to him. It seemed almost that he was hurting her, but she held his head in both hands and pressed his face down. Saqib crouched and watched, concealing himself against a tree, and it went on and on, a scene not so far away down in the clearing of cast light. Once the woman pulled him up and they kissed, and then she pushed him down again, and it was then that he saw it was Hisham Sahib and Sonya Bibi, their hostess.

What seemed to Saqib most obscene was the Sahiba's luminous pale shade smudged in the half-light, the bottom half bare, her legs, her kurta pulled up, her arms and upper torso clothed, like a doll half undressed. When Saqib crept away it was not just because he feared being caught, a hand clapped on his shoulder, and disgrace forever, thrown out of Ranmal Mohra, his father fired from his valuable job as the gardener at the house there. Sometimes families were expelled from the village, carrying their belongings away on a borrowed trolley, utterly thrown down. Watching for one long last moment, touching his hard penis through his shalvar, Saqib felt excited and also ashamed, for himself, for them. Looking down had been like looking at a dim-lit stage, mechanical actions in the dirty yellow light, captured pleasure, his and theirs.

Imagine putting your face up between a woman's legs, that secret place with monthly blood. And yet, he had seen these women at the parties in the Atars' Lahore mansion, how clean they were. And these women would allow it. He had seen a videotape, so exciting that he came without touching himself. In Lahore recently he had access to a video player for a whole week while the cook who owned it went on leave, sneaking into the man's room at night. He watched again and again the one videotape he was able to rent in a backstreet video shop, too embarrassed to go back for a second, a woman walking briskly into a room, smiling, taking off her clothes, and then allowing a man to do with her all that he desired.

✻

Silently he withdrew, leaving his master there and this woman he had seen in the drawing room at Al-Unmool, left them there as if she might make this ratcheting sound all night, imagining her like that woman in the video, a woman from some unimaginably foreign place, desirable, all that might corrupt a man and yet draw him.

He climbed down to the little terrace where Yazid lay sleeping, sprawled wide, the blanket thrown off his legs. Another time Saqib might have tucked the blanket around him again. But now he crept onto his charpoy, and when he closed his eyes he saw women's limbs tangled together and felt a drop in his stomach. He did not masturbate though he thought of it, to do it secretly, but lay there right till the dawn only half sleeping. When he woke the entire world seemed changed, the garden charged with meaning. How often did a woman and a man play out such scenes inside these walls, and what else too, tangling through the summer, this property so large that it had fruit orchards, tanks of water, tennis courts, terraces leading to terraces, so many secret arbors and gardens?

*

The next day, although they left early, Saqib loitered above and saw the woman again, as he would see her often when she and her husband stayed in the following years at Al-Unmool. That morning she wore a black velvet ribbon in her hair, smoked a cigarette on the terrace over breakfast when Saqib brought more coffee, had volunteered that errand. So much that came afterward, his longings for whatever the Atars possessed, had a basis in that vision, of Sonya Harouni sitting on the parapet overlooking a hundred kilometers of air all the way down to the twin cities, Islamabad and Rawalpindi, smoking a cigarette and idly speaking with Hisham and Shahnaz and the other guests, how pale-skinned she was, how foreign, so unspeakably distant from everything Saqib had grown up with in the dirt lanes of Ranmal Mohra. And yet this same cool figure last night lay back on a daybed in the darkness by the swimming pool and allowed Hisham Atar Sahib to give her that pleasure, while Shahnaz slept not a hundred meters away. He had idealized Hisham and Shahnaz, and although he had believed from the beginning that their sophistication had many refinements, this night gave form to his appreciation of the corruption within their world also, violations of principles and betrayals of each other, alluring, somber, frightening, and ultimately sexual, as money and power are sexual.

If at first Saqib had regarded his masters from a distance, looking up at them as at the moon, gradually they became familiar to him, approachable. He came to understand that their complexities were a matter of style as much as of substance. One of the marks of intelligence is to see likeness in unlike things, and so he understood quite soon that his acute village perceptions could be translated here and find purchase. Though initially it had been a great matter merely to serve, gradually he found himself wanting what they had in some further degree, wanted to appropriate their ways. Because of that, and because of his fine sensibility and intelligence, he quickly worked his way into their hearts. Now his suspicions were confirmed, that the world presented layers of experience not available to all, that there were secret rooms and coded meanings. Saqib was drawn to concealments and puzzles, so it pleased him in his solitude to view the world this way. His shock was bound up with his sense of being initiated into a realm of deeper experience, one made both more toxic and more beguiling by association with the sahibs, with Hisham and his charismatic powers and Shahnaz with her sophistication and subtlety.

✻

The trip to the mountains also marked another step in Saqib's rising fortunes, unprecedented in the Atar household for a servant as green and untried as Saqib. After that trip, Saqib became a settled part of the traveling team, young man perched front-seat-left in the car when the sahibs rode out from Lahore. Because he was young and yet increasingly an intimate from whom the more private scenes were not shielded, Hisham began to ask of him little services that he preferred not to impose on the older servants, and that yet required someone who understood exactly how he wanted things done. When Hisham lost his phone at two in the morning in the middle of a party, or needed another bottle of booze after he'd sent the servants to sleep, he would ring a bell that sounded only in Saqib's quarters, and the boy would appear almost comically fast, alert and unperturbed, and proceed smoothly to find the phone or locate another bottle of a particular wine or conjure up cigarettes that he stocked for such occasions, whatever it might be. Hisham took troubles with Saqib, painstakingly explained to him how to hook up the stereo system leads so that it could be moved outside, taught him how to pack an overnight bag, how to fold a suit jacket so it wouldn't get creased, how to put a perfect shine on shoes, when to serve a guest the good whiskey rather than the ordinary hooch, how strong to make the drinks on different occasions.

II

One of Hisham and Shahnaz's first acts as a married couple, soon after graduating from their American college in the 1970s, had been to build a house in the fields beyond Ranmal Mohra, designed by a society architect who worked the thin seam of rich Lahoris with restrained tastes. A modern take on a colonial bungalow, with deep cool verandas all around and tall ceilings hung with railway station fans, rooms that could be shadowed and shut in summer and cheerily bright through banks of windows in winter, it suited the landscape, shagged with greenery, overhung by rosewood trees and banyans and pipal grown tall with the passing years. They had christened the place Kèrala, drawing on the name of a nearby Machhi village, a reminder of those first riverine tribes who lived here for centuries in their little settlements perched among the creeks of the great Indus.

The ancestral house stood next to the dera—the farm stores—the master's compound at the center and the villagers' huts ringed out around it. Succeeding generations ruling over the farm had added to that original haveli, which was almost a fort, defensible. They had razed sections of the encroaching village for new wings, storerooms, gardens, sitting areas, an enlarged zenana, brothers and cousins living in that compound together. Hisham and his father, Colonel Atar, in those years were still uneasily sharing responsibility for running the farm. There would have been plenty of room for Hisham and the colonel to share the house and lead independent lives there, especially as they were rarely resident at the same time, except by arrangement.

Hisham and Shahnaz, however, struck out on their own, built their house several kilometers away, carving it into a mango orchard planted by his grandfather out toward the banks of the Indus, which served as the western border to their domains. Colonel Atar, who was concerned that he and his son should not clash over their habits at the farm, encouraged this project. The father had a habit of plucking in village maidens to his bedroom, of cuffing about his servants and the villagers too. He acted as the old feudals did, thought it his prerogative—but saw no reason to rub his son's nose in it, and, even more, no reason to court his daughter-in-law's discriminations.

Shahnaz, having been brought up abroad, would probably not have spent much time at the farm if she had been obliged to stay at the old house, plonked in the middle of Ranmal Mohra village, with smoke from dung fires hanging over the place at evening, the sounds of shouting villagers tyrannizing their wives and children, a braying village maulvi calling a distorted azaan over a cheap loud-speaker, people coming and going all about, rats and bugs that did not distinguish between the houses of master and servants.

The establishment out by the Indus River, however, soothed her after the perplexities of the city. This was the house of the early marriage, scented with that romance. There she could be free, the garden so large that they had not even troubled to throw a wall around those many acres, her roses in banks and long squares, lilies and tulips and annuals of every color that she herself carried from abroad, a whole suitcase of seeds and bulbs, trees that she planted, gulmohar, laburnum, flame of the forest, even an allée of banyans, laid out soon after her marriage to Hisham in 1978, and now, just thirty years later, grown immense, as if those elephant-trunk aerial roots had buried their tips in that black Punjabi soil and pushed subterranean feelers down to the river five kilometers away, and drank up nourishment porridge-thick with the silt of the Hima-layas. Yes, her banyans were becoming famous among her friends, city people lured south into darkest Punjab for house parties in the winter, and her flowers, the arrangement of the house. The man-sion in Lahore she took as she found it, other women had put their impress on it, and to change it was an affront. That had been the house of Hisham's mother, who died tragically and early. But Kèrala was hers.

Six years had passed since the trip to the Samarra house above Islamabad. It was spring at Ranmal Mohra, early April, the season when the covers come off air conditioners and the houses are readied for summer heat. Hisham and Shahnaz would be arriving before dusk. Saqib and Bayazid had been back and forth there all through the winter, Yazid dealing with a delicate matter—difficulties with payments following the sale of an old cotton ginning mill set up by the Colonel Sahib in the 1950s—and Saqib sent with him, now turned twenty-one and increasingly helping Yazid with business, keeping him company, keeping him engaged, if truth be told. Yazid moved a lot more quickly when Saqib set the pace.

The two servants were seated near the garages, Yazid sedately absorbing an Urdu paper, wearing a pair of battered reading glasses that strapped around his large head like aviator goggles from the First World War. Saqib, crisply dressed as always, didn't need any diversion, but simply sat and enjoyed the sound of the birds homing at evening into the trees.

"Uncle, you read so quickly, but you move your lips," observed Saqib. "It's almost as if you're reading aloud to me, but just every tenth word. It's like when Maulvi Sahib recites the Koran under his breath." Saqib was bored and wanted to get a reaction out of his mentor.

"It's impossible to get through the paper around you, I swear," said Yazid, carefully folding the paper and tucking it into the capacious pocket of his vest. "You're like a puppy, if I sit down and don't pay attention, you'll start chewing on my shoe."

"Come on, they'll be here any moment. Let's take a walk."

"Allah. All right, boy. Come on."

Yazid, who had always been tall and broad, had in the past years assumed a quite different figure, as strong as ever—his sleeves stretched tight around his massive biceps—but with an Aquarian belly that suggested a pillow, or something more angular, a box, strapped to his midriff under his kurta, the front flap of the kurta hanging down loose.

"Anyway, you know what Hisham Sahib said. He wants you walking five kilometers every day."

"Five kilometers! I'm a chauffeur, not a camel."

"I heard you ordering parathas from the old lady this morning. I should probably inform Begum Sahiba about that. She's instructed us all that you're to have only rice and a thin gruel."

"On my honor, I haven't eaten anything but rice for the past week. Those weren't my parathas, and that's the truth."

"Okay, okay, calm down."

They strolled under the trees, into the garden, knowing that they would hear the arriving jeep in good time to get back and receive Hisham and Shahnaz.

*

When Colonel Atar came to the farm the managers would line up and offer him garlands of rose petals and the guards would even squeeze off a rifle shot or two in the air, Colonel Sahib walking briskly past the assembly with a nod but secretly pleased—as they well knew. No one would have tried this display on Shahnaz, and even Hisham preferred to glide into his sanctum and head straight to the drinks cabinet, sipping down a chilled gimlet of vodka before he settled in—they invariably arrived around sunset, the departure from Lahore always later than planned.

Bayazid and Saqib hurried back when they heard the knock of the engine and now stood lined up at the end of the long drive, until the jeep came around the last bend and rolled up to the portico.

"Hello, boys," said Hisham, unrolling from the back seat—he too was developing a generous paunch. He examined his two favorites. "Look at you two, Mr. Big and Mr. Slim. You look like feast and famine standing at my doorstep."

Shahnaz's eyes drifted over her flower beds in the front, proprietary, cool as she was.

The house servants came out and made an obeisance to Hisham, both hands clasping his hand, head lowered in a bow, bending their knees. In the village the manners changed, the staff more submissive, Hisham's affect feudal, and even Shahnaz kept it up, covering her head more carefully than in Lahore and distant from the servants, an acknowledgment that before her time the women in the family had strictly observed purdah at the farm.

*

Having settled into the musty dusty cool rooms, aired and washed that morning, Shahnaz and Hisham came out into the back garden, Hisham with drink in hand, Shahnaz with shears to cut bouquets of flowers for the house. They were at their best as a couple now, Hisham having changed into a fresh white shirt and khakis, Shahnaz mazy and idle, drifting into the garden. The ice cubes in his drink tinkled merrily, and he had made her one too.

"Hold on," he said. "I've got a surprise for you."

"You know I hate surprises!"

"Not this one, my angel."

Overhead the crows that gathered each night in the surrounding orchard elbowed silently past, and the songbirds in the garden called to mark their places for the night.

"*Koi hai*, anyone there?" shouted Hisham, and Yazid and Saqib, who had been standing in the servants' area behind the kitchen expecting to be called, quickly emerged.

"Come on, come on," he said, hurrying Shahnaz forward.

"What is that thing?" she asked, peering through the trees. "What have you done to my garden?"

They walked up to a newly built wall, enclosing the swimming pool that Hisham had built soon after the Kèrala house was completed, as a present for Shahnaz. She had been complaining ever since that she didn't like to swim at the village, because the pool didn't have any screening from gardeners or some chance intruder. Hisham always pooh-poohed her, would order the staff far away when they swam. "No one would dare to come near when I've told them," he insisted, but she had her own views on what the villagers would and would not dare to do. Now he had secretly built her the wall she desired, Saqib acting as the supervisor under Bayazid's loose tutelage, his first foray into such a role, which elevated him from being merely a house servant.

"Wow, fantastic!" said Shahnaz, but tentatively. "I love the design. I like that it's not just square." She looked more closely. "What's amazing is that it looks like it's been there forever."

She was dubious, coming around to innovations and new places and new people uneasily. Hisham complained that her enthusiasms developed so slowly that neither she nor her companions ever enjoyed the full beauty of them.

✳

The wall had decorative crenellations at the top, and ran irregularly around the pool, swerving to gather in a large rosewood, flowing around the curves of the flower beds. Stepping through the gate, they found a portion of garden also enclosed, the wooden chaise longues newly painted and the pool filled that day with fresh water, a table and chairs laid in the new little garden with a tablecloth and a vase of flowers, and even fresh sod all around the construction.

Shahnaz turned to Saqib, who had lingered by the entrance. "Come on, Saqib, come forward. I recognize this. This is your work. I'm impressed."

Saqib knew his moments well, when to be circumspect. He took one step, but still kept to the shadows.

"No, Bibi Jee, this was Mian Sahib. Mian Sahib laid it out last time when he came here."

"Maybe," she demurred. "But it's the details. It's like your cooking and your driving, you pay attention."

Her praise washing over him, eyes slightly downcast, and yet a connection of feeling between them, two fastidious souls in communication, his reticence an invitation to her unwonted enthusiasm.

"Look at how solid that is!" said Hisham, patting the wall. "That's like something the Moghuls built." And truly, the wall had the look of a structure that would stand when all else around lay waste, the bricks carefully fitted and grouted, all of it precisely made and with little flourishes, the crenellations, the way in which pillars had been regularly incorporated, an arch over the gate.

"He mostly used old bricks from when we tore down one of the stores at Ranmal Mohra," said Yazid proudly. "It saved a lac rupees."

They ate dinner there by the pool, the kitchen now more or less under Saqib's supervision here at the village, for he had learned to cook, spent a month of secondment with the superb chef of Shahnaz's close friend when she and Hisham were abroad the previous summer. With typical efficiency, he had learned a round dozen or so of comforting European dishes that he knew they liked— a flan, potato cutlets, puttanesca, a roast chicken with fresh-made noodle stuffing—serving them in combinations, experimenting but within that restricted palette. The Pakistani dishes, which didn't require his magic touch, were left to the village cook.

Shahnaz, who swam as precisely as she lived, gracefully and quietly, went to the house and brought her bathing suit and changed in a little alcove built for the purpose, slipped with a tiny splash into the chill water and did a single lap, then came out and dried herself, brushing the cold water off her arms, invigorated.

"So cold! But I love it. What an improvement with this wall. That damned boy is an artist, I tell you. You wouldn't have had time to tell him all those little details. We really should send him to school, you know, he deserves it."

The previous year Shahnaz had thought hard and made inquiries about what it would take to get Saqib up to speed for the University of the Punjab, the premier institution in the province, which might even lead to education abroad. She had a ritual of going each morning to the market and buying flowers for the Lahore house, vegetables, some delicacies from the emporium that sold imported goods, and in the past couple of years Saqib had taken over from Yazid the duty of driving her on these rounds. She would go to her tailor, her jeweler's, and while he drove she would lounge in back and talk to him, making an exception to her usual reticence with servants only because he never presumed upon her confidence. Both maternal and girlish, she allowed herself to speak with him of idle matters, and he would tell her interesting facts about the people in the streets, the scams that the beggars got up to, little incidents that he could unpack for her, why the policeman motioned secretly to the man on the motorcycle, and how the motorcyclist passed the folded-up banknote for the bribe. As is often the case, her severity was a mask for her delicacy, and so when she lowered her guard she quite burbled forth, ingenuous and tentative and sweet. In any case, Saqib was the age that her son might have been, if she had one. What a fine line Saqib threaded, saying so little when she offered a little more, and covering up the rest with the stories from the village that she increasingly allowed him to tell, little snippets of humor, never anything of significance that would require her to act, certainly never bearing tales.

"Behind it all he's quite funny, you know," she said to Hisham, and he in turn joked that Saqib was her folly.

For several months she had been unraveling this plan of sending Saqib to school, until it dawned on her that the enthusiasm flowed more from her than from him. This conversation about his future, practiced between the two of them, had been the playground of their intimacy, the Memsahib and the village boy with the bright eyes and quick mind, and so it had surprised her that when she began taking concrete steps to enroll him in classes, he shyly asked her to wait, to give him a few years.

"I'm already learning so much here, here in Lahore and at Al-Unmool, Bibi Jee. In a year or two, then I will do as you like," he said, "but for now let this be."

He spoke as of a magical passage in his life, and she was touched, and after that she did not send for applications or talk to the people who could move the matter forward.

*

Now, beside the pool and private behind the walls that Saqib had built, they sat long, the mosquitoes kept away by a pedestal fan, even the wiring along the wall thought through, a plug just where they wanted it. Hisham puffed away at a cigar right to the stub, which always indicated a deep felicity in him, and Shahnaz drank slightly more than she usually did, wife raising her glass to the husband. As night fell, swallows skimmed the water and zigzagged through the air, rending the porcelain of evening, like a crack running through a cup.

*

Despite having been brought up mostly abroad—her parents were diplomats, recently retired to Canada after her father crowned his career with an ambassadorship to Vienna—Shahnaz had a better intuitive grasp of the characters around the farm than her husband did. On returning to Pakistan and marrying Hisham, she had accepted as a necessity not to be shirked the duties of being mistress to their feudal estate. She saw the position from the outside, however, through the lens of her Western politics and experience, so that she was conscious in this role, where her husband and relatives acted by instinct. This disabused her of Hisham and his crowd's belief that all the players in the game were equally satisfied with the way it was played. For starters, she didn't take seriously the lip service the managers and others paid to Hisham's feudal status. "It's an old business," she said. "The locals puffed up the Brits for two centuries and told the white sahibs how clever they were and how they couldn't be fooled—all the while plucking them thoroughly—and now they're using the same tactic on you. It's so darling of you all to believe them!"

"Stop it, you know I don't like it."

"Look at you, all ruffled feathers. Those are the ones they pluck."

The head manager at Ranmal Mohra, ever since the overthrow of the great Sheikh Abbas in the 1970s, was a massive phlegmatic figure named Rana Abdul Sattar, who had the misfortune to be the particular object of Shahnaz's satirical humor. Poor Rana Sahib (who was not, by the way, poor at all, for he'd liberally rewarded himself over the years for his loosely supervised labors managing the business) would sit in the garden with Hisham after one of their tours around the farm, pear-shaped head, pear-shaped body, looking as if he'd melted into his chair, gloomy eyes, painfully slow with his pronouncements and suggestions, and if Shahnaz happened to come by, making her way about her flower beds, she would stop and sit and have a cup of tea and crackle and snap around him and make him uncomfortable with her airy humorous manners and double entendre.

"It's indecent, really," Hisham would say afterward, but he too found it amusing to watch her rake Rana Sahib down, all of it conducted with an angelic expression. "Let him be, poor thing, he's old enough to be your father, you know."

"Just because he pretends to be slow doesn't mean that he's not crooked as a dog's hind leg. I've seen the expressions he makes behind your back. Everyone around here is terrified of him, you know. When you're not here he's lord and master, after all. And I'm sure he makes us pay for every one of my digs in thousand-rupee notes. He probably keeps track of every crack I make in that little notebook of his. I'd love to have a look at that someday, by the way. And then you're not here and—pop!—he smokes your cigars and wears your silk pajamas and sleeps in our conjugal bed."

"That's a horrible thought! Rana Sahib in pajamas."

"Oh, yes. Your pinstripe silks. And then he calls in one of those doe-eyed girls from the village and absorbs them. He envelops them—real protoplasm stuff—and then they're gone forever with a slurping sound."

All was sweet between husband and wife then; their best moments were when Shahnaz grew wicked and humorous—their marriage, more than thirty years on, had reached that stage where romance turns to guarded toleration, the pair social partners, the bower of love now a public square.

✳

Thus, when Hisham announced, a couple of days after they arrived at Ranmal Mohra, that he wanted to go ahead with a new line of business that they had been discussing, Shahnaz's first comment was, "I hope you're not planning to put Rana Sahib in charge? That man's about as dynamic as this noodle."

They were eating lunch by the pool, a puttanesca whipped up by Saqib.

Through the years, and more lately, Shahnaz had involved herself in their business affairs, for she understood that security and power ultimately derived from the business, the money. She skirmished around the edges of the enterprise, finding no direct entry because she was a woman.

"Why not? He's been running this place for thirty years, and he does a pretty good job. I make as much as any of the farmers around here."

"Don't kid yourself, my love. You make as much as any farmer around here who's a member in good standing of the Punjab Club. The real farmers around here are richer than us even though they still drive motorcycles. Or rather, because they still drive motorcycles."

"I don't know where you pick up this stuff. But I suppose you're right."

"I keep my eyes open, but most of all, I study the Russians. Turgenev. Joking aside, you should try it."

"I have, I did."

"In college, between toga parties and beer bongs. Anyway, this thing is super complicated. Rana Sahib can't do it. You need somebody young."

"Ah, I see," said Hisham, looking at his wife over the tops of his glasses. "Let me guess who you have in mind. Your Saqib project, part two."

And with these fateful words Saqib got his big break.

*

The principle of using household servants in an executive capacity had been established, strangely enough, by Colonel Atar. Colonel Sahib was old school, meaning he was trained at Dehradun and the Indian Military Academy before Partition, and had absorbed deep in his fibers a respect for British tradition and manners that could still be seen in his upright posture and choleric bearing, his bristling mustache, the silver on his dining table, his fondness for dogs, his shooting and riding, his khakis and tweeds, his accent, and, most significantly, his views of the role and bearing proper to the lower classes.

Plainly Colonel Sahib could not be considered a man of revolutionary principles, and it had therefore been a remarkable day when he took his chauffeur, Bayazid, into his confidence and even into his heart, an organ not notable for its warmth. Perhaps it was his age—the Colonel Sahib was in his graying fifties when Yazid joined his service, as a shaggy genial youth—and perhaps also that Colonel Atar had already then begun to consider himself a man of a previous era, and therefore ripe to assume various eccentricities, including dispensing with niceties of class when it amused him to. The long-retired colonel began to use Yazid not just as a personal servant, but as a source of information and even advice regarding his businesses, peppering him with questions about the goings-on at Ranmal Mohra and among his factory managers, during their long drives on the old Grand Trunk Road between Lahore and Islamabad, where the colonel intermittently served in government or played an intemperate part in the opposition. Yazid was not a tattletale, took no pleasure in exposing wrongdoing, believed in service and loyalty, and had no ambition to be anything other than a driver. These qualities, which his astute master conceded, gave his words weight.

It was in this context and with this precedent that Hisham—meaning Shahnaz, really—resolved to put Saqib in charge of the new enterprise, reasoning that Yazid would supervise and Saqib provide the energy. Though he was only twenty-one at the time, and looked even younger with his wisp of a mustache and cheeks that barely needed shaving, Saqib undoubtedly had the presence and initiative and intelligence to make a go of it.

"Are you sure? He's smart enough, but isn't he a bit green?" said Shahnaz to Hisham as they sat over toast and marmalade in the dining room at Ranmal Mohra. She had already made up her mind, and now was pretending reluctance as a way of bringing Hisham on board, these almost unnecessary subterfuges of a wife who for years had been playing three-dimensional chess with her hapless mate quite without his knowledge.

Poor Hisham, as she regarded him at such junctures, could be obtuse. "Perhaps you're right. He's just a kid, and he has no idea of business. Plus, I hate to lose such a good valet."

"Valet? Saqib? *Pffh.*" Shahnaz was elaborately buttering her toast, which she regarded as an art, one that she absorbed as a diplomat brat among the Europeans. "You're not just wasting him packing your suits and making your drinks the way you like them—you'll even be wasting him on your vegetable startup. I still say that boy should be sent to university, if only he knew English. Not that he doesn't, by the way, but I doubt his spelling."

"I suppose he learned it by watching our lips," said Hisham. "Like some super-intelligent dog."

"Dog! You're worse than your Colonel Sahib."

III

*T*he plan was this. Forty years ago, in the 1960s, the channel of the Indus adjoining Ranmal Mohra had shifted slightly to the west, toward Balochistan, exposing on the eastern bank several hundred acres of extremely fertile soil—bottomland. Colonel Atar had taken possession of this, as was his right, for the family had a long-established claim to the lands ceded by the river, among the shifting creeks and channels. There had been some trouble with his neighbors at the time, who challenged the claim, but the colonel was then in government and had swatted them down, softening the blow by not bringing the land under cultivation but using it as a *rakh*, or hunting ground. When Hisham returned to Pakistan after college in 1976, one of his first acts, in the bloom of vigorous youth, had been to clear the land and plant sugarcane there, the bristling neighbors long blunted by their patriarch's death and a subsequent political eclipse.

Driving back and forth from Lahore to Ranmal Mohra during the past year and more, Saqib had drawn Hisham and Shahnaz to observe that prosperous small farmers were increasingly planting vegetables in plastic greenhouse tunnels, bringing the produce to market in winter, when prices were several times what they were during the summer season. It cost a fortune to build the tunnels and the risk of failure was high, but managed properly the thing could make a small farmer into a large one in just a few years, for the kind of man who had the perseverance and wit to jump on this bandwagon also had the temperament to use the proceeds for buying land rather than taking trips to the city and hiring dancing girls. As they drove along, Saqib would casually point out one and then another of these enterprises, the plastic sheets that covered the long tunnels reflecting the winter light and looking high-tech and interesting compared to the green-caped fields of sugarcane, wheat, and fodder.

No one—other than one fellow over by Sargodha, who had first brought the hybrid seed and technology from Europe, and who had become a byword among farmers for his prosperity and shrewdness—had done this on a truly large scale, however. The Sargodha farmer, Chaudrey Gul Nawaz Warraich, now ran a kind of franchise, selling the imported plastic sheeting and the imported seed to new entrants, and throwing in his technical knowledge for free, for his interests were well aligned with his customers', each success story leading to more clients. Pakistan's population was booming, if nothing else in the country was, and there was little danger of the prices falling precipitously, especially because of the high barriers to entry into this business. Now, on that bottomland by the river, Hisham would establish a large tunnel farm and go dancing all the way to the bank. Saqib would set this up, with Yazid's help, starting small—say fifteen acres—and continuing till they had more tunnels than anyone but God, or at least till they were God's acknowledged munshis in all Punjab.

*

Yazid and Saqib drove up to meet Warraich in the farm jeep, a rattling vehicle that in prouder days had borne the great Zulfikar Bhutto himself through a series of meetings and rallies arranged by the colonel in the district, and now served more prosaically to shuttle the head manager, Rana Sahib, about his noodling errands to police station and assistant commissioner's office. Yazid sat relaxed in the passenger seat, hands in his lap, showing his complete confidence in his apprentice's driving skills by his inattention to the mad traffic.

"Oh God, not another one!" groaned Yazid, as Saqib turned

toward a little patch of vegetable tunnels visible in the distance along a farm track. It was September now, the weather still warm, and the farmers were just beginning to prepare the tunnels, installing six-foot-tall hoops of steel piping, like a snake's ribs, and then stretching plastic sheeting over them. This was the third farm that Saqib had turned in to visit, making what should have been a four-hour trip up to Sargodha into what would clearly be an all-day affair.

"Don't worry, Uncle. We'll reward ourselves with the meal of our lives in Sargodha. There's a place they do a famous tandoori quail there and it's just the end of the season now; the birds are still passing through. I asked this guy who comes from there. You'll see."

"Quail! What use is a quail? I feel like you've been beating me with sticks, crashing along into every farm you see, and then you talk about quail. Have you seen the size of those things? They're like sparrows."

"Well, you can have a hundred if you like. We're on the farm expense account now."

At each place they visited, Saqib would stand with the owner writing notes in a pad, his questions unfolding leisurely, not satisfied with the original answers, the farmers at first perfunctory and then animated and explicit. The sort of men who went into tunnel farming—that painstaking and risky innovation—were invariably either dreamers or cranks, the former most likely headed for failure, the latter cucumber-cool detail freaks. The former would pile on improbabilities, a fortune almost in hand, one extravagance capping another, while the latter were suspicious and taciturn and discouraging, not wanting another entrant into the business. Either way, Saqib with his notebook and his pretended ignorance and his sober, tentative manner soon had them singing out their secrets. At the second farm, Yazid settled down on a charpoy when Saqib asked to take a stroll about the place. By the third, he could barely be convinced to leave the jeep.

✻

When they reached the big tunnel operation in Sargodha, however, Saqib took a different approach. The place looked like one of the old British military farms, where paint and polish ruled, with the trunks of trees whitewashed to a height of three or four feet, the road leading to the main dera packed hard with powdered red brick dust, and a central office resembling one in a well-run Lahore business headquarters, with a tarmac car park and plantings of cypress trees in rows. There was a proper sitting room for visitors, plastic flowers in vases, walls fresh-painted, tea brought quickly and served by a peon of the sort more commonly seen in the more senior government officers' anterooms, clean-dressed and with manners. Out front, a new black Land Cruiser jeep sparkled, with a driver polishing it, seemingly catching the specks of dust before they could land.

A junior manager came in with the tea and sat down with them, but Saqib did not bring up business at all, instead chatting about general affairs, as if they had come to pay a social visit. Saqib had given their antecedents—from Ranmal Mohra, managers for Mr. Hisham Atar Sahib—and when finally the man asked their business, he said, "Hisham Atar Sahib has asked us to speak with Chaudrey Gul Nawaz Warraich Sahib personally. If Chaudrey Sahib has time to offer us, of course." Yazid said nothing, but sat immovable and placid, leaving Saqib to his maneuvers.

Slightly nonplussed, the manager went out and was gone for ten or fifteen minutes. Returning, he said, "Ji, Chaudrey Sahib will see you now."

They were led out into the gallery and then into a large and very brightly lit room, with a sofa and comfortable chairs to one side, arranged around a coffee table, and at the end of the room an imposing desk, behind which sat Chaudrey Sahib himself, two pens bristling up from an executive pen holder, and three telephones in a row before him, one of them for some reason bright red. He rose to greet them, polite, but brisk.

Chaudrey Warraich was a tall figure of fifty or so wearing an unusually fine shalvar kameez, not white but cream, and a black vest of the sort worn by politicians. Unlike most Pakistani businessman, he was slender, almost gaunt, with a long hooked nose and a bronze face, like an Afghan, his hair dyed gleaming black and parted to one side, the face made more striking by a single black mole just above the left corner of his lip, as if painted there. As soon as he sat down again, he reached forward and took an imported cigarette from a packet, lit it, and then studied the two men seated before him through a cloud of smoke.

Dispensing with the usual preliminaries, he said, "So I understand that you come from Ranmal Mohra. I visited your farm, several years ago. I didn't meet you then."

After a nod to Bayazid, who sat impassively, he addressed himself entirely to Saqib.

Saqib nodded. "Mian Hisham Atar Sahib is a progressive farmer. He has different men who work for him in different capacities."

"Yes. I recall the senior man, a Rana Sahib. He seemed more of the old school."

"Rana Sahib is the tree under whose shade the rest of us work."

"In that case you're well sheltered indeed."

This might have been taken as a reference to Rana Sahib's bulk. A look of understanding, almost of humor, passed between the two men, and Warraich now relaxed and settled back and put on a more genial expression toward Saqib.

"And you're the front man for Mian Hisham Atar Sahib's new venture, are you? I got wind of that. Well, let's see how we can work this out."

Not bad, thought Saqib. By some means, Warraich knew of their plans, which he had concealed from all the staff at Ranmal Mohra.

"You're well informed, Chaudrey Sahib."

"I'm based in Lahore, and there, as you may know, word gets around. It's like a village. Everyone speaks of each other's businesses, and Hisham Atar Sahib's business is of interest to many."

Warraich at first treated the subject of the tunnels in a superficial manner, but soon he and Saqib were discussing the technicalities in detail, Saqib giving as good as he received, and catching War-raich out on a question of the correct moment to water cucumbers in order to prevent flower drop. Warraich began to enjoy himself, Saqib moving the subject and quick with response and respectful yet firm, drawing the other man into areas that he would prefer not to touch upon, the source of the seeds in Holland, the question of other suppliers for plastic sheeting and for the nets on which certain vegetables were trained.

✶

It had not been easy finding Baba Kareem Tikka house, or, rather, it was easy to find Baba Kareem Tikka houses in general—there were five of them so named within a few hundred meters of one another—but Saqib was determined to find the real one, the original.

"How about this?" suggested Yazid, pointing to a large establishment with a plate glass front, the customers sitting under bright lights displayed to the world. "If you want fancy, that's it."

"Are you kidding? That's Baba Kareem's third cousin's younger son. They're selling rats with the front legs removed as quail, you can count on it. No, we want the grimiest one of all."

It was no use asking. The passersby would give them a flat look and say, "It's all Baba Kareem. This whole intersection. You can see."

Finally Saqib located the right establishment, the original, and they were seated on a filthy charpoy, in a filthier room.

"Why do you care which restaurant, boy?" asked Yazid. "You eat like a quail yourself."

"I'm more of a spectator. I want to see what a big man like you can do to a tiny little bird after a long day in the saddle."

A plump boy with a hardened expression plonked a metal jug of water on the table and a little steel plate with cut onions, tomatoes, and chilies. Looking over their heads, at the traffic cruising past outside, he recited in a singsong voice, no break between the words, "Chicken piece mutton piece beef chargah fish piece Kabuli pilau . . ."

He came up for a breath of air, pausing his litany.

"Fish?" asked Saqib. "Fish? In Sargodha? Is that the golden carp?"

The boy, who was barely aware of their presence, stopped at this, like a dog finding a fault in a scent.

"Golden?"

"Is the fish the one with the gold?"

"Gold?"

"Who's asking questions here, you or me? I asked about the golden carp and you just keep saying 'gold' back to me."

The boy had returned to earth and was now actually aware of their presence, as more than two mouths attached to wallets.

"We don't have any golden anything."

"Bright boy. How about golden quail?"

Off he went. "Roast quail quail pilau half quail masalah full quail masalah . . ."

Saqib stopped him. "Okay, okay, we get it. Just bring us the quail, a plate of each dish, however you do it."

Now he had the boy's attention. "One of each? You sure? What-ever you want."

When he'd gone Yazid remarked, "That's going to be a lot of food. He figures we're some rich Chaudreys from out of town."

"Well, I guess we are. And they're used to that. They'll bring us the best."

"And then charge us for it."

"We've earned it. I learned more today than if I'd gone to school to learn tunnel farming in Holland." He pronounced it "Haw-land," as Warraich had, picking up the terms of art.

"Holland? Why Holland?"

"Didn't you see? All that stuff that Warraich sells comes from Holland. That's why we have to buy through him. You and I don't know anyone in Holland."

"What about in the bazaar?"

After they left the Warraich farm, Saqib had insisted they go through Sargodha bazaar and get prices on all the equipment, the nets, the seed, the wire.

"No, the stuff in the bazaar is no good. That's why I wanted to see it. Now we know what the fake stuff looks like also. Warraich runs his business making sure we do well. He'll charge more and then we can count on it."

"You know, boy, I'm not quite sure when you learned how to be such a businessman. You're making me nervous."

"I'll tell you one thing. I'll make sure that we have the best tunnel farm around."

"What does that mean, if I may ask? Bigger cucumbers?"

"More of them. Isn't that what we're trying to do? You know how things are at Ranmal Mohra. I think it's worth shaking it up."

"Right now, at least it works. You shake it up and then suddenly the pieces don't fit anymore."

"Don't worry, Uncle. I'll catch them in the air and put them back gently."

"I keep hearing about you doing this and you doing that, my boy."

Saqib laughed. "Well, it's us together, and a lot more of you than of me. It's like the recipe for horse and pigeon pie. You know how it goes. 'Take one horse and one pigeon, put them in a large saucepan . . .'"

"Don't tell me you're going to start about my weight right before dinner."

"I'm just kidding with you, Ustad Jee. You're the bigger part of this project, joking aside. You're the one they trust. Hisham Sahib put you on to keep an eye on me."

"Then I'm responsible, but it sounds like you're doing the planning and the work."

"Lucky you! Yours is the easy part."

Yazid smiled at Saqib affectionately. "I brought you up, boy, but I'm not sure where I went wrong. You're too clever by half."

When the serving boy handed them the bill, folded on a plate, Saqib took it and then pulled a big wad of cash from his pocket, many thousands of rupees, the advance that he'd drawn from the manager in Lahore, on Hisham's instructions, and very much against the manager's inclination. He counted off the bills, intent, licking his finger to count.

"That used to be me," said Yazid, pointing at the boy, who had gone to get change. "Look at life. I used to be that, and now I drive around in a Mercedes four-door saloon."

"But you don't own it."

"I don't need to."

"Anyway, now we can say we've eaten our fill of the famous Baba Kareem quail. No one can take that away from us."

IV

A late afternoon in October, a tractor straining to pull a culti-
vator plow through the rich soil of Saqib's plot, throwing a
lace of black diesel smoke upward to hang there for a moment and
then disperse into the air, a fading memory. Munshi Abdul Sattar
had given over to him with bad grace a fifteen-acre plot, less than
Saqib had asked for, but as much as he expected—at the remotest
edge of the farm, toward the Indus, the river at that place several
kilometers wide when in spate, braided and immense, a river at a
scale greater than ordinary landscape.

By the river, though just thirty minutes of potholed road from
Ranmal Mohra, the texture of life changed, of manners even. Many
of the people there were Machhi, a fishing caste, and lived by the
rhythms of the river, patient when mending nets, knowing the
spawning times, the seasons when fish disappeared into the depths,
out early and back late, and thinking of the towns as a different
world, because the people there were not governed by the rhythms
of the great Indus, its fish and fowl, drownings and its bounty,
riches given up, enormous hauls of river carp or even valuables floating through after floods and caught by some lucky man, a Machhi,
who could navigate the catastrophe. Outlaws lived there too, men
on the run and men with bad intentions toward the settlements, the
little shopkeepers round about afraid of the gangs who camped on
uninhabited islands in the river, and whose criminality had more
bravado than substance, men desperate and steeling themselves to
stick a gun in some poor fellow's ribs on a dark night.

There stood Saqib, watching the tractor comb over the field back and forth, preparing the bed for his venture. He and Chaudrey Warraich from Sargodha were often on the phone that fall, and one fine day a truck arrived at the site laden with steel pipe, motorcycle clutch wire to pull it all taut—the best wire available—rolls of nets for trellising, plastic sheeting to cover the structures he would build, all the material he would need to move his plan forward. Saqib's new-hired men had built a little room to keep his sprays and tools and fertilizer, throwing it together of cheap half-fired bricks and mud for plaster, keeping his costs down. For weeks now he'd been sleeping there too, in the evening bicycling several kilo-meters for food to a tea stall perched at a crossroads, whatever they had, getting to know the miserable peasants who lived out that way.

✿

Away from the east, coming from the settled area, from Ranmal Mohra, he saw a cloud of dust thrown up, a car approaching along a stretch of road that had washed out in a flood years ago and never been repaired, laden trolleys stuck there after rains, the silicate dust there piled knee deep in places. Saqib watched the car approaching, to this dead end, alert because of the isolation there. It resolved into a tiny Suzuki car, then to a particular one, Munshi Rana Abdul Sattar's new wheels. Saqib had been expecting this visit for several weeks, knowing that the old man would be coming to make terms with him, especially now that he saw Saqib meant business, with all the supplies coming in like the circus come to town.

He stood there cool and upright, hands by his sides, watching the car approach and park. Rana Sahib pulled himself out—the car fit him like a box, and he could easily have afforded a larger one but dared not flaunt his riches in front of Hisham. Only when the manager had come halfway to meet him did Saqib walk over.

"Come, come, Rana Sahib. Let me send the boy for some tea."

"All right, make it tea, then."

Rana Sahib dropped his bulk on a charpoy, sideways, and Saqib pulled up his one brand-new chair, part of his shopping: that chair, some cookware, a torch.

"You're settling in here, young man." Rana Sahib seemed not too thrilled about Saqib's arrangements.

"Well, I can certainly never be as comfortably settled as you are, sir, at Ranmal Mohra."

The insinuation was not lost on the wily old man.

"This *is* Ranmal Mohra. Though now that you mention it, Balochistan is across the river, and it's not that far either. Be careful some of those Khosas and Legharis don't swim over and steal your pots and pans one night."

Now it was Saqib's turn to read between the lines. The old manager could probably find men over there in the tribal areas who would gladly be given a green light to steal away with Saqib's machinery and perhaps kidnap him along for a bonus. Across the river men were sold like sheep, passed along through the tribes till they ended up head down in a hole somewhere in Waziristan waiting for a ransom to be paid.

"Oh, they can have the pots and pans. The main thing is to keep Mian Sahib's business running."

"It is running, boy," growled the manager. "I know that, because I've been running it since well before you were pupped."

Saqib recoiled, genuinely distressed by the crudity of the manager's approach. "Please, Rana Sahib. We all know what it is. I respect you, and if the truth be told, I could have come about this all a different way."

"What different way? You're talking like that because you've managed to slip into the Sahib's ear and sit there whispering and humming."

Saqib knew he must stand up to the manager. He had carefully planned this scenario, right down to the flash of anger that he allowed himself now.

"Oh no, not at all. I'm not the whispering type. If I were, if I really started whispering, who knows what I would have to say? Let's not pretend. You've got nothing on me, but I know so much about the farm business. They keep talking about some little scheme you have with the sugar mill, and they don't just talk about your having separate permits from the mill, they keep talking about the details. You have three secret permit-books, and you send a load from the farm to be registered on one of your books every two or three days." He made a dismissive gesture. "I could tell you by tomorrow exactly how many loads you took last season. You know how it is, Manager Sahib. The higher you stand the more visible you are. And you stand highest of all."

Rana Sahib struggled to his feet. "I didn't come here to play around with a green little fellow like you. Do your worst, then. We'll see. They come and go, but I'm still in charge thirty years later. Don't forget, it's Colonel Atar Sahib that I answer to. Hisham Sahib is still learning. I know men like you. You come here and have new ideas, but in this country, there's only one idea that matters. Money. I've got it, you don't. It's not difficult to scribble out some papers and talk to a few men, and suddenly a poor fellow falls into a sea of trouble. It may surprise you to find that a lack of imagination is not one of my weaknesses, contrary to what our benevolent masters may think."

"Is that a threat?"

"Let's just say that nothing happens on this farm unless I'm part of it. Not for long, anyway."

At this dry moment the boy fortunately returned carrying a pot of tea in a yellow tin kettle and two cheap white ceramic cups printed with roses.

Saqib, who had stood when the manager did, now gestured at the charpoy. "Please sit down, Rana Sahib. We've gotten onto the wrong footing here. Have a cup of tea. The fruits of your imagination lay all around us. You made this farm, and I only want to make a small addition to that. Our interests are the same."

"Since when did a fellow like you have interests? You're a house servant, and your service there isn't much to talk about. You've been there what, five years?"

"Six years. But that's not the point. The point is that I carry some weight, and you carry some weight."

"What do you want, boy?"

"I want to be left alone. Let me do this my way."

"I want twenty percent of your little portion."

"Twenty percent of nothing is nothing. I'm not planning to keep anything on the side."

The manager seemed genuinely to find this funny. He put down his cup, which he had drained in three gulps, and grinned. "Fifteen percent then, you fox. Let's not banter here."

"I'm serious."

"Why are your books separate, then? Why not put your accounts with the rest of the farm books?"

Knowing that he would be opposed by Rana Sahib, Saqib had managed to bend Hisham's ear to his purpose, not at Ranmal Mohra, when the old munshi could be called in for consultation, but in Lahore. The upshot of their conversation was that the vegetable farm would be run separately from the rest of the operation at Ranmal Mohra—much cleaner that way—with a new bank account and separate books.

Now, sitting by the river with the victim of these machinations, Saqib knew the moment of truth had come.

"I didn't do that. Bayazid did. He insisted."

"Come on, little boy. I wasn't born yesterday. Bayazid is about as interested in this business as I am in women's footwear."

"He's the one who spoke with Hisham Sahib. You can ask him."

"I'm sure you've told him what to tell me also."

Saqib permitted his temper to rise. "Don't talk about Bayazid in front of me. You know and I know and everyone knows what he is."

"Yes, he's the big screen behind which you'll play your little game."

"Little or big, he's all the screen I need. You know that even Colonel Sahib trusts him completely."

The manager saw himself defeated, and with a gesture folded his cards. "All right then. It's almost time for my prayers. Let's leave it at that."

"But you can say your prayers here, Manager Sahib."

"I suppose someone should, since you never do. You see? I know all about it, I know if you pray, I know if you don't. For that matter, I know what time you go out to take a shit and where you do it too."

This too was a threat, to spread about that Saqib was impious. Saqib brushed it aside.

"Give me a year, Rana Sahib. You can make it very difficult for me, I know. Just one year, and then we'll speak again. I understand how the system works, and I'm no revolutionary trying to throw everything into confusion. I want to build up this business. Many mouths can be fed from a large pot, once it's full."

Now Rana Sahib did get up, and, putting his hand on Saqib's shoulder, walked back to his car. Sitting down into it with a heavy motion, he rolled down the window and said, "One year then, young man. But this isn't negotiable—you'll put two names on your payroll, and you'll send me the salaries. Make up any two names you like."

"As you wish, Rana Sahib."

✻

Next morning, Saqib pedaled to the Kèrala farmhouse, where he found Yazid still asleep in the little room that he had commandeered behind the kitchen. He was lying with a bar of sun almost across his face, massive head surrounded by curly hair on a greasy pillow, huge, cracked feet poking up, and snoring. Saqib knew that, left to his devices, he might sleep thus until noon. What an ox! He rolled Yazid back and forth, like a boat stuck in the mud.

"All right, all right, what's the hurry!" slurred Yazid, still recumbent, opening one eye, a sweet smile developing over his face. "Oh, they were wonderful. First it was little birds and then they were girls and they were singing. You shouldn't have woken me."

"Quail, I suppose."

"You and your quail," he whispered. After a long moment, he said thoughtfully, "It's true, I still remember those little things and you could even eat the bones. The only part of your damned vegetable business I've liked is that dinner we had." He sat up. "How's your operation out by the river?"

"Our operation, remember? Hisham Sahib put you in charge, and if it goes upside down you're the one with his neck in the noose."

"My neck can take it."

Saqib had gotten a cup of tea and a paratha from the girl in the kitchen, and now he produced these.

"Oh, you darling! Give that here."

Like other fat and gluttonous people, Yazid approached his food warily at first, as if addressing a problem. Rolling his legs sideways, bare feet hanging in the air and kicking idly, he took a little scrap of the paratha, then a mincing sip of the steaming sugary tea.

"So, I've had a visit from Rana Sahib," reported Saqib.

"Sit down, boy. You're making me nervous."

Saqib coiled himself down on the charpoy and went so far as to place his hand for a moment on his mentor's knee, like a jockey touching the withers of a restive horse.

"And . . . ?"

"He wants me to put two men on the payroll. Or rather, he wants me to send him the salary for two people."

"Then he damned well better send the men. I'll talk to Hisham Sahib. Anyway, I'm going to Lahore tomorrow. You don't need me here, and Hisham Sahib doesn't have a proper driver, and frankly you can keep your village life. In the past week I've seen three snakes. I'm afraid of those things, I'm a city boy."

"No, that's the point. We've won, and cheaply too. I can afford two extra *baildar* salaries, this business is big enough to handle that. But now Rana Sahib is on board. He's lazy, he won't come out and check on me, so long as I keep sending the money. And the guys I've hired can easily take up the slack. The harder I work them, the better. Get them used to it."

Saqib had taken great care when hiring men, three of them Machhi-caste boys from the river settlements, all very young: a boy of fifteen whose parents had died in a bus accident, two others of equally precarious position, and then, to break up whatever coalition these boys might devise, a Christian from a little settlement pinched there among the Muslims. They would be grateful for the job, and they would be entirely his men—no one else wanted them or would give them a chance.

Yazid shook his head. "You know, sometimes I worry about you. Why would you leave your cushy job curling around Mian Sahib's legs—I won't speak of Bibi Jee—to come out here and get chased by jackals and these snakes and by Rana Sahib and all that. You like money too much, or you think about it too much."

"It's not the money, it's the operation."

"Your problem is that you're too tight wound. It's like your driving. I tell you to keep your hands loose and sloppy on the wheel, and you shoot down the road as if you're on rails. You'll get a heart attack someday. Operation shoperation. You're growing cucumbers, for God's sake."

"I wouldn't talk about heart attacks if I were you. The only reason you're sticking around here is because that wretched woman in the kitchen lets you eat as much as you like. And then you go insulting the food too! I should warn you, she's got her eye on you. That's how these village women work, in through the stomach, out through the heart, like a needle."

V

*H*iring a tractor by the hour because Rana Sahib would not send the farm tractors on time, pushing his men, himself working into the night, Saqib got the hooped ribs of the tunnels set, the plastic sheeting pulled onto the ribs, the seeds planted. None of this was easy, for neither he nor the men had done it before. He tenderly watched the expensive Dutch seeds reaching up out of the ground, expressions of life and vitality, finding the little seedlings whimsical, their curling paths up into the light, the vegetable kingdom bearing the stamp of fantasy. His men hung netting inside the tunnels, then later carefully wove the growing cucumber shoots into the lattice of the nets, and he worked alongside them, hours and days of toil over fifteen acres. People from the area would stop alongside his fields to see this strange enterprise coming to life, and they regarded him with the skepticism of peasant farmers whose ways have remained unchanged for hundreds of years, conservative from living close to the land and barely making it pay.

Bayazid departed for Lahore as soon as he could plausibly do so and did not come back for several months, and, as it happened, Hisham and Shahnaz went abroad to New York, so that Saqib was left quite alone managing his expensive business there by the river. Though his parents' house was just half an hour bicycle ride away, he went only twice that fall, going at dusk and eating whatever meal his mother had happened to cook. She too was skeptical, and kept her own counsel, and even his father found it unnatural that his son barely into his twenties should engage in these innovations and presume to play a munshi's role, and so he kept away and asked no questions.

The belt on either side of the Indus, brushed by floods, subject to inundation when the course of the river shifts as it does through the decades, is one of the last wild places left in the Punjab Plain, and that wildness appealed to Saqib's austere soul, the shrieking of the waterbirds and the silent flighting ducks fast skimming the water or cutting along high up in their skeins. For days on end he spoke only with his men, and with them he maintained a distance, eating separately from them and taking the trouble to keep himself immaculate, fresh clothes each morning and washing himself from a bucket each night after the men left, whereas they lived in sweat and dirt, inured to it.

Although a great deal of money passed through Saqib's hands, it had not occurred to Hisham to increase his salary—advancing a servant boy so high seemed award enough—and so Saqib was still paid as a middling servant at the Lahore house. A month's salary barely covered twenty meters of white cloth bought one day when he went to Multan, twenty thousand for cloth seeming insignificant when he spent two lacs on spray that same morning, finer material than a fieldhand would wear, but he must maintain appearances, the local tailor running up seven shalvar kameez so that he could change every day. The radio he bought kept him company under the stars, after his workers went home, when he sat beside a little fire before going early to sleep, and he could hardly be expected to shuttle around on the ancient bicycle that the kitchen boys at the farmhouse used, and so purchased a new one. Saqib kept track of these expenses in a little notebook separate from his farm ledgers.

The system did not just tolerate theft on a small scale but assumed it. Without ever having given it much thought, Hisham paid his workers and servants and even his munshis on the same principle as his father and grandfather, going back to the Sikh times, when these lands were run as a little principality. He conceded something like a living wage, vaguely aware that employees might nibble off more, though not accepting it, each dependent finding his own level, cooks notorious for padding bills, thirty-year munshis accumulating small fortunes, concealing their state and retiring well-off unless they gobbled too much and were whacked down and forced to disgorge the bigger chunks. Many hundreds of people subsisted off the farm—they called the Atar family a great banyan, with whole villages sheltering under it. No feudal would offer a fair wage to all, from the small to the mighty, the cowherd to the powerful men at the pinnacle. The withered hag—Abishag—who sweeps the dera threshing floors each morning is fed rather than paid, filching away plates of uneaten food, bolting it down in corners, and secretly carrying away old bottles and old rags to the dark room where she lives out her days.

So Saqib also took what he needed, different from the others only because he kept track so carefully. During his years in the Lahore house Saqib had never handled money, and so had not been tempted to keep a little something to the side. His father, gardening at the Ranmal Mohra house, never stole anything, for he too never had any opportunity, even if that had been his temperament, which it wasn't. But all around, when Saqib was a boy, the munshis stole and were credited for it, their underlings expectant and hoping that they would be caught, and yet admiring their daring and envying their possessions. From the Atars, Saqib learned the value of appearances, of culture, the ways in which power is exercised through manners, but Hisham certainly didn't embody any high morality—Saqib had been disabused of that early on, as when he saw his master with his head buried between their pale foreign hostess's legs, sprawled on a chaise longue, so wicked and desirable. Now, toiling in the vegetable patch, doing so much and making so much for the Atars, Saqib was troubled by these little thefts, felt them beneath him, and yet also found pleasure in taking what he needed and desired. The power of these little thefts invigorated him, and though he was confused in his loyalties to Hisham and particularly to Shahnaz, at bottom he did not think himself debased.

✳

As with most new enterprises, managing the vegetables proved even more difficult than Saqib had imagined. The fifteen acres were planted to cucumber, the tendrils trained up onto netting hung in the center of the tunnels, and the plants grew so fast that soon they threatened to reach the top of the nets. When he cut back on nitrogen fertilizer, they stalled and withered. Plagues of aphids chewed the leaves, and the spray he bought from a local dealer turned out to be fake Chinese rubbish. He was keen, vigilant, present, and these challenges intensified his determination, silent and alone there out by the river. Imagining himself failing, he avoided going into Ranmal Mohra, by sheer willpower keeping the plants not thriving but growing. He made it his.

Chaudrey Warraich from Sargodha had steered Saqib right. "Stick to cucumbers, forget about chilies and tomatoes and all that crap. Some idiot's doing cut flowers, gladiolas from Holland, but that's not going to work, I guarantee—I know, I sold him the bulbs. Treat those cukes like every little plant's your firstborn son. There's one rule: Be a maniac about spray—do it every day, as if they handed out those chemicals for free—and be a miser for everything else. You're a smart boy. You'll see. You should be in your tunnels every morning and every night and all day too. You study your problem, boy, and you'll mint money, for yourself or for Mian Hisham Atar." He grinned. "Maybe for both!"

Saqib had started out too big—fifteen acres of cucumbers made him already larger than anyone for many miles around Ranmal Mohra—but he managed it, everywhere all day around the farm and half the night tending to his books, checking and double-checking the figures, alarmed by costs, the devil in the details, watering, spray schedules, bug attacks, mildew blooms, bags of fertilizer, every paisa in and out. He even kept a notebook with his observations, like a diary, schooling himself for next year. When he sent out the last bag, on May 17, he bought his men an enormous sagging carton of sweetmeats, slick with ghee, the largest that could be found in the market, coconut barfi, almond barfi, date barfi, chunky balls of sugar cooked in oil to a brown sweetness, a white sweetness, ladoo, chum chum, ghulab jaman. The four men, minus the two ghosts whose salaries went to Munshi Abdul Sattar, couldn't possibly eat it all. He sat with them after the last sacks of cucumber had been packed off to market in Multan, and they ate till their bellies squeaked, and the men then took the rest home, each carrying a bundle of sweets wrapped up in newspaper. That night maybe for the first time their families would eat as many sweetmeats as they could pack away, forcing down more with glasses of cool water, and then ramming it all home with cups of sugary tea. Yes, it had worked. When Saqib finished his accounts he calculated out that the farm made almost two lacs an acre, four times what Hisham's heritage mango orchard netted on its very best year, from trees that had been maturing since Colonel Atar planted them in the 1960s, and close to ten times what Munshi Abdul Sattar conceded to his master when growing sugarcane, wheat, and cotton.

*

A few days later, as Saqib was working around the farm with his men, dismantling the tunnels to free the land for an interim crop of rice, he saw Chaudrey Warraich drive up in his big black Land Cruiser.

"Look at you," said Warraich. "You've done it, first year. I'm impressed. Come on, I want to take you for a ride."

Hisham rarely went anywhere without a chauffeur, sitting crowded in the rumble seats far back if the master chose to drive, but Warraich had no one with him.

"Show me the way. Take me out to the river and let's have a chat."

"The road's pretty rough for taking a vehicle like this out there. I suppose it cost millions."

"Fifteen million lac plus. This is top of the line. Leather seats, full auto, all electronic. I bet your Hisham Atar Sahib doesn't have a better one. And I change it every other year."

Unlike Hisham, however, who thrashed his cars indifferently, Warraich nursed his way through till the road ended at an embankment crowned with twenty-foot elephant grass overlooking the immense river.

"Look at that," said Warraich. "That's where all the money comes from, from that water. Without it we'd be growing beans in the sand and praying for rain. It's lucky the English had a thing about building canals. We would never have gotten around to it after they left."

He stepped out from the car and stood by the bonnet, and Saqib followed, both men looking out across the glittering river toward Balochistan.

"See that?" said Warraich, pointing across to the west. "Keep going for five thousand kilometers and you're in London. Those planes you see overhead, that's where they're headed. I was in one of them just a week ago, and I could look down and see this river." He turned and looked at Saqib sharply. "Have you ever thought about that, boy? About London?"

"Yes, sir. Who hasn't? We've all seen the movies."

"The girls half naked in their dresses!" laughed Warraich. "I remember, I was brought up in a village two hundred kilometers farther up this river. I used to stand there looking up and thinking, *Someday I'll ride that bird.* Does that surprise you?"

"No, I've looked up and thought the same thing. I didn't wish to ask, but I knew you came from just like me."

"You did, did you? Anyway, give me a few more years and I'll pass. Sometimes I already do. You've got a trained eye, living in Lahore with Hisham Atar Sahib. One thing you should know. It wasn't hard work that bought that jeep. Or rather, it wasn't just hard work. That's the big secret no one tells you. Maybe someday I'll explain it. You're different than the average. Maybe I could school you up and use you some day. That would be a worthwhile education for you."

"Yes, thank you, Warraich Sahib. But I'm learning here too, and then this is my family's place. The Atars have sheltered my family for generations."

"Sheltered indeed. Just keep this in mind: There are two ways to make it, slowly or quickly. I'm pretty sure you will make it, by the way. You'll make something. But look at me. I didn't make it an inch at a time, taking a bit here and bit there. Guys like me, driving around in Land Cruisers, when their families rode on donkey carts, there are always some loud noises at the beginning when they get the whole thing started."

He paused, thought for a moment, and continued more quietly, confidentially.

"You don't look like a munshi to me, you look like a business-man. But there's more to you, I think, than the little weedy guy who scrapes and puts away ten rupees at a time and maybe steals a little bit too if he can and then sets up a cell phone shop in the bazaar and thinks he's made it. You like my wheels, don't you? Well maybe someday you can have a set of them yourself, and also the shiny metal bit on top where the seats go."

A silence hung between the two men, but Saqib didn't break it.

Finally, Warraich said, "Okay, hop in. Or wait a minute, you want to drive? I saw that you were the guy behind the wheel when you and your friend came to Sargodha that first time. You won't believe how smooth this beast is."

"No thank you, sir."

"Suit yourself. Let's go."

*

Back at the farm, Warraich asked for a tour, and seemed impressed by what he saw. As he was leaving, already seated behind the wheel and the farewells made, he rolled down the window and motioned Saqib over. "By the way, young man. I like to show my appreciation of my best customers with a little something. This is for you per-sonally." He took an envelope from the console between the seats and handed it to Saqib.

"What's this?"

"Less than you deserve. Already this year I've done a lot of busi-ness with you and your Mian Hisham Atar."

Saqib took the envelope without looking at it, smiling into War-raich's face. "I suppose this is the discount that you claim you never give to anyone."

"Sure. Call it what you like. Next time let's talk before you set up for the season. We'll figure out how to make your discount bigger by a lot." He enveloped Saqib's hand in both his large hands, several rings on his fingers, confining him, holding it an extra beat, the gesture intimate and controlling. "I think we'll do great things together."

Watching the businessman cruise away in his black chariot, Saqib slapped the envelope against his palm, wondering how far he could trust him. This shrewd man, playing a long game, had said straight out that Saqib farmed the tunnels better than anyone else in the area and farmed more of them than anyone nearby too. Later, away from his workers, Saqib opened the envelope. A hundred thousand rupees, enough to buy not merely one of those tin-and-chrome Chinese motorcycles that were just then flooding the roads of Pakistan, but the real thing, a Honda 125, best transport available short of a car.

He entered the sum into his secret book, in the column where he kept track of his debt to the farm, money drawn against future earnings. A few days later he went to Multan and bought a motorbike, but not a Honda, which would make people talk. Instead he bought the best of the Chinese ones, and though he had the cash to buy it outright he put it on installments. It would cost him fifty percent more over two years, but this way he could explain to Yazid and the rest if they asked where he got the money.

VI

*E*ach spring the Atars' Lahore household fell into a state of confusion when a team of chartered accountants invaded a suite of offices above the garages there and delved into the accounts from the textile factory and also from Ranmal Mohra. Munshi Rana Abdul Sattar Sahib and his junior munshis would bring their books, such as they were, the more professional managers from the factory theirs, Rana Sahib bearing himself for once like a villager, the factory pros wearing Western clothes, emphasizing their technocratic skills. The house servants would wait with relish for bombs to go off, themselves not in jeopardy and glad to see these princelings brought low, huddled outside doors with anxious expressions. Hisham would make glowering descents upon the offices of Shah Sahib, the Lahore household manager, where he never otherwise went, to study the offending books that were spread over tables and covered with annotations by the outside forensic accountants. Tea arrived in shuttles, lights burned late.

Invariably there were rumors of payoffs made to these bright young men, and probably this was the case, for the inquiries followed a script, with an intense period of investigation, where the outside accountants studied in sacerdotal hush the piles of account books, checking through vouchers and making lists. Then there would be a flurry, as if game had been started in a hunting field, accompanied by a new urgency among all participants, the managers sweating at the doors and waiting to be called in before these whippersnappers, Hisham irritable when he dropped in to check the state of play. Finally, a resolution followed, an abatement of tension, and the whole matter drained away into inconsequence. There might be a sacrifice, some junior manager bustled off in disgrace, and a period of unsettlement in Hisham's mood, while he digested the fact that his factories and farms had made less than he hoped, and always just slightly less than he needed.

Although he had not been summoned, Saqib determined to take part in that year's audit. Yes, it would be best to take his books there and expose them to review, figure out how to play nice with those accountant boys. In any case, he knew that otherwise Munshi Sattar would be busy about the place casting doubt on the vegetable farm and particularly on its manager. As the conclave had been called for early May, a few weeks after the vegetable crop had been harvested, Saqib had time to tie up loose ends, close down the farm for the season, and also to spend time grooming his account books, presenting the enterprise in the best light and at the same time tidying away the evidence of his little depredations. He concealed his secret debt to the farm, which came to almost a lac rupees, under various headings, and kept the lac-rupee bonus from Warraich entirely separate, referring to it nowhere.

Boarding the midnight bus from Adda Mastt Bahadur, Saqib carried his books wrapped up in a cloth bundle and a little cardboard suitcase with some clothes that he had ordered specially for this occasion, eschewing the white shalvar kameez that he would have preferred as giving the wrong impression, too immaculate, and instead choosing a neutral tan, all four sets alike. Riding a rickshaw along the canal from the intercity bus stop at Thokar Niaz Baig, at the periphery of the great city, all the way into the center of Lahore, to the tall filigreed cast-iron gates of Al-Unmool, he felt that the city was familiar to him, that he returned to it a man of substance and achievement. He peeled off banknotes from a wad, took no notice of the rickshaw driver's protests but paid what he thought right, and stepped in along the curving bricked drive. Seven years ago, when first he saw this house, he nearly slunk away in his confusion, fearing to present himself at such a palace, no matter if he had been instructed to come by Bayazid. Now as he cast an affectionate proprietary gaze over it, he found it impressive and appropriate to the family's status, took pride in it, noted a few little maintenance jobs that should be seen to, a mango tree needing pruning, flower beds that should be weeded, if that had been any of his affair.

He maintained an eloquent discretion in front of the servants marveling at his elevation, gaping at him, who had made the impossible transition from houseboy to munshi, and still in his early twenties. With Yazid, behind a closed door, he laid out his achievement like a jeweler setting out his finest pieces of emerald and gold on a velvet cloth. He had rehearsed the story and relished the telling, one that he would offer to no one else, not in such detail, how many bags he sold each day, each month, the costs, how many sprays, how much nitrogen and phosphate and potassium, the cost of clutch wire, the bundles of plastic sheeting twenty-two feet wide and a thousand feet long, and then finally, what Yazid had been waiting ten minutes to hear, the net profit, after all this ruinous outlay. Saqib's mentor gleamed with satisfaction, with something approaching love for his protégé. That moment forevermore would live in Saqib's memory, the moment when finally it became real, when he knew he'd won his game, his first smashing success with money, with business, all the days and nights he had spent for eight months, dirt under his nails, sleeping rough, out at night, up in the morning before his men arrived and already inside the tunnels checking checking checking.

"Would you like to see my books?" asked Saqib at the end, making to unwrap the bundle.

"What do I know about books," responded Yazid, chewing his mustache in the corner of his mouth with sheer pleasure. "You've told me the one number that matters, the nut, and that comes to a whacking beautiful gorgeous sum. I want to kiss you, I swear I do. You're as quick as I always thought, you're one of those rockets they show in the movies."

"I want you to talk to Mian Sahib. This is your project."

"Ho ho ho! I wouldn't know one end of a cucumber from the other. The only thing I know is that they're good nibbling next to a dish of chicken karahi. Let's send someone to ask if Mian Sahib is free."

"No! I want to do this right. Let me handle it. Good news can wait, and tomorrow's as good as today. We'll choose our moment."

"Yes, we'll do that, you fox. I hope you don't manage me the way you manage Mian Sahib and Bibi."

"Manage you? Are you kidding? That would be like trying to manage the moon. There's too much of you, and you're too immovable for a little fellow like me."

Saqib stayed out of sight all day, relaxing, lounging as he had not in many months. Only next morning did he allow Hisham and Shahnaz to become aware of his presence, as if accidentally, when he went into the kitchen and helped to prepare the breakfast, making banana pancakes as he had learned when first winning the masters' hearts, such a short time ago.

*

Having observed this drama of the yearly audit while serving in Lahore, Saqib understood the ways in which Hisham and Shahnaz did and did not pay attention to the details of their business. When called into Hisham's study that morning, he brought all his books, tied in a cloth bundle, his face shining with sincerity and a deferential calm. In his hand he carried a file folder with a summary written out in a calligraphic handwriting, this legibility important not just because it lent his work a professional sheen, but because while Hisham—with his wide knowledge of Urdu poetry and his Aitchison College education—knew Urdu well, Shahnaz did not read it with any great fluency.

Unlike Shahnaz, Hisham's aristocratic self-regard made him shy about money, a squeamishness that his managers knew and exploited. He found it refreshing to receive a packet of money from Shah Sahib the household manager and to shove it in his pocket uncounted, crisp notes blithely shucked off without consideration, paying or overpaying, say, a gambling debt incurred over whiskey sodas at the Punjab Club. At the same time, he secretly thought of himself as something of a financial wizard and delighted in catching out the managers in some petty irregularity.

"Come along, Saqib," he said, looking up from the newspaper, holding up his shining morning face, well fed and benign. Shahnaz sat on one side, reading a book, wearing a silk housecoat, a dress that she would never have worn in front of an ordinary munshi. "What news from Ranmal Mohra?"

"The vegetables are finished, sir. We're planting rice now, to leach down the salts in the land."

Hisham wore a pair of half-moon glasses, and now studied Saqib over the tops of the lenses.

"Yes, that's good, rice. What about using gypsum. We can bring down the pH with that too."

A sarcastic thought flashed through Saqib's mind. *Yes, we can, two experts like us.* It was difficult not to find something appealing and boyish in Hisham's tufts of curly hair on each side of his head. Saqib had seen this many times, the owner throwing around scraps of knowledge about business or farming proposals and the munshis egging him on, distracting him with these little toys, a scheme for growing papaya along the watercourses—"A free crop," Hisham would say through his nose, "extra income, every bit counts." The munshis' nodding faces beamed wonderment, and Chaudrey Abdul Sattar even carried around a little pad in which he ostentatiously noted these pearls from the citybound owner.

It was the Begum, however, whose gaze Saqib registered more carefully.

"And how did we do?" asked Shahnaz.

Saqib handed the file with the summary to her, and after glancing at it for a moment, she put it down.

"Well, give me the bottom line. Is Mian Sahib to be the vegetable king of Muzaffargarh District?"

"Yes, Begum Sahiba, I think so. I think it's possible. The cucumbers brought"—he squinted at the summary sheet, though he knew the number by heart—"brought 175,596 rupees per acre. And that doesn't include the rice we're planting now, between crops."

"What about the expenses, though? How much were your costs?"

"That's after all my costs, Bibi Jee. That's net." He marshaled his expression so as not to seem triumphant. Let the numbers speak.

"Almost two lacs per acre? That's incredible!" said Hisham. "It's brilliant. I'm told that Munshi Sattar's average for the whole farm won't be more than twenty-five thousand."

Munshi Sattar indeed, thought Saqib. On another day, and with better results, the master would at least have called him Rana Sahib, or Manager Sahib.

"How many acres?" asked Shahnaz, who was studying Saqib's face.

"Fifteen, Bibi Jee."

"Fifteen? At least that's something," she said. "How many can you do next year?"

"Bibi, now that I know the way I think I can do a lot more. Maybe even fifty."

She looked into his eyes. "And with the same results?"

"With God's will, yes. The same."

"Well, do it then."

Hisham looked bemused. "The Big Sahib always speaks last, meaning the Sahiba. I guess that settles the business part of this meeting. What's the gossip on the farm, then?"

"As usual, sir," demurred Saqib. "A lot of hidden vice and a lot of pretended virtue. Jhind Vadhla died, so that's to the good. He was the head of that gang stealing motorbikes and selling them across the river. No one dared to ride at night."

"Leave it, darling," said Shahnaz in English. "He's a munshi now. Don't use him for tittle-tattle."

"Why not?" replied Hisham. "I bet he could shed a lot of light on why the rest of the farm under Sattar did so poorly." To Saqib he said, in Urdu, "So what's your plan?"

"With your permission, I'll take the overnight bus tonight to Ranmal Mohra."

"Good boy."

Saqib stood for a beat, awaiting a dismissal, then went to the coffee table and gathered up Hisham's dirty breakfast dishes. Leaving, he stopped as if in recall. "Sir, should I turn my books over to Rana Sahib?"

"Why not? Those boys can go through them." Hisham looked at Shahnaz. "How are we going to do this?"

"No," said Shahnaz decisively. "No, keep Saqib's thing separate. Let's not mix him up with that lot."

"And my expenses, Bibi Jee? It's best if I buy everything now. It will cost a lot to buy so much, but cheaper now before the season. We've got the money."

"Keep it as it is," she said. "Treat it like a separate business and use the money you just earned for next year's stuff."

"There we go." Hisham grinned. "Once again, the boss has spoken."

And so, Saqib's books were not subjected to scrutiny, and, even more important, he was confirmed in his independent command. At lunch that day, Saqib served at the table.

"It's like our old times," beamed Hisham.

Saqib had always been fascinated by the way Shahnaz handled her cutlery, the rings on her fingers, and the way she took up and put down her knife and fork, a play of silver as she spoke, using her hands for emphasis. Now she looked at Saqib, who was standing behind Hisham, his posture upright, something martial about him.

"It is and it isn't," she said. "Once Mian Sahib and I spoke of sending you to school somewhere. Do you remember, Saqib? In America!"

"I can never repay all your kindness, Bibi Jee."

"Well then, this is your school."

Saqib thought of himself sitting over his account books, studying how to cover up his accumulation of little thefts. He bowed his head, covered his confusion by slipping around and picking up one of the platters, cutlets that he had cooked specially, knowing they were Hisham's favorite, and offering him a second helping.

VII

*T*hese were the days of the great intercity buses, Manthar Transport, Road Master, Faisal Movers, New Kohistan Express, which had replaced the tooting jolting unsprung blistering-hot buses of yore, the new ones expressing their modernity by more-sober paint jobs and polar air-conditioning and arrays of high-powered headlamps that blinded oncoming traffic from a kilometer away and brushed it off the road. Saqib sat next to the window, his back arched against the talkative man beside him, who had tried to make conversation. Thieves worked these buses, chatting up passengers, sharing drugged food, then taking their wallets and valuables.

He didn't sleep for several hours, ruminating on how easily he had sidestepped the audit, then dozed, rocking, thinking of the past days in Lahore, and the days to come at the farm. Being again at Al-Unmool had recalled the great contrast between his life at Ranmal Mohra, living in a rough brick hut and working day and night, and the stateliness of life at the Lahore mansion, the grace of that organization, where he had enjoyed such a privileged place. He had spent years moving through those halls carpeted in blue and red, serving at dinners where the great and good and the wickedly amusing came to break bread with his masters, reflecting a golden light on all the household.

In truth, although the thrill of serving these masters had not abated, he knew that now he would never go back. After all, Hisham knew nothing about the business, not compared to Saqib, and this engendered a certain contempt in Saqib's mind, which had become so deeply imbued with the intricacies of his farm. Even with Shahnaz, whose approval had once been everything to Saqib, he found that now he approached her from the other side of the glass, as a manager of property. He ruefully considered that if his life had forked differently, he might still have been serving them in that house, most intimate of the servants. Closing his eyes, he thought again of the household, of Hisham's lemony cologne and his good humor in the morning, as he dressed his pampered body in soft comfortable clothes and commenced yet another day devoted to pleasure, and of Shahnaz, her brittle humor and intelligence, the refinement of her manner and her taste. His mind lingered on this vision; he thirsted for that place. And then he shook his head. He had chosen a larger game, back by the river, and that enterprise seemed to him just the beginning.

The sleeping passengers around him, the smell of their feet and bodies, which wafted up all around like a loaf of warm meat, teased and stimulated Saqib's mind. For years he had been accustomed to think for long periods at night, not just of women and sex, but more, of the future, and after Shahnaz called him to Lahore, of their interests, these masters whom he studied with wonder. Often in later years he had thought of their travels, finding that he could speculate on that for hours, filling his imagination with scenes picked up from television and movies, London, and more vivid still, the lure of America. Among his marks of favor, he was of the party that went in two cars to see the sahibs off at Lahore airport when they went for holidays. The flights always left in the middle of the night, and that added to the strangeness of their exodus, driving the empty streets of Lahore, no cars, the sodium streetlights filigreeing the big pipal trees in the Cantonment, and then the moment of disengagement from Hisham and Shahnaz, who slipped out and away to their airplane, the brilliant craft knifing above the city to the West, where blonde-haired women wore no clothes at all and the poorest man drove a new car, all seen in films. The servants would wait in the parking lot until the sahibs' plane left, in case there should be a delay, Hisham calling when they were seated and the plane departing.

Soon Hisham and Shahnaz would go away for the summer, to

London, where they had a flat—Saqib imagined it like Al-Unmool, though Shahnaz had once laughingly explained, as she taught him the technique for washing a chandelier hanging in the dining room, that in England they had no servants at all, cooked for themselves, had just a lady who came in to clean. Saqib's mind moved upon a stream. An incident troubled him, an image of contrast. That evening, when Saqib went to take his leave, Hisham had stopped him at the door as he backed out, keeping his face to them.

"What do you think of all this with Munshi Sattar?"

All day it had been whispered through the servants' quarters that the big munshi had been caught out by the accountants.

"Well, sir, every year the accountant sahibs seem to find out one person or another."

He laughed. "I hope it's not quite that random a selection."

Saqib allowed himself a philosophical comment. "One man up, sir, and another one down, like a waterwheel."

Shahnaz broke in. "What about you, Saqib? Do you think that Munshi Sahib has been too long at the top?"

"Chaudrey Sattar Sahib knows the farm better than anyone. With Mian Sahib's support he could even go into politics."

"Not a bad idea," said Hisham, in English.

"I don't think Saqib was suggesting a political career for your Sattar," she responded, also in English. To Saqib she said, in dismissal, "Anyway, I suppose he and the accountants will work something out."

Saqib walked out through the house thoughtfully, stopping to rearrange the flowers in a vase, removing the wilted ones. Whatever you said about Hisham, it was clear that Shahnaz understood the games the accountants played. Evidently, and more important, this had been something like an offer to him from Hisham, to give information on Chaudrey Sattar, with the implication that he might be in line for the job.

*

Saqib alighted from the bus just after sunrise in the little town of Adda Mastt Bahadur, half an hour by motorcycle from the farm, stale from the journey but with that soaring heart of a young man in his early twenties with money in his pocket and an easy day before him. Dispirited dogs with lowered heads sniffed among the tea and samosa carts parked here and there, nosing through garbage for scraps, and early-waking villagers sipped mugs of tea despite the rising heat, the quiet of the spring dawn shattered by a tractor blowing through pulling a load of newly harvested wheat in gunny sacks piled high. He absorbed all this through his new-bright city eyes, the men wearing dhotis and long kurtas, squatting and brushing their teeth with neem sticks, the sewage that stood about in black puddles, the crash of steel shutters being thrown open as the shops came to life. The air here was so different, and he inhaled it like a pointer on a scent, his long nose upraised, the smell of home, dust and dew off the newly cut wheat fields, the quality of the light, flat on the plains. Even gone for a few days now he missed it so, feeling for the first time that he was a conqueror returned in triumph. Now in that morning light he understood that these fields and country passages still mattered to him most, that this was real in a different way than the superficialities of his old life in the city, and his emotions prickled and absorbed the bright rising day in this place of his childhood.

Even at this hour there were a couple of men with motorcycles standing about at the crossroads, and he hired one of them to drive him to Ranmal Mohra. It was exhilarating, on the motorbike, passing through cooler pockets of air where the surrounding fields were freshly irrigated, and Saqib sat back and let his arms hang loose in the spring breezes, wearing a new jacket that he'd bought in Lahore, green leather, unlike what the villagers would wear. He knew all the ruts in the road, where overladen sugarcane trolleys had destroyed the surface, knew each field as they went past. Coming on eight years now he had ridden pillion on these motorcycles during his rare home leaves, dropped off by the intercity bus at dawn, coming into this country through those last kilometers. His father would already have gone off to his duties as the gardener in Colonel Atar's village house, for he was invariably the first servant to show up in that household, not just from obligation but because he lived with the seasons, the light of morning and dusk. Saqib's powerful mother had trained her man to that soon after they wed some twenty years ago, as if she set him spinning quietly in his place then, with such decision that she need not look to him again.

Saqib planned to spend a few nights at his parents' house—a holiday from his spare hut out by the river at the vegetable farm. He had not called to tell them of this plan of holiday in their home, not so much to surprise them, but because he wished to find them exactly as he left them, in their daily rounds that he had known so well. Those rounds would have continued unchanged, just as all things in the village had continued since his childhood, marriages and deaths proceeding, but always under the same dispensations of light and color, the same mud walls dividing the houses, the buffaloes in the common yard offspring of the ones that he tended as a boy, the trees larger but the same, the pipal that spread over the mosque, the banyans in the dera where Colonel Atar's machinery stood exactly as before, right down to the bent electric pole that for some reason stood smack in the middle of the dirt street running through the village, and the single shop that Colonel Atar permitted there, with its crude wooden door leading down into the interior like a hole poked in dough with a thumb.

He patted the rough-planked door of their little compound with the flat of his hand, though he knew it would be unlocked since his father's quiet departure an hour before. All over the village cook fires of dried cotton stalks burned, the women up since dawn, the men gone to the fields. He knew, not because he could see her through the closed door but by intuition, by his bone-deep knowledge of this household, that it was his younger sister who came to the door, uncertain, for no one knocked at this hour.

"Rahqah," he whispered, so quiet because he wanted her to be unsure.

She did not open the door, and then she did, just a crack, her face sideways in the opening.

"You!" she exclaimed, and then when he pushed in a little bit she skipped back and ran to their mother, who was squatting in front of the hearth fire in a corner of the courtyard. Each of the houses in the village was more or less the same, a rectangle of hardened dirt enclosed with mud-brick walls, two mud-plastered rooms at one end, floors in the rooms of dirt, but clean, and opposite the rooms a buffalo in one corner tied to a peg, perhaps with a calf, perhaps also a goat or two, and then in the other corner a lean-to roofed with thatched grass propped at one corner with a heavy wooden branch, where cooking utensils were kept, pots and pans hung from sawed-off branch stubs, a yellow tin teapot, chipped enameled tin plates, tin glasses and cups, a few time-worn pieces, and next to that in the open the simplest possible mud-built stove on which all the cooking was done, no oven, exactly as villagers would have used when the great Alexander passed through these lands two millennia before. Most of the village houses belonged to the masters and so were never repaired, the mud walls streaked after the last rains and not replastered, doors leaning crazily, the corner with the buffalo piled with dried manure that had not been taken out for weeks. Not this one. The cleanliness of the space spoke volumes about the mother's control, her rigidity against the slop and grunge of the village, and over the buffalo manger grew a borhi tree that she had planted in the first year of her marriage—the female banyan, as they called it. It now stood thirty feet tall, the largest tree in any of the villagers' houses, except for the colossal banyans in the one much larger house, belonging to Shaikh Riaz, the son of the disgraced manager who preceded Rana Sattar.

"Look, it's Saqib!" called the sister, but his eyes were entirely upon his mother. He had known to find that figure crouched exactly in that spot, the fire smoking in front of her as she cooked for the day, an image drawing all his childhood down into it. Yes, she was there, and she looked up over her shoulder and drew her dupatta over her head reflexively, as if he were an outsider. She did not rise immediately but blew once on the fire and picked at the chapatti that was cooking on the griddle, lifted it deftly into a woven basket lying there, folded it under a white cloth, then stood with her graceful motion, a movement that distinguished her in Saqib's eyes from all other beings. Lips set, unsmiling, across the immaculate beaten dirt courtyard she studied him in a flash, all the content of his expression, his bearing, understood by her in that one appreciation. Yes, all was well, he saw that she saw that.

*

"You're back," she stated, when he walked across and stood in front of her, his sister, and then the other one, the younger, jumping around him. "You've come with the Sahib."

"No, but I made my report to him in Lahore. The vegetables." All through the fall and winter, though he had come home from time to time, he had not spoken with his family about the business, meaning not spoken to his mother. At the end of the season Rana Sattar went about telling near and far that Saqib would soon have his comeuppance, and tight-lipped Saqib had allowed the rumor to pass, knowing that the blacker he was painted the brighter his shine when he proved himself against the odds.

She glanced into his face again. "So it went well. You've won something. That's new." She didn't miss anything.

He had brought presents for his sisters, the younger one's eyes fixed on the bag that he pulled out, made shy by it and yet breathless, the elder not to be drawn into that game. There were just the three children, very unusually for a village where five was the norm and seven or eight remarked as a blessing, more children meaning more tickets in the lottery, one or another likely to do proud, or at least keep alive the parents gone old. Saqib's mother, Hasina, didn't play those odds, she had more confidence in the quality of the offspring she raised. Anyway, she would not be trifled with by fate, she could starve if must be in old age, like an iron-willed matron in Republican Rome, this a woman who couldn't read a newspaper headline and had never traveled more than fifty kilometers from her hearth fire.

Only the paratha she served him, not asking if he wanted it, the egg fried in ghee, showed her passionate love for this son of hers, few words between them while he sat on a charpoy in the sun and ate his breakfast, more than he wanted, thin-boned Saqib, nicknamed Crane as a boy. For the sisters, this might have been a city prince come down to mingle with the people, and they perched prim on the string end of the charpoy and devoured his presence. The little one, seven or eight, was called Rahqah, and the elder Nasmin—both unusual names, names of flowers, not village names, chosen by the mother, who prized a difference in herself that had no basis in her circumstances. Unsparing, critical, ardent, unfulfilled, she was romantic at the core, as are personalities that hold themselves apart.

*

Saqib had no particular friends in the village—seven years in Lahore had dulled those connections, and the past year back at Ranmal Mohra, when he rebuffed intimacies to protect his command, had added coolness to that distance. Now Saqib walked out into the orchard that surrounded the village, along packed-dirt farm roads used only in the mango season, when the fruit went to market. He remembered it so well from childhood, each tree almost, a single eucalyptus that was the largest tree on the farm, next to which the village women washed their clothes in a watercourse, that watercourse itself, the bend where it went around that eucalyptus. His bare feet in childhood had touched every bit of this ground.

Over the past months a plan had been forming in Saqib's mind, one that grew and took shape organically. It was now evident to him that, absent bad luck, he could make a great deal of money running vegetable tunnels for the Atars. Was he content, then, to be a munshi for them? If he wanted, he knew that he could take Chaudrey Sattar's position, not even by underhanded means, not by gathering information of his thefts and presenting them to the masters, but simply by supplanting him. He could engineer Sattar's downfall merely by showing himself more efficient, for he had that most valuable of all powers for a courtier, easy approach to the masters. Yet Saqib wanted more from the Atars than that. He wanted to be tied to them in some more meaningful degree, and he wanted to share in their fortune far more than he could by serving them—even if this meant by stealing from them, dipping his ladle into a large pot that he would keep at a merry boil. All this troubled him, and it was to settle his mind and develop his thoughts that he had decided to take a few days at his parents' house in the village, away from his vegetable patch.

*

After dinner that evening, his mother brought out her embroidery and sat under the single borhi tree in their courtyard, an invitation to Saqib. His father had gone to bed, as he always did immediately after dinner, and the girls sat in the second room watching an Indian movie on the television, a luxury grudgingly countenanced by the mother, though never to the extent that she looked at it herself.

"You're still too thin," she remarked. "Boys go to the city to put on flesh, and for a big manager like you're becoming it's indecent not to have a good weight."

"I'm not a buffalo, where you can judge me by the pound."

"We judge the buffaloes by the milk they give, not by their weight. But it's the least you can have from those people, since you go and live there with them in Lahore and now stuck in that shack by the river. What else are you hoping for?"

"Those people! Our ancestors served them here since long before there were roads! You mean the Mian Sahib and the Begum."

"You talk like your father."

"Well, I should and he should. He's been kept by them pretty well."

"Don't pretend. You're not like your father at all."

"No, I'm like you."

She looked up from her embroidery. "I'd like you to do something for me, since you've got all this time on your hands, and money too, it seems. I want to visit Basti Noorwala, and you can take me. Tomorrow."

Saqib saw immediately what she was thinking, a deep-laid plan.

"My mother is becoming sentimental. Usually it's only a wedding or a death that brings her over there."

"You know what I want there. It's time for you to get married, before you get lured into some attachment, running around with city people."

"You didn't bring me up to get fooled by anyone, so why should you worry? There's no hurry about this."

"I didn't bring you up to go live in the city and serve barefoot, either."

"Yet you would have me marry a girl who can neither read nor write. And then, I'm no longer serving in the city, I'm something like a munshi now." He had said it with a smile, but he knew that his mother would be inflexible in this, that he should marry one of his cousins, preferably this particular one, Fatima, the eldest of her sister's daughters.

"Are you saying you won't take me to my sister's house, then?"

"I'll take you to the Holy Places, if you like. In fact, I'd prefer that. Give me a year or two to arrange it."

"Don't you dare speak that way to me. Holy Places! You're not worthy to go to the Holy Places. I doubt you say your prayers any-more, living with those people."

Saqib had never gone even this far in crossing his mother, and his temerity surprised him.

"Ah, those people!" he countered. "Give me time. I'm going to make money. I'll be a big man someday. I've got plans, and not just being a munshi either—although being a munshi would seem a pretty good beginning. Give me a bit of time, and I'll have some-thing to show. Then you can marry me to one of those lady doctors if you wish. It's a new world, people marry wherever they like."

"That's nonsense. You live with those Sahibs and then they've ruined you. Soon I'll be gone, and then you can marry one of those filmi girls and celebrate the *nikah* over my grave."

Saqib stopped himself from laughing and thought of her with admiration. She would have her way! The light of the single bulb fixed to the wall emphasized the angles of her bronze face. Yes, she was vain, not of her looks but of her person. Call it a fault, if you like, but never a weakness. He'd always thought her superior. No one else in the village looked like her, strength in her slender-ness, grave-faced, unbending, thin arms, long feet, like a woman of breeding. Even when there was no money at all, she had never worked in the fields with the other village women.

"You've already been settling it, haven't you?"

"Why wouldn't I?"

"Marry me to the granddaughter of Sheikh Abbas, if you choose to do it now. Or later I will do much better."

He had not meant to say this, it was not like him to show his hand without meaning to. Idly during the last year, in his loneliness by the river, planning a grand future, feeling out the way, gradually it was this girl that he came to imagine resplendent beside him in his triumphs, the days when he would have cars as good as the Atar Land Cruisers, when he too would know the cities of the West.

Just at this moment, as his mother spoke, it clicked into place, and he realized that this particular girl, Gazala, must be part of his picture of the greater good, granddaughter of the great disgraced Munshi Abbas, more the ruler than the manager of Ranmal Mohra throughout the years when Colonel Atar's car flew a minister's flag, when the farm became preeminent not just in the district but in the whole division, when the autocrat Zulfikar Ali Bhutto came to a rally here in a helicopter and spent the night.

Now truly he had shocked his mother. She threw down her embroidery. "You've gone mad. Munshi Abbas! Seth Abbas? Those people aren't much better than Hindus. The old people could remember when they were baniyas."

"The old people aren't around to tell us what they think. There's a reason that Abbas and his clan ran the Atar lands back in the old days. They were the clever ones, when the rest of the people here lived in holes in the ground and couldn't afford to buy salt for their lentils."

Sheikh Abbas was a legend on these lands, sent from one of the Atar family farms near Lahore to settle the place, back in English times when there were dunes here and nothing growing but scraps of pulses in the sand watered with Persian wheels turned by camels. Later on, in the years when Colonel Atar was bringing these lands more firmly under his control, he struggled against Abbas and finally disgraced him and took back lands that he had mysteriously acquired over the years. Now the family held just a house in the village, much bigger than any of the other peasant hovels, and a dozen or two acres of land, bits scattered here and there when the clan was forced to disgorge.

"So that's what it comes to." His mother's voice seethed. "I've seen that little thing, I can see right through something like that. What do they call her? Gazala? They should call her Devi or one of their own names. Those Hindus think they're better, that little girl thinks the dirt won't stick to her."

Saqib must not yield now. "Her father spends more time in the mosque than the maulvi, you needn't call him a Hindu. And they say they have gold buried in that house somewhere."

The mother shrieked. "Get out! Gold! Of course that man lives in the mosque, he's a secret Hindu, he would. And if there were gold that girl wouldn't be making eyes at you!"

Saqib stood up. He hadn't intended any of this, he only now realized that this was his resolute desire, to marry Gazala, who had always been the most beautiful of the girls, silent and proud and distant. She stood above them all, above the dear dirty village, and Saqib wanted that pride turned in his favor.

"Please, Mother. Believe in me. Trust me. You made me, after all." He knew how inflexible his mother could be, how absolute.

"I want just one word from you. Will you take me to Basti Noor-wala tomorrow morning or won't you? Yes or no?"

With a graceful gesture, he bent to the ground and put his hand on her foot, but she pulled it away.

"Go back to Lahore then. Or go to that place they've stuck you out by the river. Have it your way."

"Please, I beg you."

"Out!" Upright, inflexible, she pushed him out the door into the night.

*

He too had his pride. Under the moon he walked all across the farm, chilled, for he had come without his chaddar, and sat for a long time beside a tube well, the water cold and black in the tank, catching the light of the stars as he studied its reflections. It was all a tangle in him, why he had challenged his mother, why he had spoken of Gazala, that girl. Only tonight had he realized that he wanted her and her alone, and only because his mother had brought up his cousin, that village girl exactly like the others, who in five years would be spoiled. Gazala would be delectable, capricious as she was, throwing her eyes about even when she was growing out of childhood and no longer allowed to play outside. Yes, he had watched her all through his boyhood, but then so had the others, for she was the prettiest of all, and had nothing to do with the villagers, kept apart, was taught at home by her father. The mother had died, and all around it was said that they lived on gold stashed away, and that's why they never mixed with the rest of the villagers. The sons were sullen, were beaten to keep them in line, two of them, and did nothing but learn the Koran all day, and Gazala owned the muddy village streets when she walked them, even as a girl of ten and twelve.

When he returned home, he feared that the door would be chained, but it wasn't, and his mother was sitting there still on the charpoy, in the same spot.

"I'll make tea," she said, after a moment's silence, not looking at him.

"Thank you, Mother."

She rose and lit the little fire of twigs and heated the water, made the tea as he liked it. He sat wrapped in the chaddar he had left behind, the warmth coming back into him. How mysterious to him their connection, how she and he were resolved together again, though just an hour before it had all seemed to break.

"I'll go with you tomorrow," he murmured, looking at her through the steam rising from the hot tea.

"No. You won't. But I don't want you staying here. You've got nothing to do, idleness is bad for you, worse than for others even. It's my fault that you're restless, I think I brought you up wrong. You go back to your place by the river tomorrow. I understand now. But don't mention those Hindus again."

VIII

A few times that year, while passing through Ranmal Mohra, Saqib had encountered the girl Gazala, being driven on the back of her brother's motorcycle. Her father had sold his car the previous winter, a subject of gossip in the village, some falling off in that household, when all the talk for years had been about their hidden riches, the gold that the grandfather had stolen, and that would someday be brought out in dazzling show, when the danger of its being forced from them had passed. Riding sidesaddle, her little foot extended out as she balanced on the narrow seat, one hand resting lightly on her brother's shoulder, her dupatta obscuring half her face, she seemed to Saqib too fine for this mode of transport, her expression suggesting that she bore the indignity of being jolted over the rutted roads exposed to all eyes with the defiance of a princess reduced in circumstances but not subdued. Once it had seemed to him that she granted him the slightest recognition, her glance just brushing past his face and pausing ever so slightly. *We'll see about this,* he had thought, and redoubled his attention to farming.

Now, as the spring weather flourished, Saqib began stopping by his parents' house more often than had been his wont, smoothing the breach with his mother. Though usually she was so intuitive in managing her son, one evening she made a blunder.

"That Gazala girl," she said. "They were trying to marry her off to some boy from Sahiwal, that's what I hear. And she refused. She's an impudent little thing, brought up without a mother. And now everybody says that she studied for some exam without her father knowing and took the test and she's become a teacher at that new private school in Adda Mastt Bahadur. She rides off in a van they send. So much for the granddaughter of the baniya Seth Abbas."

*

His mother was biding her time still, would marry Saqib to his cousin, letting him grow into the idea of having a woman in his bed, appetite sharpened by his lonely hours scratching up crops by the river.

"It's Sheikh Abbas that they called him, not Seth Abbas." His mother used the Seth appellation to emphasize the family's Hindu antecedents, the Seth caste being the Hindu moneylenders of this area before Partition. "They weren't baniyas when they came to Ranmal Mohra, whatever they were back before Colonel Sahib sent them here from the north."

"And now the granddaughter's running around alone in public vans and meeting all sorts of people in town. I know how that ends."

"It's not a public transport, Mother dear! And then, think about how she managed to educate herself. To teach at that school she'd need a real degree."

"I imagine working there the owners choose them for their looks, not their degrees."

Saqib laughed. "You're imagining wrong. That school's a real business, it's made by Lahore people. They're building them all over Punjab, and they make a lot of money. If she couldn't do it right, they wouldn't pay her. The man building all these schools is a friend of Hisham Sahib."

A few days later, developing his plan, Saqib lingered near the main road leading into Ranmal Mohra at schooltime, and saw the van, with Gazala riding inside, along with ten or twelve other women being picked up for their duties, daughters of the better-off villagers from the area, educated as was becoming the trend among this rising class. The women in the van were all carefully dressed, bright, yet even among them Gazala seemed different to Saqib, aloof from them, immaculate, superior. Unlike the others in the van, who obscured their faces as they came onto the main road, Gazala's gaze coolly passed over the people in the dirty shops piled up at the crossroads, barbers set up under trees and fruit sellers and tea stall owners who had encroached on the government land on the margins of the road.

Seeing her, thinking of her, he felt ever more strongly that his choice had settled on her years before. He cared that this decision had been formed long ago, proof that he chose his destiny. One memory stuck in his mind, when he was twelve or thirteen. He had glimpsed her through the imposing tall gates of her father's house, and as she turned to look at him, silhouetted against the sun, hair uncovered then in the privacy of her home, she had stared into his eyes with an intensity that marked him deeply. That had whispered to him deep, her boldness, and a sadness too, defiant and yet vulnerable.

Yet he could not approach the girl in the ordinary ways, through family. His mother would not help, and certainly her family would oppose any tender, both because Saqib's family were poor and unknown, his father a gardener to Colonel Atar, and also because they were of different castes, Saqib an Arain, and her family at least pretendedly Sheikhs, a business caste of some distinction. The uncertainty of her family's position, however, gave him confidence, their whispered Hindu blood, and then this change in their circumstance that led to their selling the car, and that compelled the daughter to take a job out in the world.

IX

*T*hough cell phones had become increasingly common in Pakistan during the 2000s, there had been no towers around Ranmal Mohra because there was less population near the river, no great city nearby. That year, finally, a tower had been built in Adda Mastt Bahadur, with weak reception at Ranmal Mohra and out by the river. Saqib had owned a phone for six or seven years, using it when he went to Multan or to Lahore, but now they became common around the village, the young men buying secondhand sets if they could possibly afford them. One day he saw Gazala speaking on a phone as she drove past in the school van—he had taken to loitering at the crossroads where the van turned, drinking a cup of tea.

At the same time, new Chinese smartphones had entered the market, so that the villagers could see images and not merely talk on their sets. That became the new status symbol, to have one of those, however poorly they worked. Suddenly the villagers had access to Western porn, which confettied over all those young men. Porn on videos had been available for years, but that required a TV, a player, and most of all, must be watched in a room, in a house. Now the young men could sit in hidden places and see astonishing pictures, of women whose shamelessness seemed inconceivable. All of them wanted this, more than a motorcycle, more than any other luxury. Facebook came next, and the word of it passed through the villages, impossible to explain at first, this idea of making groups and conversing through the phone, putting up pictures, reaching out, even across the world. Relatives living abroad, somehow escaped, migrants to England, to Manchester, Birmingham, Leeds, even to America, long lost and rarely considered, suddenly reentered the villagers' lives.

The phones also allowed boys and girls to communicate without meeting, and this changed the courtship rituals established for generations, mothers blind to the promiscuities their daughters practiced under their noses. Girls would be caught up in the nets of young men, boys giving phones to girls, hidden ones, and then when the smartphones came the game of sending pictures back and forth. Girls would be compromised, tricked into sending photos of their faces, even worse photos, and then blackmailed.

Saqib had not taken much note of all this, though he bought himself one of the new phones, an inexpensive one, using it for business. He was old in temperament about such gimmickry, not playful, even the way he handled the phone, the serious expression that his face assumed as he spoke on it. Now, however, he explored the parameters of the device, studied it, looked at porn and was shocked and couldn't stop himself, then learned how to use Facebook, went into town and paid a man in a computer shop to set up a page for him, with references to his farming, a photo of himself. Quick in perception, nimble-minded, he grasped the uses of the technology rapidly.

One night, sitting at a point near his vegetables, where the signal from the last cell tower just reached, he found Gazala on Facebook. The photograph showed an Indian film star, but the address was Ranmal Mohra, and looking through the feed he knew it must be her, for it identified her as working at the Lighthouse School, and then he found photos posted by another of the teachers showing Gazala with the group at a teacher training seminar in Multan. It surprised him, and almost hurt his feelings, that she looked in the photo like another of the women around her, not particularly special, perhaps not even the prettiest of the group. Yet as he looked at the photograph—it was difficult to see anything at all, it was so small—his mind flooded with tenderness and desire. She was different, only she in that line of women had a real, bright personality; the rest were all a foil to her.

Fearfully, after much consideration, after writing messages and erasing them, he sent Gazala a nudge, no text.

Two days later, a line—"Who is this?"

She wrote in Roman Urdu. "Kon ho?"

Painstakingly, he picked out a reply using the unfamiliar letters. "Saqib. Also from Ranmal Mohra."

He waited a day for a reply, then another, then a week, not daring to pursue further and so drive her away, driving to a place nearer the cell tower, where the app would load, disappointed each time. Finally—"What do you want?"

"To speak with you."

"Why?"

"I have something to say." And he gave his cell phone number.

That same night, as he sat in his room at the vegetable farm, his phone rang with an unknown number. Heart beating, he sat up, waited for two more rings.

"This is Saqib."

Long silence. He waited, then spoke again. "This is Saqib. Please speak."

"Why should I speak?"

Immense relief, flooding through his breast. A tickling, like pleasure, but too intense.

"Just for a moment, listen to what I have to say."

"Then say it."

But he hadn't prepared this part, he had not thought this far ahead.

"Aren't you going to speak?"

He answered, by good fortune, with the one best line, the one that prevented her from hanging up. He spoke the truth. "I'm sorry, I hadn't thought of what to say. I wanted simply to hear your voice. For many years I have seen you, but I've never heard you."

"Don't be rude, how dare you." But she spoke it gently.

"I remember when you were a little girl."

"Well then you must have been a little boy. Not much to remember."

"A lot for me."

Buzzing on the line, a poor connection. More silence.

"Is this any way to approach a girl?"

"What choice do I have?"

"Don't you have a mother? And sisters? And aunts?"

"You know that wouldn't be allowed. Consider who you are and who I am."

"You're the boy who's going to be the big munshi. That's what I hear."

So she knew of his position. "I will. Perhaps that's why I dare to speak with you."

"Do you think that impresses me?"

"I don't know what impresses you."

Unexpectedly, with no further word, she hung up.

Placing the phone gently on the table in front of him, Saqib rose and went out into the night. These emotions were new to him, this raw hope, pride that she knew of his achievements, fear of her judgment, her superiority. What could her life be like? Where was she at that moment? Had someone come, perhaps, and caused her to hide the phone? Or was she done with him, had that been all, and she would never speak with him again?

In the tall hollow night he walked out toward the river, the sky like a sieve pricked with stars all over, horizon to horizon, and far away the glow of Ranmal Mohra, where she would be, in the big house that her grandfather built. That house had always seemed the center of power in the village, even though the grandfather had been disgraced, lost his job, his property taken away, the great Sheikh Abbas, who settled these lands, back when Baloch from across the river came on raiding parties of twenty and thirty men and drove off whole herds of cattle. That stature seemed real to Saqib, not like this Rana Sattar, the man who followed, with his belly and his pretense of being simple.

Even in Saqib's childhood, though Abbas had been dead and gone for years, his power over the villagers still lingered, and they were more afraid of his memory than of the man he represented, Colonel Atar, and certainly more than Hisham and Shahnaz, who were so manifestly not of this place, with their dark sunglasses and poor Punjabi. Munshi Rana Sattar wouldn't hold his place much longer—Saqib had seen that in Lahore. There was a vacuum, which would certainly be filled. All this tumbled through Saqib's mind as he walked, shivering with sensation at having spoken so many words to Gazala, believing and not believing that it was true, that she had reached out to him, that she might be drawn toward a meeting, that she too wanted it.

✳

"Why did you hang up?" He asked quietly, not accusative.

She had called again, two nights later, just as he was working up the courage to ring her again.

"Someone came."

"Where are you now?"

"In a little room where we keep the flour. I'm sitting on a sack of it and it's getting on my shalvar."

"I'm sitting by the river. That's why the signal is so bad." They could barely hear each other.

"Really? At this time of night?"

"Well, I'm near it. I'm sitting at the farm I've built."

"The plastic tunnels? Everyone's talking about that. They say you've made so much money."

"The sahibs make the money."

"When they make it, you make it. Don't forget, my grandfather was the big munshi back before. I know how it works."

Though he wanted it so much, he was strangely disappointed when she agreed to meet him, not during that conversation, not in the one after, but the one after that, when they had already come to the point of speaking inconsequentially.

She was not flirtatious at all, and neither was he. "You want some business with me, I suppose?" she asked.

He had not known where they could meet and was even more surprised when she named a place far out in the orchard, safe against being seen but dangerous for a woman alone.

"You're brave to go out there so far," he said, admiration in his voice.

"Call it brave, if you like."

Village girls, and even more, the married women in the village, walked out at night and were caught doing it too—a few years ago, even the wife of the maulvi from the Ranmal Mohra mosque had been found with one of the field-workers—but Saqib had expected that Gazala would have the manners of the town class, not quite in purdah, but certainly never agreeing to meet a man without her family's permission, not so readily. As is often the case with the sons of powerful fathers, her father was weak and irresolute, cautious and pedantic, a bore, thin and stooped and silly, standing on his dignity, repeating himself, droning on, trying to insist that the villagers treat him with respect, yet unable to command it. Someone had made a joke, and then it stuck: He's the kind of guy, when he goes out to take a crap in the sugarcane, he sneaks back a couple of times to check on it. Perhaps the girl was running wild, though Saqib had heard nothing of it.

She had told him to meet her by an abandoned tube well at the end of the Atars' mango orchard that stretched far around the village. The little mud pump room, its roof caving in, stood under a huge pipal, one of the largest trees on the farm, and its fallen heart-shaped leaves crackled underfoot. He went early, expecting to wait, and instead as he approached she came out from the pump room and stood under the tree, the air still warm and heavy just at midnight. In the darkness he went quite close, to assure himself that indeed it was her, for he had been fearing that she would send some man, one of her brothers, to attack him for having dared to communicate with her. But no, it was certainly Gazala, her features now visible.

"As salaam uleikum," he whispered. He didn't know how to address her, whether to use her name.

She didn't answer for a moment.

"I shouldn't have come here," she whispered, finally. "What will you think of me."

"I'm grateful to you."

"Grateful! You think I've done this before. Let me tell you how I got away from my house. It's true, I've been here before, but never to meet anyone. This is where I've run away, not once or twice, but five times. I can count each one. Do you know why?"

Saqib sat down on the edge of the tank four paces away from her, thinking that he would be less intimidating that way, and crossed his legs, rested his hands on his knees.

"Tell me, Bibi. I came to listen."

"Yes, I wondered why you came. Why we came here."

"I've also never before asked anyone to meet me like this."

"You mean asked a girl to meet you out in the fields? Isn't that how all the village men and women do their business together?"

"Not me."

"Yes, that's why I've come now. I saw that when we were little. I thought you were different. A little bit, I watched you."

He thought of saying, I watched you too—but stopped himself. Her confession gave him an advantage.

The words poured from her. "Yes, I don't know why. And now I'll tell you the truth. You villagers think my father's a fool, and you're right. You think we have money, but you're wrong, there's no money at all. You know that we sold the car, and even before then there was no money for gasoline or to fix it. Last year my father sold my mother's bangles, it's like that. I cried for days, those were mine, you know, after she died. You all think we have something hidden, but we don't. And now I'll tell you the rest, and then you can spread it about the village if you will. My father drinks alcohol, not every night, but he drinks till he falls to the ground. That's what it is when he's sick for days and weeks. No one comes into our house, and that's how we hide it, even in this village where there are no secrets. After my mother died, slowly it began. That's how I got away tonight, by fighting with him, running away when he became like that. That's why I've run here before, and why no one follows me."

Whatever else he had expected, coming here with a shade of contempt for this girl who would meet a strange man at night, Saqib now felt pity and something like sorrow descending upon him. Walking to this assignation through the dark of the orchard, he had played with the thought that the connection to this girl could be turned to account. In Saqib's character, the strategic and the sentimental were fluidly intermixed, and so he did not recoil from the consideration—for example—that the Atars would be tied to him with an almost familial intimacy, if they were persuaded to take part in arranging this prohibited marriage. Now her confession shocked him, not that the father drank—he had even heard vague rumors of that—but that she would open herself so immediately and trustingly. It was true, then, the romance that he had associated with her. She was proud and exposed. Her voice was much deeper than he had expected, like the voice of a boy, not a woman, and angry, not at all seductive. She had a story to tell; probably she had never told this to anyone else. Only later did he wonder why she had chosen him for her confidence. Then in the night, with the water dark in the tank of the tube well and the pipal leaves overhead shivering when the breeze played in them, he listened without judgment, the yearning he had felt toward her guiding his thoughts, this same woman who over the years seemed impossibly distant as he glimpsed her going through the village.

"So there it is," she said. "Those are our secrets." Before she had been grave, but she said this lightly, as if tossing away what had come before.

She had been looking straight out into the night as she spoke. Now she turned, and under the folds of her dupatta, extending out like a hood, he saw her face and her mouth. She had one crooked tooth in front, as he knew, that slight imperfection to him proving her beauty. He had never been this close to her before, and though it was dark he could sense her body as he had never sensed it before, the solidity of her.

"May I speak?" he asked.

"You think I risked coming here to make small talk?"

"You don't want what your family wants, I see that now, I understand. Perhaps you thought that I asked you here for some other purpose. I don't know, I still don't understand. But I asked you to come because I wish your permission to arrange a marriage between us."

He had not expected to say this, not this plainly, not this soon.

She stirred, shook her head slightly. After finishing speaking, she had leaned against the tree, and was now barely visible, the buttresses of the pipal standing out in the gloom.

He continued.

"Please. It's true, I didn't know what to expect when you agreed to meet me here. But I promise, it was not for what another man might expect. Your mother is gone, your father—I suppose I can say, we all know that he's not strong. Your grandfather ruled over this place once. And now I expect that I will do that, not rule here, but I will rule somewhere, I will be much more than I am. If you think I'm boasting, well, you may be right. Perhaps I'll fail, but I won't do it like the others do. I intend that my way here will be different than anyone who has come before. And I'll tell you this too. I don't intend to be the manager here at this farm. I intend to be more. This is my beginning, but it's not my end. I haven't spoken of this to anyone, ever. If you trust me, say yes, and I'll arrange the rest. You think I can't, perhaps—that your father would never agree to give me your hand—then let that be my first test. These aren't just words. I'll move earth and heaven to achieve my way. I'll take you away from here, and I'll put gold bangles on your arms."

He stopped. That was enough, though he could have spoken more, this man usually so taciturn.

Gazala had turned her face, though in the dark he couldn't see her expression. She leaned back against the pipal, silent for a long time.

When she spoke she still didn't turn toward him, but continued looking into the darkened orchard.

"Try and find out. I won't promise anything. I don't suppose I'll say no."

It had been so simple. She slipped away without any further words, and he could see her dark figure moving against the white dust of the village road, among the looming mango trees. His hands were shaking. For a long time he sat, mind in turmoil, so keyed up before he came here, and now touched by the gloom of the trees, the pipal shivering above him in the wind. He had not expected that this future would be settled so easily, had thought it would be lighter, superficial, meeting this girl after all the years of thinking, and not even knowing that he was thinking of her. Well, let this be how he moved forward, then. For good or ill he closed upon this choice forever.

X

*T*hat Christmas, as Saqib's second crop matured, Hisham and Shahnaz came to Ranmal Mohra for a few days. On the afternoon when they arrived, he was in the kitchen preparing an elaborate tea, pakoras and samosas. He had called Yazid and asked him to bring ingredients for the dishes he had mastered back when his ambitions extended only to running the Atar household: imported cheeses, mozzarella, parmesan, olives in jars, Italian pasta, special vegetables, broccoli, and lettuce, delicacies that were unknown in these dark regions and available even in Lahore only from one shop, where a basket of Shahnaz's goodies cost more than a month of his salary.

Easing himself from the driver's seat, Yazid murmured, "Hello, boy," behind their backs, but the greeting from Hisham and Shahnaz was all he would have wished.

"Look at you!" said Hisham, clapping him on the shoulder. "Fieldwork suits you. And now I bet you've been cooking, you've got that apron on. Thank God, we're starved."

More reserved, as always, but more perceptive, Shahnaz looked at him appraisingly.

"You've lost weight, Saqib, but you're definitely starting to look like a munshi, you've got that other kind of weight."

With Shahnaz he reverted so naturally to the intimate, solicitous manner—weightlessly filial—that had grown between them over his years' service in Lahore, though his manners these past months had been quite different, peremptory and severe with his men, sharp when doing business, buying whole trucks of fertilizer, or speaking at length with Chaudrey Warraich, even going there once to ask advice and treated as an equal, despite his youth. With Hisham and Shahnaz his manners immediately became more circumspect, subdued but attentive. It filled him, this desire for their approbation, his will to please. He followed them in, taking the bags from the houseboy. Shahnaz moved through, musing, even drawing her fingers across the tops of the bureaus to see if there was dust.

"I'm impressed, Saqib," she said. "This place is cleaner than I've ever seen it."

"Ji, Bibi." He did not say anything further, but before they arrived had spent two days himself cleaning the house and arranging it as Shahnaz would like.

As they went out to the garden for tea, Hisham said, "Mix me a drink and bring it, Saqib. You know the drill. And what's for dinner?"

"Tikkas, sir. I had that sajji guy come. He's already at it. Tomorrow I'll cook with what Bayazid brought from Lahore."

"Good job, Saqib. You're the only one who knows what I like. I'm a villager at heart. It's Bibi who has the fancy tastes."

Saqib understood that his detailed preparations would annoy Shahnaz if she felt the weight of them, and so he kept himself in the background, didn't himself appear to serve the tea or the drinks, but sent out a boy whom he had requisitioned from the colonel's house, trained sufficiently to serve food, and told to dress clean and keep silent. It all must seem inevitable, as they surrendered to his ministrations, so that they should be aware only of feeling unburdened. Afterward, as night fell, he slipped again into the front garden, to light the little diyas that he had ordered from town, clay dishes filled with oil and with wicks made of cotton string, ordinarily used only at weddings. One by one he lit them, till finally Hisham and Shahnaz, murmuring over cocktails in another part of the garden noticed, and Hisham strolled over to him.

"What's this, Saqib?"

"Diyas, sir. I thought Begum Sahiba would like to see the garden lit up."

Now Shahnaz too came over. "What's next, Saqib, a band?"

He looked stricken. "It's too much, Bibi. Forgive me."

"No no, they're lovely, don't take it wrong. It's good preparation for when we have visitors, they love this kind of thing. Really, thank you."

Saqib brought them samosas and pakoras, then retired behind the kitchen and stayed out of sight, serving them dinner himself but otherwise allowing Colonel Atar's boy to answer their calls.

*

The ambient weather in South Punjab in December must be something like paradise, the cool of the morning, dew white on the grass, sweaters, and then at noon shirtsleeves, the sky no clouds except for one high wisp of cirrus that always seems there to give accent to the blue. The birds in that garden were so many and so insistently calling that it was difficult to speak on a cell phone among the trees. Saqib knew the breakfast routine so well, and fell to it, fresh squeezed foamy orange juice and farm eggs, toast made with the good bread that Yazid brought from Lahore, and tikkas, spicy things for Hisham's hangover. Yazid was still sleeping, he was off duty. "I'll drive them if they go out," Saqib said the night before. "Now you're my guest. You relax for a few days, I'll look after everything."

"What about your veggies?"

"My guys will manage, and if they don't, they'll wish they had." Already, while he had been preoccupied with arranging the house for this visit, he had made a descent upon his farm and found some slight disorder and had sharp words with a man, imposing a fine to make a point.

Yazid wagged his head and gave Saqib a smiling look. "The boy becomes a munshi. Soon you'll be buying eight or ten buffaloes and starting a little dairy. That's the first thing they do."

"What do you expect? I've got to be a munshi. My costs are five lacs an acre, and if I make any mistakes I'll be in the red at the end of the season. This is my chance."

"I know," conceded Yazid kindly. Thoughtful, he sighed. "I know. You've done well by us all."

. . .

Late on the morning of the second day, Saqib approached Shahnaz. He had seen her out and about in the garden, carrying shears and with gloves on, trimming the roses and making bouquets for the house, carrying flowers in armfuls into the pantry, working there to make up the vases. She relaxed most of all after completing one of her tasks, and this one particularly set her mind happily adrift. Now she had settled in the sun out in the garden, coffee at hand, a couple of books on the table beside her but reading one of her fashion magazines from abroad. He approached and stood quietly, till she looked up.

"There you are, Saqib. What's on your mind?"

"Thank you, Bibi. I'm disturbing you." He said "disturbing" in English, and mispronounced it "dishturbing." "I have a personal matter."

Placing the magazine on her lap, she looked up at him, waved him in front of her. "Don't be shy, stand here, so I can see you. What is it?" She shaded her eyes with one hand.

"Bibi Jee, forgive me." Unlike other favorites in such households, Saqib avoided approaching his masters on his own behalf, proving himself disinterested. Occasionally and as a matter of policy, he would intercede for the most powerless members of the household, his suit easy to grant and sure to gratify his masters' self-esteem.

Her severity relaxed, as he had known it would, for behind the unsentimental manner that she maintained with all the servants, including him, he knew that she was more compassionate than her husband, who seemed so warm.

"I suppose it's Rana Sahib, is it?"

"No, Bibi. He lets me be. I run my little corner of things, and he runs the rest. I'm too small for him to bother with."

"Your little corner made two lacs an acre last year. How many acres did you put in now?"

"I put in fifty, Bibi Jee." He allowed himself this flourish. "It's the second biggest tunnel farm in the division now."

"So what's the problem, then? You'll be the munshi who netted ten million rupees."

It flickered through Saqib's mind how instantly she had made that calculation, reminding him that in business she was the one who might catch him out.

"Forgive me. I've troubled you about something quite different. I wish to marry, and I need your help."

She examined him humorously. "It shouldn't be difficult to arrange your wedding celebrations. I imagine you're a fair prospect in Ranmal Mohra."

"Yes, my mother wishes me to wed my cousin. She's a good person, but this girl can neither read nor write. I wouldn't know what to speak with her about."

Shahnaz had been sitting with her feet up on a chair. Now she put them down, turned toward Saqib, and looked him in the face, perceiving the complexity of the matter.

"I gather you've made a choice. And of course you would have. Who is it, then?"

"That's exactly the problem. Do you remember the name of Sheikh Abbas?"

"The legendary Seth Abbas, who became Sheikh Abbas, and who was well on his way to having more land than the colonel. What about him? That drama ended years ago, and not very well."

"Yes, Bibi, he died. And even now the villagers remember that Colonel Sahib didn't go for condolence at the time. Before he died, he disgorged most of his land and much else too. They say around here, no one can digest the Atar family's money."

Shahnaz laughed. "Go on. People digest the Atar money all the time. Every time Mian Sahib opens up the books, or, rather, whenever those accountants do, they find one thing or another."

"But Sheikh Abbas's family did lose most of what he gained. I'm speaking of his granddaughter."

"I see. So she's a Sheikh, at least the family have become so. I know the background, you don't need to explain. Is the problem on your family's side or theirs?"

"Both. They're proud because of the position the grandfather held, and my family can't imagine that I would marry anyone outside my family or my caste."

"And then there's the whole murky question of exactly what that family were before they became Sheikhs of Ranmal Mohra. You're Arain, aren't you? I should think her family would jump at that connection. Your people are gobbling up the district."

Saqib stood arms straight, long hands straight down, no motion, a studied contrast to the stereotypical frenetic Arain. "In the village they are all prejudice and obstinacy, madam. If Mian Sahib can speak just a word to the girl's father, then I can bring my mother around. Bibi Jee, it's just so for me as for any man who wants to marry by his choice: The villagers all come together. My mother says they're Hindus, and they say I'm a gardener's son and beneath their daughter."

Shahnaz joined her hands together and sat thinking. "The way I see it, both sides have a reason to settle for the arrangement."

Now Saqib played his strongest card. "Bibi, it was in your household that I learned to be different from the manners of my family. The village is changing, and I suppose that my children's world will be more like yours and Mian Sahib's, and those will be better days. With the girl I want to marry a different life is possible than the one my parents imagined for me. You taught me to hope for more. It's simple prejudice that stands in my way, and that's what we need, what the village needs, what the country needs, to move past that."

"And love leads the way, is it?"

Saqib would not be drawn so easily into fatuity. "Yes, love is also part of it. But I don't know Gazala so well as that. That is her name. I seek an arrangement, and perhaps one that is not so different than the arranged marriage that my mother wants for me. But at least in this marriage with Gazala I can imagine that we will be working together. At best my cousin would not understand me and would not be able to help me, and at worst she would blame me all her days for not being a man like the others."

Shahnaz for a moment looked into the trees. "Do you know, Saqib, I really should have sent you off to school. But then—maybe this is the best education right here, running this business. Mian Sahib and I swore long ago not to interfere any more in the villagers' affairs here at Ranmal Mohra. They always blame us when it goes bad—and it always does. But maybe this is an exception."

✧

Two mornings later, Sheikh Riaz was summoned to Kèrala. Before he arrived, while Hisham and Shahnaz had breakfast in a sunny, wind-shaded side lawn, Saqib briefed them, composed and circumspect, expressionless.

"So tell me about this Sheikh Riaz of yours," began Hisham, resplendent in his landlord morning wear, a lungi and a white long kurta with excessively long sleeves, like a Mandarin bureaucrat. Preparing his ground, Saqib had made sure that morning to brew the coffee right and threw a batch of apple muffins into the breakfast mix. "I gather he's a fool, but that's about all I know. Do they still live in that unfortunate house? If Sheikh Abbas hadn't gotten all jumped up and built himself a palace, Colonel Sahib probably would have let it slide, and the old man would have kept his spoils. But then what's the point of becoming a richie, if you can't flaunt it?"

"The son is nothing to the father, Mian Sahib. There's a story that one day Sheikh Abbas was teaching the boy about business and so he brought him in while sitting with the assistant commissioner and some others. The boy mumbled and blushed till the great Munshi Abbas Sahib became so annoyed that he stood up and began thrashing him with a walking stick, and Riaz just sat there and blubbered. It's like they say, the grass doesn't grow under the big banyans."

"Excuse my asking, but why then are you so eager to marry his daughter? What good is this Sheikh Riaz to you, without property or influence?"

"It's not for him or anything he can do for me, sir. I hope I don't need any support other than what you are good enough to provide. The daughter is different than the others, however. She has the spirit that her grandfather had, she's strong and she's proud."

Hisham nodded at Shahnaz and said in English, "That's a dangerous combination in a wife!"

Shahnaz shrugged off his frivolity. "Not at all. This makes sense, Saqib. These people are Baniyas, they've got money in their blood, they know how to get on in the world. If she's what you say she is then she'll be the one you need beside you, when you reach toward your goals."

"And what are your goals, Saqib?" asked Hisham archly.

Shahnaz made a little intervention in Saqib's favor, channeling the conversation. "Leave it, darling," she said in English. In Urdu, "So what have you said to the father? Did he refuse you?"

"No, Bibi. I knew that if I approached him directly, he would not agree. He's famous both for stinginess and timidity, and even more, for his pride. I've tried to show him that I will someday be a successful man under your patronage, and that therefore I may someday be able to help revive that family's fortunes. For a man like that, who was never the equal of his father, that is the great dream."

Hisham laughed, genuinely pleased. "That's bold! And probably true. So how should I speak to him, then? It's your private matter, after all."

"Sir, perhaps you may act as if it's settled already, and that you're calling him in to congratulate him and to give your blessings. Tell him, don't ask him. His daughter has prepared the ground, so it won't be a surprise to him entirely. Say that you approve of his open-mindedness and his good sense, tell him well done, call him a man of the future, sir, if that's not too strong. He'll go along with you because he wouldn't do anything else. He's fearful and without support in this place, he has nowhere to turn, and so he'll take what he can get. Later, tomorrow, I'll go to him and do the rest. Your favor will mean everything to him."

Hisham considered, an amused look on his face. "No one can say you're a man of conventions, Saqib."

XI

*H*isham and Shahnaz's intervention had succeeded, as Saqib knew it would, and he and Gazala were married. Although the Atars never attended weddings in the village, Saqib had picked a date for the celebration when he knew they would anyway be coming to Kèrala, and so—for him—they stretched a point and attended the mehndi, Saqib taking care to invite them only to this ceremony, the part of the festivities most likely to amuse them. Having intervened with the reluctant father and then been guests of honor at this most intimate function, this made them something like godparents to the marriage.

"It's a bad precedent," grumbled Hisham, complaining about having to suit up and go watch the village girls dancing. "How do we say no to the next Notable Not-Able around here who sends us a wedding card, when word gets out we go trotting around every time one of our servants gets hitched?"

"Munshi, not servant."

"That's even worse. At least with a servant it could be some sentimental foolishness."

"Be a sport, darling. This is our Saqib. In for a penny, in for a pound."

✻

Saqib had splashed out on renting a well-built house in Adda Mastt Bahadur, drawing money from the thin dowery that Sheikh Riaz with bad grace conceded, and supplementing his own insufficient salary with what Gazala earned teaching. Although she was leaving her grandfather's imposing house, Gazala thus moved into town from the village, proof of a rise in circumstance. The gossips exaggerated the dowery, saying that finally the old Sheikh's hidden gold came to light, and so no one questioned the couple's prosperity, the munshi moving into a sparkling new development in town—at least not yet.

Now the cucumber harvest was in full swing, Saqib's second crop, and this year his men were sending three trucks daily to market, Saqib making phone calls and dispatching the loads to the far cities, depending on where the rates were good, Lahore, Islamabad, Sukker, even Peshawar far to the north.

One morning he said to Gazala as she was pulling together her books and bag, "I'm going to be late tonight. Don't wait up."

"Will they feed you where you're going, or can I make you dinner?"

She was too proud to ask further questions. He loved this in her, the long oval face that she turned to him when uncertain, her vulnerability all mixed up with her strength. She feared that he had secrets, that he would suddenly change toward her and reveal another side of himself. "After all, I barely know you," she had said once.

"I'll be back for dinner. Don't worry so much. I have to go somewhere on business."

"Do as you must. I saw the car when you came last night."

"It belongs to a guy I know. I borrowed it for the day."

Not wanting to take the farm jeep on this errand and so to face questions from Rana Sahib about his reasons for this distant excursion, Saqib had rented a car from an auto showroom and parked it inconspicuously—as he thought—in the alley beside the house.

She was not satisfied with his answer, and yet she would not ask further, and he would not explain, telling himself that he was taking a stand for his independence.

"Look, I'm leaving my keys. I'll knock and you let me in, and you can warm dinner for me while I tell you of my day."

She took the keys and wrapped her fist tightly around them.

Often he did not understand why she reacted as she did, so that he made gestures toward her without knowing exactly what he meant by them, trying to feel out her response, making spontaneous offerings such as this one of leaving the keys. He found that she unbalanced him sometimes, as when she had this distant expression, and this grip in which she held the keys so tightly.

"Go to your business," she said after a moment. But she didn't return the keys.

*

"Mubarek on your new wheels, Manager Sahib," remarked Chaudrey Warraich as he stood and held open the car door. Eager for the meeting, or wanting to give that impression, he had called Saqib twice that morning to ask how far he had gotten from Adda Mastt Bahadur, speeding him along.

"With your blessings, Chaudrey Sahib," allowed Saqib, embracing his business partner. "But this is just a rental. I didn't ask to borrow the farm jeep today, I've come on my own here, as you see. If I asked Munshi Abdul Sattar he might have wanted to come along."

"I can see that might not be convenient. Well, don't worry, someday soon we'll be setting you up with your own car. Come, after you."

He did not take Saqib into his office but led him through a dark courtyard and then along a passage that opened unexpectedly into a new and modern house at the back.

"Here you are," he said, gesturing about, opening the doors, turning on the air conditioner. "I've just had this all built last year. This is not for business, but I'm bringing you here. Stay, I'll say my prayers and be back. I want you to have lunch with me." As he disappeared Saqib smiled secretly that he hadn't been asked if he would pray. Chaudrey Sahib studied his business associates from all angles. Perhaps he'd been sniffing out information somewhere around Rana Abdul Sattar, who made an issue of Saqib's supposed impiety.

Saqib was familiar with provincial politicians' and businessmen's rooms, glimpsed over the years while going about left-front-seat beside Yazid when Hisham made calls, then a couple of times lately on his own while developing his contacts around Ranmal Mohra. There was a sameness to the decoration of those lugubrious houses, their heavy overplush sofas and armchairs in stiff groupings, covered in drab stain-resistant material, Koranic calligraphy in frames on the walls, heavy stamped-glass ashtrays, a brass tea trolley. Living in Lahore, however, had given Warraich a further polish, which surprised Saqib. The arrangement of the furniture, in several little sitting enclaves, made the room less stiff, and the surprising blue color of the Persian carpet, the diversity of the decorations, which must have been purchased abroad, including a striking pair of lamps made of wood and glass that might even have suited Shahnaz, made the room something approaching that of an upper-class drawing room in Lahore.

Settled, looking about him, Saqib thought about this, that all the money in the world would not buy Warraich what he truly wanted, and what Saqib nearly possessed, the discrimination to understand the gulf that separated people like the Atars from himself. The Atars, meaning Shahnaz, really, had imagination, and the confidence to express that imagination, when they went about making their public statements of who they were, by their clothes, their houses, their cars, their treatment of their inferiors and each other. Warraich knew much that Saqib wished to know, about money and those machinations, business here in these lesser cities. Saqib, however, knew something even more precious, something that he imbibed over the years living at Al-Unmool in Lahore, and as such a particular favorite—and such an observant one. Those mores could not usefully be learned through description, they must be absorbed living in those spaces with the people who made them and seeing how they interacted there. That was the magic, and all the rest just a way of getting there, to live like that, with that impudence and assurance, and that taste.

With these reflections in mind, Saqib studied Warraich dispassionately as he returned to the room and settled himself onto the sofa, having changed into a loose white shalvar and plastic slippers, his sleeves loosely rolled up, face still damp from his ablutions, no formalities, wearing the shriven, inward face of a man just returned from his spiritual communion.

"Well, young man," he began, "I'm pleased to say, you're the one who seems to have found the key. You've got all the pieces, a line to the money, and the brain to put the business together. They tell me you got twelve hundred bags an acre last season."

"Thirteen hundred and twenty-seven."

"Is that a real number? Are you a farmer or a businessman?"

"What's the difference?"

"Farmers inflate their numbers, because that's what they care about, growing their crops and doing it better than the others. Businessmen hide their earnings, all they care about is the cash. They hide the treasure."

"Well, farmer or not, I counted every bag."

Warraich laughed heartily. "If you counted every single one, then!"

"Excuse me saying, Warraich Sahib, but you seem to take more pleasure in it than I do."

"I can afford to. I didn't do the work, and I didn't take the risk. Mothers don't laugh when their children do well, it's a different emotion."

A boy came in and whispered something in Warraich's ear.

"Put it on, then."

As they moved to the table, Warracih said, "They made something special that I want you to try. You've maybe heard of the Baba Kareem tikkas? My cook makes them just like Baba Kareem. I hired him away, he was a kitchen boy and stole their secrets."

"Well, then, Chaudrey Gul Nawaz Sahib, I'm like that boy, and I've come to steal your secrets. That's why I've asked for your time this day. The first time I came to see you, after our meeting I went to find the Kareem tikkas, but when I got to the market, there were ten different restaurants with that name. All of them were probably quite good, but only one truly had the secret, because that one made the name first. I think your secret, perhaps, is that you were the first. You'll always have that over the other growers."

"Don't be a mystic about it," said Warraich, waving his fingers dismissively. "This is growing cucumbers, not luring customers into a restaurant. There's no reputation here."

"But everyone knows your reputation. They buy the nets and the seeds and the wire and everything from you, because you were the first. We farmers don't trust anyone else."

"That's why you'll never make real money, you farmers. You're sentimental, and you're conservative. You think because it's been done one way for a hundred years there's no reason to change. The farmers have made me rich because I've shown them something new, but in a way that doesn't alarm them. In a way, I'm the farmer, and you all are my crop."

It surprised Saqib that this cunning businessman should be so open with him. He ate carefully, not with hunger, but with artifice, as he had seen in the Atar household, eating as ceremony.

Warraich pointed at a box of tissues, and the boy standing at his shoulder leapt and offered him one. Wiping his fingers, Warraich pulled a tiny tan device from his ear.

"Do you see this? It's a microphone, it allows me to hear. I bought this in London, and I suppose it cost more than Mian Hisham Atar pays you in six months. When I was little they thought I was stupid because I didn't answer, and only later did they find out I couldn't hear. I couldn't go to school because of it, so my father put me with a cart in the market, selling fruit and vegetables. And that was my beginning, a cart, then a little stall, then a shop in the wholesale market, selling in bulk. But that didn't do it, that wasn't enough. Just once, one time, I needed to make a lot of money at once. That's the hard part, making that first chunk, when you start from absolutely nothing. Rich sons get for nothing what we pay for with our souls and consciences. It's not quite a fortune you need—only those sons of rich fathers get that—but you need enough to make more. Money breeds money, and then, if you've got the touch and some luck, the rest follows. Mind you, that first payout has to be a decent size."

Warraich stopped speaking and instead settled to his lunch, picking at the bones of the little quail and crunching them, sucking them and then lining them up at the edge of his plate. After a little while, he looked up.

"Why aren't you eating? Isn't it good?"

"It's excellent. It's better than Baba Kareem."

"It *is* Baba Kareem. Get that into your head."

He resumed his meal, saying nothing more, Saqib too picking at his meal to keep up. They finished, no further words, Warraich eating mechanically, his eyes on the wall opposite.

Finally he raised his water glass between thumb and index finger, smearing it with grease, and drained it at one go.

"All right, you've passed. I was expecting you to be pressing me about how I made that first little fortune. You're a smart boy."

Still Saqib held his tongue, impassive—a trick of his, to be silent and unperturbed, like a fish holding steady in running water.

A moment, another moment, then Warraich abruptly stood up.

"Come on, we'll have green tea in the other room. I've got some questions for you."

When they were settled, Warraich began speaking and enumerating on his fingers. "Look, I know, you've got fifty acres under plastic right now. You're already the biggest grower around Muzaffargarh, and the fourteenth biggest in the Punjab. You bought all your gear from me, and you bought the best. I suppose you made about two lacs an acre for Mr. Hisham Atar—or for somebody—last year, and your harvest this year will be at least as good. That's the situation. And what's your plan? How much will you put in next fall?"

"The same, I don't think I can manage more than that. And I don't have the market. I would have to find guaranteed buyers farther away. Locally, if they know I have too much they'll knock down the price. And it's a big risk for the farm, if something goes wrong. My investment this year was more than four lacs an acre, twenty million for the whole thing on fifty acres."

"Twenty million? And what about in your pocket? A million? Two?"

"Not quite, sir."

Warraich blew out his breath. "*Phh.* Come on. Why did you rent a car to come here? Why not use the jeep you came in last time?"

"Maybe it wasn't available. But you're right. I came here privately."

Warraich pointed his finger at Saqib.

"I'm not sure you know exactly why you did come here today. Let me talk to you seriously. In the fall I want you to double it. Go big, put in a hundred acres. All cucumbers, all in tunnels. I'll find you the seed, the plastic, the whole kit, a package. This one will be from another stock, not the one that worked so well before. The gear will last one season, and that seed's not so bad, you'll get a crop. But you write it up in your books like last year's imported stuff. You send me a check for the imported-stuff price, I give you a commission. Call it seven lacs, that's enough to set you up."

Saqib sat unmoving, betraying no response for a moment, his head cocked, looking out toward a window, which was covered by a curtain, no view. Yes, Warraich was correct, Saqib had not come to see him with any clear sense of what he wanted, other than that he wanted more, some different way of managing the business, and more to himself, if it could be done without upsetting the balance. He would have to trust Warraich, at least enough to hear him out.

✻

"The business makes lots of money, and I suppose I could make some of that too. But what's the hurry? Rana Abdul Sattar, who runs the whole farm for Mian Atar, has millions put away—just recently they say he bought a row of four shops in Multan for his son."

"Sure. But it took him forty years to do it. A guy like you needs a piece of money right away. Or not, it's a choice. Safer your way, for sure. My way, it's all quickly, all or nothing. First year you make a lot of money for the Sahib, second year you make it for him again. Third year's your chance, make a lot, take the lot, and be ready to face the music when he asks what happened. You understand the business, they don't. Do it right and they'll accept your explanations. But if you want to make a killing, it's hard to do it by halves. You buy the Dutch stuff or the Chinese, it's one or the other."

Saqib had never imagined his future being thirty years in harness at Ranmal Mohra, filtering out a hundred thousand each season, slow accumulation. "I suppose you're right. Those were the old days and the old ways."

As he said this, he was conscious with a twinge that this was one of Shahnaz's little phrases, her rare colloquialisms.

"I need to think about it. But let's just say for now, make it a ten lacs and settle it. A round million. I'm not agreeing, I'm just throwing out a number with you."

That was a bigger sum than Saqib had contemplated. It opened such possibilities. Saqib imagined business to be done across the land and on his own account, far past Adda Mastt Bahadur, to Multan, to Bahawalpur, to the cities in the north.

"All right, sure. A million then, though it doesn't leave me much. This isn't our last handshake, I'll give it to you. And I'll set you up with a buyer in Faisalabad. You'll send all your stuff to him, and he'll give you another two lacs, something like that, so long as you accept his numbers. And he'll send you all the right paperwork too. He's a good guy."

"And how will the farm do at the end?"

"Huge loss."

"And what about Mian Atar?"

"That's between you and Mian Atar. I suppose you've made a plan."

"What makes you think that?"

"Because I was just like you, twenty years ago. I had a plan."

"And now I will ask you one question, about this, since I didn't ask before. What was that plan, Chaudrey Sahib? What is the secret there?"

"No, that's different, you have to know the Sahib and his connections and his moods, get in some shelter where he can't pry you out. Covering up depends on who you're covering up from. I'll help you, I know some guys. The district police officer in Muzaffargarh is a buddy. But if Hisham Atar Sahib starts making calls to Islamabad and bringing down the big hammers on your head, the DPO won't be able to do anything. Just this one time, you have to know how to get away with it. In Pakistan incredible crimes are committed every day, in broad daylight, but no one dares to complain. But right at the beginning, just once, you'll have to face the music. They have the power. You don't."

XII

*O*nly a few houses had been built in the new development on the outskirts of Adda Mastt Bahadur where Saqib rented their lodging, poking up here and there among paved and wide and gridded streets, so that there were no people about, this solitude rare in Pakistan. Returning that evening from Sargodha, he stood a moment, weary, confused, contemplating the unfinished landscape, which corresponded with a future that he desired and imagined, gathering to be built, an aspirational colony for rising men.

How much would he tell Gazala of the scheme proposed by Warraich? Whatever words he used, he could not bear to be as plain about it as Warraich had been, to appear as a thief in her eyes. If he had married his cousin, his mother's choice, she would not have understood about Dutch seed and Chinese seed and fake invoices. He would give her the explanation that threw the best light upon it, and she would stand by him in the face of the world, because once committed to him she must share his fate wherever it led them. That would have been simpler.

With Gazala he must tell her more, granddaughter of the great Sheikh Abbas, who came from moneylenders, hoarders of gold, famous for making shrewd calculations in their heads, able to tot up interest and costs, entrapping the peasants for centuries, subject to pogroms but otherwise always a secret power. Even as she had first encountered him, a man unknown to her except by sight and something by reputation, she had been both bold and deliberate, quick. Like a groom brought up in the stables who knows how horse races are fixed, she would know all about how a munshi plays the master, and especially this girl, put to a harsh school by her ineffective father with his secret drinking and his burned-out inheritance.

And then, she went out every day into the marketplace, to her school, a sophisticated franchise that thrived all over Pakistan, made a decent salary there, and even before that had been handling money to keep her family afloat. Living with her for just a few months now, Saqib found that the merchant culture of her caste gave her insights about him and his projects that no one in his own family, certainly, could have made. He was wary of her, that apprehension softened by her unexpected sensuality, her willingness entirely to stretch herself out upon him, from chin to foot, possessing him as much as he possessed her, hungry, easily hurt, quickly restored.

Now standing among the half-built houses, he decided to tell Gazala of the scheme, and that decision committed him to following it through. Only let him see what she said. He went resolutely toward the door. No keys. He had forgotten and panicked, slapping his pockets, looking for them. But as he approached the metal gate leading into the tiny courtyard, she cracked it open, and then leaned against it, provocative, her feet bare. Just for a moment, he stood as a supplicant before her.

"And may I come in?"

"What happened to the car?"

"I returned it to the guy. I've been in Sargodha."

"So you went all the way to Sargodha. That's far away."

*

Closing the gate so no one could see, careful, sliding the hasp shut behind him, he pulled her close, kissed her hair at the top of her head. She bore the clean scent of her special apple shampoo, not the one his mother and sisters bought in the Ranmal Mohra shop, a block of soap that foamed up blue-gray and smelled of wet ink.

In the rooms, the rich aroma of food. She cooked different dishes than the villagers did, the old dishes of her grandmother from back in northern Punjab. Now, she had made a feast, a more elaborate meal than she had ever prepared before. Tenderly she brought in smoky eggplant in tomatoes, black beans in a cream sauce, a beef shank nihari cooked in a sealed pot, which before he had tasted only in Lahore, the dishes so much more sophisticated than the lentils and curries his mother would make. These lineaments of culture gratified him, refinements confirming that the possibilities he had imagined in her proved true. He thought of the quail that Warraich had served him, Baba Kareem. Gazala knew even better than that.

"So what's the occasion, my queen?" he asked, pleased and hungry.

"Nothing. Maybe to keep you running back after you run away."

She couldn't possibly know of the Warraich deal, this must be something else.

Cross-legged on the bed, he prickled with consciousness of her body as she sat on her knees and rose to put the food on his plate, choosing out special pieces. Her body already had become so well known, her physicality, a whole head shorter than him, small-breasted. They made love so often in these days, again and again he had moved inside her. These seemed to him all the flavors of love that he had imagined, the couplings. She had put henna on her hands, so that the palms were orange-yellow, the color of her skin showing through underneath, little moons of her fingernails stained also, that color erotic to him. It was too hot for the overhead light, just one burning bulb in the hallway. In the May heat there were beads of sweat on her upper lip, and he imagined how moist and sticky and delicious her body would be if they lay clasping and unclasping in bed.

He finished, drank the glass of cool water she offered.

"Come sit up here," he said, and she rose onto the bed, sat across from him.

"There's something that you're hiding," she said, playing with the hem of her kurta, wearing a queer expression, uncertain.

He paused. It had all seemed so much more plausible sitting in Warraich's house with all the rich markings of success around, the trappings and position that Saqib himself intended to gain and surpass, at whatever cost.

"There is a man named Chaudrey Warraich who sells me all the things for my vegetables, seeds and nets and wire, from abroad. It costs more, but it's better. He and I met today in Sargodha. Now with him I'm going to make the vegetable business much bigger, and when he sells me all those things, he'll give me a portion of the profit too."

"And he'll get more?"

"Yes, he shares with me."

"And Hisham Atar Sahib will get less."

"That's true." She instantly grasped the essence of it.

Leaning back on her arms, she stared up at the ceiling for a long moment.

"And what if they find out? With my grandfather they took back what they could, but he had many years to hide what needed hiding. And even then we found ourselves poor after he died."

"Poor, but richest in the village by far, and quite rich even by comparison in the whole area. I'll take it with great care, and I'll hide it better than your grandfather did. And I won't take as much. He was there for many years, but I don't intend to be. All I need is one chance, a bit of money—a lot of it, if you count it another way—and then we'll have our own, I'll build it up. Someday I'll have what Hisham Atar Sahib has, I wouldn't be the first to become that big. Even this Warraich came from nowhere. For me this is the beginning, for your grandfather that was the end. What I take is just to lift me up once, so that I can build all that I want to build. For us, for you."

"What about the police? They'll take you, and I'll never hear from you again, or you'll come back all broken. Colonel Sahib took my grandfather away chained in the back of a jeep, and after they brought him back, he did all that the Sahib demanded. They drove him through the village like that to show the people."

"You saw that Hisham Sahib and Shahnaz Bibi came to our mehndi. I was brought up by them and with them. They wouldn't do that to me. They won't be sure whether it was a bad crop or bad seeds or bad diseases. I'll make the books look right, and they'll accept that proof and let me off, because they want to. I've studied them, lived with them. When Hisham Sahib can't decide who is right or wrong, he does nothing, that's a big difference between the Begum Sahiba and him and these waderas around us who become the parliamentarians. They beat their people for exercise. Even with your grandfather it was different. Colonel Atar was a different kind of man, and if your grandfather hadn't given back so much the Colonel Sahib might have locked him away forever. But Mian Hisham Atar thinks like people from America, from abroad."

✳

Instead of continuing the conversation, she rose, took the empty dishes into the kitchen, then returned, and quite unexpectedly slipped her kurta off over her head, there in the shadowy light. Her breasts were small, her rib cage showing. She might have been one of the girls seen coming from the canal in the summer after bathing, the ones just adolescent, their wet kurtas clinging to them. Her unexpected nudity a little bit shocked him, had surprised him from the beginning, when they made love those first nights, that she was resolutely not shy, presented herself naked in front of him without any concealment.

Sitting down on the bed next to him, she took his hand and put it to her breast.

"I have something to tell you also. I wasn't planning to tell you until I was sure, but now I will." Taking his hand, holding one of his long fingers, she put it on her nipple.

"See this? My grandmother taught me her cooking, and she taught me this. It hurts a little bit now, and these are bigger and darker."

Saqib stiffened for a moment and didn't know where to look, though this bold woman stared straight into his eyes. What he thought of saying was, *You frighten me.* Her grandmother seemed unnatural, the one who had kept the hidden Hindu figurines after the family converted to Islam. His mother too had powers, but not like this—though strange and secret, hers possessed nothing of the occult.

Gazala still held his finger upon the areola of her nipple.

"See, it's hard." She traced his finger in circles. "Do you know what it means?"

The emotion rose up in Saqib's body, up up through his head, and then collapsed down like cards. His shoulders slumped. Fathering a child so soon had not entered his calculations, although he had made love to her every night since the wedding, attaching himself to her right at his belt and core.

She looked at him steadily, calming him.

"Yes? Are you ready?"

Unexpectedly, again these emotions he didn't control, a panic. He turned his head sideways, turned over and lay on his back, looked up at her. "Are you sure?"

"Shhh," she quieted him. Looking down at him, she asked, "Weren't you prepared, then?"

He couldn't lie, he felt it too much, the day had been long, he had been thinking with such perplexity of Warraich, and now this. "Of course," he said heavily, but no, he hadn't been prepared. He felt that he should be more in command, and yet she was the one composed and holding him, untroubled and soothing him. "Yes, of course. Yes, yes." Saying it made it so.

"I went to Sargodha to speak of making money from the Atars, and now I've come home to this. All my thoughts are confused. Are you sure?"

"My grandmother would help with woman from our people who were having babies, and she took me along. I can't be sure, but . . . No, I'm quite sure, my breasts hurt and they're growing. That's how my grandmother always knew. She was the one they came to if the child must be ended, that was her secret also. They would call her even back to Lahore, after Colonel Sahib brought my grandfather here."

"What does it mean?" said Saqib, more to himself than to her. "I've been scheming to gain us something like a fortune, on the day you tell me this, about our child. I wonder how it ends."

"But it all fits together. Isn't it because of this plan with your

Warraich that you wanted so much to marry me? If the Sahib hadn't spoken to my father, he would never have given me to you. The Sahib made the marriage."

Yes, it was true. It was also true.

"Maybe. Partly. Remember what I told you? That when I was a boy, I saw you standing in the gate of your father's house. After that I always wanted it to be you."

She pushed her hands against his chest and fixed him with an expression much harder than any he had seen in her face before, a force unsheathed and swaying above them. "Then don't hide your thoughts from me! I was brought up with such plans, hearing of these things, knowing where the money comes from. That night when I met you under the pipal tree, you said that you would put gold bangles on my arms. Do it, then."

Hiding his confusion, unbalanced, Saqib sat playing with her feet, bending each of her toes back one by one.

"I know what this means," she said finally, gently, her expression again the one he knew, the pretty one, the girl one. "Always, when you start touching my feet."

"I'm just counting," he replied, embarrassed, himself uncertain of his thinking. To cover his confusion, he blurted out, "I haven't yet got you gold bangles, but there's something else. I bought it and put it away."

"Oh?"

"But you're like my mother. You don't care about presents."

"Depends on the present."

He rose, went to the trunk where he kept his papers and valuables, and brought a white box.

"How about this one?" he said, sitting down again cross-legged, their knees touching.

"What is it?"

"What do you think?"

"I know, actually. I know from the apple."

He looked sharply up at her. "And you don't like it."

Truly, he was hurt. All the months working morning and night in the fields, desperate in wind and hail, he had been thinking of this moment. She had mentioned several times that the headmistress of her school, a woman who owned a car and drove it herself, had one of these iPhones, which cost over a lac rupees, what no ordinary man could afford, more than a year of Saqib's salary. Everyone knew the price.

"Open it at least."

Fiddling with the box, prying it open, very carefully lifting out the contents, she arranged the phone and the other pieces on the pillow.

"They pack it like jewelry."

"I think I should have bought you jewelry."

She was silent, had not thanked him. Finally she said, as if this followed naturally, "Why do you never speak of your work, what you do out there by the river?"

"I have enough of my work when I'm in the fields."

"Don't think I don't understand, Saqib." Her using his name added weight to her words. "Someday everything will come out."

"Shall I not do this, then? With Chaudrey Warraich, I mean? It still is not too late."

"No, but understand me now. You know what you married. You married a baniya. We've hidden gold for as long as there has been gold to hide. Do you know why?"

"Tell me."

"Because when the people see how much we have, they take it from us. We are not warriors, we are baniyas, we lend money, that's our weakness, that's how they find out what we have. My grandmother told me, 'Gold is gold, and it rules the world, but for one matter. Gold doesn't breed.' The gold we hide drives us mad, until finally we bring it into the light, where the people see it. We make it breed by lending it, and then they see how very much we have." She picked up the phone, which still had on it the plastic sheet to protect the screen. "Take this back, don't buy me anything yet. It's bad luck, before whatever you've taken is proven to be ours. Taking is one thing, keeping is another. In a year you can buy me whatever you like."

But Saqib didn't take the phone back; he himself had been long-ing to have one like it, for he had seen that Hisham and Shahnaz always owned these phones with the apple engraved on the back. Gazala saw that he kept it, but she said nothing, as he had known she would not.

XIII

*M*unshi Abdul Sattar had fallen seriously ill that year, his dia-
betes uncontrolled, suppurating sores on one leg, with the
word going about the area that he was finished. This made it easier
for Saqib to take over an additional fifty acres of land from him, in
the spring, after the harvest of the wheat.

Calling on him one morning in the dera at Ranmal Mohra, a time
when he would likely be alone, Saqib found him reduced greatly,
sitting with one leg up, and making no effort to hide the wound,
wearing a dhoti, the leg swollen up, tubular, with a weeping sore near
the ankle. Seeing Saqib, he made a movement, as if to rise in respect,
and Saqib knew then that he could do as he wished with this man.

"Please, please, Chaudrey Sahib, please sit," Saqib remonstrated,
and placed himself on a little stool, almost at the munshi's feet.

"No, no, boy, come, don't sit there." He called over his shoulder,
"Hey, you, donkey, bring a proper chair for Saqib Sahib."

Sattar had lost flesh, his once magnificent stomach now flabby
under his kurta, all of him looking like a man wearing someone
else's skin, even the face melted downward, the flesh around the eyes
settled into the hollows, and his mouth working, as if he were chewing. Along with the chair of honor, he had ordered tea brought, a
courtesy never before offered to Saqib.

"This is nothing," he said with a hollow gesture, pointing to the
leg. "I'm going to Lahore next week. Hisham Sahib and the Begum
Sahiba have been so good to me, so very kind. So appreciative."
He paused, chewing his gums, nodding his head, looking into the
distance as if seeing his future there. "I'm to see all the great spe-

cialists. In a month I'll be back as good as ever. I'm going to speak to Hisham Sahib about planting another fifty acres of orchard, over at Hotu Wali. You know that land, it's well watered, the trees would do well there."

He knew all about Saqib's plans for that land, and looked away from Saqib's face as he made this statement, throwing it in. That was the site of the additional fifty acres of tunnels.

"Very good thinking, Chaudrey Sahib. That is good land. In fact, that's why I've come to you. You see, Hisham Sahib has asked me to increase the size of my project. I'm adding fifty acres, and that's the place I intend to do it."

"Fifty acres!" Sattar threw up his hands. "Another fifty acres! Are you mad? They say that the markets were already too full with your cucumbers last season. I saw it myself, cucumbers everywhere. Tiny little things too."

"That's the size people want. But no, there weren't too many." Saqib was not pretending any deference now. "In any case, I have the market, and it's my job to do as Hisham Sahib tells me. He wants this, and I obey."

Sattar for a moment let his temper overcome him, the old Chaudrey Abdul Sattar, who beat the peasants himself, the terror of the village, the one who called in wives of the villagers at night, the one who had told them how to vote, and threw them off the lands if they failed to follow his instructions to the letter.

"Hisham Sahib told you? Or you told him?"

"Please, Chaudrey Sahib. Don't upset yourself now. If you like I can go to Lahore and speak with Hisham Sahib directly. It sounds as if you'll be there anyway."

The old munshi knew he was defeated, he could hardly go to Lahore in this state and argue against the young manager who had just earned all those millions.

"So how much more of Hotu Wali will you need? I've already ordered the cotton seed for most of it, in fact I was planning to send them in today and begin preparing."

That's a lie, thought Saqib. He had been planning to take only fifty acres, but now he changed his mind.

"Oh, I'll need all of it. Fifty acres for my new tunnels, and then the rest for fodder. What is the whole thing? It's seventy-seven, isn't it?" Both men knew exactly how many acres in that plot. Saqib continued, "I'll be bringing in some animals, beginning to set up a little dairy. That's the next thing, animals, buffaloes. Over by the river it should go well."

"All the munshis end up with cattle, don't they," cracked Sattar, his laugh crude and without humor. "They all start so well, and then they end up with a herd of buffalo."

"MashAllah, Chaudrey Sahib, certainly your herd is second to none. But let's not quibble here. I'll tell you exactly the deal. As before, I'll add the salaries for two men, and send you that, it's only fair." (He had intended to send four, in fact, but that certainly wouldn't be necessary.)

"Two? And eighty acres of my land?"

"It's not your land, Munshi Sahib. It's Hisham Atar Sahib's land. I shouldn't be sending you anything." He made a movement as if to stand up.

"No no no, I'm just old-fashioned, you see. Sit. Come, shall I ask them to make some food? We can talk. I could help you manage this thing. We can even be partners!" He said this with a childish enthusiasm, as if believing it himself.

"It's not really time for a meal," said Saqib, feeling something like pity now for this pathetic old man with the suppurating leg, distaste mixed with contempt. Fading power should have its dignity. "And I don't need any help. It's fine, I'll send you the salaries of four men, as well as the two from before."

And that was that, and the great Chaudrey Abdul Sattar almost wept with gratitude, insisting despite the pustulant leg on standing when Saqib cut off the conversation, turned his back, and left the old man behind.

XIV

*T*he gear for the farm, when it arrived from Warraich, was really even worse than Saqib had expected.

"I'm not sure this stuff will stand the first breeze," said Saqib on the phone. It offended him to do the job as badly as it must be done.

"Come on boy," laughed Warraich. "Don't get water in your veins now. We're committed to this. The gear will be good enough for what we plan. Just patch and fill, patch and fill. The plastic is thin, but you can get your men to sew it up well enough when you need. And the seed actually isn't that bad. I tried a bit of it myself last year, it's some new thing they have in China, they've copied the Dutch hybrid. Anyway, don't go wobbly on me now. You'll keep the sheds standing somehow, and you'll get seven or eight hundred bags an acre off it, and that's your cream, you send that to my Faisalabad guy, like I told you, and he'll give you the invoices you need. Be tough, this is your moment, remember. It's never pretty the first time."

*

Even with this gear, especially with this gear, Saqib worked as if possessed that fall to build this massive operation, a hundred acres of plastic tunnels, though he ended up by calling it a hundred and eleven in the official set of books to make the per-acre cost seem less. The books would be central to his defense at the end, and so he pored over them each evening before he allowed himself to go home, building his paper trail. He knew that most of all he must be sure of the new men he hired, as before, men who would leap to his instructions and keep their mouths shut. He selected the ones in the area who needed a break, very young ones, orphans, and men from the Indus who could no longer find fish, the water polluted and increasingly barren. They came to him, silent, filing in, and he examined them and looked into their faces, reading them, this discernment one of the qualities that would serve him so well all his life. With the men he was rarely harsh, he had no need to be, and pointedly he thought of the enterprise as a challenge, as their game, together with them, the impossible equipment and all.

Soon after the season began, in the late fall, just as he sent his first cucumbers to market, an unknown man arrived in the evening at the farm and asked for Saqib.

"From Warraich Sahib," he said, handing Saqib a sealed envelope. Going into the privacy of the hut, Saqib counted the money, a million rupees in five-thousand-rupee notes. Just two hundred bills, a bundle so small that it fit easily into his pocket. When he built the little hut, Saqib had carved out a little space above the beams where he could hide valuables, sealed with a loose brick. He concealed the money there, knowing that he must not put it into his bank account, for the bank manager would gossip if a man like Saqib deposited so much.

"Welcome," messaged Warraich laconically, when Saqib sent a cryptic thanks, as if it were nothing for a man of Saqib's background to receive such a fortune.

Working through the fall and winter, Saqib changed nothing about his habits, bought nothing, never touched the money. He didn't even tell Gazala of this treasure, and that was hardest of all, sitting eating every night the meals she lovingly prepared, love in her hands. The man who bought the cucumbers in Faisalabad did as Warraich had promised, sending invoices showing the cucumbers selling for a pittance, and wiring the money to Saqib's account in small increments that wouldn't be noticed, another two hundred thousand rupees.

✳

One morning in May, Saqib arrived at his farm just at sunrise, as he always did, parked his motorcycle in its usual spot, and walked over to his *pyada*, who managed all the men, eleven of them, very few for so large a project. Two days before, they had sent the last of the cucumbers to Faisalabad. In the far distance, the Indus brightened the horizon as the first sun lit the water.

"How's it going, Zafar?" Though only half a dozen years older than Saqib, this grizzled rogue had gray in his thatch of hair, a big square head, and enormous feet, which all the other *baildars* made a joke of, calling him the biggest peasant of all—following the saying, The sahibs have big heads, and the serfs have big feet.

"Look at it, sir. It breaks my heart to see it, the way it looks now at the end, and then all the trouble we had. We just couldn't make anything of it." The cucumbers at the end of the season all died back, the leaves yellowing in the heat. When the spring heat came the men pulled the plastic off the tunnels, so there was nothing left of all the structures they had built but the steel ribs, a hundred acres of it, like a ruined city. He laughed. "All the work we did putting it up. But for you, sir, it's nothing, I suppose, you only look at the business."

"What else would I look at? Anyway, this isn't just business. Send a message to your people in Machhi Vala. You can have all the cucumbers left in these fields, tell all your women to come tomorrow morning, the whole lot. There'll be a couple of pickup loads, if they go through it carefully. You've got till tomorrow night to do it, before I plow it under."

"And then?"

"Whatever you make is yours, you and the *baildars*. That's something like twenty thousand rupees. There are going to be changes around here."

"That's more than they deserve. You'll spoil them." He paused for a moment, as if it just occurred to him. "And the rice? When will we begin planting?"

He was a shrewd man, despite his stubble of beard and rotten teeth, the back ones all pulled out when they troubled him, so that he had difficulty chewing meat.

Thin-faced Saqib, a head taller than Zafar, understood what his *pyada* meant. "You're right, we may not put in rice. We may."

"There's no seed yet, and we need to sprout a nursery."

"Not yet. Keep your mouth shut. There's more. While your womenfolk go through and take the cukes, I want the *baildars* to pack up everything of value as fast as they can. I mean everything: pipes, wires, clutch wire, right down to the anchor spikes. And pack it up carefully. I'll be in and out, but I'm leaving this to you. Think of it as your final exam. In three days, some trucks will come and take it all away. And when the trucks come, I don't want anyone around—no one, get it? Just the men. The trucks will come on the third night, on Friday. Late. Can you have it ready?"

Once sold off and dispersed in the secondhand market, no inquiry could show the quality of the gear Saqib had bought from Warraich.

"That's new, sir, you asking not telling if we can get something done on time. We'll manage."

"I'll come and go, but it's on you."

"That's new too, sir."

"Don't be too smart." For a moment, he rested his hand on his man's shoulder. "You've done well, Zafar. There may be trouble coming, who knows? But at the end of it all, I'll take you with me wherever I end up. Will you come?"

"Why wouldn't I, sir? I'll follow you to America if you like."

"That may just be where we're headed. And now I'm leaving for the day. And don't you dare say, 'Well, that's a new one.'"

XV

*S*aqib spent the next few weeks grooming his books. Though he continued as if he intended to erect a hundred acres of tunnels again in the fall, meanwhile going through the motions of preparing to plant rice—the usual bridge crop—he assumed that, when the extent of his losses came out, he would be fired. Saqib had two qualities that are as important to a businessman as to a general—he planned carefully and improvised quickly. Now the crux of the matter had arrived. After squeezing all the juice from his secret books, anything that would add plausibility to the official ones, he burned them.

Throughout, whenever he doubted or feared, one number was glowingly present always in his mind. He had nearly a million and a quarter rupees stashed away, a fortune to make a fortune, a spark for an explosion—of wealth. He had told no one about it, not even Gazala, especially not Gazala, who must know nothing if they pressured her. He was certain of being spared the worst, what happens to men without protection who fall afoul of the powers in these Punjabi towns, the leather strap and the block of ice that men are made to sit on naked, or even worse tortures that leave no visible marks, chili peppers, electric boxes with cranks. The Atars would never have the stomach for the worst—he was certain of this.

Moving the issue along, he began to instigate the inquiry that he knew must come. Since leaving household service in Lahore, Saqib had nurtured and paid in all sorts of currencies a man from Ranmal Mohra who worked in Hisham's stables, a groom for the polo ponies. This boy, too insignificant for anyone else to pay mind to him, could easily be pumped for information about the Atars' movements. Saqib therefore knew that at the time he planted his third crop—the one that would make his fortune—something dramatic had happened between the Sahib and the Begum, and they had gone off very suddenly to London. Saqib, their intimate, felt certain of knowing what it must be. Shahnaz had found out Hisham's mistress—Saqib had known of her over the years—a close friend of the family, a distant cousin of Shahnaz, a poor relative, a great beauty, and a snake. There had been others, before and during, but this one was different, a rival, one who might even lure Hisham away. The only surprise, for Saqib, was that it had taken Shahnaz so long to unearth this cunning creature. Learning of this, just as he was putting up his tunnels ten months ago, Saqib had taken comfort. If it must be so, if master and wife must part, at least it would be useful in Saqib's enterprise. Shahnaz would leave him, and Hisham would be too broken to react when the veggies failed. Even if they reconciled, the bond between them would be so much less as they reacted to the bad news from Ranmal Mohra. She would keep aloof, and Saqib could handle Hisham so much more easily if he were alone and grieving.

٭

The only remaining question was the vector for the bad news—and that, of course, must be Rana Abdul Sattar. One night and then another, Saqib dropped by the unfortunate man, asking the news of his health, dropping nuggets of truth about his parlous affairs, the great hopes he had entertained of showering the Atars with zillions, and the fears that troubled him now, how he would tell them of losses almost beyond reckoning. Consoling, considerate, Rana Sahib wept crocodile tears with Saqib. Within three days, Bayazid called.

"Hello, dear boy," he began. "What's the news from the Vegetable King?"

"All is well, Uncle. Or rather, not well, but I wish it were, and I hope it can be fixed. Things have gone upside down this year." Though he had been preparing himself for this conversation, telling himself that it must be done, that Bayazid too must be disappointed and deceived, it seemed very difficult indeed when he heard that easy, generous voice.

"You better come," he suggested, as he had planned. Best to have him alone and without his suspicions aroused. Saqib would play upon a character that he knew so well, his indolence and his impulse to see the best, his affection, even his humor, and had often painted for him the difficulties of this business and the many ways it might go bust, making a show of his careful bookkeeping. Yazid knew nothing of accounting, but he understood the culture of corruption around the farm much better than Hisham and Shahnaz did. He must continue to judge his young favorite as an exception, for as a rule all munshis stole.

"Oh, well, it can't be as bad as that. Bad years come after good years. The Sahib and Bibi Jee are in London, and I wouldn't trouble them for the world. Something should be done right away. I'll come there."

"I'd appreciate that. Thank you."

XVI

*S*aqib met Bayazid at the bus station in Adda Mastt Bahadur, having taken care to remove all glitter from his appearance. His shoes were down at heel, his clothes clean but the collar frayed from washing. The motorcycle fortunately had gotten so banged up over the past year, running back and forth from one place to another, used even to pull a little cart when anything needed fetching from town, that Yazid the mechanical wizard might feel the urge to pull out some tools right there and then and tune it up.

As soon as Yazid stepped down from the bus, Saqib began describing his ruin. Yazid took the steps one at a time, noted quick-eyed Saqib, grown ever heavier in the past years, his preoccupation drawn ever more inward to his belly.

"Leave it, boy, leave it. Let's have food and then we'll talk."

Grim, Saqib said, "Okay. But it's difficult to hold off speaking. No need to pay for another bike, I can fit behind you."

"I don't think this thing could pull us both to the end of the bazaar. You better take a rental. I'll drive myself."

Saqib had insisted they go straight to the vegetable farm, and Yazid was forced to accept this.

"I've told them to make some food. It won't be much, but then, we never have much."

✻

The *pyada* and the men had done as Saqib asked. The pipes and wires and all the kit had been packed up and sold in the market, leaving just the trash of the dried cucumber plants and holes in the ground where the tunnels had stood. It didn't look good, certainly not to an untrained eye.

Yazid whistled. "What happened?"

"Nothing. Everything. And then, wind. Whatever didn't go at the beginning went at the end. I'm ruined. But that doesn't matter. This will cost Hisham Sahib so much, enough so it makes a difference."

Although the food was plain, it was plentiful, and Yazid had tucked in like the serious trencherman that he was.

"It takes a lot more than a cucumber patch to ruin Mian Hisham Atar. Tell me the numbers."

Refusing to eat, calling the boys for more chapattis, declining to speak in front of them, Saqib sat with a pile of dog-eared ledgers in his lap.

"No, forget the books. Tell me everything, holding nothing back. How did this happen?"

And so Saqib wove his tale. Yazid knew him so well, but then, Saqib knew Yazid so well. He was almost his son. It broke Saqib's heart to do it, right there as he spoke the grinding in his chest was almost audible. But he had known for months that this would be the worst of it. Like parents who have planned a divorce for months and years but fear one thing most—to tell their little children—so Saqib had dreaded telling this man of his heart, deceiving him, disabusing him at the very least of his belief in Saqib's abilities. Yes, it must be done, and it was done well.

At the end, Yazid fell silent, then clapped his hands on his knees and struggled heavily to his feet.

"It's not as bad as all that. I'll have to go back to Lahore and speak to the managers there from the factory. I'm going to leave tonight, I can't wait here. They'll have to prepare money to make up the balance till you put it right here at the farm. When Hisham Sahib returns from London we can decide the next move. The problem isn't the lost income. It's that you've lost all that investment too. When it costs so much, and then you go and do a hundred acres. It makes a hole."

He put his arm around Saqib, who had stood up also.

"I'll go with you. I should be there when the Sahib comes back."

"No. Let me deal with it at first. You wait, they'll call you to Lahore, I suppose. Make sure all these books are perfect, everything added up right. Even if this wasn't your fault, they'll make a full inquiry." But he didn't go on, he stopped there and thought for a moment. "This is all so strange." He was embarrassed. "It all looks so wrong," he said finally. "Come on, let's go back to the house. I can't stand it here. Truthfully, I can't stand you right now. You're an idiot." Sharp now, he looked Saqib direct in the face. "You know it doesn't look well?"

"I know."

"Yup. You know. You knew too much. It's all right. You're young, and they can take away your polish, but they can't take your heart. Come on."

Saqib rode behind Yazid, stuffed there like a sack of wheat going to market—they had sent away the man with the rental motorbike. Resting his hands lightly on those massive shoulders as they bumped along, he became thoughtful, then elated. Okay, he'd done it. Nothing else would hurt like this.

Yazid slept in the afternoon, and when he woke was quiet, saying that he would take the evening bus, though Saqib pressed him to stay. There was too little between them, still that sense of embarrassment and also a closeness, as if they had fought or one of them had been slightly ill. Saqib had waited till Yazid woke, then went in himself with tea.

"Look at you," Yazid had said quietly as he brought it in. "This is my fault, boy. You shouldn't have had all this responsibility so soon." They left too early for the bus, so that they were forced to wait in the bazaar, making small talk, which had never been their way. Finally the conductor called, the driver honked the horn, and Saqib helped Yazid to climb up the narrow stairs. His knees were going, and with all that weight he already was becoming invalid, the big brave man no longer mobile.

It was over, the first impression had been made. Yazid gestured farewell without looking Saqib in the eye, then made a show of leaning his head against the window and closing his eyes, making a pillow of his sweater.

Relieved, as the bus was leaving Saqib took out his phone, his iPhone. Gazala had said, "Call me the moment you can and tell me it's okay."

Looking up, he caught Yazid's eyes in the window, shock and then a clenched jaw, eyes blazing at him. Blown up with anger, his head suddenly had become much larger, dangerous, looming. He had seen the phone and recognized what it was. A hundred and fifty thousand rupees glowing in a slab of white metal.

That was all it took, Saqib knew then. That was the trigger, for the understanding that had been creeping over Yazid from the morning. For days Saqib would see in his imagination that over-sized face in the window, the expression of wildness. He would regret this moment bitterly, that he had not waited to make the call, not left the phone behind. Yet also the best in him had shown itself, overmastered him, balking at concealment, defiant and intentional, to prove to himself he was not like the other munshis. Taking out the phone, he had looked up at Yazid, almost willing him to open his eyes and look back, seeking his complicity. He had wanted Yazid to know but not to tell; that would be his absolution.

The bus rolled away, diesel smoke and the grinding of gears, huge beast shouldering out of the bazaar, and Saqib stood with his hands at his sides, wanting to call the bus back, to call Yazid back and make him understand. Yazid so good, so beloved. Saqib's past and perhaps his future massively rolled away down the road, the square back of the bus drawing away. Oh, that was so bad! Saqib walked the bazaar stamping his feet, shaking loose his thoughts, the dusk like rainfall on him.

XVII

*H*e thought about Yazid obsessively then for the next days, as if by remembering the past he could change the present. He remembered himself slim and delicate around Yazid's bulk, and the fussiness of the big man around him, the ways in which he played to Yazid by his daintiness, by his considerations, by his intuition. Even now he did not believe that Yazid would expose him directly. Saqib would make up something about the phone, say that he had bought it secondhand, that it was an old one with a cracked screen. It had never been Yazid's way to carry tales; he didn't take sides. If he had been inclined that way, he might have been a great figure in Hisham's household, and in Colonel Atar's household before him. There were no secrets on the farm, everyone knew who took what and how, and yet Yazid had never tittle-tattled.

A day, two days, Saqib heard nothing. A groom whom he had emplaced in the Lahore stables told him only that Yazid had returned in a dark humor, and that one of the managers from the factory came a day later and sat with him for a morning and then left. Dispirited, Saqib did not call, and then when he did call, Yazid didn't pick up.

Finally: "What is it, boy?" His abruptness spoke volumes.

"I'm worried about how to go forward, sir. The rice is all set to go in, whatever we decide about the farm next year. Shall I come to Lahore to explain and make the plan?"

"No, you stay there. Mian Sahib is back in a couple of weeks."

"But about the rice and getting ready for next year?"

"Well, do whatever you can."

This, anyway, seemed a concession. When the inquiry began, he would already have planted the rice, would have done it to perfection. At the same time, he would set in motion the preparations for next year's vegetables, which no one else could manage. Maybe it would blow over, hard questions and cool answers and much puzzling over the books and then his restoration. Next year no fooling about, give the Atars a big profit—Saqib already had what he needed, he wouldn't be greedy—and then withdraw and use the money that he had laid by to lay the foundations of his fortune. He thought of the old Punjabi proverb, *Kill the snake, and not even break the stick.*

✳

The day the stable boy in Lahore messaged him that the Atars had landed back from London, Saqib went to the Kèrala house and found it empty and locked, just the gardeners there, sweeping leaves across the lawns, as they did all day throughout the year, as his father had all his life in Ranmal Mohra.

"Where's the key?" Saqib asked. "Where's Sadiqa?"

The woman came, a plump pretty thing who had once caught Colonel Atar's eye. She'd held his attention for several years, his little dish whenever he came to the village, then was pensioned here when the jaded colonel found it burdensome to keep her around his own place.

Saqib told her, "They're coming in a few days."

"Good to hear." She spoke with the insolence of knowing that she could always fall at Hisham's feet and cry favor in the father's name if she was found amiss. "Don't worry, I know how they like it. I'll fix it all up before they come."

"Let me have the key, I'd like to see."

"Suit yourself."

Saqib walked through the darkened house, making note of all that he wanted to do. In the bathroom he washed his hands, his fingers scented with the expensive soap that Shahnaz brought not just from Lahore but from abroad. He thought of the little touches by which she marked this place, brightly colored napkins, pillow covers, pillows also from abroad, stuffed with feathers, and also a blanket filled entirely with tiny duck feathers. The bed mattered to her, and this was one of the mysteries that drew his attention, a sensual appetite, her ways mysterious and yet familiar.

In her absence, in Hisham's absence too, their properties lying about the house glowed with meaning, Hisham's guns in a steel cabinet, with the keys hidden in a box pushed among some books, foreign cartridges in boxes, expensive and heavy, her toiletries, bottles that glinted, lotions. Saqib was brought face-to-face with his past in this household as he wandered through the rooms, feeling privileged there and yet uncertain, not there on command, like a schoolboy kept home by sickness listening to the sounds that ordinarily he would not hear, routines maintained in his absence. He would lose this now, this part of his education was finished, after the inquiry, when he would be dismissed or later would withdraw. The poignant, melancholy rooms lay drained of motive in the masters' absence. On a rosewood bureau Shahnaz kept a collection of mirrors large and small, silver framed, or framed with milky-green stones, like jewels. These troubled his wandering mind, because he couldn't understand why they should be there, why a jumble of old mirrors should be a sophisticated decoration; and yet he knew it was. Of course there must be money, and a great deal of it—but that was not the key.

After many months living in the hut by the river, his mind felt refreshed and surprised by the little graces that made this house so different from anything the locals could conceive, even the wealthy ones, the politicians. Roughened by those months working the vegetables, he had almost forgotten the refinements of Hisham and Shahnaz's lives and manners, and this made him smile, a little bit grim, a little bit proud of himself, for in fact these people, his masters, were quite superficial. They didn't understand where the money comes from, not as he increasingly did, nor just how much it takes to earn the rupees that made their lives possible.

✻

And yet, and yet! As Saqib moved through the rooms, he understood then that if he had betrayed the Atars' trust, he had done it in this good faith, that with the money he had taken, and with the money that he could thus earn, he would someday not merely have many possessions, he would be able to take the one great step that a man like Chaudrey Warraich never could. His star shone more brightly than others, shone as his mother and perhaps even Gazala could never understand. His life work might even be to make Gazala understand, that he had not merely emulated the Atars and the few people they accepted without reservation, but that he one day had become one of them. This would be his fortune, this his genius.

Next morning he returned with one of his men and set to work, first on Yazid's little room, airing it out, sweeping it, even whitewashing it, establishing a base. Though Yazid didn't care for refinements of living, Saqib calculated that he would be softened to find these fresh rooms. Then he rolled up his sleeves and his shalvar cuffs and threw himself at the greater problem. He would make the house more immaculate than ever before, for that was what truly mattered to Hisham and Shahnaz, their immediate comfort. He toyed with ordering the public rooms repainted, but time was short, and that might be too striking—balance and subtlety was the currency with which he had gained their extraordinary favor. Instead he contented himself with touching up where most needed, and then repainting the master bathroom walls, which were flaking from moisture. If he left the windows open until their arrival, the smell of paint would be fresh and pleasant. Two days before they arrived, he took all the furniture into the garden and washed the terrazzo floors with a hose, squatting and pushing the water out with a broom of reeds, splashing about in the cool, leaving the rooms deliciously chill and sweet with the scent of fresh water.

XVIII

*J*ittery, manic, on the morning of the Atars' arrival Saqib found
fault with the workers at the farm and made them again
rebuild a watercourse, though it would have served perfectly before.
Returning to Kèrala, he spent the day ministering to the house,
preparing it for the Atars' arrival like a hostess before a party. Then
he bathed and changed, chose a white shalvar, polished his shoes.
He must look contrite, efficient, and grave but not repentant, for
they would find against him proof only that he had failed in a difficult business. In the characteristically neat toilet he had built at the
vegetable farm, where he continued to live and sleep, he regarded
himself in the mirror. What would be the face with which he would
regard himself next morning in that mirror? Would it be a face of
triumph? He felt that he had done so little wrong, when he had
done so much right, giving Hisham extraordinary profits for two
years. It even seemed that the successes he imagined—expected—
for himself in the upcoming years, with the money that he had
taken from the Atars, would rebound to their credit, and that his
achievements would be theirs too, raised on their lands, their stock,
and then creature of their hands. If he and they must scissor apart
for a moment, they soon would be rejoined. He narrowed his eyes
and smiled at himself in the mirror. That tuft of hair standing up,
as if he were still a boy.

Having gone to the bazaar himself and cunningly selecting the
best of what was available, Saqib had been cooking at Kèrala since
the day before. He had grown up a great deal these years managing
the farm with all its difficulties and extent, had become accustomed

to command, and his successes had further developed in him a belief in his own star. Well before the Atars could possibly arrive, he stationed himself at the front of the house, planning where he would stand, how he would salute them. He imagined himself not penitent, but like a sentry awaiting his officers' inspection. Any disorders would soon be forgotten.

Yet he was stricken with remorse when he heard the car approaching, that it should have come to this, when always before he had been golden in their eyes. Leaving aside what he had taken, he had failed in a project they'd entrusted to him, for the first time ever. When the jeep came around the final curve of the drive, he expected to see Hisham beside Yazid in front, where he always sat when they were traveling alone. But that seat was empty. So Shahnaz Bibi had come too. He had not expected to confront her; the pleadings he had crafted in his mind over the past weeks were all addressed to Hisham. As a pair they were more formidable, Hisham's Punjabi willingness to cut corners and avoid unpleasantness tempered by the steel of her resolution. Perhaps this would work in his favor, nevertheless, for she was the one who had first taken Saqib into the household, then raised him up further. He made an obeisance to her as the jeep glided to a halt, her face obscure behind the glass now milky at dusk. She didn't turn to him, and when he opened the door, she swept past without acknowledgment. On the far side of the car Hisham received the salaams of the household servants and then also withdrew into the house, more quickly than he would have usually, not taking a moment to stretch and look about at the garden and the trees, to inhale the country air and take possession of the farm. He glanced at Saqib, but no more, and his usually genial face, which was the face of good fortune, appeared more like the face of command.

Slow to emerge from the Land Cruiser, heavy, Yazid came out and regarded Saqib with a quizzical expression. Rumpled, ungainly, his down-at-heels shoes made him roll as he walked, and the waistcoat that he wore despite the heat was wrinkled at the back from sitting rigidly for hours in the driver's seat. He seemed pathetic, despite his great size, and Saqib felt ashamed now of his own brightness and slenderness, his sharp dealings, contrasted with his mentor's shaggy rectitude.

"As salaam uleikum, sir," said Saqib, tilting his head down in salute. Absurdly, he wanted to fall on his knees and make the peasant submission, his forehead to Yazid's feet. All this conflict might be relieved in a gesture, or at least Saqib wished it so.

Yazid didn't respond, but again looked hard into Saqib's face, as if not recognizing him clearly, and Saqib thought back to his blazing dangerous expression in the window of the bus that disastrous evening when he had seen Saqib's iPhone.

"So you're here, are you?" He turned toward the servants' area, and when Saqib followed, he stopped and turned. "Stay by the car, boy. They'll be calling you."

"But I've made a dinner, sir. I'm cooking for the Sahibs. It'll be ruined."

"That's the least of it for you right now. Do what I say."

✻

Yazid made his way around the corner and then the dusk settled over the garden. A servant came out and walked in hush around the veranda that ringed the house, turning on lights in the gloom one by one. How sad it felt, to be excluded. Saqib was so unaccustomed to this loneliness, of sitting out while Hisham and Shahnaz were inside, where he should be tending to them, movement seen through the windows. He didn't sit down, not wanting to appear like the supplicants who squatted out by the cars in the driveway, hoping to catch the sahib's attention when he came out. Inside now Hisham would be nursing his second drink, rattling the ice cubes to catch Saqib's attention when it was empty. Shahnaz would have distributed her things around the bedroom; she always did that first, unpacking to make the place hers again. And the food, the meal that he had been preparing all day, would be ruined by the village cook. Worst of all, the household would know of something very much wrong when he didn't return to the kitchen but stood out by the cars.

After an hour, which seemed so much longer, one of the serving boys came out. Preparing himself for the inquiry to begin, mentally organizing his statement, Saqib moved toward the door.

*

"No, not that way," said the boy. He studied Saqib with interest. "No. They say you should go to Ranmal Mohra and tell them to open up the *baithak* there. Wait there, they say. And call your father, he's to be there with you."

Surprised, Saqib betrayed his emotion. "To the *baithak*? Why there?"

The *baithak* was the hall at Ranmal Mohra used for political gatherings or formal meetings with large crowds. It was also where Colonel Atar and the owners before him had adjudicated disputes between factions or met their political allies. But Hisham never went there, not since he abandoned politics.

"No idea," said the boy. "I'm just the messenger." He grinned, impertinent. "Doesn't look good, does it?"

Of course word would race through the house, then the village, then the whole area, that Saqib the jumped-up servant had come to a crash, their spirits feasting upon him.

"Stay out of it, kid, and keep your mouth shut." What a sour business! He would have liked to teach this boy a little lesson. Here in the villages no one showed mercy when the mighty fell. The fallen were torn apart.

Mounting his motorbike, Saqib bumped along the farm road to Ranmal Mohra, then into the dera, and told the watchman there to open up the *baithak* and turn on the lights.

"And call my father," he said.

"Your father?" asked the watchman.

"Just do it."

XIX

*L*ike a temple on a plinth, the *baithak* in Ranmal Mohra stood large and rectangular, commanding Ranmal Mohra village with a public air, a place for gathering and ceremony, with one very long central room, space to hold a hundred men seated on the floor at a jirga. Its tall carved wooden doors revealed high ceilings paneled with wood, colorful patterns of vines and flowers painted on them, and chandeliers brought from abroad hanging down, one in the center and one at each end. It had been built a hundred and fifty years ago, not by the colonel or his father but even before that, back when there had been a fort there, when the Atar family ruled, when they fought against the tribes from across the river, when the Atar lands had no fixed boundaries but stretched into the wastes all around, which in those days were as unsettled as they had been when Alexander the Great marched through with his army. Tribal sardars had been welcomed here in state and cases had been heard here that ended blood feuds or began them. Even in the colonel's time men had been thrashed with wooden rods in the courtyard and their screams hung over the village. Since the colonel passed into senescence the *baithak* had sat empty, but these walls still held that.

Defiant no more, Saqib crouched on the ground, which was covered with an ancient threadbare carpet, and after a few minutes his father came in, hesitant and looking very small in this shadowed hall, wearing his dhoti and a loose much-washed kurta, a pitiful figure. Saqib stood and embraced his father, not expecting any succor from that wasted presence, whose connection to him had been thin as a rope always, paternity alone. Yet whatever else, the Atars should never have implicated this blameless old man.

His father, who had lost whatever force he had years ago, becoming a vegetable himself through years of silently tending the gardens here, didn't question Saqib at all.

"Salaam," he said, as if they were meeting anyplace, in the tea stall or along the road. Embracing Saqib, he then sat down cross-legged on the floor in an inferior position near the wall, accepting whatever should befall him. He knew there would be trouble but awaited it as if it didn't concern him. What could he know of his son's predicaments, this boy who had grown so high and far from his own purview?

Yet the presence of his father emboldened Saqib and increased his resolve to bear this trial. He had sat down on his haunches next to the withered old man, whose cracked bare feet with toes splayed from going barefoot all day for years, and his bowed head, and the poorness of his dhoti and kurta, proved how little his life-time of service in this house had gained him. Saqib thought of the wonders he had seen in Lahore, generals and ministers coming and going, dinners that cost a year of his father's salary and more, flowers imported from abroad still fresh, lilies, and Shahnaz's emer-alds, her pearls being restrung while Saqib sat by and kept watch over the jeweler. That trust they placed in him would never have been rewarded, their trust enough reward in their eyes. He thought grimly of the million and a quarter rupees hidden behind bricks in the ceiling of his little hut at his tunnel farm, where it could never be found.

He must at least call Gazala, later they might take his phone—he saw that now. He had concealed the iPhone, replaced it with a sec-ondhand Chinese device.

She picked up on the first ring.

"Is it over?"

"Not yet."

"And?"

"Don't worry, but I think they'll keep me here."

"What about your ledgers and books and showing that and your proof?"

"I don't know. They've sent me to wait in the Colonel's *baithak* at Ranmal Mohra."

"Why the *baithak*? Are they going to lock you in that jail in the dera?"

"I don't think so."

"Why else would they take you there?"

Just then, he heard the car in the courtyard.

"They're coming. Listen, don't worry, it'll be fine. I have to go. If there's trouble, take Jehan Shah and return to your father." Saqib had chosen this grandiose name for his son.

"I will never go back to that house!" she cried and hung up.

*

Saqib and his father stood when Hisham and Bayazid entered, Hisham looking bleary and annoyed. His father held his hands in front of his chest, like a squirrel holding up its paws, an attitude of submission, his head bowed, and Saqib too bowed his head, then stood straight.

Throwing himself down in the thronelike chair at one end of the room, extending his legs, Hisham didn't speak for several moments. Saqib had never seen him like this, quite transformed, seeming larger, and his face pointed and gathered, triangular toward the mouth. Even when angry, Hisham had always retained his jocularity behind his frown, his anger a mask. But this was no mask, this radiated from within.

"What have you done, boy?" he said finally. "What the hell have you done?"

Saqib stepped forward, placed his account books on the table in front of Hisham.

"Sir, I can show you exactly the details here. It's all written down. Twice there were storms that ripped up the tunnels, and then the cold burned the crop. The prices were bad, and the yield low. This is the difficulty with these tunnels, there's a great profit, but the chance of great loss. I spoke with Your Honor about this and explained the dangers."

He bent down and opened one of the ledgers, placing it before Hisham.

"Books!" exclaimed Hisham, and slapped the ledger shut. "Yazid, say again what you told me before."

Yazid had stationed himself behind Hisham's chair when they entered the room, his face set in repose, indomitable. He stepped forward now, hands linked across his belly. "Sir, you know what this boy has been to me. I take no pleasure in seeing this happen. I brought him up, I brought him out when he came to Lahore and for several years after. He reads and writes well because I taught him. The fault is mine. And I heard him tell of his losses, and then I saw him in the bazaar carrying a phone that costs lacs. I have stood behind your father the Colonel Sahib for many years and seen how business is done, and now I have been with Your Honor for many years. This is not right. There was no loss as he tells it."

"Be plain, Yazid."

He looked stricken, but he whispered the fatal words. "The boy stole the money."

There was no triumph in his voice, only conviction.

Hisham looked up at Saqib. "What do you say to that?" His voice rose almost to a shriek, and Saqib understood that not only was Hisham angry, but he was also hurt. "Is Bayazid lying?"

"Sir, the phone was secondhand and with a broken screen, it cost no more than another phone. It's not a question of his lying. With all my respect, Bayazid is mistaken. Let the accountants in Lahore see my books, and they will prove me right."

Hisham now stood up, with one hand swept the pile of books onto the ground, went around the table, and stood directly in front of Saqib.

"If there were any doubt Bayazid would not speak against you. He's the one who fucking taught you everything, you snake. Forget about your loyalty to me or to this family. How could you do this to Begum Sahiba? She trusted you, she brought you so far. And this is how you repay her?" His voice rose to an uncharacteristic shrillness.

Saqib kept his gaze quite steady, allowed himself to look into Hisham's eyes, and found no comfort there, no flicker of uncertainty. He expected to be hit, slapped, as he knew Hisham had been wont to do in the early years after he came to the farm, as his father had done, and his father before him, the masters striking their servants. Later he would be ashamed and would regret it, that would work in Saqib's favor.

Instead, Hisham walked over to Saqib's father, who had not moved when Hisham and Yazid came into the *baithak*, and now his wrath increased further. When Hisham approached him, the old man put his forehead to the floor, as if in prayer, and then sat up with his head at Hisham's knee.

"And you, old man, how did this happen? Your people have lived on our land for generations. I give you shelter, grain, protection. You serve this house, your family has eaten our salt for generations. Is that how you brought up this boy of yours, to steal from my hand?"

"Sahib," he whispered, head bowed. "I am your servant. I know nothing of any such things." His voice rose, something like dismissal in it. "The boy grew far beyond me long ago." It surprised Saqib how resolutely the old man spoke, his father, who might pass from one week to the next without uttering a half dozen words, other than the ones he offered to his maker when saying his prayers.

As Hisham pulled back his hand, as if to slap the bowed head, the old man sat up and looked once at Hisham's face, then put his head on his master's feet.

"Sahib, yes, I've eaten your salt, my father and his father before. We belong to this household, with all the rest. Kill me if you like. Take the boy and do with him whatever you wish."

"I will."

Saqib thought that it had ended. Hisham turned, looked at Saqib, who was sitting still on his haunches, watching this transpire. And then, still looking at Saqib, he kicked the old man, once, twice, not hard, but as if lightly kicking away some clod in a field. The old man made no sound, he cowered and kept his posture, and then after the second blow he again put his forehead to the ground and whispered, "Allah, Maulah."

Saqib made no move to protect his father, not a twitch, not a gesture. He kept his eyes downcast, while Hisham stared at his face from across the room. Yazid stood ready, and later Saqib understood that he would have leapt upon him if Saqib made any threatening movement.

Then the tension left the room. Saqib's fingers had been bunched upon his knees. Now he straightened them, his only reaction to the humiliation of his defenseless father.

"Put the boy in the strong room," Hisham said, quite without emphasis, an easy word of command. "Send the old man home."

Without looking at either Saqib or his father again, Hisham departed the room, the long empty *baithak* like a stage after a violent enactment, the atmosphere stunned, the three remaining men alone there, no center of authority, and even Bayazid bowed and reduced. Saqib's father still had his head to the ground, and made no sound, prepared to accept more blows, from Bayazid, perhaps, no resistance in him.

Saqib went over and knelt and lifted him. "Abba, get up, you must go home."

The old man raised his head but said nothing. His face bore no emotion, and he looked neither at Saqib nor at Yazid, but across the room, as if this assault had passed before him without registering at all. Saqib knew that he might never speak of this again, simply go home and settle to his hookah, beyond grievance, centuries of submission expressed through him.

Yazid was gentle with him too. "Come on, Baba, let's go out."

In the courtyard people had gathered, the watchmen and a few others, drawn to this activity in the dera so late in the evening.

When the three men came out, they stepped back, and then all eyes were drawn to Saqib's father, who was now snuffling, in shock.

"Go on," said Yazid to him quietly, touching his shoulder. "Go home."

"What of my boy?"

"He'll stay here."

That was the worst image of Saqib's young life, his father limping and shuffling away out through the gate of the dera, making little noises and not looking back. He could not imagine making any protest, not even to protect his own son, bent to obedience all his years, all these people here on the farm the same, all implicated in these histories.

✻

The old watchman had misplaced the key to the strong room, and so Yazid and Saqib stood awkwardly in the courtyard waiting, not speaking to each other. With all the people about, hovering in the shadows, Saqib would not allow himself to say anything, although the insult to his father burned him now. Finally, the watchman brought the key.

Saqib would not be pushed, he walked himself into the room, Yazid behind him.

"Leave us," Saqib said to the watchman.

The watchman looked at Yazid.

"Do you want him tied up?" He would relish doing that, the old ways.

"No. It's fine, go, leave the key."

Except for bars on the windows and a door reinforced with steel, the room was just like the other farm stores. There were piles of empty fertilizer sacks on the floor, and empty pesticide bottles heaped up, giving off an acrid smell.

✻

When they were alone, Saqib sat down on his haunches, hands resting on his knees. Softly, without looking at Bayazid, he said, "What have you done to me, sir? How could you say that to them?"

Yazid stood over him and put his hand by Saqib's face, finger pointing.

"What do you mean, 'them'? Watch how you talk. You mean Hisham Sahib and Shahnaz Bibi?"

Saqib was lost in his train of thought. "And why did this happen to my father? Who knows nothing and can't write his own name and signs his pay receipt with his thumbprint?"

"A father is the head of a house, whatever else he may be. Your disloyalty is his. Who are you to question what Hisham Sahib does? You should look at yourself. Where is the money?"

"There is no money. The crop failed, I'm not a magician, I'm a man. I did what I could."

"With someone else, I might believe that. Not here, not you. I think back and I see you preparing for this. I was blinded by you. Enough. I'll still be driving the car tomorrow, but you'll be somewhere else."

"They can leave me as long as they like in this room. That won't fix anything. I'll make it up. I'm planting the rice, and I'm already getting set for next year. The profit from next year will more than make up this loss."

Looming over Saqib, now Yazid stepped back, stepped to the door, and closed it partway.

"You still don't understand. The Sahibs have already decided. Hisham Sahib made a call to Islamabad, to Shah Vali Shah Sahib. I don't need to tell you what that means." This was a sitting minister in the government, an old family friend of the Atars', and one of the two or three most powerful men in the country.

Saqib stood up slowly. "Why? Why speak to Shah Sahib about something so unimportant?"

"I heard Hisham Sahib make the call and explain exactly about this thing you think is so unimportant."

So then the police would take him away and pressure him, hold him, bring in his family and hold them too, perhaps even beat him, until he gave up the money, and even if he gave up the money they might beat him still, when the order came from so high. Saqib had lost his bet. All his effort and deception had been for nothing.

"But that's not possible. Shahnaz Bibi would never let this happen!"

"They made the phone call in the jeep coming here. Hisham Sahib wanted to let it go. It was Begum Sahiba who insisted he make the call."

XX

Yazid left without any further words and locked the door behind him. Why lock it? As if Saqib could run away from all this. He turned from the closed door and walked toward the opposite wall, the room furry and vague with darkness, the air sour with the smell of farm chemicals. How long before the police came? This all had happened so quickly and had turned so wrong. Just hours ago, he had stood smartly by the cars at Kèrala, under those familiar trees, impatient even, his account books under his arm, the numbers running across the pages so precisely, the totals all correct, the final page signed by him with a little flourish, despite the large final number in red showing the loss. In the supporting ledgers he had used different pens to suggest that the figures had been entered on different days, and he had obtained bills and receipts for every expense, all corresponding exactly to the totals. Standing there awaiting them he had dared to hope that before the evening ended there would be forgiveness, acceptance, that Hisham would become sentimental, that Yazid would perhaps apologize for having doubted him. He had counted on his star, the one his mother spoke of since he was a boy.

How was it possible, then, that Hisham had thrown those books from the table as if worthless and—so much worse—kicked his father as he lay prostrate on the ground, just another landlord beating his peasants? The dull thud of Hisham kicking his father's ribs seemed a madness, the father more vegetable than man, who timelessly swept the lawns at Ranmal Mohra, and might do that forever without thanks. *I am still that Saqib who came to you as a boy,* he would tell them, if he could. *Insult me as you wish, but I remember. . . .*

What did he remember? He remembered everything. He remembered Shahnaz very sick, when Hisham had stormed off to Karachi after their biggest fight of all, one that had been building for weeks. That night she was so weak that she couldn't walk from the toilet to her bed. She had taken some pills, the ones that made her sleep, the bottle lying on the ground where she had thrown it, the pills scattered across the floor. He had stationed himself outside her bedroom door, and she had called from the bathroom and was not properly clothed but called him in anyway. As she hobbled along, held in his arms, her body had been so thin and light, like his young sisters when they were sick. How grateful she had been, in her sickness and sorrow, and Hisham not coming back for two days, though the manager Shah Sahib had called and reported that Shahnaz was ill. It had been about a woman, as Saqib had known from hearing their shouting, for even that they didn't conceal from him.

Later he brought her clear soup and tidied the room around her while she sipped it, staring dully at the dark wall opposite over the edge of the spoon, sick and thin and sad and vulnerable, girlish, eyes large, as if she had suddenly become much younger, her shoulders rounded as if she feared a blow, drinking the soup as if afraid it might be taken away. All night he had stood sentry outside her door, not allowing himself to sleep. He had imagined that he held a sword in his hand all night and would have given his life and had wished that he could.

From that to this.

⁎

An hour or more later, Saqib heard vehicles driving into the dera and rose from the corner, where he had been sitting in confusion, and went to stand exactly in front of the door, offering himself up, no fight in him.

The policeman who threw open the door startled back when he found Saqib a foot away, arms by his side, impassive. These policemen begin their sessions with an access of fury, getting warm, like a fighter who enters the ring and immediately throws himself on his opponent. Mistaking Saqib's stance for defiance, he reacted with a fury that seemed perfectly genuine, scowling, hauling back his fist and punching Saqib in the face so hard that it staggered him to the ground and bloodied his nose, bloodied his kameez, so that already he looked as if he had been beaten. Several more policemen rushed into the room, thinking Saqib had attacked their officer, and roughly pushed Saqib's face to the wall and handcuffed him behind the back so tightly that the pain of that exceeded the pain of the blow to his face.

"Don't tell me the motherfucker came at you," grunted the sepoy as he ratcheted down the cuffs. "Should we start?"

"No," said the officer. "In the truck."

The sepoy grimaced. "The fucker's getting blood all over me."

Although he knew that it would go better for him if he cowered and begged, Saqib allowed himself his dignity. At least that way, with a crowd of villagers in the dera gathered in the dim lights, he would not be ridiculous, not any more than he already was. When the sepoys manhandled him in the storeroom one of his shoes had come off, which seemed worst of all, to hobble across half barefoot to the battered blue pickup that idled there under the lights.

"Will you bring my shoe from inside?" he whispered to a little boy who gravely peered from the side of the door, and when the boy did dare to go into the strong room and retrieved the shoe and dropped it by his feet, Saqib felt gratitude flood him almost to tears. *I'll remember you someday*, thought Saqib, looking carefully at the boy's face, comforted at the thought that he would return from this martyrdom one day and reward this one who served him in his fallen hour. One of the sepoys helped him to put on the shoe, and that too seemed a victory to Saqib. These men were no different than his workers, than other villagers. There would be a way to negotiate through this.

They threw him roughly into the back of the pickup, under the metal bench that had been welded there, and then the constables crowded in, three four five six of them. What a party, but then, Saqib knew the drill, these men lived for the hunt, going around the villages and picking up men and making a great deal of money off it. He had expected to see Bayazid, but did not, just the villagers, hushed and slightly awed at this proceeding, knowing what happened when men were taken away. A couple of the bolder ones sidled over and peered at him lying bent under the steel benches, one leg at a bad angle.

A jolly party indeed! The sepoys were in high spirits. They kicked him once or twice, as if to reassure themselves that he was under their command, and then settled back, the officer in front, the truck rattling and squeaking merrily along, for of course the policemen stole all the repair money. They stole even the government fuel ration, would stop at farms and demand diesel and be given it by the farmers, who wanted to curry favor. The blood had crusted in Saqib's nose, making it hard to breathe, and his arms manacled behind him hurt terribly with each jolt of the wagon.

*

Saqib had expected to be taken to the central police station in Ranmal Mohra, but instead he perceived, from the twistings and turnings and the unpaved roads, that they were going out somewhere by the river. Was it possible that they would kill him? That's how they did it, stop the truck in some wasteland and pull out the bound prisoner, let him run chicken wild and shoot him down, and report that he died escaping. After half an hour the truck drove into a gate, which was closed behind them, and the men clambered out, then dragged him out too.

"You're a quiet one," said the sepoy who had been sitting over him. "If I were you, I'd loosen up my tongue now."

They threw him into an unlit room, face down, locking the door. He rolled over, managed to get his legs under him by pushing against the wall, and looked about. As his eyes accustomed to the dark, which was broken by light from under the door, he saw that the room had a desk and chair, some sacks of wheat in the corner, and nothing else, a concrete floor, a sour smell of urine. The wheat would be from the farmers, at harvest now the police went around and demanded it. A rope with a hook hung from the ceiling in front of the desk, and under the rope a stool, and that looked awful in this gloom.

All winter, as Saqib had furthered his scheme, each step of the way, as one false invoice after another came from the market in Faisalabad, each time the cheap plastic over the tunnels tore, each time the inadequate wire snapped and a section of tunnel went down in wind like a thrashing wounded animal, his orderly mind had placed his qualms on one side and his fortune on the other, looking up at the hiding place of the money up in the beams of his little room as he labored over his account books, telling a fanciful tale. That had been an education too, he began the season as a boy and ended as a man, each untrue mark that he inscribed in those books another step in his emancipation. Looking at that rope hanging from the ceiling, he thought that this too then must be part of his plan. His mother's star shone over this scenario too. They had not shot him along the way, and so they wouldn't now. He terribly feared the pain that might soon be visited on him. And what of Gazala? Who would come and pay these men to secure his release? With what money? She sat at home, his wife, nurturing his child, and he prayed devoutly there in his loneliness and fear, O that his love were in his arms, and he in his bed again.

XXI

*T*he little police thana where they had brought Saqib had only a central corridor and four rooms, as he had seen when they marched him in, an outpost perched out by the river to control the dacoits who hid out in those wastelands among the creeks of the braided river. He wondered why they had brought him there, rather than to the main police station in Adda Mastt Bahadur, fearing that it must be because they intended to use those loudest methods upon him that couldn't be enacted there in the city with houses all around. Half an hour after they threw him into the room, he heard the truck outside start up and drive away, voices joking there before the doors slammed, and then silence, a couple of men making desultory conversation in another room. He had not eaten, felt terribly hungry, and he needed to pee. Hours passed, until finally he knew that it must be coming on morning, though the room had no windows. They had taken his phone along with his wallet. He could no longer feel his hands, bound by the steel manacles behind his back, and he kept shifting back and forth, trying to get the blood moving. It had become entirely still, and then as morning came he heard the sound of men moving about, hawking and spitting, the creak of a hand pump outside, a news report on a radio. Finally, when it must have been afternoon, a vehicle again drove into the enclosure, and he heard the slamming of its doors and then voices of greeting in the other room.

Suddenly, the door was thrown open, blinding Saqib in the dark, and then very bright lights flipped on, blinding him further. All through the night and the morning Saqib had been expecting this, that the policemen would come in and question him harshly. All his plans and expectations had been overthrown. Though he had known that there would be an inquiry after Yazid saw the iPhone at the bus station, he had not planned at all for this extremity, that he would be exposed to the methods of the Punjab Police. All night too he had been thinking of the million and a quarter rupees tied up in a bundle in the beams of his little shack by the vegetable farm. Whatever they did to him, he must not divulge that. He imagined himself tying it to a string and lowering it far far down into a well, deep in his mind, heart, soul, into dark water there, all the way to the bottom, and then into a little cave, as he had seen on the television, caves in deep water where strange fishes lived. There he would keep it. He would tell them everything else, anything they asked, there would be no limits to his confession. But that would be his keep, he would not allow them into that underground cave. If he could somehow keep the money from them, then all this would be worth it. All night to stave off despair and terror he made brilliant plans, how he would build up a business, how he would trade commodities, have money to buy low and then sell high, he who understood the markets so intuitively. He could double the money, double it again, and then he would be on his way. Warraich would help him, he would make bank on those promises.

This reverie had kept his spirits intact, and when the policeman burst in Saqib was quite prepared to be shouted at, threatened, even slapped. He had never found himself wanting, he had worked in heat and cold. He had stood in wind and rain and kept his entrusted business intact. Now he would prove to himself that he could defy pain as well, better than another man could. And then, as he promised to himself, the Atars had turned him over to the police, but they would not expose him to the worst of it, not to those tortures from which men never recovered.

The bristling, glittering man who strode in wore civilian clothes, immaculately white, and highly polished Peshawari chappals, his handsome square face ornamented with a mustache just bordering on extravagance, and he shone with youth and energy.

Sitting down, cracking his knuckles, he turned a wolfish gaze on

Saqib. "What's this?" he shouted, outraged. "What's this? What have you savages been doing to Chaudrey Saqib Sahib? Don't you know he's your guest? Don't you know he is a munshi of the Atars from Ranmal Mohra? Untie him immediately. Hurry, you idiots!"

A police constable came into the room and helped Saqib to stand up.

"Take off those handcuffs immediately. Chaudrey Sahib must have been extremely uncomfortable, lying like that. But what do you buffaloes care about that. And why is there blood on his kurta?"

The constable took off the handcuffs. The man indicated to Saqib the stool placed in front of him.

"Please, Chaudrey Sahib. Have a seat." To the constable: "Leave us."

Saqib hobbled across, shaking his arms to get the blood flowing, sat down gingerly on his aching legs, the stool low and pitched at an angle, so that he leaned forward at chest height to the policeman. The relief of being unshackled filled him with gratitude, the cessation of pain. Almost as bad as the pain had been the humiliation, of having his hands twisted and tied behind his back, rendering him defenseless.

"So, Chaudrey Saqib, have you seen the Inspector Sahib yet?"

"No, sir. I've seen nobody."

"Do you mean you've been here all this time, and you haven't seen the Inspector Sahib yet?"

"No, sir."

An enormous happy smile blossomed on the man's face. "Oh, Chaudrey Sahib, Chaudrey Sahib! But now you *have* seen him! I am the inspector. I am Inspector Aftab Shakil Janjua. That is me!" He rocked in his chair with pleasure, with this gift that he was offering to his prisoner. "Yes. That is me! Here seated right in front of you."

Despite his qualms and his crumbling tremulous mood, after the long night and the extreme discomfort, Saqib smiled at this sympathetic policeman, feeling shy, wanting to share his indignation, for yes, he had been treated quite roughly. "As salaam uleikum, Janjua Sahib." He wasn't thinking very clearly, it had all been too much, his mind darted about unfocused.

The policeman seemed all of a sudden to find grave fault in what

Saqib had said. "No. No no no," he admonished, pained, shaking one finger theatrically in Saqib's face. "Not Janjua Sahib. Inspector Sahib. You will always call me Inspector Sahib. We will be good friends. Longtime friends. And always. Always! You will call me Inspector Sahib."

"Yes, Inspector Sahib."

"And when I tell you to shit, you will say, 'Yes, Inspector Sahib.' And then you will shit. In your pants. On the floor. A nice shit."

Saqib thought he must have heard incorrectly.

"Shit, sir?"

The man roared in anger, half rising from his seat, electrified. He leaned forward and pulled back his hand as if to slap Saqib.

"What is this? What happened to Inspector Sahib? I treat you like this, as if you were my brother, my friend, not some thief, and then already there's no more Inspector Sahib? I see what I'm dealing with now. You're one of those. They can't be trusted. You give them a finger and they take the whole hand." Now he did slap Saqib, very hard, so hard that Saqib was thrown to the ground. It had been so sudden that he hadn't put up a hand to defend himself.

The policeman shouted, "Come on, boys. We've got one of those ones. The ones that like to spit in my face. Come on, right now. Put the cuffs back on. No more coddling this piece of shit."

Two constables who must have been standing just outside the door came rushing in, slammed Saqib against the wall, yanked his arms roughly, and put on the handcuffs again behind his back. They were extremely quick with this and wore grave expressions on their faces, performing a vital task.

"String him up!" roared the inspector. Who would have thought that such a fine-looking man could become so very upset so quickly?

"Tighter," he shrieked. "Higher! Pull it! Don't be afraid. I'll cover for you!"

The constables had hooked one end of the rope from the ceiling onto the handcuffs behind Saqib's back and now yanked from the opposite end, so that Saqib's arms rotated backwards and up. He hung there swaying. Immediately he thought his shoulders would break, and just as it seemed his arms were popping out of their sockets the men slightly eased the tension and let him down so he could stand on his toes.

"Is that all the pull you beauties have in you, or shall I come give a tug?" shouted the inspector.

"Sir, he'll break."

"That's the point, you lovely man. We're breaking Chaudrey Sahib. We're making a nice meat chops out of him. He's lunch for the fishes out there. And also the birds."

Again, as suddenly as he had become unhinged and swollen up like an angry cat, the inspector settled back and his face shone with mildness. "Do you like birds, Chaudrey Saqib?"

"Sir?"

"Sir?" shrieked the inspector. "Sir? Is that what you think of me? You think a man like you can't shit his pants? Shall I show you how your head can touch the ceiling? Do you think the ceiling is dirty and you want to polish it with your head?"

"Sir?" whispered Saqib. The constables had pulled on the rope again, so that the pain was almost unbearable. It danced through his whole body."

"Inspector Sahib!" roared the inspector. "Inspector Sahib. Are you stupid? Or do you think it's funny to disrespect the Punjab Police. You don't salute the man, you salute the rank. However funny you think I am, however much you think I'm some sort of clown, however much you want to fuck my sister and my mother, I cannot allow you to disrespect me, because thus you disrespect the institution that I am so fortunate as to serve. The Punjab Police is like my mother and father, but for you it's a joke and you want to fuck it and you say sir sir sir."

"No, Inspector Sahib," croaked Saqib.

"Oh, thank you, thank you," whispered the inspector. To the constable: "All right, please, let's allow our guest to take his place on the chair again, now that he has decided he no longer wishes to insult the Punjab Police." He had shouted the words "Punjab Police."

This man is insane, thought Saqib. He sat precariously on the stool, his arms still pulled behind him at an unnatural angle, as if he were praying behind his back, still hooked up to the ceiling, with his body then leaning forward at an acute angle and his head thrust forward.

Now the inspector wriggled on the chair a bit, patted his pockets, brought out some cigarettes—imported—a gold lighter, and lit a cigarette with great relish. He took one puff, another. He shook his head. His expression reminded Saqib of Hisham Sahib when he lit one of his cigars brought from America in a wooden box. "Oh, I'm tired," he complained. "I've been running around all night. What a job!"

"Do you smoke, Chaudrey Saqib?" he asked offhandedly.

"No, Inspector Sahib."

"Does your mother smoke?"

"What do you mean, Inspector Sahib?"

"Answer my questions, you fool. I ask you a simple thing, to answer my questions. You disappoint me." He shook his head, bitterly disappointed.

"I'm sorry, Inspector Sahib."

"I'm sorry too. I really am. I thought we were going to be friends."

He sighed theatrically, put his feet on the desk, winsome, offended, smoked some more. He flicked imaginary ash from the end of the cigarette.

Finally, as if he had reached some profound resolution, he said, speaking quite rationally now, "I have a question for you, Chaudrey Saqib. Where the fuck is your *biradri*? You're an Arain. You belong to the most successful and the most prosperous and in a sense the most powerful caste in this district and probably in all of Punjab. The proud Arain *biradri*! We brought you as a guest to this rather remote little thana because we expected vast crowds to besiege the Ranmal Mohra station, if we took you there. I wouldn't hurt your feelings for the world, Chaudrey Sahib. But not a single fucking person has been there to ask about you, since your legitimate master Mr. Hisham Atar Sahib asked us to host you for a while. I ask again: Where the fuck is your *biradri*? You're a big enough fish so that Mian Hisham Atar uses you with trust. Even more than that, my senior officer the SP Sahib received the gift of a personal phone call from Islamabad, from Mr. Shah Vali Shah Sahib himself. A very very busy man. It appears that Shah Sahib knows your name, or at least knows of your existence. How is it possible that an Arain whose crimes are of some sort of interest to Mr. Shah Vali Shah Sahib himself does not have enough connection to the Arain *biradri* that you are sitting here as our guest for a day and a half now and not a single fucking person has come to inquire about you? We invite a fucking fruit seller from the roadside to one of our events, and if he belongs to the Arain caste, within an hour there are five hundred people shouting outside and threatening to set fire to our offices. You, Chaudrey Sahib, are a singularly unpopular Arain."

Saqib all night had been thinking of the choices he had made, of the path that had brought him finally to this little police check post by the Indus River. How right it all had seemed not so long ago. He had terribly miscalculated, thinking that Hisham Sahib and Shahnaz Bibi would remember against his failure in the tunnel farm that they had stood witness to his wedding, had arranged the match, more or less. All night and morning a second great realization had been dawning on him, one so obvious that it seemed inconceivable that he hadn't considered it. He had gone to Lahore at the age of thirteen. He had never cultivated friendships or connections in Ranmal Mohra. When he returned to the farm and set up his vegetable operation, he had intentionally kept himself quite apart from the people around, because he wished to protect his command. He had thought that his connection to the Atars would be all the protection he needed. He had despised the chaudreys and all the others. And now, in his moment of need, when the Atars had spurned him and thrown him in prison and put him at the mercies of this diabolical policeman, he had no one to come to his aid. He had been stupid beyond measure. All his plans had been wrong. He felt immeasurably weary. He had thought himself a new man, in a new era, with new manners, not subject to the laws that governed before. Look at the new man now.

"I have lived in Lahore since I was a boy, Inspector Sahib," he said ruefully. "I am nothing to my *biradri*. I am a creature of the Atar family. It is true, you can do with me as you like, if they have abandoned me. I have no one to call."

The policeman sat back, looking up at the ceiling. "Interesting," he said. "So very interesting."

He rubbed his chin, like a caricature of a man thinking.

"And did Mr. Hisham Atar Sahib trust you so very much as that with his businesses? I have heard tell of a large tunnel farm over by the river."

"I was a servant in his household, Inspector Sahib."

"Answer my question. Were you trusted?"

"Yes, Inspector Sahib. I had that good fortune."

Suddenly, the policeman stood up and snapped to attention. "Right," he said to the two policemen who had been hauling on the rope, and who had been watching the whole proceedings with great interest. "I'm off. Remove the cuffs, leave him in here, leave him alone. Feed him."

✵

When the policemen had all gone, Saqib did not dare to sit in the chair behind the desk, nor could he bear to sit again on that stool. They had left one light on, which hung over the desk and over the rope hanging from the ceiling, from which he had been hung just a few minutes before. He felt no anger, but rather gratitude that they had not again put on those wicked handcuffs. Somehow he must get a message out, but to whom? He knew that Gazala's father would not raise a finger to help, nor any other, really—for who would side with him against the power and glory of the Atars? It struck him that for exactly this reason he intended to become a great man, that he might never again be brought to this room, the ones like it, where men like him might be beaten into fortuitous shapes. Would Yazid take pity on him? Shahnaz Bibi? Gazala must be frantic, but she had nowhere to turn. He could imagine her in the bazaar, seeking to sell her pitiful wedding jewelry. Even with money she would not be able to buy his release, for these policemen would want more than she had.

Hours passed, till the room became familiar. A sepoy brought in food, so little of it that it only increased his ravenous hunger, half a plate of watery lentils and a single chapatti.

"How long will they keep me here, brother?" asked Saqib of the young constable, who wore his uniform shirt untucked and plastic chappals with his khaki pants.

The constable, a boy less than Saqib's age, studied him from top to bottom, as if weighing his fate.

"For you? It's a special case. That's only the second time that I've seen the Inspector Sahib come here and do so little and then leave the guy behind. Usually he's at it for a while."

"I'll give you five thousand rupees if you let me make a phone call." Saqib knew he mustn't offer too much, for if he showed he had money they would begin to work on him in earnest.

"I'd love that. But the Inspector Sahib warned us not to fuck around. It's worth my job. And Inspector Sahib knows everything and finds out everything. I wouldn't even try to hide it from him."

Toward evening the constable brought in a metal apparatus with a hand crank on one side and two long wires coming out of the other.

"This is for you to think about," said the constable. "Study it. Don't touch it."

"I need to use the toilet."

"Go in the corner."

"I already peed there. But I've got to do the other."

"If the Inspector Sahib comes back and smells anything you're really in for it. Hold it if you can, that's what I always tell them. I can't let you out."

$\mathcal{A}$ ll through that night and the following day, whenever he heard movement around the station Saqib expected that someone would come and relieve him of his anxiety. Toward evening the same constable came and brought exactly the same meal again, but when Saqib tried to engage him in conversation the man looked at him and put his finger to his lip.

"Nope. Nothing. The Inspector Sahib called and told us again to be very careful around you. I shouldn't even be telling you this."

After dark a vehicle drove into the courtyard, the doors slamming, then a bustle of sound outside the cell. Saqib stood up from the wall, where he had been sitting, bored now rather than fearful, all his contemplations having led him nowhere, and with no idea of how he could relieve his distress. This would be his third night held in this secret prison, and the thought of Gazala's state as she searched for him, alone and with the baby to care for, lacerated his heart.

As before, the door was thrown open, the lights blazed on, and the inspector walked in, muttering to himself.

"Well, well, well." Sitting down at the table, he opened a pink folder that he had carried in and pulled out a pile of papers. "These, Chaudrey Saqib, are your bank statements from the time that you opened your personal account at the Muslim Commercial Bank in Muzaffargarh. I see that you have been receiving wires of money from a vegetable wholesaler in Faisalabad for the past five months. The buyer has sent you"—he looked at a figure written on one of the papers—"has sent you two hundred and sixty-eight thousand four hundred and fifty-one rupees."

"I can explain that, Inspector Sahib."

The inspector sighed in frustration. "Please, Chaudrey Sahib. We're not children here. Let me finish."

He very carefully gathered the statements, tapped the bundle on the table to align the edges, and then with a casual wave of his hands threw the papers into the air and watched them confetti to the ground.

"So much for the paper trail. Next we come to the human intelligence, as we call it in my business. When I say the name Zafar Machhi, I'm sure you know who I mean."

"He was the *pyada* at my farm."

"A lovely man. A rough exterior, but a very keen eye. In my business, as I call it again, we appreciate these qualities. He tells me you promised to take him to America."

"America?" spluttered Saqib.

"You've heard of it. A country. Your friend Zafar Machhi told me that you're planning to go there soon. Out of curiosity, business, or pleasure? Tourism? I was there recently, in fact. My cousin lives in Houston. Have you been to Houston, Chaudrey Saqib?"

"No, Inspector Sahib."

"Once he and I got all talkative, your friend Zafar also told me how you conducted your business. Two good years, one bad year. Up and down. It's an old story, Chaudrey Saqib. But enough of that. Now, let me bring your attention to this little apparatus sitting on this table in front of us. Do you know what it is?"

"It seems to be some sort of generator, Inspector Sahib."

"Clever man. Usually they don't get that. Yes, it's a generator. I believe they used them once upon a time to power telephones. Now, do I need to explain how we in the Punjab Police use this device in our investigations?"

"No, Inspector Sahib. I understand what this is for."

"Excellent. Then I will ask you, and ask you once only, before I fire it up. Where is the money? I know that it's not in your bank account, there's not enough there. I hope for your sake that it's not in your house, where your young wife and even younger child are at this moment sitting and wondering where you are."

"What money, Inspector Sahib?"

Without another word, the inspector stood up and went briskly to the door. "Okay, guys, let's do this. I'm in a hurry here, I need to be in Multan."

Two men came in, also wearing civilian clothes. They brought with them a chair that was fitted with leather straps on the arms and the legs, and with this they pinioned Saqib, so that he was seated but could not move. They muttered to each other as they worked, "There we go, just a bit tighter. Good. Now the other one." Afterward, Saqib remembered as most terrifying of all their remarkable gentleness, like a doctor fitting a patient for a medical test.

"Nice and tight, it's better," said one to the other. "There we go."

They took the leads from the hand-cranked generator and clipped them to metal plates encircling his ankles. Saqib watched all this with disbelief more than panic. He thought of his sweet flesh, no sweeter to be found than what stuck to his own back. Could they possibly be doing this to him, to little Saqib, this body that Gazala had shown him how to love, this father, this mother's son?

He thought of the butcher who came to cut the throats of sacrificial animals at Eid, how businesslike and unhurried he was around the victim, petting it, easing and then suddenly cinching the bindings so that it barely struggled.

"Righty tighty," said one man to the other, testing the straps at Saqib's wrist, then making a loose informal salute to the inspector. "All done, sir."

"Well, let's try it out!" said the inspector with enthusiasm. "Give it a whirl."

Now Saqib began burbling, the words foaming out of him. "Please, sir, ask me what you like, sir."

"Sir? What an idiot!" he said, and he gave the crank a vicious twist.

Saqib had never felt anything so remarkably strangely painful before in his life. The current made him jolt and quiver and seemed to course through his body, not hot or cold but like a living burning wire being twittered and jerked and rammed through him. His sphincter loosened and he shit his pants.

"Oh no!" said the inspector. "Right, just for that . . ." and he began cranking the handle energetically and continuing and continuing and continuing and continuing, till the room turned purple and then black in Saqib's sight and the men and the inspector all seemed very far away and all the time that terrible wire was being shaken and pulled through his body, as if he had come alive to another diabolical tune, the shaking and the pull and the pull and the pull, and his teeth ground so hard that he broke a tooth, felt it snap, and then in all the burbling jerking foaming confusion he swallowed the little niblet.

He had closed his eyes and gone far away into some purple room of pain. His flesh was all like a snake, turned inside out and eating him bit by bit and all at once. His limbs all were broken, his eyes were broken, his every finger and every toe and every bone and every muscle screamed and jerked as if he played to a terrible tune, a music that sucked inside from outside and made his body a surface all wet.

*

When he opened his eyes, the inspector was sitting back in his chair and looking into his face with a mild expression, as if looking for an answer there to some unimportant question.

"You okay? We've just begun, you know. Just so you know. That was just a taster. We have a whole menu for you tonight. This is our littlest machine. We have lots of others, and I want to introduce you to them all. Every. Single. One." As he said these last three words he hit the table with his hand, once for each word. Every. Single. One.

With the convulsions Saqib had danced the chair away from the table, almost to the farthest extent of the leads that were tied to his ankles. Now the two constables picked up the chair and moved him again close to the table. Saqib's head seemed to be loose on his neck, he couldn't lift his chin, and he had drooled and pissed himself and the shit in his shalvar felt wet and warm and had spread all over, he could feel it slippery under him.

"Get ahold of yourself," suggested the inspector. "Straighten up. I'll give you a minute."

"No," begged Saqib.

"No what? No who? No where?"

"I beg you, sir."

"Sir?"

"Inspector Sahib, sir, Inspector Sahib, Inspector Sahib, Inspector Sahib," he babbled. It mustn't happen again, nothing else mattered, he mustn't let it happen again.

The inspector had his hand on the crank and was looking directly into Saqib's eyes.

"You were saying? About the money?"

"The money?" He was pulling it up from that deep well where the fishes were. Nothing must stop it. It must come up.

The inspector turned the crank just a little, just a buzz, a snap, a jolt.

"Where is the money?" How powerful seemed the inspector to Saqib then, and yet almost a friend to him, a lover, a brother—who could stop the pain, and all he needed was to have that money.

"It's in the beams of my little shed where my tunnel farm is. Look above the center beam. There's a thin metal box, if you move the bricks. Everything is there."

The inspector still held the crank. He gave it a twitch, and again Saqib's body jolted against the restraints.

"Everything?" he purred.

"I swear. I swear on the Koran. I swear on my wife. I swear on my child. I swear on my mother's head. Every single rupee is there." He was sobbing.

"It better be," said the inspector, and he touched the crank again and gave Saqib a tiny jolt, and then stood up.

He turned and paused at the door, absent-minded, as if he had just thought of this.

"By the way. How much would you have put in your little box, Chaudrey Sahib?"

"Sir, Inspector Sahib. So much. A million and a quarter, sir. Almost thirteen lacs."

"Oh!" The inspector really was delighted; this was not feigning. Now they were getting somewhere! "That's not bad, not bad at all. For a first timer, too. You're a natural." He stood, thinking. "You know, you and I can definitely work something out. Even better, I think I'll have the whole thing, just this once. You don't seem to have a lot of friends to harass me about it, anyway. All for me just this once!" He said it singsong, like a little boy, happy at the thought of a new toy, a plaything, or like a guest committing to a third slice of pie. Why not?

He again turned to leave, then stopped a second time.

"Listen here, Chaudrey Sahib. I don't want to hear about this ever again, not from you, not from anyone. Not what happened tonight, not the money. I'll be the one to talk. Whatever anybody says, you just keep your fucking mouth shut, today, tomorrow, and till the end of time. There never was any money, that's your new religion."

To the policemen he said, "Clean him, feed him, leave him alone. Find some clothes for him. Maybe he's done."

Finally, to Saqib. "And you, sonny boy. You shut up and you keep your nose clean."

They took him outside and stripped him and washed him with a hose. It was dark by the river and hot and he lay on a cracked concrete pad and had not even the strength to raise his hands to protect his face when they sprayed the water right into his eyes. The one detail that kept coming back, that he had eaten his tooth. His tongue kept searching along the jagged spot where the tooth had broken, and that was where it hurt most. He had memories, but they were smoking and vague. Later, inside, he struggled to dress himself. They gave him a shalvar kameez too big for him, something from a taller and much fatter man. Who was taller than him, he stood almost six feet tall, two meters? On the floor of the room, he sat with his head hanging between his legs and this time they brought food in plenty, though no better in quality than before. But he ate nothing, he put it to his mouth and then coughed it out. The water tasted strange, that too had electricity in it. He was beyond exhaustion, beyond the world really. All his muscles hurt. The thought of what had been done to him stunned him still. They took him into another room with a charpoy and despite the heat he slept under a blanket. When he woke, it was late morning and he was immaculate, or so he thought, but then he smelled how very filthy the blanket was. The room had high windows, and through them he heard many sparrows chattering, playing in the dust. His sense of smell had become extraordinarily keen, he could smell the river. It wasn't far away, he knew that.

They brought him tea, steaming hot, and a little basket of hot chapattis.

"Inspector Sahib sent this for you, and a message. He found the thing you mentioned. No one must ever know what you told him, about the box. He said that he has many other instruments to show you, if the first time wasn't enough."

XXIII

A few months after Gazala and Saqib married, Saqib had taken her to Kèrala, choosing a time and making provisions so that no other servants would be there. They sat and walked under the trees, and he told her of playing in the garden at the old Ranmal Mohra house when he was little, having the freedom of the place when the sahibs weren't present, because his father worked there. That had been his first exposure to their world, that lush green enclosure set in the village but forbidden to the villagers, the flower beds his father tended through the years, all his labor to please the sahibs when they happened to come. He showed her the Kèrala swimming pool and the elaborate curving wall he built for Shahnaz, telling her that story of this first elevation. He even took her into the house, treating the rooms with familiarity, opening Shahnaz's cupboards and allowing Gazala to feel between thumb and finger the rainbows of her kurtas, to lift and hold the objects with which she surrounded herself, the ivory paper knife and the peacock-feather ceremonial fan from some far country. He had spoken of Shahnaz so often, explaining the connection that had brought him so far, that Gazala had wanted to see the properties of her rival, whatever rivalry there could be in a match so unequal. That had been a moment of tenderness between husband and wife, in those early days when they were coming to know each other, his gift to her, showing his world from before they met, showing off too.

It had been important to him that Gazala should not think Hisham and Shahnaz were like other landlord couples. They were a unique pair, he had said, calling them a jori, the Punjabi word for a matched pair, as of a span of horses, a mare and a stallion. He wanted her to see the complexity of his attachment to them, the ambiguities, his role more than that of a servant, making a shadowy obscuration as he described his management of the vegetable farm, wanting her to distinguish the money that Warraich gave him from the thefts of munshis before him. Romantic about them and sentimental, he showed Gazala how deeply they had scored his heart and mind, as if that would mitigate his offenses against them. This connection must be judged differently, he told her, because Hisham and Shahnaz were not of any temper known here before, bringing here not just city ways, but the ways of abroad, of the airliners that cruised forty thousand feet above the Indus—and which he described to her, as Warraich had described them to him.

All these fine explanations had fallen in a heap when her father phoned on the evening that Saqib was taken to the *baithak*, not so drunk as to be incoherent, but railing, despairing, strangely triumphant, pulling the house down around his own head, telling her of Saqib's disgrace, the father beaten—he exaggerated as the villagers had exaggerated the story, but giving it his particular venom—and, worst of all, saying that the police had come and found Saqib lying in that guardroom and beaten him there and then taken him away. She had married against his will, he screeched, and now she had disgraced him, put him at risk of losing what little he had. He would stand by the Atars, he shouted, he wouldn't be ruined by her husband's crimes.

And so she had sat expectant all the next day, desperate and not knowing where to turn, awaiting some signal, isolated, proud, her defiance threadbare. Then the second day that Saqib had been jailed away in some secret place passed. In the afternoon she had been finally to beg for word of him at the police station in Ranmal Mohra and been laughed away by the constable on duty. Aloof princess of the village, renegade from her caste, she had nowhere to turn.

She must chance a throw of the dice. On the third night she crept up the drive to Kèrala, hesitant and small in the darkness under the mango trees. It had been so difficult to get there—no one could know, and she came with the child—had hired a car from the bazaar to bring her from Adda Mastt Bahadur to Ranmal Mohra, telling the driver she had a sick relative, then walking the last four kilometers out to Kèrala, turning her body against the lights of the few cars that passed, covering her face with her dupatta, the wonder of this woman out on the road toward the river so late, where dacoits moved under cover of darkness. Her grandmother had taught her a trick for traveling with infants, one grain of a sleeping pill, the ones that the pharmacist sold under the counter, warning his clients not to take them for more than a few days or risk dependence. The child slept heavily, beloved weight in her arms, like a sleeping rabbit along the length of her embrace, and she was not frightened that he did not stir, for she knew her grandmother's spells and serums from being a braided little girl rapt at the old crone's knees.

The bright moon spread light around the shadows of the trees, and her eyes were well accustomed to that dark, yet she crept alongside the bougainvillea that overhung the drive, and only felt secure when approaching the little landing where the cars stood gleaming, Hisham's dark blue Land Cruiser and another from the farm, an old Willys, one of Hisham's expensive toys. She took her phone, the glow of it lighting her face, afraid but daring to call there in the darkness of the orchard. A few months earlier Saqib had managed to install one of her little nephews as a houseboy out there. Now, hidden along the driveway, she phoned him, told him to go outside where he would not be overheard.

"I need you to do something for me, something important. Go into the house and find if the Bibi is awake. Make some excuse."

"But, Auntie, how can I possibly do that? I don't dare go anywhere near the house at this hour, much less inside."

"What about the watchmen? Who keeps awake around the house?"

In this she was lucky. "They've put in old Baba Mehr, the one who used to fall asleep at the dera but couldn't be fired because he's Rana Sahib's cousin. You can say there's no watchman at all. Baba Mehr is asleep with a fan. Everyone else went to their rooms."

"Does the Bibi go to sleep early?"

"I don't know. I think not. Sometimes the Sahib and the Bibi even go to the swimming pool late at night."

Saqib's disgrace had already filtered down even to this boy. "Are you here at the house, Auntie? They say there's trouble with Uncle Saqib. Will I be all right?"

"Go back to your charpoy and don't make a peep. One word of this and you definitely won't be all right."

❋

Gazala, like Saqib, had from childhood found the darkness a place of refuge, running away from the village at night when her father's drunkenness made him intolerable. They had shared these stories, and Saqib had even told of that night up at Samarra when he spied on Hisham with the foreign woman. He described it to her as a witches' sabbath, when some part of his repose as a boy from Ranmal Mohra fell away—and that same night, when he told her that tale, she allowed him to kiss from her lips to her breasts to her belly and then to that so carefully epilated notch that he longed to kiss and lick—and allowing him that liberty too had been a sabbath in the closeness of their bodies.

So it came to her easily to slip around the house, the child inert as a knotted rag in her arms, keeping beyond the light thrown from the windows, which cast a hazy powder of white onto the bougainvillea, the rose beds, and all Shahnaz's plantings, hibiscus, champa, verbena, and then—in April blossom time, when the night flowers are so fragrant—the night-blooming jasmines, raat-ka-raja, king of the night, and the raat-ki-rani, queen of the night. She stole through this confusion of scents, mélange, and peered into the curtained rooms one by one. It did not surprise her finally to see, glowing and lit as if on display, Shahnaz sitting alone in a large, darkened room, so close that it surprised Gazala and made her wish she had been quieter, a single lamp behind her shoulder, absorbed in a book, seen through a plate glass window. Yes, it seemed inevitable that the night should conspire with her, the watchman asleep, and the person she sought alone now and so visible, as if awaiting her. This was not like men fighting with their sticks and pistols, but she came here with a purpose no less grave.

✳

Any little mischance now would have ruined Gazala's mission. Carefully she placed her hand on a branch of a frangipani tree that hung over the patio in front of that plate glass window, and made it move unnaturally, but only slightly. Shahnaz indifferently looked up, cocked her head at the window, the view out into darkness obscure, continued reading. Then, when the branch swayed twice more, she stood up, walked over to the window, tried to see through—a pair of sconces barely lit the patio, throwing patterns onto the brickwork.

She's brave! thought Gazala when Shahnaz opened the door and emerged into the night. She wore a shalvar and a long kurta, hair loose, arms bare, and was smaller than Gazala remembered her, compact, maidenly, when Gazala thought of her as attenuated, a sweep of her.

"*Kon hai?*" she called, firm and loud. "Who's there?"

She stepped out farther, while Gazala kept perfectly still under the frangipani.

Tentative, she came out still farther onto the fan-shaped patio, with a circle of chairs at the center, where the sahibs would take their meals or meet their intimates.

Gazala imagined an elastic thread pulling Shahnaz back into the room, stretching behind her as she stepped forward into the night, and just when the thread pulled taut and Shahnaz turned to go back in, Gazala stepped out from the shadows.

"What's that? I'll call the guard." But already recognition showed in her attitude, the tension subsiding. A woman, not a man.

"Gazala?" Her voice was so loud in Gazala's ear, who imagined the household awakening and ruining her plea.

"Bibi Jee," Gazala whispered. "Bibi Jee, I am alone. Look, I have my child with me."

She held up the sleeping child in its bundle, and even pulled back the cloth to show its face. "It's sleeping. He's sleeping."

Wary, Shahnaz stepped forward.

"Jehan Shah," said Gazala, holding the child up and then protectively drawing it closer into the fold of her arms when the other woman approached.

"Who let you come here? Where is the guard?"

Gazala stood unmoving. She must not break the tension of Shahnaz's interest.

"Speak up!" Peremptory, angry, unsympathetic. But she had come close and was peering down at the unstirring child. Still Gazala remained silent, and in that prolonged moment Shahnaz became sensitive to the night, the scent of the flowers, the slight breeze in the trees, banyan and rosewood, that guarded that patio.

"My husband brought me here once not so long ago, Bibi Jee. We should not have come, or we shouldn't have come without permission. Our excuse was that we had just married, we had been living in the same house just a few weeks, when neither of us had ever lived with anyone before. And he wanted me to know what his life had been like before, with you and the Sahib."

Again she stopped, feeling for a response, no disturbance now must be allowed, now it must be quiet between them. Gazala remembered her grandmother then, her healing, which had been accomplished so much with words.

And it worked.

"It will be too loud here," said Shahnaz. "Come with me."

She led across an open expanse of moonlit lawn. Already there was dew, Gazala felt the grass wet on her feet.

Two steps led up to the pool, the door rattling when Shahnaz drew the latch, and then they were two women alone inside the enclosure, the whitewashed walls glowing, a table, chairs, underwater floodlights shimmering blue.

Now it was Shahnaz's turn to be silent. She walked over to one of the chairs and leaned down on the back of it with both arms extended.

Collecting herself, inflexible, she began.

"I know why you've come. Your husband's a fool. He's hurt Mian Sahib. Not very badly, because it isn't in his power to do that. But enough so that everything from the past is wiped away. You've wasted your effort."

"Saqib spoke to me many times about that past. I know that my husband has hurt you, and more badly than you say. That is why I am here. That is why I dared to come. You have not been toward my Saqib as with your other servants."

This was a part of Gazala's speech that had been prepared—more than prepared, the sentiment deeply contemplated in the long walk along the black road with her child in her arms, all the way out four kilometers from Ranmal Mohra to this compound concealed in its orchard.

"You dared to come," echoed Shahnaz, musing. The girl had struck home, for yes, she was more badly hurt than others might imagine. Only now these past days had she understood how Saqib had penetrated her reserve, touched her secretly. She had come now to an age for great decisions, past childbearing for many years, and nearing sixty she was beginning to feel that it had come to final things, her last chances. Her lover, fourteen years younger than her, had finally given up and in turn married a younger woman that winter, and although she had not cared for him so very much as that anymore, still afterward she felt as if she looked at life through a pane of ice skimmed from a puddle, her vision unclear looking forward. And here was this girl, so young to have this child. They say that couples grow to resemble each other, but this girl already resembled Saqib, and she could imagine them paired for a lifetime. Bitter pairings, and yet what better offer would they find?

"Yes, I suppose you're right. There is more to this than ordinarily when servants steal. But that makes it worse. You've come here to beg, but it's too late for that. You're the granddaughter of a great munshi, you know how this plays out."

"Yes, I do know. I cannot imagine my Saqib in that room where they take them and where they do all those things. I beg you, let me say my piece. You know who I am, Bibi Jee, at least this much, that I am the granddaughter of Sheikh Abbas. At one time he held all the power here, as the instrument of the Atar family, though he was thrown down before I was born. My childhood still had some of that."

"The gold in the walls," said Shahnaz. "Even I've heard the stories."

"There was no gold in the walls, Bibi Jee. I wouldn't be standing here before you with my infant child in my arms if there had been."

"No gold, then. But that excuses neither him nor your husband."

"I admit that, Bibi Jee. My grandfather failed and was punished because he took what Hisham Sahib's father and grandfather had, not all of it, not even very much of it, but more than they wished him to have. The lines were not clear about how much they gave him, but if they had rewarded him in the same measure as the power they gave him, then he took only his due."

This annoyed Shahnaz. "Don't speak in riddles, little girl."

There were dangerous currents here, Gazala's imagination fanning back and forth in the background as she shaped her rhetoric.

"Forgive me, Bibi. I will be plain as I can. I do not know my husband's business. We have been married barely a year, and then, perhaps you know how closely he governs his tongue. But about his sincerity I can be certain. Saqib is sincere with you. He speaks of his gratitude to Mian Sahib and to you, when we are alone, when he speaks his mind truly. You raised him from nothing, you taught him, you made him different, and he is different—that is why you chose him. No one here from Ranmal Mohra ever before dared to want what Saqib does. No one else has Saqib's ways. I am his wife, but I think that even now after more than a year I understand him so little. I have never seen him anywhere but here, leaving before dawn and returning after dark, working so hard that already he has lines around his mouth and at the corners of his eyes. But I'm certain that he is capable of all you saw in him."

Gazala had been standing three paces in front of Shahnaz, both of them aligned with the edge of the pool, Shahnaz alternately resting her two hands on the back of a chair, then standing up straight, Gazala holding the child, which grew heavy, so that her shoulders settled down, and when her dupatta fell into her face, she did not lift a hand to brush it away.

Shahnaz stepped forward, with one finger rearranged Gazala's dupatta, and then looked squarely down at the unmoving face of the child.

"You are so far above us that I dare to say this, Bibi Jee. I am jealous of your perfections in my husband's eyes, because I can never have what you have. You gave him too much. You said he could go to the big university in Lahore. I am educated too, Bibi Jee, I know what the Government College in Lahore is. You said he might even go to America."

Gazala raised her face to the light, now softening as she imagined these possibilities. "He might have become what you proposed. It would take so much strength, but he has that, he would not be stopped by the difficulty or the distance."

Her thoughts turned inward, and for a moment she seemed to forgot herself and her purpose. Quietly, she said, "And if you had not sent him back here, he would not have married me."

And then she composed herself again, spoke as if describing something in front of her eyes.

"Imagine he came back, all full of education and thinking himself different than anyone here at Ranmal Mohra. Then what? Without money, what is a man with a piece of paper from Government College or even another piece of paper with different words from some other country? He would perhaps be worse than before, with foreign tastes but no way to satisfy them. It is true, a man like Saqib is capable of doing more than others, doing things well, doing them badly. You recognized that in him. You made that in him."

Now she broke down, emotion and design inextricable.

Falling to her knees, she held the child in her outstretched arms, laid it at Shahnaz's feet. She was weeping.

"Mehra ki kasoor. Bachay da ki kasoor." These words between women. "What fault of mine? What fault of this child?" She continued, "You married me to Saqib, Bibi Jee. You were at my mehndi. I could not have married Saqib but for you, and this child would not have

been born but for you. If you destroy my husband, you punish us cruelly."

"It's easy," replied Shahnaz. "Tell him to give back the money he stole."

"I don't know anything about that," sobbed Gazala, shaking her head, small-shouldered there at Shahnaz's knees. "But I've seen what these men look like after the police is finished with them. They will take everything he has and then more. Saqib is young, I am young, the child is not even one year old. All three of us will be finished before we began. You didn't marry me just to the man, you married me to his life."

Shahnaz waited for her to continue, but the girl hung her head and still wept silently, no display now but absorbed in her grief alone.

The child had still not stirred, and then it did, smacking its lips, turning its head, gliding back into consciousness, that grain of sleeping pill metabolized away. And something like victory flooded the scene, the blue shimmering pool, the underwater lights in the pool kept on all night just in case Shahnaz wished to swim, water-proof lights imported from the West, and the woman at her feet, Saqib alone that night in a cell somewhere ruing his infidelity.

"All right," Shahnaz said, finally. "For your child, then. Saqib will not be harmed. He will be released."

Slowly uncoiling, Gazala rose up on her haunches, lifted the child, held it up.

"Bless my child, then, Bibi Jee. Give your blessing to my Shah Jehan."

And Shahnaz did, she touched its warm forehead with the flat of her hand, and then she turned and walked away.

XXIV

S aqib lay in the little room until midmorning, exhausted still, the world heavy around him, as if at the edge of his vision a gray leaded curtain hung circular on the horizon, his body heavy too. The insult had been to his mind as much as his body. His mind snagged on little observations, the delicate lacework of the white-wash flaking off the wall opposite him, as he sat up cross-legged on the bed with the filthy blanket reeking around him. The metal door stood open just a handsbreadth, a sly invitation. Way out here by the river, where the roads ended, how could he make his way back to town, wearing this oversized baby-blue shalvar kameez that hung around him looser than an elephant's skin, all in bunches, and the fabric washed so many times that it was soft as a bar of much-used soap. Who would stop for a man so dressed in this remote place? He could not hear the waterbirds, but he knew that nearby the immense river flowed, the one that watered all this flourishing land, kilometers wide in places, the current making boiling huge whirl-pools and then lazily meandering into oxbows and bends, where the fishermen cast their nets and sometimes pulled out fish as large as a little child.

Finally, unsteadily, tentatively, he pulled himself together, went to the door, peered through it, and then stepped out.

"Hello?" he called.

No answer.

Barefoot, for he could not find his shoes, he went to the end of the corridor, then through the open front door into a little veranda. Before him lay a large open space, bare dirt, a mud wall thrown around it to the extent of a whole acre, and to one side a line of ten or more tethered buffaloes, each with a wooden trough to hold its feed, and three large pipal trees under which they could find shade. A stooped, thin, graying sepoy worked unhurriedly among them, wearing his khaki uniform pants and a faded torn red T-shirt, gathering manure into a pile with a long wooden scraper. Saqib noticed that the buffaloes were in good condition, fat and glossy. They would be, the local people would bring feed in any quantity that the police demanded. This was not just a couple of buffaloes to give milk for the policemen's tea, this was something like a dairy farm.

The constable glanced over at Saqib, then continued his work. Was it possible that in this very place last night Saqib had screamed in agony and felt himself turned inside out, like the intestines of a butchered sheep turned inside out for washing under a faucet? How nice it felt to be warm in the sun, too warm, but it healed his bones. Yes, the river nearby made the light dance in the sky, like water roiled in a basin under sunlight.

Saqib made his way over to the constable, picking his way carefully to avoid impaling his bare feet in the fallen thorns from an acacia tree that cast its spotted shade over the scene.

"Hello, brother," called Saqib to the man, embarrassed, for he must know what had transpired last night, Saqib's humiliation and torture, although he had not been present.

The man looked up at Saqib with a friendly smile. He had tight curly black hair, like a Makrani tribesman, and very white teeth.

"You're up," he said pleasantly.

"Where is the Inspector Sahib?" asked Saqib.

Now the man gave Saqib a hard look. "Do you think that they tell a man like me where the Inspector Sahib goes? They went somewhere on a raid, that's my guess. They call him 'Inspector,' but he's a lot more than that. They're not locals, you know, the inspector and his team. They sent them from up north. Encounter specialists. The less you ask the better."

"Can you help me find my shoes?"

"They're over there, by the hand pump."

Just then, a vehicle honked outside the gate, one tentative beep. The policeman carefully leaned his implement against a feeding trough, then padded to the gate and opened it. In drove the little red farm jeep from Ranmal Mohra, with Bayazid alone behind the wheel, too large for such a small vehicle. The jeep had a ragtop and the canvas doors had been removed because of the heat, so that Yazid seemed to bulge out of the sides, with his billowing shalvar and his wide shoulders, his immense frame. He parked far away, emerged in sections, so large as he was, and then made his way toward Saqib.

Saqib did not move but watched him approach. What to make of this? And what to say to this beloved man who had turned him over for such treatment? The author of his torments.

"Have they turned you to keeping the buffaloes now?" commented Yazid. He could see from Saqib's apparel, and more, from his broken stance, that there was not much cause for humor in this moment.

Saqib's throat felt so dry that he could hardly speak. The reproaches he might have uttered stopped his throat, like a plug of mud swallowed there.

"Have you come for me finally in the morning?" he whispered.

Yazid shook his head. "Yes, I have." He strolled up to the policeman, as surely in control as he always was, this imperturbable mountain of a man.

"Where are your officers?"

"Gone, sir. They might not be back until long after dark."

"And what of this man?"

"I was told to set him loose at the gate."

"I'll take him then."

* ✳

"Suit yourself." Not wanting any further part of the business, the sepoy rudely turned his back and resumed collecting the manure, his wooden paddle scraping the dirt there under the trees, leaving the two men to whatever their terms might be.

Saqib hobbled over to the hand pump, put on his shoes, which glowed there in his eyes with portent. The world seemed to Saqib portentous that morning, even the crows in the pipal trees seemed there with purpose. For many years he would not forget the ringing of the skies that morning, the meaning fitted into the world, perfectly elusive and yet incontrovertibly expressed in every shake of the trees when the breeze worked among the branches. Yazid sat in the jeep, watching him through the windshield without moving at all, not moving as Saqib painfully hoisted himself into the doorless jeep. The policeman, more a cowherd perhaps, laconically strolled over and pulled open the creaking gate. Yazid backed out, the little four-cylinder engine of the Willys jeep burbling.

They were very far out by the river, after a moment Saqib recognized the place. Three nights ago, when they brought him, it had not seemed so very remote. This chilled him, like a little jolt of electricity again running along his shoulders. Yes, they had brought him into the wilderness. No one came here.

Yazid worked the gear with his usual precision, his care, negotiating potholes in the dirt road. Finally, he spoke. "What did they do to you? Where are your clothes?" Without waiting for an answer, he continued. "Neither Mian Sahib nor Begum Sahiba intended so much as this, that you should be brought here. We did not know the reputation of this inspector. He was sent here from Jhang side to control those Motu gang dacoits. They say he's killed many of them, he stages encounters every night."

Saqib said the thing that mattered to him most. "Did the Begum Sahiba send you to get me?"

Yazid shook his head slowly. "That's a strange thing to ask. Mian Sahib spoke with me this morning. He said to bring you out."

When Saqib said the words "Begum Sahiba" he had choked up and almost begun weeping. It seemed very hard, that he must still control his emotion now, when he had not cried so very much that night before, when the pain had been so great. They had not wrung that from him, perhaps that had been the thing that he kept hidden deep down inside him in the well where the fishes were, where the money had been, the money that left a hollow there.

Gradually they entered more settled country, driving under

hundred-year-old rosewood trees now, massive along both sides of the road, trees that had been planted back in British times, growing here as a memorial to the vision of some colonial administrator now lying buried in a faraway English country churchyard. The vivid green sugarcane fields began, the cane fronds waist high in the hot May weather, a haze above the fields that had been watered.

Yazid began to speak. "I was blinded by you. Thirty-nine years of service in this family and now you bring this shame on me."

Saqib had been thinking only of himself, of what he might say in explanation, to win back respect in some measure. Now he asked, "What fault was it of yours?"

"Look at me. Look at this belly. I also was a slave to my appetite. I've eaten away my lifetime and have nothing to show for it. I never got married. I never had children. And so this belly, this is my child. I remember that first time when we went to Sargodha and you took me and we ate those quail from Baba Kareem, all that food."

Yazid had always been subject to emotion, would weep over Punjabi films, bearing along his sentimental old heart—Saqib had loved him for that.

"What did that matter?" begged Saqib. "That meal cost a few thousand rupees. What difference did it make? And even this. Will anything change for Hisham Sahib because of a bad year at my vegetable farm?"

Yazid was lost in his own thoughts. He began to blubber, heart-breaking to Saqib. "Thirty-nine years of service and what I have is this belly. That's my fucking family. That's my daughter and my mother and my son." He stopped himself, wiped his face down with a broad hand, turned and looked at Saqib once through bleary, reproachful eyes.

As they came into Adda Mastt Bahadur, the traffic increased, unruly and irritating to Saqib. The noise seemed like an affront. He and Yazid should go to some watered green place and sit in silence for a long time. Though he had never been a boy given to embraces, nor had his mother nurtured him that way, yet now Saqib hopelessly imagined that Yazid might so easily stop the jeep and turn to him in forgiveness. As if removing a feather-plumed helmet,

Bayazid might uncrown and lay aside his loyalties and his powers and embrace Saqib as a father, almost a father, Saqib almost his son.

But the world is not so forgiving, as Saqib understood then. The world is governed more by chance than by intention, as if a madman or a child were sovereign. What if Yazid had not seen the iPhone that day?

"Take me home, Bayazid, I beg you," Saqib said finally, wearily. "I have my wife and child. Don't mess with me. I can't go back to Ranmal Mohra."

"You need not beg. I'm sorry for what happened to you. I see how much they did to you. The Sahibs did not wish or order this. They don't care that much about the money. They never did. Remember this. Whether or not you and I are for sale, what they have, it was never for sale. Let's not speak of this again."

"I doubt we'll speak of anything at all," said Saqib quietly, a final gesture to this faithful man, devotee of a faith he no longer could share.

Bayazid piloted the little red jeep through the bazaar of Adda Mastt Bahadur, the fruit sellers and store owners shooing away flies with their hands or with switches tied with rags, and none of them knew what a rich caravel rode past that forenoon, loaded with Saqib's heaviness and his knowledge too, and the love he bore for Yazid just then, which felt to him like music all around. He was a little bit insane then, and remained so for days, had lost his bet, lost his money, lost his place, lost his integrity too. He would need to find this all again, but now he needed silence and the hand and body of his wife, his Gazala.

They didn't speak again, and Yazid dismissed Saqib with just a touch on the shoulder. Their parting could not have been simpler, there in that little flourishing colony, with roads laid out but only a few houses yet built, like teeth in a child's mouth, one here and one there.

A NOTE ABOUT THE AUTHOR

Daniyal Mueenuddin was brought up in Lahore, Pakistan, and Elroy, Wisconsin, and is a graduate of Dartmouth College and Yale Law School. His stories have appeared in *The New Yorker*, *Granta*, *Zoetrope*, and *The Best American Short Stories 2008*, selected by Salman Rushdie. His collection *In Other Rooms, Other Wonders* was a finalist for the Pulitzer Prize and the National Book Award. For a number of years he practiced law in New York. He now divides his time between Oslo, Norway, and his farm in Pakistan's South Punjab.

A NOTE ON THE TYPE

The text of this book was set in Centaur, the only typeface designed by Bruce Rogers (1870–1957), the well-known American book designer. A celebrated penman, Rogers based his design on the roman face cut by Nicolas Jenson in 1470 for his *Eusebius*. Jenson's roman surpassed all of its forerunners and even today, in modern recuttings, remains one of the most popular and attractive of all typefaces. The italic used to accompany Centaur is Arrighi, designed by another American, Frederic Warde, and based on the chancery face used by Lodovico degli Arrighi in 1524.

Typeset by Scribe
Philadelphia, Pennsylvania

Book design by Pei Loi Koay